THE BUILDING THAT WASN'T

THE BUILDING THAT WASN'T

ABIGAIL MILES

CamCat Books

CamCat Publishing, LLC
Fort Collins, Colorado 80524
camcatpublishing.com

Hardcover ISBN 9780744309850
Paperback ISBN 9780744309874
Large-Print Paperback ISBN 9780744309911
eBook ISBN 9780744309898
Audiobook ISBN 9780744309959

Library of Congress Control Number: 2023950763

Book and cover design by Maryann Appel
Interior artwork by George Peters, Natrot, Supermimicry

5 3 1 2 4

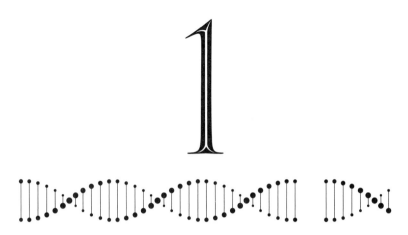

1

The room was white—almost blindingly so, with surfaces that had been scrubbed to a shine, so that by staring at the floor or a wall it was nearly possible to see one's own reflection. It was clean and fresh and sterile. The perfect canvas.

The most beautiful aspect of the white room was how stark contrasting shapes and colors appeared on the initial blankness. This was an aesthetic quality that the man found particularly pleasing to explore, and so he did as such extensively, to a near-compulsive rate. He fancied himself an artist, with the borders of the room providing the ideal location to bring his masterpiece to life.

Keeping that in mind and aiming for the truest form of artistic perfection he could conjure, the man gripped the tool in his hand—his paintbrush of choice—and hefted it before him. His arm dropped in an almost graceful fashion as he completed a full swoop, similar in form to that of a baseball player setting up to bat. Then, pausing once to allow the moment to settle in its resplendent glory, the man slowly lowered his arm, tool in hand, and looked around at what he had created.

The white backdrop truly was perfect, he thought. It made the red look so much fresher—sharper and more potent. And the shapes the droplets formed, the pattern they enacted across the room. Perfect. The man admired the final product and couldn't help but think that this may have been some of his finest work yet.

Not to mention the added pleasure derived from the screaming.

While some find the sound of a human scream to be unpleasant, the man found it to be more precious than music—a chorus of varying pitches and volumes coming together in a resounding crescendo at the final moment. He would do it all for that, for the symphony that was forged as a result of the fear, the excitement. The pain.

That's why he was there, after all. To create such a stupendous pain in the people they supplied.

Well, that was not technically true. Technically he was there for many, many more reasons. Glorified kidnapper being one, rubber duck watcher another.

But the pain. That was his favorite.

Though usually the pain was accompanied by a distinct factor of *more* —the unraveling of the universe and all that.

Not this time. This was only an ordinary body, with no spark of the otherworldly in sight.

The man didn't care.

Maybe others would, but he found purpose enough for himself in the beauty of what he could fashion there, with or without the ulterior motive. In some ways, one could say that having a secondary reason for the pain only tarnished it, whereas this belonged solely to him. This moment, right here.

The man took a deep breath, savoring the complete ambiance of the space he was in, before he turned back to his subject and assessed his options. Settling on a different, more precise tool—one with a much sharper edge—the man once more lifted his arm and continued with his ordained task.

From a different room, a set of eyes casually observed on a screen as the man set to work on his masterpiece, nodding once in approval before turning away. The screen left on displayed the white walls, no longer pristine, which echoed back the horrendous chorus the man's work produced.

2

There was an elderly man Everly had never seen before standing behind all the black-clad patrons, and his eyes had been focused on her for the duration of the service.

She blinked and realized that wasn't quite right. There was an elderly man Everly recognized, as if from a dream, as if from a memory, lodged deep and low down in the recesses of her brain. She squinted at him, because if she could just . . .

She blinked again, and of *course* she knew him, why wouldn't she know him, why would she ever not recognize—

Blink. Everly shook her head. The man was still there, and she didn't know why a second before she had recognized him, because she did not, though she felt oddly unsettled by the memory of recognizing the man. Not as unsettled as she was, however, by his mere presence or by the fact of his staring at her.

He was too far away for her to actually see his eyes, to know for sure, but she could feel his attention pierced on her like a dagger through her spleen. The sensation was disconcerting, but in a strange way she appreciated the man and the mystery he presented. It gave her something to focus on. Something to puzzle over.

Someone to look at other than the form in the coffin on the elevated platform in front of her.

The man wore a bowler hat over his tufted gray hair, and a brown tweed coat, which worked even further to set him apart from the sea of faces that encircled him—the rest of whom were all adorned in shades of black or blackish blue, all at least a little familiar to Everly. The friends, the coworkers, the distant acquaintances and associates.

But not the family. There was no other family. None but her.

The preacher had finished speaking, Everly realized with a start, and was gesturing for her to step forward. She didn't want to. She wanted to go back to pondering the mystery of the peculiar man in the bowler hat, trying to work out how he had found his way there, and why, but they were all staring at her, so she stood, refusing to breathe as she crossed the distance between her chair and the platform ahead of her. A sharp pang flashed through her skull when she reached the front. Everly gritted her teeth, resisting the urge to lift a hand to the side of her temple.

She couldn't look at the body. They had asked if she wanted to beforehand, to make sure he looked okay—like himself, she supposed—but she knew it would be no use. He would never look like himself. Never again.

A car accident had led her here, to this raised platform, in front of all the vaguely familiar forms in black and the solitary strange one in brown. Or at least, that is what they had told her, when it was already too late for the cause to even matter.

But according to them, it had been a car accident, and so he hadn't been quite right. Or his body hadn't been. They told her it would be okay if she didn't want an open coffin, but she wasn't able to stand the thought of locking him up in there any sooner than she needed to.

So even though she refused now to look, she kept him out in the open. She kept him free.

Afterward, Everly was ushered to a dimly lit reception room, where she had scarcely a moment to herself before the other mourners came flooding in to report how very sorry they were, how devastating of a loss it must be, how much she would be kept in their prayers. Everly hardly heard any of them. She leaned against one of the whitewashed walls of the hall and rubbed her temple, trying not to close her eyes, though she wanted nothing more than to shut out everything and everyone around her. She wanted them all to go back, to their lives and their families and their homes. She wanted to go back.

But back to what, she couldn't help but ask herself. Back to the empty house with too many rooms and the life that she wasn't sure she could picture any longer in his absence.

Her father's absence.

She was too young, all of Everly's neighbors had tried to claim. Too young to be all alone. But at twenty-four, she was hardly a child anymore, and really, what would anyone have done anyway? Where would she have gone?

She had nowhere else to go, no one else to go to, and they knew it as well as she did.

She was on her own.

Everly considered leaving. She thought better of it a moment later, looking around at all the people who had come out to celebrate her father's life, but an instant after that she realized she didn't even care. None of them had truly known him anyhow. They had only come for the cake, which was now set out on a plastic folding table by the door, the words *Our Most Sincere Condolences* traced out in poorly scripted black icing across the center of the buttercream sheet. They probably wouldn't even notice if she left, Everly thought, and even if they did, she could see no reason why she should care. No reason at all.

Everly stood up from the wall to leave, trying to appear as nonchalant as possible as she walked between the well-wishers, making her way toward the doors of the reception hall.

As she stepped out into the deepening evening air just beyond the doors, she caught sight of a blur of brown fabric far ahead of her. Straining her eyes against the dusk that was swiftly descending, Everly could just make out the shape of the strange man from before—the one she remembered and knew yet was certain she had never met—as he strode off into the night, the shadow of his curved bowler hat protruding distinctly above his head as he left without so much as an insincere commiseration offered her way.

3

It was his own fault, and he knew it. Luca shouldn't have told Jamie that he'd take on the second shift, but he hadn't been able to resist. It had felt like the right decision at the time, and like all the worst decisions, it was only through the harsh lens of retrospect that he could see how little he had thought this through. After nearly a full twenty-four hours in front of the screens set up around the cramped surveillance room, Luca's eyes had more than glazed over, and he was becoming afraid they'd get stuck that way if he stayed in there much longer: frozen in a state of half-awareness.

Struggling—failing—to suppress a yawn, Luca leaned back in his chair and ran his eyes over the screens again, searching for anything he might have missed the past thousand times he had scanned the camera feeds. It was proving to be an unusually dull shift—doubly so, for the added hours of monotony. Despite the long hours and unending boredom, it was almost worth it for the chance to be alone, if only for a little while.

To be the eyes instead of the watched.

(As far as he was aware, at least.)

And to use his eyes for his own purposes.

If only he could stay awake to use them. Luca could feel himself fading, and every few seconds he had to jerk his head up to prevent himself from collapsing from exhaustion. If only something interesting would happen, he thought. Something to wake him up.

Unbidden, his mind began to drift, in a half-conscious state, to the dreams that haunted him during the night—not the only reason, but certainly one of the reasons that had driven him to make the ill-guided decision to stay awake through the night in front of those awful screens.

Though, perhaps *haunt* wasn't the right word. Haunting implied ghosts from a past lived through and regretted. If anything, Luca's dreams hinted at something that hadn't yet come to pass, if he was feeling high-minded enough to label himself as being prophetic.

And really, would he have been that far off?

He was never able to place a finger on what it was about his nighttime visions that unsettled him so, but more often than not, Luca would jerk awake during the night, drenched in sweat and with fleeting images filling his head, then vanishing moments later. He didn't ever retain much from them—mostly just a feeling of dread—but occasionally he would find something tangible to hang on to, something that he thought he could remember, if only for that brief instant.

Sometimes he saw her. She was always different: sometimes a child, with strawberry-blond pigtails and a lopsided grin; sometimes older, with a sharp chin and mouth perpetually turned down on the ends; most of the time she was a young woman in her twenties, around his age—fierce, tall, defiant.

Always she burned.

Last night she had returned, the auburn hair a fiery halo encircling her head, her eyes burnished with their own kind of flame as they met his in sleep—and in memory. But she always left far more quickly than he would have liked, and in her absence Luca was always more shaken than he could reasonably account for. He didn't think she was the cause of the fear that always gnawed at him after such dreams—though he could not have said why—but nonetheless, where she walked, so did the shivers that racked his body the next day, casting all his thoughts into a shadow of doubt and worry.

They were getting worse. When he was a kid, Luca would find himself awoken by a fiery nightmare once, maybe twice a year. They were always vague, already distant by the time he had shaken himself fully awake.

That changed years ago, for no clear reason that Luca could think of, but now they were arriving more and more frequently.

Most days now, he was afraid of closing his eyes for too long, afraid that that alone would be enough to hurtle him back into the dreams.

So, to avoid further encounters with the girl and her flaming hair and everything else that would inevitably follow, Luca had volunteered to stay on watch well into the night—long past when his normal shift would have ended. It gave him time to think, he had tried to tell himself. But really, by that point he would have attempted nearly anything to evade the dreams.

(A secret unbeknownst to Luca: he wasn't the only one in that building to dream.)

Luca didn't have a way to track the passing of time in the surveillance room (clocks in the building had an uncanny knack of being disobedient), but he knew that the night must have faded away when he heard the sharp beeping of the alarm that signaled the start of the morning. A few minutes later, the door behind him creaked open, and with the sound, Luca tensed, sitting up straight. Pretending he wasn't doing anything wrong. Even though, for the moment at least, he wasn't.

Taking in shallow breaths, Luca steeled himself, then turned his head, slumping immediately back in his seat when he saw that it wasn't one of the building's runners, but rather Caleb's slim form stepping into the room.

Cast in the pale lights emanating from the wall of screens, Caleb Arya looked cold, in the way that he always seemed to lately. Racked with shivers from an invisible force Luca never felt himself, his friend held his arms tightly wrapped around himself even now. Adding to the ensemble that was Caleb were the permanent dark circles painted beneath his eyes, the clammy sheen to the skin of his forehead, the hitch in his breath every few seconds that was only audible if you were listening.

And Luca was listening.

"Long night?" Caleb asked, trying to arrange his features into a smile. He was always trying, for Luca.

As Caleb settled into the seat next to his, Luca tried to return the favor. "Not too bad," he managed, though he knew it couldn't have sounded all that convincing. "Nothing interesting, if that's what you mean."

Caleb offered a mock sigh, tilting his head toward the ceiling. "Shame. I know how much you value your midnight breakouts and breakdowns."

Luca knew he was joking, but it still struck a chord in him. That was the other reason he took the night shift, though he hadn't been as productive in that regard lately.

His illicit use of the surveillance room's cameras was his most treasured secret. And his most dangerous one.

"Roll call?" Luca asked, without looking at Caleb.

"Five minutes."

"Right. Well, I'll be there soon. Need to wait for one of the blues to come in here and relieve me."

Caleb sighed. "Don't be too late this time. You know how the runners get when you aren't in the lineup. You don't want to anger them, Luca."

"I know," Luca said. "I'll be there. I promise."

Luca heard more than he saw Caleb get up and leave. Alone again, if only for a few minutes, Luca took one last opportunity to glance over the screens in front of him. His eye caught on activity in one of the uppermost screens, and he paused, watching.

"Sorry, Caleb," Luca mumbled to himself. For a moment, his mind sliced to what the repercussions for not showing up to roll call could be—Caleb was right, he really couldn't afford to anger the runners—but he steadied his resolve, bracing his fingers on the keyboard. "I'm going to be a few minutes late after all."

4

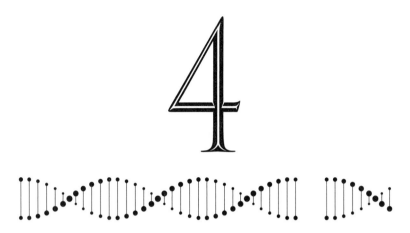

A PERSON FINDS THEMSELF AT the building through one of three means.

One: They walk in. This used to be the most common ground by which new residents arrived at the building. They would be strolling along, enjoying a beautiful day, when suddenly their feet would take them on a new path, through grass a little browner and more dried up than the surrounding lawns, down brick lanes that felt out of place in the city or suburb or rural area that they had previously been strolling through. It doesn't matter which of the latter is true; the brick lanes always feel out of place. Then, rising before them like a beacon out of the mist: a towering structure with gray paneling and darkened windows. And an allure, a call, a feeling of rightness that leads them up the endless steps, through the opaque glass doors, and into the lobby within.

No one finds the building who isn't supposed to.

Two: They are brought in. This is a feat far more easily accomplished when the person being brought in is a child: smaller, lighter, more easily convinced to get into the van with the strange man because, hey, do you want to have an adventure, young man? When this is the method of transport, they usually do not have the opportunity to see what the outside of the building looks like as they are brought in (usually because they are in some phase of unconsciousness), so all they know is what they see inside: gray walls, small rooms, endless hallways.

Three: They are born in the building. In the history of the building—which is both unfathomably long and hardly anything at all—this has only happened once.

5

She was being followed.

Everly could think of no other reason why the man from her father's funeral would appear here, in her neighborhood park. He was even in the same outfit he had worn at the funeral—the same outdated bowler hat and faded tweed coat. The only difference from their first noninteraction was that now she *knew* he was looking at her. Not twenty feet away from where she stood, the man had halted in the middle of the path, his eyes unwavering as he watched her. Everly knew she should have been more alarmed at his repeated appearance in her life—knew that she should have run, should have called someone, should have hidden. But against her better judgment, Everly instead found herself pulled toward the stranger, and she didn't know why.

No. That wasn't quite right. She did know why, or at least she thought she did. Now that she was seeing the man again, and much closer than before, when they had been separated by a church's worth of mourners, she could see his eyes. They met her own, and she felt like she knew them—like she knew *him*, despite the undeniable fact that before the funeral she was certain she had never seen him before. She also had that terrible sense of déjà vu again—the same as she had felt at the funeral. It nagged at the back of her mind, like a string begging to be pulled, like static wanting to settle into place, like an itch needing to be clawed out.

It was more than feeling like she knew him—it was feeling like she had spent her whole life with him, like she knew his darkest secret. Like he knew hers.

But not even Everly knew her darkest secret.

For a minute the man only stared at Everly, and then he smiled. It was a slow smile, a kind smile—almost even, one could say, timid. He removed the bowler hat, held it between both of his hands, and took a tentative step forward. All the while, Everly didn't blink. She stood frozen and waited while the strange man approached her, curiosity now taking over in the roots of her mind, overruling any lingering sense of unease.

The man paused about two feet away from Everly and stood looking at her for another moment before he began to speak. "You look just like her," he said, and his voice was far softer than she had been expecting, full of a warmth that nearly caught her off guard. Everly was so mesmerized by these observations that she nearly missed what he said.

She scrunched up her brow. "Like who?"

"Like your mother," he said.

Now Everly knew the man before her was mad. Or a liar. Or both. No one knew her mother, and if they did, they would know that Everly looked nothing like her. "No," she said back to the man. "I don't. My mother was fair and blond. She was petite, and beautiful. I'm none of that." She knew all of this because of the smattering of memories that she still retained from her early childhood, those which she hadn't lost or closed away over the years since her mother's passing. She didn't really remember her mother anymore—not in any tangible sense. But she remembered enough to know that the man was wrong.

"No," the man agreed. "You're not. But you have her eyes. And her spark."

"Spark?" Everly bristled, wondering if this was a snide remark against the reddish auburn of her hair.

"Your life," the man said. "The energy you radiate. I can see it now. It's vibrant, just like you. Just like her. You're marvelous, my dear."

This made Everly pause, at a momentary loss for words. "How did you know my mother?" she finally asked, once she found her voice.

The man seemed to hesitate for the first time, but only briefly. He looked Everly directly in the eyes, and it gave her a chill—that same uncanny sense of déjà vu. "Your mother," he said slowly, "was my daughter. Everly, my name is Richard Dubose. I'm your grandfather."

Everly took a step back. "No," she said, shaking her head. "You can't be. My mother didn't have any family."

"She did," the man said, almost sadly. "She does. Though, I'm afraid, you and I are nearly all there is left."

Everly kept shaking her head, backing away from the man and his words, his impossible statements. She knew her mother hadn't had any family because her father had told her so, and if someone had been out there, they would have found her long ago. She would have known.

The man's presence in front of her was irrefutable, however, and now Everly began to realize why his eyes seemed so familiar, so much like a ghost from the past. They were her eyes—the exact same deep blue, with a hint of green around the irises.

Her mother's eyes, if what the man claimed was true.

Everly's breath caught, and she looked closer at the man, searching for further clues, further proof that this unlikely miracle might be true. That someone else may abide within the nonexistent circle that she could call her family.

The man didn't say anything else while Everly examined him. "How?" Everly finally asked.

Again, the man hesitated for the span of a heartbeat before speaking. "When your mother . . . we weren't on good speaking terms, when I last saw her. She blamed me for many things, most of which she probably had a right to be angry over. Your father, too. I wasn't a very good parent, and so I figured it would likely be for the best if I stayed away from you and your father in your grief. Better if you didn't have me interfering in your life as I did for your mother."

Everly, still not convinced, crossed her arms over her chest. "So why now, then? If you thought it would be better if you stayed away, why did you come here?"

The man searched Everly's eyes. "Something has happened," he said quietly. "Or something is going to. We're going to need each other, very soon."

She couldn't understand any of this—couldn't understand why this man whom she had only just met could need her help, could need anything from her at all. Keeping her arms crossed, Everly cocked her head and narrowed her eyes. "What could you possibly need me for?"

He opened his mouth, closed it. Pressed his lips together in a firm line, furrowed his brow. "I think," he said slowly, "it may be easier to show you. I want you to understand, I want you to be able to see the whole picture, and I don't think I can do that right here."

"You want me to go somewhere with you?" A twinge of alarm flared through Everly. With it came the familiar flash of a headache—quick and fierce, like a sharpened fork being jabbed between her eyes. Everly grimaced; she'd been getting more and more of them recently.

"I want you to meet me somewhere," he said, still twisting his bowler hat between his hands.

Everly wiped her face blank, trying to banish any evidence of phantom pains as she considered the man, considered his proposition. She thought about what her dad would have said, if he could have seen her with the man and all the impossibilities he had presented. Her dad would have told her not to go. Would have said to stay home, to stay safe.

But her dad wasn't here. She probably had dozens—hundreds—of reasons why she should say no. But in that moment, she really couldn't find it in herself to care about any of them.

Slowly, as her headache abated, Everly began to nod. "All right," she heard herself say. "Where do I meet you?"

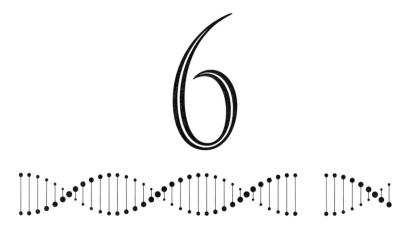

6

In the building, buried two levels beneath the ground, was a dark room hidden on a dark floor. The room wasn't very large—few rooms in the building were—but it was full.

On one wall: screens. Nearly identical to the wall a floor above, in the surveillance room that at that very moment Luca Reyes sat in. The difference was that here, in this black room, this secret room, there were a few more screens than Luca was privy to.

On one such screen was an image of Luca himself—his tall, lean body reclining in a chair, his dark hair splayed haphazardly over his eyes, his mouth set in a firm, determined line. It could be almost hypnotic at times, that line. That mouth. The face it was set into.

On another wall: a door, the only way in or out of the room, and in front of the door a canvas divider that stood nearly from floor to ceiling, shielding the rest of the room from the vantage of one standing in the doorway.

And in the middle of the room: a desk, large and wooden and ornate. Too large for a room that size, one might argue, but then one wouldn't understand the value of a quality desk when one spends one's whole life behind said desk. Atop the large wooden ornate desk were few items, all things considered. A small stack of papers, files. A lethally sharp letter opener. A lamp that was heavier than it looked. Behind the desk sat a person dressed in all black—black blazer over black collared shirt, with black trousers hemmed around the ankles and black socked-feet tucked into shiny black loafers.

The person in black had eyes trained on the wall of screens. Well, not the whole wall. That would be ridiculous. One particular screen.

The screen showed a small boy with dark hair and blue eyes—though you couldn't make out the specific shade of his eyes through the camera feed.

He wasn't doing anything, really. Sitting on a narrow gray bed in a narrow gray room. His room, the person in black knew.

He had been sitting there for a little over an hour now. This might not have been perceived as unusual, if the person in black hadn't known where the boy should have been instead.

And where he had been an hour before.

Luckily for that boy, he had a guardian angel looking out for him.

And unluckily for the guardian angel, the person in black was also watching.

The person in black observed the small boy for a while longer, wondering idly what might happen next.

For the first time in a long time, the person in black did not know.

7

Another long night, nearly over.

Luca's eyes trailed over the screens before him half-heartedly, knowing that he only had another minute left on duty before a runner came in and relieved him. Maybe Jamie would let him have the day off. Doubtful, but even the reds had to have a good day every once in a while.

At least Michael hadn't gotten out again during the night.

Luca's eyes shuttered as he recalled the last night shift he had worked. You wouldn't know it to look at the kid, but he was always finding himself in more trouble than anyone in that building could afford. It was good he had Luca to look out for him, to protect him.

Whenever he was on duty, at least.

Luca had seen Michael wandering, as he too often did, down the halls that were off-limits and away from where all the other children had assembled to line up for roll call. Working fast, Luca had diverted all the cameras pointing at Michael, scrubbed any record of the kid being where he shouldn't have been, and then he'd counted down the seconds until the morning shift runner came in to take over for Luca. The instant he was free, Luca ran in the direction he had seen Michael heading, catching up to him on the steep incline that led up and out of the sublevels.

"Michael," Luca had gasped, out of breath from running half the length of the floor, and he pulled at Michael's arm, causing the boy to jump.

Michael had blinked, like he always did when Luca had to come find him, and he stared up into Luca's eyes in fear. "Luca," Michael said in a small voice, his eyes searching around the corridor they stood in. "I—I didn't mean—what—"

"Shh," Luca said, grabbing the younger boy to himself. "It's okay. They didn't see. You're fine."

(Of course, someone did see—a certain someone dressed in all black and seated in front of a wall of screens one floor beneath the boys—but they could not have known that.)

Michael hadn't said anything else, but he had let Luca lead him back to the center of the floor, where they slipped in line behind the others who were already amassed for roll call. Across the room, Caleb caught Luca's eye, raising his eyebrows in question. Luca just shook his head. They had made it. That was all that mattered.

Now, Luca checked over the cameras one final time, spotting Michael sitting on his bed in his room, his back pressed up against the wall, his arms wrapped around his knees. At least he was safe, Luca thought.

Safe. Such a relative term.

But yes, in that moment, one could call Michael safe. As safe as anyone in the building could be.

They had both been lucky. Michael hadn't been seen, and Luca hadn't gotten in trouble for showing up late to roll call. He knew he couldn't keep taking risks like that, knew that they were bound to catch up with him someday.

But did he have a choice, really?

Behind him, Luca heard the door opening and knew it was time to go. He straightened and said without turning back, "That time already."

He received only silence in response. Twisting around in his seat, Luca saw the stoic figure of the runner who had entered the room, dressed in their signature blue scrubs, with a black mask covering the lower half of his face. The runner did not speak—they never did. He stared straight ahead with such a vacant look in his eyes that Luca wondered, as he often did, at the runners' ability to monitor the camera feeds at all.

"Well, all right then," Luca mumbled to himself, standing up. As he moved to pass the runner, though, the blue-clad figure held out a hand, halting him. Luca looked up at the runner with some surprise, a tendril of dread spiking in him, but then he saw something in his hand. A piece of paper, folded carefully in half. Frowning, Luca took the note out of the runner's hand and opened it to Jamie's slanted handwriting. *Testing Room.* That was all it said.

Luca's blood chilled as he read those words, but he managed a nod. "Right," he said, mostly to himself. "Sure. I'll head there now."

Of course he would. He always would.

And the knowledge that he would go there on his own with no urging or forcing was why Jamie had sent this runner with this note, rather than showing up himself to bring him there.

Trust. What a tenuous idea.

But Luca received trust in the building, and he had very little else that he could call his own. So, he left the surveillance room, pretending his hands didn't have a slight tremor, and made his way to the testing room.

▪ ■ ■ ■ ▪

LATER THAT AFTERNOON, Luca sat on the floor of the dome with his back against the wall, watching the younger kids as they played. He liked being in here—seeing the freedom that still existed behind the eyes of those younger than him. He liked to think back to when he was that young and carefree, but more often than not when he tried to remember those wayward years, he came up empty, and so instead he came here.

Standing next to him, empty eyes looking out over the room of children, was a runner Luca had taken to calling Julia. He didn't know her real name—didn't even know if runners *had* names—but she was always there when he came to the dome. She never sent him away, even though he technically wasn't allowed to linger there long. She carried the same bulky, almost malformed frame as all the other runners. The same distant expression. But Luca always liked to imagine he could see a soft side in her, somewhere. He liked to think that sometimes he caught her watching the children with something like wistful affection in her eyes, rather than the blankness that he knew should have been there.

On the other side of Luca, a new figure plopped down on the floor. Michael. Luca smiled down at him, but it was a pained smile, laced with the memory of the other night, of what could have happened. Michael didn't seem to notice, and instead he propped his chin on his knees and looked at Luca.

"Don't you have to go?" Michael asked. "You're usually working right now."

"I know, kid," Luca said in a tired voice. "I know. Thought I'd come in here first. See your beautiful face." He made his eyes cross, and Michael laughed, the sound of which drew out a small smile from Luca. It fell away an instant later as the weight of what he was avoiding settled over him again.

It was always hardest for him right after being tested. The pretending. Acting the part of a loyal, happy resident. He could usually forget, or at least tell himself that it wasn't all that bad, living there.

The lies were never strong enough in the wake of the testing, though—with the pain still lacing his arms and the memories of that room still lacing his mind—and so Luca was afraid of what he might do or say if he went back there, back to the surveillance room and the confidence of the runners and the position where he was given (theoretically) so much, and in response expected to (theoretically) trust them in return.

And the truth was, there could be much worse in store for him than the testing. It was painful, but it was expected. It was the thought of the *unexpected* the runners could throw at him—dangers beyond the scope of imagination—that lingered on his mind with every camera he redirected, every kid he rescued just in time.

People who defied the building didn't get hurt. They vanished—went missing from the feeds in the surveillance room, and never showed up again. Luca didn't know where they went, what happened to them. But he couldn't imagine anything worse than that: disappearing one day without a trace, and without anyone to miss him, much less find him.

But even the threat of ceasing to exist wasn't enough to make Luca stop.

Though maybe it should have been.

His hands were still shaking in the aftermath of the testing, so he kept them clasped in his lap. His shoulder was still aching, his arms still trembling. It would go away in a few hours, he knew from experience. But not the memories of that room.

White room, silver tools, white chair, silver smile. Jamie's. All Jamie's.

And right now, he couldn't pretend any of that away.

So instead, he was here, with Michael and Julia, as far away from his responsibilities as possible.

If Michael registered any of what was on Luca's mind, he didn't show it. He leaned his head back and closed his eyes, and Luca couldn't help but wonder how long ago the kid had gotten a good night's sleep.

And he couldn't help but wonder if some part of Michael knew what happened in the testing room. If perhaps he had been in there, even.

They usually didn't start bringing the kids into that room until after they were ten—apparently the equivalent of adulthood within the building. Luca didn't know Michael's exact age, but he would guess right around ten. Young enough, in theory, that he might not have been brought in for testing yet.

In theory. That was always the key, wasn't it?

"Do you have to go back?" Michael asked without opening his eyes, and Luca thought he heard something in the kid's voice. Something small. Something scared, maybe. So he observed Michael, with his eyes still closed, for another moment, then leaned his head back and shut his own eyes.

"Not yet," he said. "Soon."

8

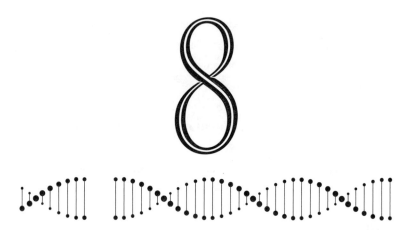

Everly sat in the dark, her back hunched over the kitchen table that was scattered with various stacks of envelopes and crumpled-up papers. Her elbows were propped up on the table, right over twin bills that screamed *Overdue* at her in bright-red letters. She wasn't looking at the bills, though. Her head was buried in her hands, her eyes clenched tight in a futile effort to stop the tears that were never far away these days.

Sucking in a ragged breath, she jerked up, another headache coming on. She'd been getting them for years, but they'd been growing so much worse recently. Just one more problem plopped onto the growing mountain of problems that was her life.

None of it really mattered anymore: the bills, the house, her headaches.

Her dad had been all she'd had. Twenty-four, and Everly still lived at home, bouncing around from part-time job to part-time job. Oh, she'd tried things, sure. Spent a year at a college three hours away, and when that didn't work out, she'd tried her hand at a few internships, traveled for a while. Nothing stuck. So she'd come home and had jumped from one brightly colored smock with a name tag to another for the four years since, waiting for something better. That something better had yet to come along, but all that time, Everly had always had her dad. While any past friends had long moved on and nothing else in her life ever seemed to line up right, her dad was the one constant that she'd come to rely on. She'd taken it for granted that he was always there, that she could always turn to him.

But *always* can be such a flimsy word.

"Evs, you can only ever be yourself," she could remember him saying to her, time and time again, when she thought she was failing at making the life she was supposed to live, at becoming the person she was supposed to be. "So, it's up to you to make sure you become the best version of yourself," he would say. "And that's all you'll ever need to be."

As she stared upward at the flickering yellow ceiling light above her table in the kitchen, Everly thought she could remember a time before when she had been just as alone. More than that, when she had been aching, bleeding, crying, fighting. Fighting? She had been scared, uncertain, and alone. Just like now. It was just like now. It was—

It was not real.

Behind Everly in the kitchen, a whistle began to sound, sharp and insistent, and it made her flinch. She had forgotten that she put the kettle on, but now she gladly took the opportunity to move, to shake herself awake.

None of that had been real. She didn't know what she had been remembering, but it didn't matter, because it wasn't real.

The bills were real. The red warnings splayed across them were real.

The heat of the stove was real, and she paused for a moment in front of it, hand outstretched so that it was an inch away from the blistering steel of the kettle, trembling there as the kettle continued to scream at her. Closer, closer, closer. Then: blink. Snap. Hand pulled away, head shaken awake. Blink blink blink.

She pulled the steaming kettle off the stove, listening as the biting whistle finally died down, and poured the water into a mug that was set on the counter with an old tea bag sitting inside. While Everly bobbed the tea bag in and out of the hot water, her thoughts began to trail toward the strange man from the day before.

Her grandfather, if he was to be believed.

It was absurd—she had no other word for it. The thought of meeting a stranger who may or may not be her grandfather at some strange building with an even stranger name.

The Eschatorologic, she thought. *What kind of a name for a building was that?* What struck Everly was not only its unorthodox name but also the fact that she had never heard of this building, which supposedly stood less than two miles from where she lived.

After she'd left the park, Everly had ventured to the nearest library, intent on finding answers. A clue, a relevant detail—something. Nothing about what the man told her made sense. And if anything, her trip to the library only left the whole ordeal murkier than before.

She'd searched for the building itself first. The Eschatorologic was a unique name; if it existed, surely it would have shown up.

Internet searches bore no fruit, so she'd turned to physical, paper accounts. Building records, maps of her town, receipts for past realty sales. Nothing. As far as proper records could indicate, the building didn't exist.

Next, she'd tried searching for the man. Dr. Richard Dubose. He, at least, definitely existed. She found a microfiche for a scientific article, half a century old, stating briefly how Richard Dubose, PhD, had been given a grant of such and such amount for research in the field of molecular biology and cell research within the realm of abnormal genetic output. Whatever that meant. There was an even older clipping with a picture of him in a well-pressed suit, smiling broadly next to a woman in a vintage-style white dress. The caption on the image listed them as the newly married Dr. and Mrs. Richard and Miranda Dubose. Her grandparents, supposedly. She'd tried to look more closely at the faces in the picture. The man was definitely Richard—a much younger, much happier version of him, with a full head of dark hair and an almost boyish grin that stretched ear to ear. The woman was more subdued, but undeniably beautiful. In the black-and-white image, it was impossible to tell the shade of her hair, but it floated around her shoulders in stylish waves. Everly struggled to see any of herself in the faded image of the young married couple, any hint of a relation between them.

That was all Everly was able to find on Richard. She'd then hesitated before deciding to type in one more name. Mary Dubose Tertium. Her mother.

The only result for that search was an obituary, dated twenty years earlier, in which Mary Dubose Tertium was listed as having died at the age of twenty-five to unknown medical causes, leaving behind a husband and a daughter.

Twenty-five. A few more months, and Everly would have outlived her own mother.

If her trip to the library had shown Everly one thing, it was that pieces were missing from the story Dr. Richard Dubose had offered her in the park.

And then there was the matter of her dad.

Everly shook her head, dispelling phantom memories from the week before, from what her dad had been like leading up to . . .

There has to be more to it, a voice whispered in her head now. That voice had been whispering to her all week, only growing louder after her encounter in the park.

She knew, in her core, that it hadn't been a car accident that killed him. It just didn't line up, didn't sit well with her. And so, if not that, then what?

Richard Dubose might know. Somehow, impossibly, he just might.

That nagging voice in her head told her it couldn't be a coincidence: her dad dying, and then one week later Dr. Richard Dubose tracking her down in a park to tell her about a building that she couldn't find any record of.

Maybe none of it was connected, and she was trying too hard to find an answer where there wasn't one to be found. Maybe it really was all about a lonely old man seeking out family, trying to form a connection where he never had before.

Or maybe she was onto something and this man, this Richard Dubose, knew more about what happened to her dad than she did.

Whatever the case may be, Everly couldn't put off anymore the one thing she did know: she had to go to that building.

Headache finally slipping away as she sipped her tea, Everly picked up the phone to call work, informing them that she'd be out a few days longer.

She was going to pay a visit to the Eschatorologic.

9

Everly Tertium entered the building for the first time fifty-three years ago (by some accounts). She didn't know why—it wasn't a very attractive or appealing building from the outside, by any means. Old, tall, decrepit. The kind of building you walk by on the fringes of city limits as a child and have adults quickly guide you away with furtive looks over their shoulders and a mumbled, "Let's not go this way." The kind of building you wouldn't be surprised to find a smattering of spray paint adorning one side, perhaps a few shattered windows on another. The kind of building you didn't willingly approach, at any rate. Certainly, the kind of building you didn't enter.

Everly Tertium was walking, and at some point her mind and her feet weren't synchronized any longer, and after a while she found herself there, standing before the glass front doors of the building. A sign hung out front—large, tattered. Hand lettered? *The Eschatorologic.* Strange, Everly Tertium thought. What a strange name.

She put her face up against the glass panes that made up the doors and squinted her eyes, trying to peer through.

Nothing. Just her fogged-up breath, filling the space between her face and the door.

Everly Tertium would later like to tell herself that she considered walking away at that point. That she paused a moment before she made her decision. But this would be a lie. Here's how it went instead: the squinting through the glass, peering, trying to make out anything. And then a shrug, so fast it was barely even there, and both hands braced on the glass where her face had been, pushing, and then she was inside.

Inside there was: nothing.

It was dark and empty. No desk yet, no benches, no chandelier. Just sprawling, barren space.

And then: a noise.

She thought it was a screech at first, until her nerves settled a tad and she realized that it had been a cough.

Not that that was much better. Where there was a cough there was a cougher.

Another moment passed when Everly Tertium did not pause, but rather she stepped farther into the open room—not exactly a lobby, yet—and walked in the direction of the cough.

What she found: a hallway, hidden on the other side of the wide-open room, that led back to an alcove with gray paint and gray carpets and gray doors.

And a man.

He was young in a wiry and mature way—wide glasses, knit vest, domed hat, wrinkled trousers. Dark hair, blue eyes. She had to squint to make out his eyes in the dimly lit hallway, but his machine helped.

It was small and boxy and covered in flashing lights that were either assessing with terrifying accuracy or completely for show. It also beeped, which she felt to coincide with the flashing in a way that the man holding the box probably understood, but she found just irritating enough to clamp a hand over one ear.

The man was fully absorbed in his flashy-beepy machine, so much so that Everly Tertium was watching him in the hallway for nearly a full minute before his eyes lifted, and froze, and widened.

Another ten to twenty seconds, and then the man spoke, in a soft and lyrical voice that Everly Tertium thought might be more suited for poetry than flashy machines. "You saw it?"

Her eyes leaped to the contraption in his hands. The man, noticing her expression, shook his head.

"The building. You saw the building."

"Oh," Everly Tertium said. "Sure."

"Do you know how?"

Did she know how she found the large, gray building that her feet somehow directed her straight to? "I walked?"

The man stared at her some more. "Marvelous."

"And you?" she asked, thinking there must be a reason for his fascination. In response, the man lifted the contraption.

"Electromagnetic pulse. Very unique energy signature. Very strange. I walked past the building at least five times before my eyes landed properly on it."

"Strange," was all she could think to say.

The man studied her from across the hall, then took a tentative step forward. Everly ducked her head, trying to hide what she knew the man would be able to see if he got too close. The bruising beneath her left eye, the marks she could still feel roughing up the side of her face. She retreated a step, but as the man approached her, he didn't even seem to notice.

When he was close enough, the man held out a hand, shifting the small machine around to be under his other arm. "Richard. Dubose."

She grasped his hand in hers, noting that it was unpleasantly clammy. And in that fleeting second, with her hand tucked inside his damp one, she remembered for the first time that maybe she should be afraid. Or at least moderately cautious. On a whim, she decided on a fake name, and offered it to him with the confidence that she hoped would assure him it was true.

It took a few seconds for the man to smile, but when he did it was wide and bright, stretching across the center of his face. "Welcome to the Eschatorologic."

10

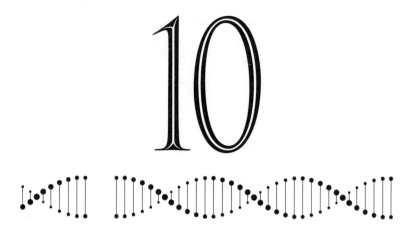

Everly Tertium entered the building for the first time two days after meeting Dr. Richard Dubose in the park by her house. Her grandfather. Two days after meeting her grandfather in the park, and being told that she had a grandfather, and being told that an inexplicable building existed not two miles from where she had lived all her life.

She was struck first upon entering the Eschatorologic by a low hum that seemed to rise out of the floor, resonating with every step she took into the lobby. A lobby that was possibly the most expansive room she had ever stepped foot in. Or at least, she supposed it was a lobby. Standing there in the entranceway, it felt more like a ballroom, with its domed ceiling that sported a chandelier the size of a small elephant, glittering so high above that she had to crane her neck to see it. Large wooden benches with intricately carved designs were pressed back against the walls on either side of the glass doors that Everly had pushed through, and marble tiles lined the floor, leading up to a large desk in the middle of the cavernous room.

There was a woman behind the desk. She sat rod-straight, with her eyes facing forward, not reacting at all to Everly's entrance. Cautiously, Everly began to walk across the lobby toward her. The woman was striking, with carefully carved features set into golden-brown skin and silky dark hair that hung in loose waves around her shoulders. Her exceptional beauty was almost entirely overshadowed by her clothes, however, which were abhorrently bland (beige on beige on beige). The beautifully beige woman still didn't acknowledge Everly or even so much as blink, really, so Everly cleared her throat and waited.

Still no response. "Excuse me," Everly tried. "I'm here to visit"—a beat of hesitation—"my grandfather. Maybe you know him?"

The woman didn't move. Chills ran up Everly's spine watching this woman who was so still she could have almost been a statue if it weren't for the slight rise and fall of her chest. It was unnerving; Everly wondered if something might be wrong with the woman.

"His name is Richard Dubose," Everly pressed on. "He told me to meet him here?"

The woman gave no indication at all that she had heard Everly. At a loss for what to do, Everly looked around the rest of the lobby, searching for some sign that Richard had been there, that she was in the right place. Off on the side, against the far wall, she spotted an elevator that she hadn't noticed before. *Maybe I can find him,* she thought.

Abandoning the woman and her desk, Everly walked toward the elevator. Halfway across the lobby, though, her feet stalled in place, her mind jarred by that uncanny feeling from before, from so many times before.

The déjà vu, if that's what it should be called.

The sense of reliving.

Of doing over.

Of experiencing a dream that she'd already had, again and again.

She had been here before. She had stood in this lobby before, talked to that woman behind that desk before, strode toward this elevator before. She had ridden in this elevator, up and down (down?), she had been here with Richard before, she had done it all. Before.

Blink blink blink and no she hadn't. Of course she hadn't. Everly put a hand up against her head, shaking it slightly. Why would she think she had? Except this time it didn't immediately clear away like it usually did.

Rather, the feeling of redoing felt stronger with every passing moment that she stood in the lobby. The harder she tried to focus on the feeling, the more abstract her thoughts and supposed memories began to feel.

She was old and young and a stranger and a friend and important and insignificant and everything and nothing all at once. None of the flashes lined up smoothly or made sense at all, but they pressed in against her, more and more insistent.

A small gasp escaped Everly's lips as she clenched her eyes shut and tried to push it all away, to steady herself. But the harder she tried, the harder the intrusive thoughts fought to overwhelm her. Or so it seemed. They were building, growing, spreading, overtaking. They were—

The elevator's ding cut through everything in Everly's mind, and she used that distraction to pull herself back to her present, to the place she was now.

The Eschatorologic. She was in the lobby of the Eschatorologic.

Blink blink blink blink.

Everly's eyes slowly came back into focus and, shaking away the rest of her unease over whatever *that* had been, she glanced up at the opening elevator doors in time to see a man stepping into the lobby.

He was easily the tallest man Everly had ever beheld, and she couldn't help but stare at him, her mouth agape. He made the lofty ceiling seem a reasonable height by comparison. The man then caught sight of Everly, who had taken a few steps back toward the woman's desk, and he walked up to her.

As he approached, Everly took in the details of his appearance. He seemed to be around middle age—mid- to late thirties, if she had to guess. He had pale skin and equally pale hair that had been shaved with military precision, framing a kind, boyish face, and he wore red scrubs that hung loosely off his gangly form.

The man glanced back and forth between Everly and the woman at the desk, a question on his face. "Is there something I can help with here?" he asked.

And just like that, Everly remembered why she was in that lobby at all, why she had been headed toward the elevator before the man had arrived in it himself. "Y-yes," she said, voice wobbling slightly. "I'm trying to find my grandfather. He works here, and I was just about to go look for him upstairs." She pointed weakly at the elevator doors, and the man glanced back that way.

He lifted his brows, studying Everly. "What did you say your name was?"

"Everly. Everly Tertium."

The man's face immediately cleared. "You're Richard's granddaughter, then," he said, declaring more than asking. Everly managed a small nod in response. "He said you might be coming by," the man went on. "And you said you were going to go upstairs?"

Everly nodded again, feeling small next to the man's looming height, but she was somewhat comforted by the fact that he knew who Richard was. At least she was in the right place.

"Well, I'm afraid that probably won't work out too well for you just yet," the man said. "The elevator, that is. But not to worry, I know how to fix that."

"What do you mean?" Everly asked, following the man as he retreated toward the elevator. "What wouldn't work?"

"Well," the man said, pulling a small device from one of his pockets and fiddling with it, "there's a facial recognition software programmed into the elevators. Assuming this is your first visit to the building, you won't be in the system yet, so the elevator won't let you move through the building."

"So, it's basically a program to keep people from breaking in?"

"Something like that. Now," the man said as the device began to light up in his hand. "This should do the trick. Say cheese."

Everly only had time to turn in the general direction of the object before a blinding flash went off.

"Got it," the man said. He then pulled a short cord from another of the overly large pockets in his uniform and proceeded to push the elevator button. It opened for him, and he stepped inside, placing his foot out to stop the doors from closing behind him. "All we have to do now is attach this to the elevator's control panel." Everly watched as he plugged one end of the cord into the device, the other into a slit below the elevator. "We upload you into the facial recognition program, and then you should be good to go."

Everly saw the man frown slightly. "What?" she asked, trying to see what he was doing.

"It looks like you've already been programmed in. Odd. Your gramps must have done it before you got here." For a moment, the man stared at the paneling inside the elevator. Then, his eyes lifted to Everly's face, and she saw—or thought she saw—them widen, ever so slightly. Thought she saw his mouth making a soft sound, an *oh*. But then, she thought she must have imagined that, because he shook his head and grinned up at her from his crouch on the ground. "Well, at any rate, you are now free to use the elevator."

"Thanks," Everly said, smiling back at the man as he stood up.

"No problem." He slipped the device back into his pocket, and then held out his hand. "I'm Jamie, by the way. Jamie Griffith."

Everly took his hand and shook it. "Thank you, Jamie," she said.

"Anytime," he said brightly, stepping back out of the elevator. "It is my job, after all."

"Wait," Everly said, putting a hand out to stop the elevator doors from closing. "What is this place, anyway?"

Jamie cocked his head, a strange smile on his boyish face. "Don't you know?"

"Not really. I was told to come, that's all."

"Well, who am I to ruin the mystery, then?" Jamie said, backing away from the elevator. "It was a pleasure meeting you, Miss Tertium."

Everly frowned at the doors as they closed, then her eyes slid over to the wall of buttons. The building, it seemed, went up one hundred floors, and Richard could have been on any one of them. There were also two basement floors, she noticed, but it looked like those levels required a key to access, so she just had to hope that he wasn't down there. She didn't have any good options; Richard really could be anywhere.

Everly decided to start at the bottom, and hope she'd either stumble into him, or into someone else who could help her navigate the Eschatorologic. And in the meantime, maybe she could try to learn something about this building. So Everly pushed the button for the second floor and held her breath as the elevator began to hum gently, going up.

When the doors slid open again a few moments later, the first thing Everly took in was gray.

Gray walls. Gray floors. Gray doors that lined the single hallway on either side directly across from the elevator, going back, back, back, morphing into an endless expanse of nothing.

Everly stared at the gray hallway and had no idea where to begin. Before she could think too much about all the gray doors and what might lie behind them, one of the doors near her opened, and a man dressed in red stepped out.

He was so different without the tweed, the coat, the hat. Nonetheless, it was definitely him, dressed in identical red scrubs to Jamie.

Richard Dubose. Her grandfather.

The man she was looking for.

It was almost too easy, Everly knew. One hundred (and two) floors, and she found him within five minutes of entering the building? It was almost like he'd known where she'd go, or like he'd known she'd show up today, of all the days.

Everly shook her head, trying to clear it as she waited for Richard to catch sight of her. As he turned toward the elevator, he halted, confusion turning to delight as his face lit up.

"Everly," he said, walking swiftly toward her. "You're here!" He stopped in front of her, brows furrowing again. "But how did you get up?"

Everly blinked, trying to clear away the disorientation that had followed her since she entered the building. "There was a man," she said. "Downstairs. He said his name was Jamie. He programmed the elevator to let me ride in it. But," she said, thinking back, "Jamie told me that I had already been programmed in. He thought that maybe you had done it."

Richard's smile faded slightly. "Right. No, no, I didn't think to do that earlier. But Jamie is a bright man. He is the primary software engineer in the Eschatorologic. I mentioned to him that I might need him to help me with that very thing at some point today, when you got here. But you're here early!"

He said that as if she'd agreed to come today, but Everly herself hadn't been sure until the night before. Her brows drew together as she studied the man in front of her, weighing the merit of all the questions that bubbled beneath the surface.

"Richard—" she started.

"You can call me Grandpa. If you want."

Everly stared at the man. Was that what she wanted? All her life, she'd dreamed of what it'd be like to have more family. Aunts and uncles, cousins, siblings. Grandparents. And here it was, an offer for something that could almost be seen as a hand reaching out, ushering her into a family she'd never known.

Yet, that voice was still in the back of her head, telling her something was wrong here. Telling her not to trust Dr. Richard Dubose.

"What is this place?" she asked instead, the same question she'd asked Jamie, hoping now for a more straightforward answer.

"Why, it's a building," was Richard's response.

Everly bit her lip in frustration. "Well, yes, but what kind of building? Why did you bring me here?"

"I suppose the easiest answer would be to say that this place is my life's work, the culmination of years' worth of research and study. More than anything, however, this is a building full of people, some of whom I would very much like to introduce you to today, if you'd care to join me?"

He lifted an arm, gesturing toward the long, gray hallway beyond where they stood.

She wanted to ask so much. Why now, after all these years?

What had kept him away, why hadn't she ever heard anything about him? She also wanted to ask about her mother. It had been dangling around the back recesses of her mind since that day at the park, though she hadn't wanted to admit it to herself—didn't want to admit that she had been drawn here, to this building in part by the base desire to hear Richard talk about her mom.

This man had known her mother—and no one knew Everly's mother. But how do you ask someone you barely know what might be the most important questions of your life?

Before she was given the chance to formulate the right words, Richard cleared his throat. "Come," he said to Everly, already walking away. "I have someone I want you to meet." He gestured again to one of the gray doors down the hall—not the first door, but the second in a long string of tightly shut doors—and Everly, deciding questions could come later, followed as he walked over, and then paused, in front of the indicated door.

"A woman lives here—a woman who has gone through a great deal in her life. Her name is Lois," he said without conviction, "and she has been in this building for a long time, nearly as long as I have. Be careful with her. Her mind is fragile these days."

Not knowing what to say, Everly simply nodded, wondering why Richard wanted her to meet this woman, whoever she was.

Richard pushed open the gray door and stepped inside. Following him, Everly found herself in a very small, sparsely furnished gray apartment.

The space seemed to consist of three rooms: a cramped bedroom that Everly could see behind a partially opened door to her right; a meager kitchenette in the corner with only a microwave, a stove with two burners, and a mini fridge balanced precariously on the countertop; and a sparse living room that consisted of nothing but four blank walls surrounding a single gray couch, on which sat a very old woman.

Everly supposed this was Lois. She looked to be about her grandfather's age, but her eyes read as being far more ancient. When she saw Everly and Richard enter the room, Lois struggled a bit to sit up straighter. She was outfitted in scrubs that were nearly identical to those worn by Jamie and Richard, except that hers were a very bland shade of gray.

Her hair was completely white, and her eyes were a cataract-coated blue that momentarily caught Everly off guard as they looked at her. Pierced her. A shiver shot unbidden through Everly, and she swallowed thickly before following Richard over to the woman's side.

"Good morning, Lois," Richard said, his voice bright and cheery. "How are you doing today?"

Lois didn't seem to hear him. Her focus was still caught on Everly, eerie in her unwavering intensity. Richard gestured for Everly to move closer, offering an encouraging smile.

"Lois, I want you to meet my granddaughter. This is Everly."

Everly offered the woman a weak smile, lifting a single hand in greeting. "Hi," she said. "Nice to meet you."

The woman started blinking rapidly, and her breathing became ragged. "You," she said in a thin, shaky voice. "You . . . you're . . ." She trailed off, blinking faster still. Blink blink blink. "What did you say your name was again?"

Everly gulped, rubbing her hands over the gooseflesh that had risen on her arms. "I'm Everly," she said softly. "Everly Tertium. I'm Richard's granddaughter." She gestured to Richard, hoping that might help.

The woman's gaze cleared ever so slightly, and then her eyes widened, her face bleached suddenly of all color.

"You," she said uneasily. "You're—you're not supposed to be here." She met Everly's eyes, her expression pained. "It's not your time."

"I—" Everly took a step back, suddenly afraid of the elderly woman in front of her, unsure what was happening or why she felt so wrong.

Richard hurried forward and sat down on the gray couch beside Lois, gently touching her shoulder. "Lois," he said calmly. "Lois, it's okay. You're okay."

Lois was still shaking, but she turned to look at Richard, leaning her slight frame into his and sobbing uncontrollably.

"Richard, oh Richard," she gasped between sobs. "I thought, I thought . . ."

"I know, Lois. It's going to be okay. I promise." Richard turned his head up suddenly. "Everly, go look in the cabinet over the sink in the kitchen. You should find a small bottle of pills. Bring it here, please, as well as a glass of water. Quickly," he said as she hesitated, and Everly rushed over to the cabinet he had indicated, hastily finding the pills and bringing them back. Richard took the bottle and shook out a pill, offering it up to Lois, who obediently swallowed the medicine.

She immediately began to settle down, not crying anymore but still leaning into Richard's shoulder. As she tilted her head down, eyes closed, Everly thought she glimpsed a thin, silvery line running up the back of Lois's neck, disappearing into her sparse, white hair, but before Everly could look too closely, Lois shifted, sinking deeper into Richard's side as she fell asleep.

Easing Lois onto the opposite cushion, Richard extricated himself from her grip and edged off the couch. He stood up and walked slowly over to Everly. Then, he signaled for them to leave the apartment and went back out into the gray hallway. After closing Lois's door, Richard turned around to face Everly, wearing a weary smile. He leaned against the wall next to the door, looking older than he probably was for the first time since Everly had met him. She waited for him to speak, to explain what had just happened. He looked up at her with tired eyes but managed a smile.

"I'm sorry," he said. "That—Lois is a woman who is very easily distressed, and who has lived through her fair share of difficulties. I didn't expect the intensity of her reaction, and I am sorry if she scared you."

"She didn't scare me," Everly said, thinking back on what had happened. "More unsettled, I guess. What made her so upset? Did I do something wrong?"

"Wrong?" Richard shook his head. "No, not wrong. None of that was your fault, not at all. But I needed you to meet her, and her you, before I could begin to explain . . . anything else." He sighed deeply, looking down. Despite his apparent exhaustion, however, Everly sensed an undercurrent of energy in his posture that she was struggling to reconcile with their interaction with Lois moments before.

"Okay," Everly said slowly. "So, explain. Why did you bring me here? What is this place?"

Richard met her eyes, and there it was again: that strange energy pulsing through him. "I need you to know that Lois is a very dear friend of mine. I've known her since the beginning of all of this. But she is only a fraction, the smallest piece of anything here. And she was only the beginning."

"What do you mean?" Everly pressed. "The beginning of what?"

"Everly," Richard said, "the people here are special. My *work* here is special. It's all connected, and I promise that someday this will all make sense. What you need to know right now is that you are an important part of this."

"Me?" Everly asked, dumbfounded and barely able to follow Richard's frenzied whispers. "What do I have to do with anything?"

"Everything," Richard said, then shook his head. "I promise you, this will all make sense eventually. For right now, what I need you to understand is that Lois is only one of many people who are kept here in this building."

The word he used—*kept*—snagged in Everly's mind. Like they were possessions or pets owned by someone. She stared at Richard, trying desperately to understand.

"Why are they here?"

"They're here to change the world."

But Everly didn't hear her grandfather's response. Her mind had fallen backward again—or forward, so hard to tell. Standing in front of Richard—of a man who looked an awful lot like Richard, only with brown hair instead of gray, only with no wrinkles or age spots, only with brighter eyes. Standing in that building. Or a building an awful lot like that building—only with no people in gray apartments and no woman sitting frozen behind a front desk and no scientists with wide smiles and fancy gadgets.

Everly blinked and she fell further, further, further.

Blink blink blink blink blink.

11

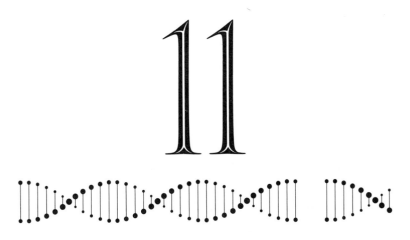

Everyone is special, in their own right, but some determinedly more so than others.

Dr. Richard Dubose was not special—at least not in the way that the building recognized as being so. From a genetic perspective, he was spectacularly, ridiculously, overwhelmingly ordinary.

So how had he discovered the building in the first place?

You could argue his fancy device had something to do with it: electromagnetic bloodhound doodad, or whatever he called it.

You could say it was intuition. Spend enough years studying a thing, the thing might begin to study you.

You could say it was luck. If you were to say that such a thing existed at all.

You could say a lot of things, but you couldn't prove any of them. The building was funny like that. It liked being obvious, and opaque, and an absurd combination of the two.

You could say he was meant to find the building.

He'd like to say that, at any rate.

In the lengthy-short-eternal lifespan of the building, Dr. Richard Dubose was one of the very few ordinary people to ever stumble across its premises.

Maybe it meant he was extraordinarily brilliant.

Maybe it meant he searched farther and wider than anyone else would have had the gumption for hunting down a nonexistent building.

Or maybe the building just wanted a friend for once.

But honestly, who's to say?

Regardless of the means or reasons behind Dr. Richard Dubose's presence in the building, there was no denying the fondness he held for the Eschatorologic, or the fondness that was reciprocated in return. He loved the gray walls that held all the potential imaginable (in his opinion). He loved the mystery of it all, even when he had spent so many decades searching to unravel as much of it as he could. Above all, he loved the people in the building.

And he loved what they could do.

Everly Tertium departed from the building—though she would return, Richard knew, if history was to be any indication—and Richard found himself nearly giddy. This was why he loved it, his role here. All the threads and pieces and links that formed the longer you sat with the puzzle that was the building.

He never would have guessed, fifty, sixty years before, upon beginning his great search for answers. He never would have guessed about her. Yet there she was—at the beginning, at the end, and in all the cracks and crevices in between. She was everywhere, and he never would have guessed.

His granddaughter.

And now he was close, *so close*, to fixing everything. Making it all right. He'd found her, he'd gotten her to come. Now he just had to make sure she returned.

And then he could save her.

Her very existence nearly defied all logic. Now, it was up to him to ensure she continued to exist.

He wouldn't fail.

I'll make it right, he thought. *This time, no mistakes.*

He hadn't wanted to tell the Warden, not right away.

He'd wanted to be sure. But now, after meeting her so many times and having so many identical conversations, he knew beyond a shadow of a doubt.

It was her. It would always be her.

Richard was high with the possibilities of it all as he stood in the elevator, inserting the key into the narrow slot by the button labeled B2 and riding it down into the very heart of the Eschatorologic. He was jittery with anxious energy as he walked down the black hallways of the building's lowest level. As he reached the office's door, he made a concentrated effort to stifle his nerves, settle his resolve.

It was always slightly jarring, coming into the Warden's office—being affronted with the screen that was set up between the door and the rest of the room, blocking much of the light that was cast from the desk lamp on the other side. Richard always felt the smallest pinch of annoyance when faced with the screen. In a certain context, he understood the necessity for it. The Warden held a power in the building that was hard to define and would be harder to retain without the distinct level of mystique that was cast over the role by the lack of knowledge as to the Warden's identity.

But Richard knew—of course he knew. Richard, in many ways, had helped to shape the position of the Warden. He should have held nearly as much credit as the Warden did, yet here he was, separated on the other side of the screen.

He supposed he should be grateful. So few even made it to this side of the screen at all.

From across the room, he heard the shuffling of papers. He knew the Warden heard him come in and was listening, so Richard cleared his throat and tried to speak with as much authority as he could muster. Always so much harder with that screen in the way.

"We had a visitor today."

Silence. Richard cleared his throat again, determined not to be deterred by such a nonreaction.

"My granddaughter, as it happens." He paused before saying, "Everly."

From the other side of the room came a new kind of silence. He wished—oh, how he wished—that he could see the Warden's face right now. Could see what would be splayed across it.

"I believe she will return," Richard plowed on valiantly. "And then I can test her, of course." Not that he needed to, really. "This is a good thing, you know," he continued when the Warden remained silent. "For all of us. You, me, her. The building. We all stand to profit from this. I know you value your . . . privacy, but you have to understand that Everly coming here will only benefit us all."

Everly, Richard thought. She had always used a different name, and he had always known that it was a fake, but now, having heard her true name from her, it rang so bright and real for him. He was tempted to repeat it aloud, but he knew that the Warden wouldn't appreciate it, so he bit his tongue, deciding not to push his luck.

Finally, *finally*, a voice came from the other side of the room. "Very well. Keep me posted."

That was all the Warden had to say. Richard opened his mouth, feeling like he should have been entitled to more of a conversation. But it was clear that the Warden was done, and so he was as well.

Besides. There was more work to be done.

Always more work to be done.

12

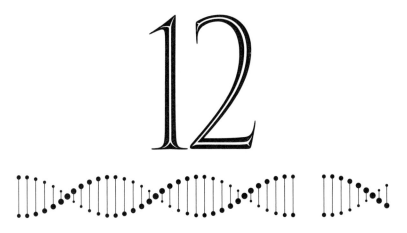

The black paint of the walls around him was hard to focus on after so many hours in front of the brightly lit screens of the surveillance room, but Luca didn't mind.

Jamie had pulled him out at the end of his shift, and Luca had been certain that he was being sent back.

To the testing room.

To that hard metal chair.

To . . .

But that wasn't what Jamie wanted him for. He had asked if Luca still had the keys, and then sent him down here.

The black floor.

Very few residents knew enough about the building to even be aware of the black floor's existence. Luca didn't know of anyone else who came down here. He knew the runners and reds alike probably had access, but he had never run into another soul while traversing the black halls of the basement level.

His feet tapped off the black tiles of the floor as he went—the only noise in the abandoned corridors—and he relished the sound. It meant he was alone, which was a novel concept within the building.

Though he knew that would never entirely be true. His eyes traced over a spot on the ceiling where he knew an invisible camera was planted. He could visualize the angle from the other end—from his chair in the surveillance room that he had sat at nearly every day for years now—and he knew that whoever was in there now was watching him as he made his way to the back of this floor.

Luca was glad Jamie had sent him down here. It meant that they still trusted him enough to send him off on his own within the building. Six months before, Jamie had approached Luca and presented him with a ring of keys that he said could unlock nearly every door in the Eschatorologic.

Not every door, he had implied. But enough. He wasn't allowed to keep all the keys—Jamie always took back the ones that were too valuable, too dangerous. But access to anything beyond the door to his room was more than Luca had been privileged to before—more than he knew any of the other residents had access to. He knew it was so he could carry out roles around the building without needing a runner escort—like the job he had been given now—but it still felt like a taste of freedom to him. One of the first he had ever been given inside that building.

Depending on the day, Luca was sometimes asked to go up, either to bring or take away something from the residents who lived above ground. They never remembered him, but he enjoyed getting to talk to the older residents, nonetheless.

Other days, Jamie would send Luca to tell someone—usually either a runner or Dr. Dubose—a piece of information. Luca never really understood the messages but was happy enough just being able to roam around the building.

Today, he had been asked to go down to the black floor and retrieve a file for Jamie. Luca didn't know what most of the rooms on this floor held—too many of the locks didn't belong to any of the keys on his ring and too many of the rooms didn't have cameras—but usually when he was asked to come down here it was to retrieve a file. No one told Luca what the files were for or what was within them, but to the best of his knowledge this floor was nothing more than a glorified filing cabinet. The first few times he had come down here, Jamie had shown him the rooms he would have access to, and how to know where to pull the files from. Now, Luca was sent out on his own, and he was taking the opportunity to drag his feet far more than usual.

The longer he lingered on this floor, he knew, the longer he could avoid his regular duties.

The longer he could avoid the surveillance room.

The cameras.

Her.

Impossible, incredible, intangible *her*.

One hour before, Luca had been working.

Just working.

It had been fine—normal, uneventful.

And then he'd just . . . seen her.

In a camera feed. On a screen. Like she was anyone else.

The girl from his dreams.

He knew that it couldn't be real, that dreams didn't manifest themselves like that, out of nowhere. Especially not for him—Luca had never really been the type to have dreams come true.

And yet.

She *had* been there—he was certain of it.

In the lobby of the building.

His building.

Luca had been reeling over this, over the stupefying sight of her face, a face that he thought he knew so well, reflected as if straight from his dreams, and there, into the building's lobby.

And then Jamie came in, yanking him out of the daze he had fallen into upon seeing the girl's face on the screens of the surveillance room.

Luca was glad for it—the distraction. Glad to have something else to focus on. Except that now he was alone with only his thoughts, his memories, his dreams, and so there was nothing to stand in the way of him thinking back to her face, only an hour before.

So close to where he had been seated a floor below.

Luca shuddered internally. It was possible that he hadn't seen her—that it had been someone else entirely, or that his mind had made her up. He didn't think he wanted to know the truth. Didn't want to know yet if it was real or not, if *she* was real or not.

So instead, he was down here, avoiding reality as thoroughly as he could.

Luca came up to the door he needed to access. None of the doors on that floor had any labels, but he came and went so often that by now he knew this part of the floor well, and knew which doors were the ones he would be able to go through. The key ring jangled in his hand as he pulled it out of the deep pockets of his gray scrubs. His key ring had far fewer keys than the ones belonging to the runners, but Luca still relished the sight of all those small pieces of metal, strung together and belonging to him. As much as anything could belong to him. The proof that, to a limited extent, he could leave the narrow world that had been built up for him.

He found a thin silver key on the ring and inserted it into the lock, twisting it once and hearing the satisfying click of the mechanism within turning.

Inside, the room looked the same as every other room on that floor that Luca had been in. There were rows and rows of tall, metal cabinets with drawers that extended nearly from floor to ceiling. The cabinets were labeled with letters and numbers, none of which Luca understood. Jamie had given him the information he needed to find the file he was looking for, so Luca meandered between the cabinets, searching for the right one.

It didn't take as long as he would have liked, and soon Luca was sliding open the indicated drawer, ruffling through the files until he found the one with the right label.

He was always curious. Luca knew a camera was directed right at him within that room—knew that the instant he tried to open one of the folders, an army of runners would be upon him. It had to be important—the information he was sent down so often to retrieve, that was kept so locked down and hidden on that floor. He wondered what it would mean, if he were to open it and read what was inside. Would it change anything for him, to know what they were doing there?

Maybe. Or maybe he would lose the small amount of freedom he had worked so hard to gain over absolutely nothing.

Luca didn't open the file, instead navigating his way back through the twisting black halls, heading for the stairs. He didn't know why they wouldn't let him use the elevator—maybe that would have been too much freedom. The stairs were usually fine, at any rate, until he was asked to go up to the ninetieth floor, where he would find himself red-faced and huffing, the muscles in his legs burning from the exertion. Going up from the black floor to his floor wasn't too bad. It was only one flight.

One flight in the dark, though, which he wasn't always that thrilled about.

With a sigh, Luca reached the door that would lead him into the staircase. He pulled out a new key—this one larger and bronze in color—and he entered the dark beyond, the manila file with all its secrets clasped in his hand.

13

Dust clouds permeated the air, filling the room with the musty scent of something forgotten, something unused. Everly coughed, waving a hand to dispel some of the particles.

She was spending the afternoon going through her dad's things—both because it needed to be done, and because it gave her something to do with her hands while her mind tried to piece together what she had seen while visiting the Eschatorologic.

Their house was a single floor, divided into four spaces: kitchen, living area, bedrooms, and storage. She was starting with the room they used for storage; his bedroom had remained closed up like a vault since his death, and she hadn't been able to force herself to enter it yet. Later, she kept telling herself. That could come later.

The storage space might have once been set aside as a third bedroom or an office, but Everly and her dad had taken to filling it with sporadically labeled cardboard boxes of keepsakes and tossed aside trash bags of everything they'd never gotten around to donating or throwing out.

So far, Everly had made a rather substantial pile of all *her* old things that she'd long forgotten were even in that back room, but she had found surprisingly little of her dad's. She'd never considered him to be much of a minimalist, but box after box of miscellaneous junk seemed to be all hers, none his.

As she sorted through a box of old sweaters from her high school years—setting aside one or two she thought she might still be able to pull off—Everly reflected on everything that had happened the day before. Everything she'd seen at the Eschatorologic.

They're here to change the world, Richard had said. It was nonsense, pure and simple. What could he possibly mean? Nothing Everly had seen remotely suggested the magnitude Richard seemed to believe he was working with.

She ran through a list of what she knew about the Eschatorologic. The building had a hundred and two floors, two of which you needed a key to access. What would warrant being kept locked up like that down there? Could there be dangerous chemicals stored in the basement? Or contraband of some kind? Or maybe it wasn't that illicit, and that was just where they stored cleaning supplies. Regardless, the building had one hundred and two floors, and thus far Everly had seen exactly two of them.

A lobby, with one strange receptionist. And an all-gray floor, consisting of a hallway lined with doors.

The only room Everly had entered was a dwelling of some kind for a very old, very disturbed woman. Taking a small leap in assumption, Everly would guess that other rooms in the building likewise housed other people—perhaps equally old and disturbed.

She knew no one was telling her the truth—that much was evident. Neither Jamie nor Richard would give her a straightforward answer when asked what the building was, which could only bode poorly for whatever truth they were trying to cover up.

Everly tried to think of a logical explanation for everything she'd seen. It could be some kind of nursing home, or a hospital. An asylum. A prison?

None of it quite fit, which she knew, but she couldn't think of anything else it could be. Trying to banish further thoughts on the building—for now, at least—Everly shoved aside a rather heavy box and found an old wooden crate. It was soft and spongy around the edges, like the wood had been left in a damp space for far too long. Everly nudged aside another cardboard box so she could sit on the floor in front of the wooden crate, and she pried off the lid. The interior of the box emitted a musky odor as Everly peered down into the contents. She stuck a hesitant hand inside, wary of anything that might have been overtaken years ago by mildew and age.

The first item she pulled out of the box was a photo album. One she'd never seen before. Everly opened the cover and stared in shock as she was met with the warm blue eyes of her mother. Mary Tertium smiled up at Everly through the fading picture, a floppy beach hat drooping over her forehead and a bottle of what looked like champagne in her hands.

It had been a long, long time since Everly had seen a picture of her mother. A piece of her was relieved to see that her scarce memories lined up fairly well with this tangible image of her.

Flipping the page, she found more images that reflected a time she had little to no memory of. Several of her as a baby, dressed up in frilly clothes, the occasional bonnet, and more than one animal costume. A couple of a very young version of her dad, with a full head of hair and, to her shock, in some a bushy beard. She also found some pictures of all three of them—Everly and both of her parents. A family that used to be.

At the end of the photo album were several blank pages. Everly ran her fingers over the edges of the pages, checking if there was anything she had missed. From between two of the last pages, an image fell out, landing in her lap. Everly picked it up, and the breath froze in her chest.

It was a picture of her. Not her as a baby, as in the rest of the album's pictures, but her now. In the picture, she was seated in a nondescript area, looking away from the camera so that the shot only caught the side of her face. But there was no denying that it was her—Everly knew herself, knew that it couldn't be anyone else.

So why did she have no memory of this picture being taken?

Shaken, Everly hastily set the album back in the crate, shoving the photo of herself back in between two random pages. She rummaged again through the rest of the items in the box, none of which she recognized from her childhood: a rose-colored sweater, a fountain pen with a university's insignia carved into the side, several novels that she couldn't imagine her dad ever reading.

Eventually, Everly began to suspect she had found a box of her mother's belongings—things her dad had decided to keep stored away in here rather than throw out.

The items in the box painted the edges of a picture for a woman whom Everly had never been given a chance to know. This box said she had been a woman who enjoyed small comforts and little moments. Soft things and memories. The items told a story of a woman who loved her life.

And had it taken from her all too soon.

At the bottom of the box, crushed beneath a hefty volume of short stories, Everly noticed what looked like a crumpled-up piece of paper. She pulled it out, frowning as she tried to smooth out its edges.

There was no date on the piece of paper, so no telling how long it had sat at the bottom of the crate. Someone had scrawled out a note in wide, looping handwriting across the white piece of paper. But it wasn't addressed to her mother—it was addressed to her father.

Jacob,

The time is drawing near. You know it is. You need to make a decision, soon. Come and visit me—you remember the way, I'm sure. I think you know what has to happen.

There was no signature, not even so much as initials to go by. Everly hadn't the faintest idea what the letter was supposed to mean. What decision was her dad being asked to make? What did this person, whoever they were, think had to happen?

She read the letter again, hoping for some other clue to pop out, but there was nothing. It was too vague, too nondescript. With care, Everly folded the piece of paper, then set it back inside the crate.

Why was her dad receiving mysterious letters at all? She had always considered him to be an upfront, straightforward kind of man, but recently she wasn't so sure.

Could this letter be connected somehow to what happened to him?

Everly shook her head. That was too much speculation, even for her. This letter could have been in that crate for decades; there was nothing to suggest it had anything to do with her dad's death.

But still, she couldn't stop thinking about it.

The week before he died, there was something off about him. He came home one day acting strange, and he refused to tell her where he'd been or what he'd been doing, only turned aside and walked away. She followed after him, and he shook her off, leaving her standing behind in the hall as he closed himself in his room.

A few days later, he left again—went out without telling her why. When she'd seen him that morning, the sight of him had left a twisting in Everly's gut. He hadn't looked like her father. His eyes were sunken in, empty, frantic. His skin—so wane, so sallow. He left quickly that morning, running out the front door without noticing Everly standing behind in the shadows. Afterward, she tried to banish the image of her father escaping the house like a wild animal set free—but then she had walked into the kitchen and found the note.

Don't follow me, it said. *I will be home soon. I promise.*

But he'd lied.

The police found him later that afternoon, and she was so unable to reconcile the image of the man she had seen that morning—the man who hadn't looked or seemed at all like her father—with what they said happened to him.

They said a car accident, and who was she to question that? He had been found in his car, after all, and it had been totaled. Wrapped around a tree, according to the cops.

She didn't know much, but she did know her dad was always a careful driver, the kind who never went more than three miles per hour over the speed limit, who used turn signals when there wasn't another car within five blocks of him.

Not the kind of driver to wrap himself around a tree.

And Everly didn't know much when it came to injuries, but she didn't think his sounded right.

Lacerations up and down his arms. Burns covering his whole body. More skin damaged than not.

He wouldn't have been so careless as to wreck his car like that.

And he was supposed to come back. He always came back.

He had promised.

Something had rattled her dad that week, and somehow, because of all that, he died. The explanation could have been as simple as he hadn't been in his right frame of mind, and that led him to swerve his car off the road, but she didn't believe it, not really. The man she'd seen that week, the one with the crazed eyes and frantic energy, hadn't seemed at all like the man she'd known all her life.

But he had seemed like the kind of man who might receive ominous, unsigned messages and not tell her about them.

Everly placed the lid back on the wooden crate. Her dad, Richard, the Eschatorologic. This box full of her mother's keepsakes.

It was all too much, all at once.

And what about her? It was undeniable that something was also happening inside her head—something beyond the headaches. Visions, memories she shouldn't have, images that made no sense.

Her thoughts strayed to that picture of herself found in the back of the old photo album. The one she had no recollection of being taken.

Maybe she was losing her mind. Maybe that's all this was—her own slow descent into madness.

Everly didn't know what was happening to her, or what had happened to her dad, and she didn't know what was happening in that building.

But with a sinking in her stomach, Everly understood that there was only one place she could go to get more answers.

▪ ▪ ■ ▪ ▪

As EVERLY APPROACHED the Eschatorologic the next day, she saw Richard waiting outside. She waved a hand in greeting, trying to smile despite the anxious energy that coursed through her.

"You're waiting for me today," Everly said.

"It's a large building," Richard said as she reached the top of the stairs, falling into step beside him. "Easy to get lost. Dangerous, in fact. I didn't want you alone in there anymore, so I figured it would be easiest to wait out here."

"What if I hadn't come back?"

Richard glanced down at Everly. "I had faith that you would. And besides," he said, gesturing around them, "it's a beautiful day to wait outside."

It was a beautiful day, but Everly could see there was something Richard wasn't telling her, a tension to his posture that hadn't been there the day before. "Are you okay?" Everly asked. "You look a little pale."

Richard shook his head, face suddenly serious. "I want you to meet a few more people today," he said. "Some really amazing people, actually. Men and women I have come to care for greatly during my years working here."

As she followed Richard into the Eschatorologic, Everly again felt the floor buzzing beneath her feet, as if the building itself were rumbling from all the pent-up mysteries stored within its walls.

The same woman as before sat behind the desk in the lobby, and Everly glanced at her uneasily as she walked toward the elevator with Richard. The woman didn't acknowledge either of them, continuing to sit straight with her head lifted high, her eyes unblinking.

Once in the elevator, Everly turned to Richard. "Who is that woman?" she asked, indicating the direction of the lobby beyond the closed elevator doors. "The one who's always behind that desk. She seems . . . I don't know. Strange? Yesterday, she wouldn't even look at me when I tried talking to her."

Richard's face softened, his eyes going distant. "That's Sophia," he said. "She's . . . very special, very dear to me. She's one of our runners. More or less. Was the very first one, actually."

"Runners," Everly repeated. "What does that mean—" Everly started to ask, but then the elevator chimed as the doors opened to the third floor, and Richard cut her off, exclaiming, "Here we are!" as he strolled out. Everly stood where she was a moment, watching him walk away, before huffing a sigh of frustration and following behind.

This floor was identical to the second floor in every way—same gray walls, gray floors, gray doors going all the way back to the end of the lengthy hallway. Richard passed by the first door in the hall, stopping in front of the second.

Inside was another bare apartment, this one with a man who sat at the small wooden kitchen table. He was slight in stature and hunched over, staring at a plate in front of him with something that looked almost like mashed potatoes. His head was bald and shriveled, reminding Everly of an overly large raisin, and he wore a gray uniform identical to the one Lois had worn the day before. Also identical to Lois was the thin, silvery scar that Everly could see running up the back of his neck—much more visible on this man, with his bald head, than it had been on Lois. Everly wanted to ask.

Everly was afraid to ask.

The man didn't appear to notice Everly or Richard as they came in, continuing instead to stare at the plate of food in front of him.

"Hello, Maurice," Richard said, approaching the man. "I hope you're doing well this morning. I see one of the runners has already paid you a visit." He nodded at the plate of food and then turned to Everly. "The runners are what we call the workers here," he said, answering her half-asked question from the elevator. "Among other duties, they are responsible for bringing food to the residents on these floors. Many of those living here can't handle even feeding themselves on their own."

Everly watched as Richard sat down in the chair across from Maurice, smiling kindly at him.

"I brought someone here to visit you today, Maurice," Richard said, and he gestured over to where Everly stood. "This is Everly. She is my granddaughter, and she is excited to meet you." He looked pointedly from Everly to Maurice and so, taking the hint, Everly walked around the table and took one of the remaining empty chairs.

"Hi," she said, voice small and uncertain. "I'm Everly. It's nice to meet you."

Still, Maurice did not move from where he sat, continuing to stare down with a vacant expression. Everly saw Richard's smile tighten, but then he leaned forward and continued to talk to Maurice in an upbeat voice.

The man remained unresponsive through the rest of the visit. Richard kept up a lively one-sided conversation for about ten minutes, then bid Maurice a good day and got up, signaling for Everly that it was time for them to go.

Out in the hall again, Richard paused to look at Everly, asking, she assumed, if she was all right to go on.

Everly nodded once, and they continued.

They spent the day like that, going from room to room—or floor to floor; Richard never took her into more than one room on each floor before they went up another level—visiting numerous residents in varying states of awareness and sanity. All seemed to be at least sixty, some probably much older. While a few of the residents more or less recognized Richard, none of them were able to completely understand who Everly was. A good number of people were like Maurice, barely able to look their way when they entered the room. Others were like Lois—responsive but unintelligible, and sometimes hysterical. Richard went into each and every one of their rooms with the same wide, open smile on his face. He talked to them. *That's all,* Everly realized. He wasn't doing anything special or medical. He was just talking to them.

She wondered briefly if that was why he had asked her to come with him—if he just needed another person to help, to share the burden. Assuming all the floors were full of apartments like these, housing people like those she had met, there had to be hundreds, thousands of people living in that building. They had only been able to visit with a dozen or so residents—who went to all the other people during the day?

Everly kept trying to bring it up. In the hallways after they left a room, she'd turn to Richard and open her mouth, prepared to ask him again why these people were here. Why *she* was here. But every time she tried, he blew her off or walked away or spoke over her, loudly and enthusiastically about something entirely different. As they ascended floor after floor, visiting more rooms, Everly's frustrations grew, becoming nearly suffocating as she tried to shove them down, at least long enough to get through the day.

After a couple of hours spent visiting rooms, Richard stopped Everly before they could get back into the elevator. "I think that is enough for today," he said. "Do you want to go somewhere else with me? I—" He cut himself off, eyes scanning the hallway. "I want to talk to you about today, but I know you'd probably rather do so someplace else. The Eschatorologic can be . . . a bit much, at first."

Heart racing, Everly nodded. *Finally,* she thought. Finally she could get some answers out of him.

Richard told her to wait where she was for a few minutes, and he left her, standing alone in the empty gray hallway on the fifteenth floor—the highest they had managed to get that afternoon, visiting one room per floor. About ten minutes later he returned, adorned in the tweed coat and bowler hat she had first seen him in, and he ushered her back to the elevator. They exited into the lobby, and Richard began to quickly walk toward the door, Everly trailing in his wake. Before they could reach the door, a voice called out from across the wide room.

"Richard!"

Everly turned and saw Jamie's tall form striding toward them, hand outstretched in greeting. Richard paused where he stood, hesitated for half a second, and then spun to face Jamie, a new smile plastered on his face. To Everly, the smile was tinged with a hint of something insincere, and she watched him closely as he walked over to Jamie.

"Jamie, how nice to run into you." Richard put an arm around Everly. "I hear you've already had the opportunity to be acquainted with my granddaughter. Thank you, by the way, for being willing to help her with the elevator."

Jamie waved him off. "Just doing my job," he said, repeating the words he had told Everly the day before. "Though, you must have beat me to it; I didn't have to do much for her."

Everly saw Richard pause for a second before responding. "Right," he said. "Well, at any rate, it was good you were down here when she came in."

With a grin, Jamie turned to Everly. "Nice running into you again, Miss Tertium."

Everly offered him a tight smile in return. Something about this was off. Richard, who was so friendly and open all day with the people they visited, suddenly seemed closed off, distant, despite the relaxed air he was trying to give off. Something about Jamie had set him on edge.

"Listen," Jamie was saying, "if you both have time, there's something I'd really like your eyes for, Richard, and I figured I could give Everly a tour of some of the lab space, too, in the process." He winked at her. "Might be something she'd be interested to see. What do you say?"

"Oh, I'm sorry, Jamie, but we were on our way out for the day. I have to take Everly home before it gets too late. But I can come find you tomorrow, if you'd like." Richard spoke with ease, but there was still a certain tension, a rigidity to his spine, that kept Everly watching Jamie closely as he responded.

"Is that so," Jamie said. He grinned again. "No worries. There'll be another day, right? Well, I don't want to keep you. I'll see you tomorrow, Richard." He nodded at Everly. "Miss Tertium, a pleasure, as always."

And then Richard was steering Everly away, out the front doors of the building, waving back briefly to Jamie as they went. Once outside, Richard looked like he could finally breathe again, like a noose had been released from around his neck.

Everly watched him carefully, walking beside him as they descended the long trail of steps down to the road.

"What was that about?" she asked him, once she thought they were far enough away from the building.

He shook his head, not answering at first. "That was Jamie," he said, then sighed. "Suffice it to say that while Jamie and I have similar goals in mind when it comes to the Eschatorologic, he has a very different preference of methodology. I would rather if you didn't spend too much time around him while you're in the building. That's all."

"Methodology? What do you mean?" All she'd seen Jamie do in the building was fix the elevator to let her use it. She couldn't think of what would cause Richard to be so edgy around him. Jamie seemed nice, and so far he had only been helpful to her; but then again she'd also say Richard seemed nice enough, and what did she really know about either of them?

"It doesn't matter," Richard said sharply. "He just doesn't . . . value the sanctity of what we're doing as well as I do."

"And what are you doing?" Everly pressed. "All you've done is show me rooms full of people who probably wouldn't remember me if I went back tomorrow. What does any of this mean, Richard?" She saw him flinch at the use of his name.

Richard stopped walking, looking—really looking—at Everly for the first time that afternoon. "You're right," he said. "I owe you some answers."

Everly crossed her arms, waiting for him to continue. Richard had taken on a look as though he were gathering all his thoughts together like yarn in a basket, trying to pull apart one strand from the rest.

"When I was twenty-six years old," he began, "which is not much older than you are now, I stumbled across a genetic anomaly."

That term—genetic anomaly—tickled at something in the back of Everly's mind. She remembered the snippet on Richard that she'd found at the library. Something about a grant, right? Something to do with genetics?

"I was in the final year of my PhD program at the time," Richard continued, "and found it without realizing I had been looking. At first it sounded outrageous—impossible. But it intrigued me, and so I began to spend more time searching for it, studying it, trying to understand it.

Eventually, my studies with this genetic anomaly led to my discovery of the Eschatorologic."

"What is it?" Everly asked. "This . . . anomaly. What does it do, exactly?"

"A good question." Richard paused. "The anomaly is very special, and exceptionally difficult to explain. It is also rarer than I have ever heard of a genetic trait being among humans. If I hadn't been so actively searching it out, for so many years, it is unlikely my research would have ever come to anything."

A gust of wind blew between Everly and Richard then, nearly knocking off Richard's bowler hat, and he clamped down a hand to keep it in place. His eyes had gone distant while he spoke, and Everly took this moment to study him. In the building, he had seemed so at ease, so content to move from room to room, speaking with the elderly residents and being among them. Out here, in the real world, she suddenly saw how out of place he appeared.

"I say all of this to you," Richard continued, "because I have strong reason to believe that you have this genetic anomaly. That you are what we in the Eschatorologic refer to as *enhanced*. And so, I want you to come back—I want to test you."

"Test me?" Everly repeated faintly. "I'm sorry, you want to *what*?"

"It's a simple enough process. Not too invasive." Which implied that it was, at least a little bit, invasive. Everly's pulse spiked, trying to process what Richard was telling her, what any of this was supposed to mean.

"Why would you possibly think I have this—this anomaly? Why me, Richard? You don't even know me."

Richard turned his body then so that he was facing her more directly. His eyes had lost the far-off glaze that had filled them only moments before. Now his attention was sharp, pointed. It reminded her of the funeral, when she had known he was watching her even when she couldn't really see him. "Because your mother was enhanced," he said. "And while it is not always a genetic trait that is passed down by birth, it does drastically increase your odds."

Her mother. Everly thought back to the box of her mother's belongings she'd found the day before. Thought of the photos of the woman with the coy smile and bright eyes.

Were you part of this? Everly found herself thinking.

"There's more to it than that," Richard said, eyeing Everly closely. "Your headaches cease when you're inside the Eschatorologic, don't they?"

Everly stared at him in shock. "How do you know about those?"

She hadn't noticed before, but he was right: she'd never gotten the headaches while inside the building.

Richard continued by saying, "It's all connected, you know. Return to the building, and you can keep the headaches away for good. They're only the start; it'll get worse from here on out. I should know, I've seen it before." He paused very briefly before adding, "It's imperative you return. You don't understand how important you are, Everly."

And that—that was what shattered the illusion, what went too far. Because Everly was many things, but *important* had certainly never been one of those, especially not to this man who hadn't wanted to be part of her life for the first twenty-four years.

"No," Everly said, shaking her head. "I don't know what's going on in that building, or what you've gotten yourself in the middle of, but I want no part of it."

Richard opened his mouth to interject, but Everly plowed on, saying, "*Test me?* What does that even mean? You have no right to march in now, twenty-four years late, and tell me I'm important and decide that that's enough to pull me into all of this. So unless you can give me a reason—a real, concrete reason—why I should go back, I'm done—done with that building, done with those people, and done with you."

Sucking in a deep breath, Everly paused her tirade. She had never spoken like that before—to anyone. Staring at Richard, waiting to see what he would do, she expected to see shock in his eyes, or surprise at her outburst. Instead, she saw something she almost would have read as anger; anger, perhaps, that she'd dare to stand in the way of his progress, in the way of everything he'd been working toward? Oh, he masked it well, putting on a somber face a moment later, but she'd seen it. He couldn't hide who he was, beneath all his pretty and kind words. She might not know what he wanted with her, but she knew it was all for his own gain—knew it had nothing at all to do with helping her, even if he wouldn't acknowledge that to himself.

But oh, he knew what he was doing. Richard looked at her with those faux-kind eyes and he said, simply enough, "I can tell you what happened to your father. He came to the building, you know. Only a few weeks before you."

It was like a sledgehammer to her gut. Everly nearly bent over from the weight of Richard's implications. *He did know. He knew what happened to her dad. She was right, there really was more to it.*

Everly studied him for another moment. This man to whom she owed nothing. Every survival instinct in her told her to run, to go home and never look back. It didn't escape her that he still hadn't even told her what this genetic anomaly was—he hadn't told her *anything.*

But he knew what happened to her dad.

And he knew that would be enough to pull her back in.

"Okay," she said. And that was that.

14

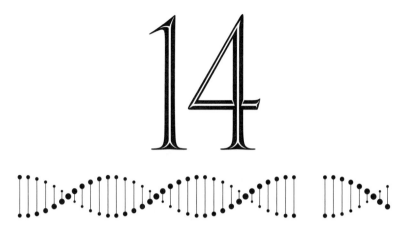

A SNAPSHOT OF A MOMENT:

Floor one: one life form, a frozen receptionist sitting regally behind her desk, staring out at empty air.

Floor two: six occupied rooms, a dozen empty ones. All occupants shared unsettlingly identical blue eyes. The hair was different, though. White for the first two, then mostly auburn with streaks of white, then red enough to burn the building down (hypothetically speaking, of course).

Floors three through one hundred: similar enough to floor two, with distinct variations in gender, eyes, hair, skin, height, weight, etc. But the pattern was the same.

Floor negative one: children. And mysteries.

Floor negative two: something deeper than a mystery, the negative space around a secret that no one even knew was a secret. Let's just say there wasn't anything down there. Nothing at all.

Except we can mention the black office with the person in black who still sat behind a too-large desk and still watched over a wall of screens, staring at the people trapped within.

And we can also now mention a second office. More of a lab, really. It contained a narrow metal desk with a single desktop computer sitting in the center. Shelves with organized boxes of equipment along one wall. Wobbly filing cabinets lined up along another.

And a chair. A chair that was sometimes empty, but right now held a scientist with unkempt gray hair and deeply blue eyes and a face that was buried in his hands as he bent over in that chair, eyes clenched shut, tongue pressed against the roof of his mouth, fingers like claws that were in danger of digging into the skin of his face from how tightly locked in place he had them.

He had to be careful going forward. He had to be so, so careful. He'd almost lost her that afternoon, and he knew it. He couldn't make any more mistakes.

She didn't understand yet, but he'd make her see the truth. He'd make her see how valuable she was to the building and how much she needed to be there. How much he could help her, if only she'd let him. For the time being, he'd dangle what she wanted to know just out of reach, long enough so that he could get her to understand. Long enough for her to see there was no other way. Long enough for him to save her.

The scientist rolled his chair over to one of the filing cabinets and opened it. Inside was row after row of leatherbound notebooks. His prized possessions, he'd say on days when he was feeling overly sentimental.

Opening an unfinished volume, the scientist put pen to page.

We have so little time left, he thought as he wrote. So little time to do what must be done. It must happen now.

He knew what had happened before, all the other times, but with her it was different. There was precedent, but there was also a whole lot of chance. And scientists don't like leaving much to chance.

One thing this scientist knew: he wouldn't repeat his mistakes. He'd learned from his past, and this time, it was going to go right.

There was no longer any room for error.

15

Luca Reyes entered the building for the first time as a five-year-old boy with eye boogers crusting his eyelids shut and hair greasy after four days of no washing and a shirt that was stained from the breakfast that had been thrust at him that morning and then promptly spilled straight down his front. He was carried in the arms of a man with a tweed coat and a bowler hat—back then, there was no one else suited to the task—and was ushered into a gray room a level beneath the ground. He was given a bed, a uniform, an identity, a purpose.

He was the seventy-third to be found, so they had it down by then.

The best age to find them, the best words to say to reassure them, the best time to test them, the best way to stabilize them.

Luca Reyes didn't cry that first night, for which Dr. Dubose was thankful. Number seventy-two had been a screamer. But Luca Reyes also wasn't leaving much behind.

That first time around, Luca Reyes found a sort of peace in living in the building, unlike most other residents. He felt a sense of belonging, an understanding between him and the building that went beyond their communal existence outside of typical conventions of space and time and all that. It was the knowledge that he was where he was meant to be, and even at five years old he had realized that he never would have experienced that anywhere but in that building.

The first time around—for Luca, at least—had also been when he first met Everly Tertium. Everything the first time around was imprinted on the building like a tattoo dug into the skin on the back of a wrist, like a Sharpie message penned onto freshly painted drywall, like a pocketknife carved through the door of a bathroom stall: there once and then there forever.

Because Luca Reyes met Everly Tertium that first time, he met her every time.

Because Luca Reyes fell in love with Everly Tertium that first time, he fell in love with her every time.

And because Luca Reyes was killed by Everly Tertium that first time, he would be killed by her every time.

But Luca didn't know any of that, at the start. Neither did Everly.

At the start it was always mysterious, unexpected, strange.

No one ever fell in love in the building.

No one except Luca Reyes and Everly Tertium.

16

When everly found herself standing in front of the glass double doors of the Eschatorologic, she wondered, yet again, why she was here.

It felt wrong to be back, like she was intruding on someone else's fate.

It felt right to be back, as that noose of inevitability was knotted around her throat and secured to the front doors that she now stared at.

She wasn't here for herself, she reminded herself. She was here to learn about her dad. To finally learn the truth.

Everly took a deep breath, pushed open the doors, and stepped into the domed lobby.

The woman, Sophia, still sat behind her large desk dressed in the same dull, beige clothes. Ignoring her, Everly headed toward the elevators but paused when she realized that, once again, she had no idea where to look for Richard.

One hundred (and two) floors.

He could be anywhere.

Before she could decide what to do, she heard footsteps and, turning away from the elevator, realized someone was walking toward her.

No, not toward her. Toward Sophia. It was a young man who looked to be about her age, early to midtwenties, who was lean and wiry with unkempt dark hair that hung down in his face. He could have been anyone. If it weren't for the uniform.

He wore the same gray outfit as the other residents in the building—a matching pair of faded scrubs. The marker, Everly recognized, of someone who lived there. So, who was he?

The man was talking to Sophia, who seemed to be pointedly ignoring him. Everly couldn't say why, but she felt slightly reassured by the fact that she was not the only one the woman was set on ignoring. She inched closer, wanting to hear what he was saying, but not necessarily wanting to be seen yet.

His voice reached her, soft and amiable. "It looks like the cooks really outdid themselves for you today, Sophia." He glanced down at the plate that he had just set on the woman's desk in front of her—what looked like some generic slab of meat and something green and wilted. "They clearly value your skill set above mine here," the man continued lightly.

His eyes flicked up then and he caught sight of Everly across the room. There was an instant in which he seemed to freeze, and Everly felt something rising inside her, with his eyes caught on hers—dragonflies, molten lava, exploding bubbles of air.

But then the man blinked, shaking his head slightly, and Everly had to take a step back as the strange spell broke.

"Who—" the man started, then stopped. With his eyes still latched on Everly, he took a breath, then started again. "Who are you?"

It almost sounded like he was asking the question to himself rather than Everly, though clearly it was about her. Everly frowned, then crossed her arms over her chest and walked a few steps closer to the man, recovered now from whatever it was that happened a moment before between them. Maybe it hadn't even been anything, she thought. This building was good at playing tricks on her mind.

"I'm Richard Dubose's granddaughter," she said, frustrated that she didn't have anything better to offer. "And who are you? I haven't seen you in the Eschatorologic before." She hadn't seen anyone near her age—only older residents who had lost their minds (or had them stolen from them) and scientists (of the maddest variety).

The man leaned back against Sophia's desk and crossed his arms. The secretary didn't seem to take notice.

"Oh, I'm nobody," the man said. "Just another set of eyes." He said this with those very eyes still pinned on Everly—dark eyes, she noticed for the first time, dark-brown eyes—and she resisted the urge to shiver beneath their gaze. There was something about the way he was watching her, like he was afraid to look away, even for a second. Like she may vanish if he were to blink for too long.

"So," Everly said, "you work here?"

He shrugged, watching her uneasily now as she got closer to him. "In a sense." He nodded at the woman behind the desk. "I bring Sophia her meals. And do other . . . tasks, for the Eschatorologic."

"Well, do you at least have a name?" she asked him.

He seemed to consider her question carefully before responding. "Luca," he finally said. He raised an eyebrow expectantly. Everly took one final step toward him and stuck out her hand.

"Everly," she said. The man—Luca—considered her hand for an instant before he took it, shaking it gently.

With his hand still wrapped around hers, Luca's eyes leaped from the clasped hands up to Everly's eyes and back. He opened his mouth as if he wanted to say something (*I dreamed of this,* he would say, and wouldn't say, and would dream of saying, and would never admit to dreaming of saying), but before he got the chance, a piercing ding echoed through the lobby. An instant later, the elevator doors slid open, revealing the tall, pale form of Jamie Griffith.

Jamie's eyes focused on Luca first, who had dropped Everly's hand and moved a foot away, then jumped over to Everly, then swung back. "Mr. Reyes," he said, and Everly took that to mean Luca. "I think it is time you should be heading back down, don't you?"

Luca straightened and nodded once without speaking.

He started to walk away but turned back briefly, eyes again catching Everly's for an instant.

"And Miss Tertium," Jamie said, drawing Everly's attention back to him. "I see you have returned to us. Are you looking for your grandfather?"

"Yes, actually," she said, then glanced around, realizing that Luca had left, though she hadn't heard the ding of the elevator doors opening. "Do you know where he is? I need to talk to him."

"Of course," Jamie said brightly. "I can take you right to him. In fact, I can give you that tour I suggested before, if you're up for it."

Everly considered his offer. She remembered Richard's hesitation around Jamie, the way he had pushed against going with him. But she did need to find Richard. And maybe she could get Jamie to tell her what Richard was clearly keeping to himself about this place.

Besides, she tried to reason with herself, Jamie didn't seem like a bad guy. (They never do.) He was nice to her, at least. So maybe Richard was wrong about him.

"All right," she said. "I'd like that. Lead the way."

Inside the elevator, Everly was surprised to see Jamie pull out a key ring from one of the deep pockets of his red uniform, selecting a small silver one that looked suited for lockets and music boxes. While neither of the latter were available inside the elevator, there were the two circular key holes on the elevator's wall panel, and Jamie inserted the dainty silver key into one such hole next to a button labeled B2. Everly did not say anything, but her insides buzzed. What was important enough to warrant being kept so locked up?

(Black offices with screens, white rooms with tables, furnaces wide enough for a single body.)

As the elevator began to descend, Everly looked over at Jamie, studying him closely as she asked, "Jamie, did you ever happen to meet my dad? His name was Jacob Tertium. He . . . he . . ." *died,* she couldn't bring herself to say.

Jamie tilted his head, as though considering. "Nope, can't say I've had the pleasure. Why do you ask?"

"Oh," Everly said, "no reason." If she was honest with herself, Everly didn't know why she had asked Jamie that. Some part of her thought maybe, maybe Jamie could be the person to send her dad the anonymous letter she'd found? Not that she had any reason to suspect that. But despite what Richard had told her, she wasn't convinced he'd offer her the answers he'd promised. She'd been hoping Jamie might be able to.

The elevator doors slid open as they reached their destination, and Everly exited onto the floor beyond.

More halls. Always more halls.

These halls were black rather than the bleak gray that permeated through the rest of the building (except where it didn't).

Unlike the upper levels, this floor did not run straight back in a single-file line, with doors uniformly paneling the walls on either side in a two-by-two pattern. Rather, down on this black-painted floor, the halls seemed to spiral away from the elevator's focal point like roots seeking water by growing far and fast away from their source. She couldn't see where they all went, or how far back the halls stretched, and this filled her with a distinct and unnameable queasiness: distinct because it was similar to the feeling of standing on the edge of a lofty bridge and having vertigo wash over you; unnameable because Everly had never stood on the edge of a bridge, and so she wouldn't know that this was precisely what she was experiencing.

To reconcile the odd sense of unwinding Everly felt as her eyes tried to take in the entire black floor at once, she chose instead to focus on the black tiling that her feet treaded across as she followed Jamie down one of the paths, and then another, and finally a third, at which point Jamie halted. He placed a single palm flat against the black-painted frame of the door and then pushed gently against the door's surface, stepping into the space beyond. As Everly joined him she realized that it was a lab of sorts. The only labs that Everly had seen were of the high school biology sort, but she thought this was probably close enough: brilliantly white walls that contrasted starkly against the darkness of the hallways just outside; rows of long stainless steel tables covered in beakers and test tubes; stacks of papers piled up on the stainless steel tables and in corners on the white-tiled floor and propped up haphazardly in the cubbies of shelves that lined the back wall of the room.

"This is one of the open labs," Jamie said, gesturing around the room. "Available to the few of us who may need it."

"What are the labs for?" Everly asked, gazing around the space, looking for some indication of why a lab would be needed in a building that otherwise could pass for an unorthodox apartment building.

"Think I'll leave that one to your gramps to answer," Jamie said with a chuckle. There was an edge to his laugh. Something Everly didn't understand yet.

"So, Richard works in this lab?" Everly asked, pressing more.

Jamie tilted his head to the side. "Sometimes. He mostly stays in his private lab. Says it's easier to get work done that way." Another chuckle. "Can't say I blame the man. Sometimes the noise in this place can get to you. Come on," he said, stepping back toward the door. "I'll show you where I spend most of my days, and then I'll take you to where your grandpa is probably camping out."

Everly followed Jamie as he wove through a series of interconnecting halls, all painted the same impossible black that made the floors and walls and doors all blend one into another, like an endless sea of ink. Finally, they stopped in front of another door, and Jamie again laid his palm flat upon it, pushing the door open.

"Here we are," he said as Everly came in after him. "Home sweet home."

It was a much smaller room than the lab he had first shown her—to the extent where she was almost hesitant to call it a room at all. Far more like a closet—a very dark, cramped closet.

A large table took up the middle of the room/closet, upon which sat numerous computer monitors and hard drives, all blinking ferociously up at Everly with their flashing lights and muted beeps. Set up perpendicular to the first large table was a second desk, covered in just as much hardware and cables, and between the two was a chair that could swivel back and forth between the two workstations.

"This is where you work?" Everly asked, going over to inspect a rubber duck that was positioned at the base of one of the screens on the desk.

The correct answer would have been: yes, and no; yes, this was where Jamie worked, but no, this was not *only* where Jamie worked—there were also the other rooms, the (usually) white rooms, one of which was, in fact, only one hall to the left and currently empty, but also currently not white, because it had not yet been sanitized after his most recent . . . session in there.

But instead, Jamie responded by saying, "Yeah," and then he rubbed the back of his neck, as though self-conscious of the half-truth he was choosing to share. "I know, tech nerd, right?"

"No," Everly said. "I think it's great. What do you do in here?"

"Well, I was brought in to speak computer. Essentially, people like your grandpa find data, and I upload it into a program I developed that assesses the information for viability. I don't understand what half the data means, but I guess that's what the others are for."

Another partial truth: some of the data came from men like Dr. Richard Dubose, but some of the data also came from actions that Jamie himself carried out in rooms like the currently not-white room a hall to the left. But again, Jamie chose to edit this facet of the truth out in his explanations. For now.

Everly slid her hand along the top of one of the monitors. "So, all the data you look at," Everly said, watching Jamie as she spoke, trying to gauge how much he might know. "What's it all for? I mean, I know you don't understand all the science behind it and everything"—(an understatement)—"but you must know something, right? What you're working toward?"

Jamie smiled as Everly spoke, the same as ever, but his face had assumed an inscrutable expression now, and he shook his head.

"Sorry," he said. "Even if I did know, I doubt I'd be able to explain it well. I'm horrible with words. That's why I'm the computer guy, right?"

Everly nodded but bit the inside of her cheek in frustration. "Right," she said.

Then Jamie's smile widened into a more genuine expression, and he waved toward the door. "I'd better get you to the old man," he said. "I've got work to do, and you're probably bored to death looking at all this junk."

"Not at all," Everly said. "In fact, I think this is all fascinating. Any chance you'd let me come back sometime? I would love to learn more about what you're doing, even if I don't understand any of it." A truth and a lie: she would like to come back, but not at all because she was fascinated by computers and completely because she was fascinated by everything else in the building.

And Everly was ever so slightly better at people than she was at technology; she knew that Jamie had kept his half-truths from her, now what she wanted to know was *why*. More than that, she wanted to know the other halves he was keeping to himself.

And also: what did a building like this need a person like Jamie for?

"Sure," Jamie said, smile brightening to an even higher wattage. "If you're ever around here and want to come by, don't hesitate. You can ask old Richie to show you the way; he knows how to get in here."

"Really?" Everly beamed at him—overkill, perhaps, but effective, nonetheless. "Thank you, that would be perfect."

"Right," Jamie said. "Well, shall we then?"

▪ ■ ■ ■ ▪

SHORTLY AFTER LEAVING Jamie's office, Everly stood beside Jamie as he knocked on another black door. He turned to her and winked. "Something really cool about this building's security system," he said. "There are certain doors in the building that are coded to only open at a particular person's touch—it recognizes their fingerprints. My office, for instance, wouldn't open for you, unless I let you in, and it wouldn't open for Richard, either. Just like his lab here won't open for me."

Everly started to ask how that worked, when the door sprang open and revealed Richard standing on the other side. His mouth was open, as though he had been about to scold them. He looked back and forth between Everly and Jamie.

"Everly," Richard said, his expression somewhere between pleased and bewildered.

Before Everly could speak, Jamie jumped in. "I found her stranded in the lobby, figured I'd show her down to your lab. Hope that was okay and all."

Richard pushed the door open slightly wider. "Of course, thank you." He looked at Everly. "Well, come on in."

Everly stepped inside the lab, and Jamie made as though to follow, but before he could Richard started to close the door. "Thank you, Jamie. I really do appreciate it." And then the door clicked shut—locking Jamie out, if what he had told Everly about the fingerprints was true.

Once they were alone, Richard spun to Everly. "You came back."

"I said I would," was all she said.

She then took the opportunity to look around the lab. It was different from the other two rooms Jamie had shown her. There were labeled bins with items varying from syringes to hydrogen peroxide, a desk with a single computer on top, an entire wall covered in tall filing cabinets. It all looked neat and orderly, but at the same time she could sense a tumultuousness underneath it all—probably due to Richard's inherent chaotic energy.

"Before we begin," Everly said, walking around the space, pausing to peer into boxes and pull open unlocked drawers. "Tell me what you know."

Richard blinked. "What I know?"

"About my dad. You said he came here."

"Yes," Richard said. He was standing far away from her, she noticed. Like a man afraid of a rabid dog. "He did come here. Shortly before he died."

"Why did he come?"

"He came here for you, Everly. To help you."

"Help me? What do you mean?"

There was a weariness to Richard's stance, like he knew the questions she was going to ask and wasn't happy about having to answer them. "I mentioned before your headaches," he said. "They were a sign, an indication that . . . it was time to bring you here. To show you this place. On that count, your father and I agreed."

"A sign of what?" Everly asked, pressing. "How did he even know about this place?"

Richard ignored her first question, but replied, "He had come here before. With your mother."

Everly's head snapped to him. "My mother came here, too?"

"Years ago. Before she had you. They both came and saw the work I did here."

"And that's when you tested my mother?"

Richard frowned. "What do you mean?"

"You said she had this . . . genetic trait. Anomaly. Whatever. So, you had to have tested her, right?"

"Not . . . exactly," Richard said. "It was different for you mother."

"Why?"

With a sigh, Richard said, "Let's just say I had other reasons to suspect she was enhanced. I didn't need to test her formerly—as you have promised to be—to know that she had the genetic anomaly."

"But—" Everly started.

"Now before I answer any more of your questions, I'm going to insist that you sit here." Richard gestured to a chair that looked like something out of a dental office. "We'll do the testing, and once I have the results, then I will answer all of your remaining questions."

Everly scowled at the man. She didn't trust him—she wanted to insist that no, he would answer all of her questions *first,* and then, only then, would she allow him to test her. Whatever that meant.

But almost against her will, she felt herself acquiescing. She had to admit, she was curious. She wanted to know what all of this meant: tests and genetics and enhancement. She wanted to understand. So, she sat in the chair Richard had indicated as he walked swiftly over to one of the labeled boxes, rummaging around for a moment before standing straight with a scowl.

"I seem to have run out of clean needles. You stay here, I will return momentarily." With that, he dashed out of the lab, barely sparing Everly a parting glance.

As soon as he was gone, Everly leaped out of her chair. For all his promises, Richard had yet to give her any tangible answers. If he wouldn't give them himself, then maybe his lab would.

She walked swiftly to his desk, clicking for the computer to open and then frowning when she saw it was locked. Opening the first drawer in the desk, she found nothing out of the ordinary—extra pens, stationery, paper clips. Conscientious of the seconds ticking away until Richard returned, Everly yanked open the drawer below that and suppressed a yelp of victory when she found it filled to the brim with thin, leatherbound notebooks. She pulled one out at random, flipping it open to scan its contents. Below a date of 1952 scrawled at the top, she read:

> *I believe that I am finally beginning to understand. With the help of my darling Miranda, I have begun to conceptualize the function of the genetic anomaly, and I think that my plan may be able to work. I am feeling confident for the first time since this project began.*

What is this, Everly wondered. It seemed to be some kind of journal. She looked back into the open drawer, overflowing in identical journals, and yanked out a handful at random, shoving them against her back, into the waistband of her pants. Hurrying back to the chair she'd been sitting in before, Everly just managed to situate herself before the door opened with a rush of air, and Richard entered, holding a very daunting-looking needle.

"Now then," he said, "we first need a sample. We'll need to test it for the genetic anomaly, make sure you have it. Then we can decide how to proceed."

Everly's eyes were latched onto the medieval-looking syringe in Richard's hand, and so it was with a certain amount of queasiness that she said, "You never really said what it is. The genetic anomaly. What it's for."

Richard busied himself in setting up the equipment he needed to draw Everly's blood, speaking as he worked. "We call it STM," he said. "Or at least, that's what I call it. It's all very hard to explain, but that stands for Space-Time Modifier. Essentially, the anomaly allows enhanced individuals to release extremely high levels of energy, energy that, as far as we have been able to decipher, defies certain laws of space-time."

"Right," Everly said, feeling dizzy with this explanation, and not at all satisfied. "Energy. Space-time. Got it."

There was something else too, right alongside the dizziness from Richard's words and from the very large needle that he was now inserting into the vein running through the crux of her elbow.

It was that same sense of falling, of plummeting, of rising, of realizing.

The same sense that she had been here before—in this lab, in this chair, with this needle (the same needle?) being inserted into the soft flesh of her arm.

Hearing the same words spoken out of Richard's mouth in the same tone, at the same pace, with the same doctoral level of serenity that he used now to calm her nerves as he drew out the enhanced blood from her enhanced veins.

She thought she knew what he was going to say before he said it.

It went like this: "It is exceptionally rare," she thought.

"It is exceptionally rare," she heard Richard say aloud right after.

In her head: "As of now, we have only ever successfully identified about one hundred unique genetic codes carrying the anomaly."

Out loud: "As of now, we have only ever successfully identified about one hundred unique genetic codes carrying the anomaly."

And then she knew what she was supposed to say next, as well as the response that would follow:

"And are you one of them?"

In her head first and then from her mouth.

"No," Richard said, silently first inside Everly's mind, and then out loud into the echoing lab space. "No, I am not."

Richard was watching her curiously now, which was different from the way the scene progressed in her head.

In her head: He was excited, bubbling over in pent-up enthusiasm over the research that he hadn't been able to share with anyone, or with very few someones, and now he had her, or a slew of hers, or all of the runners and residents filling up his building.

But with her eyes she saw Richard pause instead, contemplative rather than enthusiastic. For a moment she could see both Richards—the real and the imagined—and this strange doubling broke her free of whatever it was she had fallen into.

Again.

Blink blink blink blink.

Everly blinked. Richard blinked. They blinked at each other, and then Richard turned back to his work. When he was finished drawing the blood he required, Richard withdrew to the other side of the room, to his computer and a boxy machine that was set up next to it, and Everly watched at first as he fiddled around with various knobs and keys, but then the weight and dizziness from the episode before must have caught up with her because the next thing she was aware of was the darkness of her eyelids closing, followed an instant later by the stark whiteness of the lab as she opened her eyes, and a sharp beeping sounded close to her ear.

"What happened?" Everly asked, rubbing at her eyes and struggling to sit up. The stolen journals pressed limply into her spine as she propped herself up in the chair. "Did it work?"

Richard nodded absently, scrolling through a list of data that appeared on the computer before him. "The results are in," he mumbled, still scrolling. Then his hand paused, and she saw him nod once, almost to himself. He looked at Everly, his features set and expressionless.

"I was right," he said. "You have it. You have the genetic anomaly, Everly."

17

RICHARD DUBOSE ENTERED THE ESCHATOROLOGIC for the first time four years after securing his PhD in molecular biology.

Alternatively: Four years before Richard Dubose entered the Eschatorologic for the first time, he had secured a PhD in molecular biology, writing his dissertation on a rare genetic anomaly that somehow no one before him had discovered, or at least no one before him had thought interesting enough to dedicate their life's work to.

He had so little proof of said genetic anomaly at the time of writing said dissertation, however, that his adviser only barely allowed him to receive the desired degree. It's just a blip on the scans, he was told so many times, but so what? What does it mean?

He did not know, but he loved that he did not know, and he did not understand why they (the proverbial "they") did not love that, too.

Here's how it went: for three years in grad school, Richard Dubose had taken interesting but predictable classes and received high but predictable grades and had learned about the human body at a fast but predictable rate. Except that he had chosen a STEM route more for its unpredictabilities than the alternative, so there was a flavor tinged with dissatisfaction about the whole endeavor.

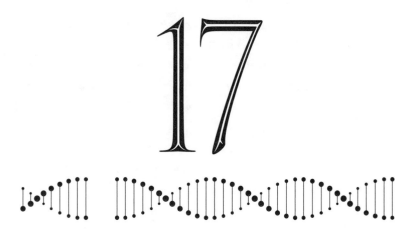

Then one day: the discovery. Something that wasn't supposed to be there. A blip, his adviser said, but the blips weren't supposed to exist without explanation.

Finally: unpredictable.

Richard Dubose then spent every waking moment with the blip. And trying to find the blip again.

It didn't happen in graduate school.

It didn't happen, in fact, until three years after graduate school, and then it wasn't at all on purpose, but rather by the best kind of accident.

He was in Malaysia, on grant money that he had been reluctantly offered because still he was the only one to believe in the significance of the blip. What he had discovered in the three years since barely receiving a doctorate: it was something about energy. That's it, but that was almost enough, at least to his ever-hopeful and overly idealistic heart, and so he built a device supposedly capable of detecting unique fluctuations in energy patterns.

So far, it had yet to do anything other than squeak loudly and uncomfortably upon being turned on.

Until Malaysia. Richard Dubose—recently made Dr. Richard Dubose—was trying to find lunch. As he meandered through stalls manned by people with loud voices and bustling tables of produce, trying and utterly failing to remember enough Malay to ask to buy a star fruit or a durian, he happened to stumble over something in the road. A pebble? A misplaced shoe? A tiny bit of fate? Who's to say, really, but whatever it was, it caused Dr. Richard Dubose to fall, landing facedown in the street, where the crowd of shoppers kindly parted around him as they went on their way. In a panic, Richard sat up, searching around for his machine—which, of course, he carried everywhere, despite the odd stares that were often cast his way as a result. Just as he was beginning to hyperventilate, not able to locate the machine, he heard something. A bleep. A ding, a whirring, searching cry that perked his ears and caused him to swivel his head where he came face-to-face with the sight of his machine, lit up like he had never seen it before.

Holding the machine out to Richard was a small girl with small hands that were struggling to stay firmly wrapped around the handle well enough to keep it up. She smiled at Richard when she saw him looking, her eyes darting in the light of the machine. Now speechless, Richard took the machine back from the girl, his eyes remaining focused on her all the while.

She gave him her name. He gave her his. She pointed at the machine and asked a question he hated himself for not being able to understand. He asked if she wanted to see it do more, which he didn't know if she could understand, but she smiled and nodded just the same.

Feeling only the slightest twinge of apprehension, Richard led the girl back to the room he had rented for the month. The room that he was calling a lab, even though it was hardly even a room in the first place. The floor was dirt and the ceiling had holes, but it was all he could afford with the remaining funds he had from his university. No one wanted to see him succeed, and if not for the girl following behind him, even Richard likely would have given up in due time. But the fact remained that the girl *did* follow him. She entered his room and sat down on his bed as he fiddled with the knobs on his machine and opened his suitcase to fish out a needle and syringe. The girl eyed these warily, but also, perhaps, curiously.

Richard did not expect the girl to agree. In fact, he expected her to run the instant the needle was anywhere close to her skin, and so it was with a hearty deal of shock that he realized she wasn't going to flee. Not when he approached her, not when he gestured between her arm and the needle. Not even when he pricked through her skin, drawing from her vein a thick slew of blood that he then bottled up, staring at with uninhibited adoration. Unfiltered hope.

In his hovel in Malaysia, Richard did not have nearly the amount of equipment that he would have liked. He did, however, have just enough to look at the girl's blood, and to determine all he needed to know.

All he needed to have hope again.

And to go in search of a place for that hope to rest.

In search of a building.

18

THE PERSON IN BLACK THOUGHT it was a good idea.

"Yes," the person in black replied to Dr. Dubose's suggestion. "Yes, I think you're right. She'll do better without you here."

"So, I'll step away then," Dr. Dubose said. "For the time being."

"Yes." The person in black had accepted that what Dr. Dubose had said before was true—it was good that this young woman, *Everly*, had arrived. And now the person in black was thinking rapidly through possibilities and scenarios, calculations and stray factors. "You have become a comfortable figure for her. We need to take that away, see how she reacts. We need to give her the freedom to become lost in the building on her own." That was how it had happened in the past, after all. Patterns were made to repeat.

"What would you suggest in the interim?"

The person in black shrugged, though Dr. Dubose, on the other side of the canvas divider, could not see this. "We have spare rooms down here, for emergencies. Take up residency in one of the vacant apartments, wait out the month. I will continue to observe her."

"And then?"

"And then when she is cast free in the building without limitations or expectations, we will see where she goes. I know her, her mind. Sooner or later, she will find herself in a scenario where she cannot leave. Or wouldn't want to. And then you may return—for the grand conclusion."

"In the meantime," Dr. Dubose said, "I want to increase the testing."

"We have already been increasing it. You know this."

"Yes, but now it is more important than ever."

The person in black paused. "You cannot be seen. Not by her, at least."

"Then have Jamie do it. He has more of a stomach for those affairs than me, anyhow. But this is just as necessary as securing her presence here."

"Very well," the person in black said, contemplative. "Since you are so sure it is necessary."

"I am," Dr. Dubose asserted fervently. "Oh, I've never been more sure of anything."

19

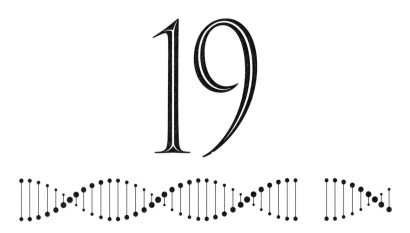

Luca went to work that day, like he was supposed to. He sat in the chair of the surveillance room like he was supposed to, and he stared at the hundreds of screens spread out in front of him. Like he was supposed to.

He would always do what he was supposed to.

But his thoughts were far from where they were supposed to be.

They were focused on a fiery girl with fiery hair.

Real. She was definitely real, and here, and not a figment of his most buried imaginations.

Everly.

She had said her name, and he could have sworn he already knew it, though of course that would have been impossible.

No more impossible than knowing her face, he supposed.

She hadn't seemed to know him, and in fact, the more they had talked out there in the lobby, the more she had diverged from her dream self. No longer was she mysterious and elusive, accompanied by that ever-present cloud of dread.

Now she was just a young woman. And he was almost relieved.

But she was Dr. Dubose's granddaughter.

Luca certainly had not anticipated that development.

For him, she had only ever been a figure cast in flames and smoke, born to life out of ether and desire. Realizing that, instead, she had been born to parents, had grown up, had lived a life outside of that building—it broke, in some ways, the spell that Luca had imagined her casting over him. In other ways it made her all the more real.

And all the more impossible.

He was not trying to find her. As his eyes traced over the screens with half-hearted effort, Luca was willing his vision to avoid her, even though he knew she had to be somewhere in the building, and so she had to be somewhere on the screens. He knew that if he found her, he wouldn't be able to look at anything else for the duration of his shift.

Fortunately for Luca, there were too many screens to count, and so even if he had been intentionally seeking her out, it likely would have taken a considerable amount of time to chance upon her. So, he continued to glance across the rows of tiny screens, relaxing as more and more of his shift passed without catching sight of her. He watched runners bring trays of food up to the older residents, children group together in the mess hall for lunch, Sophia sit stoically behind her desk. People worked, and slept, and sat in rooms and stared at the air around them. There were hundreds of people living in the Eschatorologic, and Luca fell into an easy rhythm of watching them all go about their routines.

It was nearing the end of his shift when his eyes traced over one of the small screens, and he kept going before his mind caught up with what he knew he had seen.

It was not the auburn of her hair, which he had so been dreading finding, but rather movement in one of the other nearby screens that drew his eye.

After watching the screen for a moment, Luca cursed and shoved away from the desk. He ran out of the room, down the halls, making his way across the floor as fast as he could without drawing any unwanted attention. The only comfort he had as he pivoted around corners and down new corridors was that, with him out of the surveillance room, there shouldn't be any eyes on him.

(None except those of a person dressed in black who, once again, was fixated on the screens through which Luca now ran.)

When Luca flung open the door, he found Maurie in a ball on the floor, rocking back and forth and sobbing uncontrollably. Luca cursed again under his breath, then quickly entered the room and shut the door behind him. He stepped over toward the kid—a boy no older than eight or nine—and sat down on the floor next to him, placing a steady hand on his shoulder.

"Maur," Luca said in a soft voice. "Maurie, you have to snap out of it. Do you hear me?"

But the boy made no indication of having registered Luca's words. His wails only became louder, more frantic, and so Luca took the boy by the shoulders and pulled him up into a sitting position, shaking him twice.

"Maurie, you can't do that. Not here. They'll *hear* you. Are you listening? They'll *come*."

That, at least, seemed to get through to the young boy, for his breathing began to calm marginally, though wet tears still streaked down his thin cheeks. Eventually, his sobs turned instead to hiccups, and he sat there, with Luca's hands on his shoulders, heaving silently until he could breathe normally. With a sigh, Luca removed his hands and looked the boy in the eyes.

"Are you okay now?"

He nodded once. "I—I don't—"

"I know," Luca said. "It's okay. They didn't see. It's going to be okay."

And Maurie nodded again, though neither of them was entirely convinced of this.

Luca left once he was sure Maurie wouldn't break down again, and he headed back to the surveillance room, hoping no one had noticed his absence.

It was happening more and more often. More of the testing, and also more of this: the breakdowns. First Michael and now Maurie, in the same week. Something was happening to them, the people living in that building. Luca didn't understand it, but he knew whatever it was, it couldn't be good.

(And, as was often the case, Luca was right.)

20

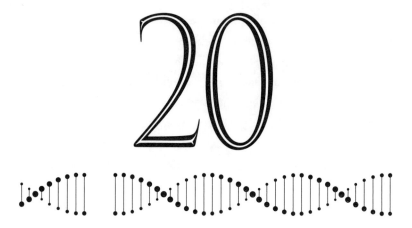

This is what Maurie saw:

Himself.

Maurie was preparing to return to his shift in the laundry room when he stumbled to his knees in his bedroom, overcome with . . . something.

Dizziness, one could say.

Pain, another might add.

The blinding torrent of uncertainty, a third might pipe in.

All of the above, really.

Maurie was overcome with a painful dizziness that accompanied the blinding torrent of uncertainty that was heightened by him having no idea what was happening to him.

It was getting worse for everyone in the building, after all.

And then he clenched his eyes shut to block out whatever it was that had overcome him without his consent. Only, rather than blissful darkness behind his eyelids, he instead saw his own face, reflected back at him.

This is not entirely correct. He saw his own face, but about twenty or thirty years older. It was hard to say, but Maurie could tell—as one can often tell their own face, even when others couldn't—that it was him.

And he was screaming.

Not the real Maurie, crouched on the floor of his very gray bedroom. Well, that Maurie, too. But first, the one painted on his eyelids, who was strapped to a chair in an all-white room that Maurie himself had not yet been brought to (he was still too young, even by the building's loose interpretation of "young").

This Maurie had a blade to his neck that wasn't meant to be felt, but oh he could feel it.

The slick cut that scorched through him as the blade ran up from his shoulder blade to the base of his skull, obliterating all other thoughts and logic in the face of the blinding pain that followed.

And because the other Maurie felt it, this Maurie did, too.

And so, he began to scream, clawing at his still-shut eyelids until they flung open, and he returned to the banal floor of his gray bedroom.

(Cell.)

The screaming cut itself off once the residual pain left, but then the tears came in its place.

This is how Luca found him: racked in uncontrollable sobs as the vision of what happened to the other Maurie was forever locked in place at the very front of his mind.

He thought that he had somehow seen his own future, which is not quite right.

But it's not quite wrong, either.

21

Maurice thompson entered the building for the first time as a twenty-four-year-old man with wide spectacles that covered half his face and a prematurely balding head that offset the amount of face that was covered by the wide glasses. He thought he was arriving for a job interview, but this was only because his ever-logical mind was trying to reconcile the direction his feet had guided him, and he didn't understand why they would have taken him anywhere other than the building where he was intended to arrive at eleven thirty for his scheduled interview.

Maurice did, in fact, have an interview that day—an interview that he missed, to the bewilderment of the recruiters who had been inspired by the promising young upstart they had been talking with for months leading up to that last interview, only to be stood up at the final hour.

But Maurice did not, in fact, realize that he missed his interview. Not at first, at least.

At first, he was drawn into the building, where he encountered one Dr. Richard Dubose, as well as one person dressed in black, who by this point was already being referred to as the Warden—both of whom welcomed Maurice with wide and open arms, distracting him in the miraculous buzz that filled the building until it was too late for him.

What neither the Warden nor Dr. Richard Dubose realized at first was that Maurice was already twenty-four years of age when he first entered the building, nor what the unfortunate repercussions of entering at such a late stage would prove to be.

Needless to say, the first time Maurice entered the building, he only lasted a very short time on the lower levels before being repurposed for the upper floors.

This was a lesson to Dr. Dubose and the Warden both, of the value of younger residents, and when to bring them in to best suit the purposes of the building's patterns.

This was not a lesson to Maurice, as he could no longer even process what the word *lesson* meant.

22

After having her blood drawn and confirming the very otherworldly significance of her genome, Everly did not go back to the Eschatorologic for a week.

There was something about having a needle stuck in her arm that gave her more pause than before.

She still didn't understand what the building was. Not really. Something about genetic anomalies, something about changing the world.

Nonsense, really.

That day, when she'd been tested, she'd had every intention of sticking around and pushing Richard to tell her more. To tell her what he'd promised: the secret to what had happened to her dad. The reason why he'd died.

Afterward, though, she'd barely been able to string two thoughts together. It was an effort to walk back to the front doors of the Eschatorologic, an even greater effort to walk all the way home. Even now, days later, Everly still felt sluggish, like more than just blood had been drawn out of her. It was unnerving, feeling that way. It was unnerving to know she'd willingly let Richard do that to her, let him stick that needle in her arm. And why? Why hadn't she run away from all this yet? Everly knew Richard needed her for his little science experiment. She knew all the people trapped there—because she was becoming more and more sure that's what they were, trapped like lab rats in an elaborate cage—were twisted up in the game Richard had set the board for, and were being used to satisfy his own means, whatever those were.

What she didn't know was why he needed her, specifically.

Or how her parents fit into all of this.

She'd looked through some of the pilfered journals from Richard's office, when she'd been able to stomach reading about everything Richard had been doing in that building. So far, she hadn't found much of substance—mostly Richard romanticizing his work, singing his own praises early on using vague, murky language. But one thing was immediately evident to her.

It was the handwriting. The same wide, looping letters filled Richard's journals as the note she had found among her mother's things, addressed to her father. *You need to make a decision,* the letter had said. A decision about what?

What had Richard needed her father to do?

Desperate to learn something, anything, about what her dad had to do with all of this, Everly had flipped through journal after journal, not reading the contents so much as scanning for a name.

When she found it, she stopped. The entry was short—far too short.

I have found that I quite like Jacob. He is a pragmatic young man, with a good head on his shoulders. But he's too inquisitive, which doesn't suit my purposes here. I can't have him poking around where he ought not be—and I can't have him dragging Mary into anything she shouldn't be. It's a shame he can't stay. Neither of them can.

What had her parents gotten into, all those years ago? Why had her dad been there, at the building? And what happened to him—what *really* happened to him, the truth that Richard had promised, and still withheld from her. Adding to the jumble of questions she couldn't begin to think of the answers to, why didn't the people in the building leave? What was keeping them there? Why play into Richard's hands, Jamie's hands, whoever's—why not get far, far away from all of this? For that matter, why wasn't *she* getting far, far away from it? Or, better yet, why wasn't she calling the police, telling someone what she'd seen?

Everly didn't know if she could fully answer those questions. Even now, back at home, away from the building, she could feel it pulling her back. Each time she went, she left with a new ribbon attached to her chest, connecting her to that place. And she didn't know why. But she could feel it, now more than ever.

A new thought popped into her head, more frightening than all the other unanswered questions piling up around her. What if she became like all the other people in that building, trapped without knowing why?

This—along with the memory of a sharp needle being jabbed in her arm—was the thought that kept her away from the building—away from Richard—that whole week. Instead, Everly spent the week watching movies in bed—movies she used to watch with her dad, that used to make him laugh, and made her laugh at him—and she made pancakes like he used to, and sat wrapped up in his favorite blanket, trying to find any lingering traces of his scent in the well-loved fabric of the patched quilt. The whole time there was that dull thudding at the back of her head; it only made it worse to know that the headaches would go away the moment she stepped back into the building.

It was while curled up like that on the worn cushions of her living room couch, gripping her head with one hand, that Everly finally allowed herself to remember.

To remember her dad, as she hadn't been able to since before.

Since before there was a before.

She remembered a warm Saturday afternoon, years and years ago, when her dad had encouraged her to give bike riding a chance—*It will be easy, you'll see*—and she had fallen on the pavement with her first attempt. He had rushed up to her, trying to suppress a laugh, and her eyes had burned with embarrassed tears, until he scooped her up and swung her around, coaxing a reluctant smile out of her. She remembered picking strawberries on the first of May, as they did every year, eating the red fruit as she went about filling up her plastic bucket so much that by the time they were finished her stomach was as full as her bucket, and her fingers were stained a sticky red.

She remembered when she had walked across the stage at graduation and looked out across the sea of faces, her eyes instantly snagging on her father's lone standing figure as he cheered and clapped louder than all the other families.

She remembered the last morning she had ever seen him, and she remembered the desperation that had traced his features as he set out into the bleak, rainy dawn. That whole week before had been an unpleasant one for her. The headaches had gotten so bad, she'd had to call out of work for a few days. And so, she hadn't been herself—hadn't noticed what was going on with her dad until it was too late.

She remembered thinking that she should do something to cheer him up when he returned. She remembered staying awake late into the night, waiting for him to come back, and then falling asleep wrapped in the same quilt she now clung tightly to herself while she stood vigil through the night, only to be woken too early the next morning by a fierce knock on the front door. She remembered wondering if her dad would get it, then realizing she hadn't ever heard him come home.

She remembered the look on the officer's face when she opened the door. When he asked if anyone else was home. When he told her what had happened.

And then she told herself to stop remembering because she couldn't do any more than that, she couldn't, she couldn't. Only the memories didn't want to stop. Instead, they seemed to multiply, to expand within her head too far and too fast for her mind to properly keep up with.

The same memories, only . . . warped. Shaded with a distinct hue of *other* that Everly could neither put a finger on nor name.

Riding her bike, but her dad didn't laugh. He walked slowly over to her with a stern expression, arms crossed fiercely over his chest as he leered down at her, watching as she stumbled gracelessly to her feet. Picking strawberries, but quickly, joylessly, aware that she only had so long before he took her away from there and refused to let her continue. Then feeling the cold clasp of a hand wrapping around her arm, yanking her upward when she lingered too long. She remembered thick bruises in the shape of fingers that took weeks to fade from her arm.

Graduating, but with no one there to cheer for her. Coming home with a diploma in hand to receive a cuff to the head in congratulations.

Except that behind each of those false memories, there was yet another buried memory. Another lie.

The lie was a woman. Slender frame, blond hair, blue eyes rimmed in green.

Her mother.

There and then vanished. A phantom lingering on the outskirts of each of the forgotten childhood dreams that Everly both knew and didn't know anymore.

Blink blink blink.

Everly blinked. She shook her head. She pressed her hands up against the skin of her forehead and tried to calm her breathing, tried to bring herself back to the present. Her present.

This. This was happening more now, too. Whatever *this* was. And Everly knew—she *knew*—that it was getting worse because she was spending more time in that building.

But she also knew that it would probably get worse regardless.

She would rather go, and risk whatever *this* was, for the sake of determining that for herself.

And if no one would tell her the answers she was seeking, well, then she'd just have to dig them up herself.

So, seven days after she'd had her blood tested in her grandfather's basement laboratory, seven days after she had learned that her DNA held something special, almost magical, Everly left. Without really thinking too much about it, she shoved the collection of journals she'd stolen from

Richard back into the waistband of her jeans before walking out the door, irrationally afraid to leave behind her only real evidence, lest something should happen to them while she was gone. So, journals nestled against the small of her back and head held high, Everly walked toward the looming, hidden, nonexistent form of the Eschatorologic.

Arriving at the building, Everly was not sure whether she was surprised to find the lobby distinctly lacking in Richard's presence. It had been a week, after all, and she'd made no further promises. She waited for ten minutes, sitting on one of the uncomfortable wooden benches that faced the woman at her desk, before she decided it was a lost cause—the waiting, that is—and so perhaps she would be better off searching for him instead.

Or searching for something, at least. There were many floors in the Eschatorologic and she had only visited a handful in the company of Richard. *You can find your own answers,* Everly reminded herself.

Inside the elevator, Everly assessed her options. Alone, she could not descend toward either of the basement levels—they both required a key that she did not have. And she knew what the first few levels contained—only small apartments housing elderly residents, as far as she could tell. So then, it seemed reasonable to her that if she wished to discover something new, going to the top floors of the Eschatorologic held the most promise. One hundred floors, the buttons on the elevator panel told Everly. She chose the top one.

When the elevator doors slid open a minute later, Everly couldn't help the twinge of disappointment she felt upon realizing that it looked exactly the same as all of the other residential floors she had visited with Richard. The same single gray hallway, shooting straight back with doors lining the walls on either side.

Deciding that she had nothing to lose, Everly walked up to one of the first doors on the left, pausing for the briefest of seconds before pushing the door open.

(An important detail to note: it was not actually the first door on the left that Everly chose, but rather the second. This was as a result of her grandfather following the same pattern: always selecting the second door along the hallway to guide Everly into, and never the first. If she had chosen the first door at this point in time, many events may have transpired differently thereafter.)

Inside the second door on the left, Everly was initially struck by another wave of disappointment. It was just another apartment. Just as small, just as gray, just as dismal as any of the apartments below.

Sitting on the gray couch in the living room of the disappointingly normal apartment was a woman. Old, frail—no different from any of the other residents Everly had met already. She had a long trail of straight, white hair that cascaded down her back, and skin that was still fair and smooth, despite the wrinkles that were beginning to crease the edges around her eyes.

Her eyes that, Everly could tell, were more ornamental than functional, as the woman gazed blindly across the sparse living room. Nonetheless, at the sound of Everly's entrance, the woman turned, pivoting her body as she remained seated on the couch so that she was facing Everly, even though she could not see her.

The woman did not say anything. She sat there, facing Everly, as though she were waiting.

And also.

There was something about the woman. Something that nagged at the back corner of Everly's mind.

It was on the tip of her . . . the edge of her . . . the precipice of her . . .

Everly closed the door back with a snap and found to her surprise that she was shaking. She wrapped her arms uselessly around herself and stared at the gray door she had just closed behind herself.

That woman. She had . . . she had . . .

Everly shook her head. She did not know that woman, and she did not know why she thought that she might, and it was useless to think on it any further, so instead Everly turned to the next door down the hall, braced herself, and pushed it open.

Inside it was the same. Gray walls gray floor gray furniture. Gray scrubs on the sagging gray skin of another woman.

White hair vacant stare eerie stillness. Faster than before, Everly slammed the door back.

It was the same—

It was the same woman.

It wasn't the same woman. It couldn't be the same woman.

Everly went to the next room. Gray walls gray floor gray furniture gray scrubs white hair sightless eyes.

Slam.

By now, Everly's breaths were coming in ragged gasps as her mind struggled to process what was happening. One more room, she told herself. One more.

So, she went to the next door. She opened it. She looked inside.

It was the same the same the same the same.

Except.

Except this woman's hair was not as white—it was streaked with nearly white-blond hair that was nonetheless more golden, more vivid than that of the other three women Everly had seen on that floor. And the wrinkles around her eyes were less prominent and she could—

She could see.

She could see Everly, and Everly saw as the woman saw her, and she saw as the woman began to stand—to move, perhaps, in Everly's direction—but before she had the chance, Everly had closed the door sharply and moved on down the hall.

Here, she paused. There were more doors—countless doors, it felt to Everly—but what was she accomplishing, moving so erratically from room to room like this? So, instead, she found her feet moving, almost as though by their own volition, down, down, to the very end of the hall, to the final door before the endless gray hallway came to an all-too-abrupt end.

Everly opened the door.

Gray walls gray floor gray furniture gray scrubs on—

Gray scrubs on a different woman.

A younger woman, Everly realized with a start. She looked to be in her midtwenties, thirty at the very most, which felt so out of place in the building where Everly had never encountered anyone who seemed younger than sixty.

Except for that man. Luca.

But this was not Luca, it was a very confused-looking young woman whose head swiveled abruptly upon Everly's entrance, and she stared at her so intensely that for a moment Everly was almost afraid.

Until the moment stretched on. And on. And on, far beyond when any normal person should have been able to stare without blinking, or shifting, or speaking into the empty air that sat between Everly and this strange young woman.

Tentatively, Everly took a small step into the room, keeping hold of the other woman's gaze all the while. "Hello," Everly said, and her words sounded to her like they cracked apart the atmosphere in the room, breaking it dangerously into shards. "My name is Everly."

The woman did not respond, only continued to stare, and so Everly took another step toward her, speaking in a cautious, almost soothing tone. "Can you tell me your name?" she asked.

Nothing. There was no response, and the closer Everly got to the other woman, the better she could make out her features, the more she could see that maybe there wasn't anything there for her to respond with. Her eyes were empty, lifeless.

And blue. Ringed with the slightest tinge of green.

Everly's breath hitched, and faster than she had entered she retreated from the hall's final room, closing the door sharply and resolutely behind her.

There were two things that Everly thought she knew, and both terrified her in equal amounts.

One: that woman, the one in the final room, was the same as all the others. She was younger, to be sure, less withered. But she held herself the same way, and her features carved the same expressions into the lines of her face. And her eyes . . .

Two: she knew why that woman, and all the others before her, had unnerved her so badly, and why seeing them had created an unscratchable itch in the pit of Everly's memory. It was because she knew them. Her. That woman—all of them, really, but especially the last one, the youngest one—looked like her mother.

Was her mother.

Couldn't be her mother.

No, Everly scolded herself. They really couldn't be her mother, first because there were too many of them, and second because none were the right age, and third because her mother was dead.

And dead was dead was dead.

And yet.

Everly suddenly thought back to the photo album she'd discovered. To the picture of her mother, with a floppy hat on her head and a bottle of champagne in her hand.

Blond hair, blue eyes.

It couldn't be.

Everly forced herself to walk down the gray hall, away from the final door, and all the other doors and all the hidden women they contained. Forced her mind to shut off, to stop thinking for once, and to stop spiraling so deeply out of control.

Before she reached the end of the hall, Everly heard a thud—the very distinct and obvious thud of footsteps—nearby. She still wasn't thinking—couldn't stop to think—and so instead she ran, pushing herself until she reached the elevator that felt so much farther away than it had moments before. Once inside the elevator, she slammed her thumb on the button for the first floor, and then waited, waited, waited as the steps became louder, closer, coming from a room not too far away from where she cowered in the elevator. And then the doors were closing, and she was safe—had she ever not been?—and it was okay. The final second before the doors met in the middle, Everly caught a glimpse of someone walking into the hall—the owner of the heavy footsteps, presumably. It looked like a man, cloaked in a deep-red uniform, but she didn't catch his face.

Right then, she didn't care. She was too relieved at having gotten away. And also, she still was not thinking.

No thinking.

No more thinking.

No more no more no more no more—

▪ ▪ ■ ▪ ▪

Everly tumbled out of the elevator and into the lobby, panting hard and struggling to keep her feet from tripping over themselves as she escaped far from any reminder of the hundredth floor. She had to walk over to Sophia's desk and lean against it while she caught her breath.

She still was not thinking about what had happened, or what she had seen, but one thing was becoming ever clearer the longer she tried not to think and tried not to process all that she had been exposed to on the upper floor of the Eschatorologic: she needed to find Richard. She'd thought she could do it on her own, find the answers on her own, but it was all too strange.

Too impossible.

She needed to find him, and she needed to force him to tell her the truth—whatever that took. She didn't know what to believe anymore, whom to turn to, whom to trust, and could feel herself spiraling. But then she heard the elevator doors opening behind her, and after flinching briefly at the sound, she turned around to see Jamie stepping out.

He looked at her curiously as he approached, and Everly gulped, certain that all her fears and suspicions were splayed across her face. Jamie smiled, though, and came up right next to her.

"Miss Tertium," he said brightly. "What a pleasure. Looking for the doc again?"

Everly cleared her throat, trying hard to banish the tremor she could feel raking her body—the thoughts, the thoughts, she was banishing the thoughts. "Yes," she managed to say. "Do you know where he is?"

Jamie's brow furrowed slightly as he frowned—an expression that looked odd to Everly on his usually cheery face. "He didn't tell you? Look, I'm sorry you came all this way, but I don't think Richard is available." Everly opened her mouth, but Jamie cut her off. "He's not in his lab, I can tell you that, but he is pretty wrapped up in his work today. I can make sure to tell him you stopped by, if you want."

Now it was Everly's turn to frown in confusion. "What's he working on?" she asked, but Jamie shook his head.

"Couldn't say. I don't understand half the projects that man involves himself in."

Everly bit her lip, frustrated and unsure. She wasn't ready to leave yet.

A lie. She had been ready to leave since she had entered that final room upstairs.

But she knew there was much more to it than that.

A thought struck her, and she lifted her head. "Jamie," she said, trying to strike a level of intentionality in her voice. "Since Richard can't show me around the Eschatorologic today, do you think you could instead? I know you said you would be up to showing me more of your work, and I would still love to see, if you're willing."

A half-truth. She would love to see more of the building, more of the parts that Richard hadn't toted her around to yet. She did not, however, have any care or interest in computers, or programming, or rubber ducks.

All a means to an end, she told herself.

Everly could see Jamie's hesitation, could see the rejection building in his mouth. But then that hesitation froze, shifted over, was transformed by something . . . else. Something that Everly couldn't read.

(That something, by the way, was the voice of the Warden in Jamie's head, telling him to distract Miss Tertium, distract her at all costs. Keep her engaged in the building, whatever you do.)

"You know what?" Jamie said, his smile slowly returning to his face. "Sure, why not? You can come down with me to my lab space if you want. I'll show you some of what goes on behind the scenes as far as the tech side of the Eschatorologic."

Jamie started walking back toward the elevator, gesturing for Everly to follow. He inserted his key into the slot by the B2 button. They exited a few seconds later into the sprawling black floor and headed all the way back to Jamie's office.

"Here we are," Jamie said, letting her in. "Home sweet home. Sorry it's a little cramped; I'm not exactly used to visitors down here."

"No, it's great," Everly said, stepping over a jumble of cords that lay haphazardly on the floor.

"Here," Jamie said, moving a stack of papers off one of the chairs. "You can sit. I'll get everything set up."

Everly sat down and watched as Jamie booted up his computer, then proceeded to type rapidly for a minute or two, fingers flying over the keyboard as he brought up whatever he wanted to show Everly.

"So," Jamie said when he was done typing, and he spun around in his chair to face Everly. "This is the core program I've been designing for the last few years and working with. See this here," and he pointed to a string of code that looked like gibberish to Everly. "That's where I input the data from each round of testing. Essentially, the information your grandpa provides me. Then it runs through this string of commands," he slid his finger down the screen, "and spits back some statistical data that I then share with the boss. Energy readouts and all that. Pretty cool, huh?"

Everly leaned closer to the screen, as though assessing the code. "Very interesting," she lied. Then, without turning to look at Jamie, she asked, "So who's this boss of yours anyway?"

"Oh, the Warden? Well, no one knows, really," Jamie said in an altogether unconvincing voice. "I send over the data as encrypted code and then the Warden sends back messages if there's any further information. Not much of a people person, I gather."

"The Warden," Everly repeated, trying out the sound of the title in her mouth. "You've never met him? But he is in the building somewhere, isn't he?"

"I assume so," Jamie said, but Everly thought she saw him look down, evading her gaze. "All our servers within the Eschatorologic are connected, and the data is sent back and forth on the same receiver, so the Warden would have to be somewhere in here to be able to get it. No idea where, though."

"What does this person do? This Warden?"

"The Warden guides us all," Jamie said, as though reciting from a liturgy. Everly stared at him, but he didn't elaborate.

"So," Everly said, trying a different tack, "what kind of data do you process?"

Jamie opened his mouth to respond, but before he could, a sharp beeping started to ring from the computer in front of him. Jamie turned back to the console with a frown, typing out something quickly, and then spoke toward the computer. "What happened?"

Everly jumped slightly when a voice came back at them from the computer. "Sir? You should come up here. It's—well, he tried to leave. Again. It's all under control, but I thought you should know. The runners have all shown up, for whatever good that does."

"Fine," Jamie snapped at the voice. "I'll be up in a minute." He pushed a button on the computer that made the screen go dark, then got up and swept out of the room.

Jamie was clearly frazzled. He kept running his hands over his buzzed hair and twitching his head back and forth. It was perhaps for this reason that he didn't notice, or didn't care, that Everly followed him. They got back into the elevator, and Everly was surprised when he took out his keys and pressed the button for B1.

As the elevator doors slid open again, revealing a new level, Everly's breath caught. Floor B1 was not what she had been expecting. For one, it had color. Too much color, Everly thought, as she followed Jamie down the hall. The wall to her left was a bright red, to her right an equally vibrant blue. The ceiling was green, the floor purple, and as Everly walked down it she couldn't help but feel as though she were in a tunnel barreling toward the center of a carnival.

Jamie took them on a path that wove through more colorful hallways, until they reached a bronze door that he shoved open, pushing his way into the room with Everly unnoticed at his heels.

"What happened?" Jamie asked sharply to the people inside.

Everly saw three figures in the room, two of whom were burly men dressed in dark-blue uniforms with black masks that covered the lower halves of their faces. There was something about the men that made Everly's stomach churn, that made her do a double take, as though there was something off about them. Something in their stature, maybe, or the way they stood as Jamie barreled toward them. Or maybe something about the way that neither of them spoke, or moved, or even seemed to breathe.

Behind the two eerie men dressed in blue was a wall of screens. They covered an entire side of the room, and looking more closely Everly realized that they showed video of different locations throughout the building. She noticed the lobby, a series of gray hallways, even bedrooms of the residents she had visited with Richard. Everly was so caught up in taking it all in that she almost failed to notice the third person in the room, until he was at her elbow, pulling her to the side.

With a start, Everly realized it was the man she had met in the lobby the week before. Luca.

Luca put a finger to his lips and led Everly to a far back corner of the room, away from Jamie and the other two men. Everly looked at him, bewildered.

"What are you—" she started to ask, but then Luca cut her off with a hush. He looked over Everly's shoulder at the others, then back at her.

"You're not supposed to be down here," he said, eyes jumping around.

Everly shook her head. "It's okay," she said. "I came down with Jamie."

Luca's eyes widened slightly, and he let go of Everly's arm. "You came with him?" He sounded incredulous, and Everly nodded slowly.

"He was showing me some of his work when he got the call to come down here." She turned to look at Jamie, who was studying something on the screens with rapt attention. "What's going on, anyway?"

Luca ran a hand absently through his hair, hesitating. "There's a kid," he said after a second. "It looks like he tried to . . ." Luca trailed off. Everly stared at him intently, waiting for him to go on, but he pressed his lips together, shaking his head. "It doesn't matter," he said. "They're taking care of it now."

Everly looked more closely at Luca, then at the room around them, filled to the brim with computers and screens. "What are you doing in here, then?" she asked. "Do you work here or something?"

He choked out a laugh. "Yeah, or something," he said. Then Everly saw him tense up suddenly, standing straight. She was about to ask what was wrong when she heard a voice behind her.

"You shouldn't have followed me here."

Jamie's voice, colder and harder than she was used to from him, froze her blood. Luca met her gaze briefly, and she thought his eyes looked apologetic, but then she turned away, instead looking up at Jamie.

"I'm sorry," she said, voice quiet. "I was interested, is all. I wanted to know what was happening and see more of your work in action."

Slowly, Jamie softened slightly, sighing. "It's fine," he said. "Let's go. My work here is done, anyway." Then he looked behind Everly, to Luca. "You," Jamie said, voice rising again. "Why are you just standing there? Don't you have work to do?"

Luca gave a single terse nod, not a hint of amusement on his face. "Yes, sir," he said, then walked away, meeting Everly's eyes once more briefly before going over to where the other two men sat in front of the monitors. Everly stared after him, but Jamie had started walking toward the door, making it clear that she should follow behind. Reluctantly, she did.

Right before she left the room, a figure on a monitor caught Everly's eye. It was a boy, no more than ten, alone in an empty room. It was small, practically a cell, with no furniture and no other people. He stood in the middle, looking down, and she didn't know what it was, but something about him struck her. He felt familiar to her, and as she was led out of the room by Jamie, she could still feel herself being drawn to the screen, and the small boy trapped within.

Blink blink blink.

23

There was fire.

There was always fire.

Sometimes it was real fire, sometimes metaphorical, but it was always there.

This time, it was all too real, and it scorched anything in its path to dust and ash.

The fire rose like a steady giant in the distance, getting ever closer, closer, closer.

It was here. And standing in its midst—summoning or enduring the flames, it was not clear—was her.

Fiery hair to join the fiery backdrop.

She smiled. Kindly? Wickedly? Cunningly? Innocently? It was hard to tell. But she did smile, and reached out a hand, and though she did not step any closer, the hand seemed to transcend all by itself across the space where the fire ended and the emptiness began.

Her smiling mouth moved—with words? It was impossible to discern, as the rage of the flames behind her drowned out all other sounds, but she seemed to be speaking in earnest. *Come,* the rounded sides of her mouth seemed to be saying. Or maybe *run*—really, there was no telling.

It didn't matter, anyway. The flames were getting closer, and with them so was she. Now, her eyes were more visible, and so it was easier to see what rested behind their blue depths.

Fear.

"Run," she said again, a whisper drizzled into his ear, and Luca awoke.

· ■ ■ ■ ·

"Careful," caleb said, placing a steadying hand on Luca's back as he jerked upright, out of the dream.

The dream. Luca looked around. He was still in the surveillance room. He cursed beneath his breath and pushed his chair away from the desk.

He had fallen asleep.

Luca blinked rapidly, trying to banish the memory of the flames, the woman. Everly. It seemed that knowing she was real did nothing to halt her appearances in his dreams. If anything, this one had felt worse than the others. More visceral. Foreboding. Luca's head spun and he gripped it with one hand, looking at Caleb, who was standing next to the desk. "How long was I out?"

"No idea," Caleb said. "I came in just a minute ago. Found you passed out like that." He gestured to the desk where Luca had previously been slumped over. Caleb's eyebrows furrowed and he studied Luca's face—seeing the shadows beneath his eyes and the lines traced into the skin of his forehead, Luca was sure, so he turned his head down, away from the inquisitive eyes of his friend.

"Have you been sleeping?"

"I'm fine," Luca said, perhaps too quickly. He took a steadying breath, then tried to school his features into something like reassurance. "Really. I'm okay." He wasn't okay—he was exhausted. What had happened earlier with Michael had drained the last reserves of his energy. Luca felt lucky to be able to string two thoughts together.

"Luca, if a runner had found you instead of me—"

"But they didn't," Luca snapped. He sighed, ran a hand anxiously through his hair, tried not to grimace. Tried not to let on how shaken he was himself, thinking of how bad that could have been. "It's okay, Caleb."

Caleb looked like he wanted to argue further, but instead he dragged over a second chair so that he could sit next to Luca.

This morning had all been his fault; Luca knew that. He hadn't been able to get the what-ifs out of his head: if he had been faster, if he hadn't been so distracted, then he would have seen it sooner. He could have helped Michael. Instead, he had to watch while the runners took him away. He knew it all came down to bad timing—if the runners had come in even a few minutes later, he might have seen first, he might have been able to do something. Instead, the two burly men dressed in blue entered and immediately caught sight of the boy, wandering aimlessly toward hallways he should have been nowhere near.

Of course, he had to bring Jamie in. To the runners, and Jamie, this was only Michael's third incident, which was infrequent enough to warrant raising a warning signal. Luca had been quick enough to catch most of the others—fortunately for Michael—but it was getting worse. Luca didn't know how much longer he would be able to keep Michael safe.

He didn't know if he *should*. The kid headed the same way, every time. Maybe it wasn't obvious from the two or three instances the runners had caught, but to Luca, who had watched Michael try to leave time and time again, it was impossible to miss.

He was headed to the lobby.

He was trying to get out, and Luca had no idea why.

There was nothing out there for him, and Michael had to know that—they all did. More than that, there were the rumors, rumors of dark and dangerous things that kept all the residents pinned to their beds at night, kept their feet on the well-trod hallways they were supposed to walk, rather than the ones Michael tried to take, the ones that might lead away.

The rumors that warned against leaving. The ones that would be enough to fill a person's nightmares and haunt their every waking breath.

If Luca's nightmares weren't already haunted, that is.

They all knew these rumors, the ever-present threats that loomed around them like unfulfilled prophecies begging to be enacted.

Michael couldn't leave. So why did he keep trying?

"What are you doing here, anyway?" Luca asked, shaking himself back to the present. Usually at this time of day, Caleb was cleaning bathrooms with Anker. Runners didn't like for them to bail on their assignments.

Caleb was quiet for a moment, which set a thin trail of dread leaking into the pit of Luca's stomach. "Jamie came in."

Luca's dread exploded, and he opened his mouth, but before he could say anything, Caleb cut him off. "He took Anker. Said I could be done for the afternoon since it's harder for me to do the work without someone else. So I came here."

Conflicting thoughts spun through Luca. Pity for Anker, who had been taken twice already this month for testing—more than anyone should have to endure. Relief that it had been Anker and not Caleb. Anger more than anything—at Jamie and the Warden and this building they were all trapped in together. That they had no way out of.

"You okay?" Luca asked, not able to put words to any of his other emotions.

"Sure," Caleb responded lightly. "Who wouldn't appreciate a day off?" But Luca could see through his friend's bravado; people were being brought in more and more often for testing now. Luca hated it, would choose never to go back if he was given the option. But he knew that for Caleb it was worse. The last time he had been tested—nearly six months ago now—had taken such a severe toll on him that he had been left unconscious for a week. Caleb had barely survived that round of testing, and Luca knew there was no guarantee he would live through another—a realization that Luca was sure Caleb was more than aware of himself.

Without the testing, though, they were worthless in the eyes of the runners. The Warden. And so, what would that make any of them, as untestable residents?

"So," Caleb said, interjecting neatly into Luca's downward spiral of thoughts. "Anything interesting happen in here?"

Luca thought about the woman. Everly. He thought of Maurie. Michael. He thought of everything that was going wrong in that building, the danger he could feel now looming around every corner.

"I saw someone," he found himself saying. "A woman. She came in with Jamie after—"

"She was with Jamie?" Caleb asked, skepticism rising in his tone. "Who was she?"

"She said she was Dr. Dubose's granddaughter."

Caleb's eyebrows shot up. "Dr. Dubose has a granddaughter? I didn't know he had any family at all."

"I guess most of them probably do, they just choose not to talk about it. Her name is Everly."

"Why was she here?"

"I don't know," Luca said. "She didn't say."

Caleb hummed thoughtfully. "Keep an eye on her?"

"Yeah," Luca said distantly. "Yeah, I will."

24

Jamie guided Everly away from the room full of screens, leading her by the elbow back to the elevator and up to the lobby. He deposited her just outside the elevator doors, then spun on his heel and retreated back inside, pressing another button so that the doors soon closed in front of him.

Standing alone—not counting Sophia, who sat stoically behind her desk—Everly closed her eyes and tried to think.

It was clear Jamie wanted her to go home. He hadn't said anything to her since they'd left that room, but from the stern set of his brows, the downward cast of his lips, she knew he'd been unhappy. She'd pressed her luck too far and was now expected to leave.

Which made her want to do the exact opposite.

She glanced around. There really was no one there to stop her. She couldn't get back down to that room, the one with the screens, with Luca, with the unnerving image of that young boy . . .

But she could always go up.

The more she thought about what she should do, the more she became aware of what she was still blatantly *not* thinking about, and the more she became aware of what she was not thinking about, the more her mind insisted on thinking about it again.

The hundredth floor.

No.

Everly squeezed her eyes shut, trying to block out the voice in her head that was begging her to go back up.

It didn't work.

Behind her eyelids, she only saw that woman's face, plastered there and staring at Everly in accusation. Blond hair blue eyes fair skin. Her . . .

No.

But it was. Everly *knew* it was.

She needed to close herself off from that vein of thinking; she needed to retreat and leave the building immediately, just like Jamie wanted her to; she needed to forget she had ever seen anything at all.

She needed to go back up.

Everly returned to the elevator and pushed the button for the hundredth floor.

When the doors slid open a minute later, Everly again didn't let herself think as she headed straight down the long, gray hallway, all the way to the back, to the very last door.

To the woman inside.

Everly opened the door.

Inside, the same woman was sitting in the same position as before and staring just as vacantly as she had been earlier. The woman didn't flinch, or shift, or react at all as Everly stepped closer, closer.

She tried comparing the woman before her to the vague and fuzzy image she still stored in her memories. Warm summer days with a bright-eyed, fair-haired woman standing behind her. Smiling. Laughing. Wrapping her arms tightly around Everly's waist and spinning her around.

The woman before Everly now was nothing like that: cold and lifeless and immobile as a corpse.

And yet.

And yet the resemblance was undeniable.

Everly wanted it to be true too much.

And Everly wanted more than anything for it to all be in her head.

Because what would that even mean?

For this to be her mother.

Or . . . some *version* of her mother.

But Everly didn't even know what she meant by that as she thought it. She just knew that this woman, this strange and still and silent woman, was important, and now that she had opened the floodgates, she needed to know why.

Everly took another step closer, and then—

Thump.

Loud, abrasive, close.

Noise, coming from just down the hall.

Footsteps.

The woman still did not move from her perch on the gray sofa, but Everly thought that perhaps her eyes widened a fraction. If such a thing were possible. That was urging enough for Everly, who knew that she was not meant to be in that building at all, much less up there on that floor, in that woman's room.

So Everly dove behind the couch, hoping that whoever was heading down the hall wouldn't be all that perceptive and wouldn't see the edge of the shadow cast by Everly's bent over form as she huddled behind the gray sofa.

Everly could not see the door, but she heard as it was flung open and someone walked in. The sound of the footsteps crossing closer to where Everly hid made her flinch, and she clamped a hand over her mouth, hoping to cease the erratic breaths that were heaving in and out of her chest. But before the footsteps could fully cross the room they halted, and Everly heard a sharp gasp that she took to be that of the woman.

"So, what would we like to do today?" The man's voice came out in a sneer, his words cruel, rotten. But also vaguely familiar, and Everly strained to think of where she would have heard that voice before. It was so hard, so cold. She thought that a voice like that should be impossible to forget.

The woman did not seem to respond to the man's taunt. "No suggestions?" the man growled. "All right then."

Everly heard something crashing across the room, followed by muted thuds that sounded awfully like heavy boots being kicked into soft flesh. It seemed to go on for ages.

This triggered something in Everly: another memory that didn't belong to her.

Heavy boots being kicked into *her* soft flesh.

Heavy fists raining down.

A hand, wide and flat, slamming into her cheek.

Crouched down behind the sofa, Everly clenched her eyes shut, trying just as much to drown out the false memories as the sounds coming from across the room. She felt like a coward, turning away from the woman and whatever it was that was being done to her.

Eventually the awful repetition of the man's kicks died down. In its place, Everly heard what sounded like a series of manic beeping, shrilly ringing out in the otherwise heavy silence that had fallen over the room. It went on like this for some time before abruptly cutting off. "Always a pleasure," the man said gruffly. And then Everly heard his heavy stride as he crossed back across the room, opened the door, and closed it sharply behind himself.

And then he was gone, the heavy tread of his footsteps carrying down the hall, fading the farther he moved away from them.

The whole incident could not have taken more than a few minutes, yet Everly felt shaken, both by these new, unsettling images of abuse she never experienced and from having been so close to unmasked brutality. She wasn't sure what to do. As her senses began to return, Everly crawled out from behind the sofa and went over to the woman's still form. She touched her shoulder lightly.

"Miss?" Everly asked. "Can you hear me?"

The woman released a small groan, and her eyes fluttered open, looking up at Everly. With a sigh of relief, Everly helped the woman into a sitting position and took in the damage the man had done to her. The woman had a bloody lip that trailed a thin stream of red down her chin. A large gash on her forehead that looked ragged, torn apart. Countless bruises that Everly knew would blossom come morning.

Slowly, painstakingly, Everly shifted her shoulder under the woman's arms and supported her as they made their way toward the bedroom at the back of the small apartment. Everly propped the woman up on the bed and then went in search of anything to bind her head wound with.

There was nothing. The apartment was nearly barren, and there was nothing that Everly could use, save the clothes already on the woman's back. So, with a lack of any other options, Everly took the sleeve of her shirt and rolled her fist up in it. She gently dabbed at the woman's bloody forehead, enough that she could see the wound really was only surface level, and then she helped the woman to lie down fully beneath the gray sheets of her gray bed, turning off the light as she left the strange woman's small, gray apartment.

It was only once Everly was already in the hallway that she thought to consider if that man might still be on this floor, might be in one of the other rooms that encircled her, and might come marching out at any second. Might catch her standing there, frozen with one hand still on the door handle to the woman's apartment. Might do the same awful things she'd heard him doing to the woman.

Holding her breath, as if that would keep her from being heard, Everly started walking down the hall, trying to move without letting her feet make any sound, but striding as swiftly as her legs would allow her. Her ears twitched at the smallest hint of a sound, head swiveling at every creak in the floor or gush of air from the air conditioner in the ceiling.

She had made it almost to the end of the hall when the elevator bell dinged. It rang out sharply across the floor, rushing against Everly, sending a spike of adrenaline through her.

She needed to move. Hide. She did not know who was in that elevator, or what it might mean if they found her, but after seeing what happened to the woman who lived at the end of the hall, Everly was certain she did not want to find out.

So, without really giving it much thought at all, Everly dove for the first door she saw, which just so happened to be the very first door on that hall, and, thankful to find the room unlocked, Everly sunk into the darkness of the room within.

25

Happening at the same time, one hundred and two floors below Everly:

The Warden was watching a screen.

It just so happened to be the very screen that Everly moved within.

The Warden saw Everly go into the room with the frail blond woman, and the Warden saw what happened to the frail blond woman (which, to be clear, not even Everly bore witness to), and the Warden saw as Everly walked back down the hall toward the elevator.

And then the Warden saw as Everly dove into the first room of the hallway.

This made the Warden smile.

And the Warden almost never smiled.

Despite his nagging ways, the good doctor was right: they did need her. The Warden, perhaps, more than anyone. And so, this development was good. Very good.

The Warden next typed out a message into the computer on the desk:

Have the boy come down here.

There was other information in the message too—the excuse they would give him, surely—but that was the important part. They needed someone to find Everly, someone to keep her here even longer.

And there was only one person well suited to that task.

The Warden continued to smile, and continued to watch Everly Tertium on the screens, and continued to think about how perfectly everything was falling into place. But of course, didn't it always?

26

Everly couldn't see anything. The room she had fallen into was pitch black, and she stumbled backward, trying to move away from the door and the person who surely by this point was out in the hall, perhaps mere inches from where she stood.

Her foot slipped on something that was coating the floor, and Everly fell to her hands and knees. Before she could get back to her feet, she heard loud footsteps rapidly approaching the room she was hidden in. Quickly, Everly scooted backward, feeling the same slick substance that made her fall covering her arms and legs as she scurried to move as far back into the room as possible. She touched something that felt like the leg of a table and, heart pounding, pushed herself under it, moving until her back hit the wall. Then she sat, curled in on herself, breath abated, as the footsteps stopped and the door clicked open.

Everly couldn't see who had come in, but whoever it was must have flipped a light switch because instantly the room flooded with bright, blinding light. Everly blinked, trying to make out anything she could about the room she had chosen to take refuge in, but then she instantly had to bite back a scream.

There was blood.

There was blood *everywhere*—on the floor and the walls and, Everly realized with sickening horror, all over herself. It was coating her hands, her clothes, her skin. She swallowed thickly, feeling dizzy, and had to close her eyes, trying desperately to steady herself.

When she could breathe again, Everly opened her eyes, fighting against the nausea that still rose at the sight of the room around her.

The man—she could not see his face, but she was fairly certain he was a man—was on the other side of the room, still near the door. Everly was relieved to realize that she was, in fact, under a table of some sort, which seemed to shield her at least partially from the man who had come in. He hadn't noticed her yet, which Everly thought of as a blessing.

Another detail that Everly took in while observing the room: beneath the splattered crimson, the room was entirely white. Now that she saw it, the whiteness of the room seemed almost shocking to her.

(*The room was white—almost blindingly so . . .*)

(*White room, silver tools, white chair, silver smile . . .*)

The blood, and the presence of the man across the room, was still making Everly dizzy, and so she could not think about why this room alone of all those she had encountered would be white.

She desperately wanted to close her eyes, to block out the room around her, but she was afraid that if she did that the man would find her. So instead, she counted her breaths, and she waited. It felt like an eternity, sitting there, crouched under the table, and Everly was certain that he would never leave.

But then: the man's feet, barely perceptible from Everly's position beneath the table. Moving away from her. Toward the door. The sound of the door opening, a flash of the hall outside.

And then the man left, flicking off the light behind him and throwing Everly back into perfect darkness. Right before the blackness set in, though, Everly looked over her shoulder, to the wall that she was crouching against, and saw another door. She stared at it for the second that she could before the lights cut out, and then she sat where she was beneath the table for a minute, two, three—afraid to crawl out lest the man return.

When she thought that enough time had gone by and was sure the man was not on his way right back to that room, Everly slowly made her way out from under the table, far too aware of the slickness of the floor beneath her feet. Carefully, Everly moved toward the door she had seen at the back of the room. She felt along the wall until her hand connected with the cool metal of a doorknob.

None of the other rooms she had seen in the Eschatorologic had a back room—at least none that she had noticed. There had to be something behind there, Everly thought. Something important enough to hide behind a room drowning in blood.

Holding her breath, Everly turned the knob and was half surprised to find it unlocked. Slowly, she opened the door, discovering only further darkness beyond. Everly took a tentative step forward, arms held out in front of her, trying to find anything within. She took another step, and nearly tumbled down as her foot met empty air. *Curious*, she thought, and carefully she sank down onto her hands and knees, inspecting the space where she had stepped.

There were stairs, she realized. This was a set of stairs, heading straight down. Hidden stairs. Everly hesitated for only another second before she got back to her feet and began to slowly progress downward.

There had to be something at the bottom of them, she reasoned. No one would hide a staircase for no reason. Whatever was hiding down there, it had to be worth it.

And so it was that Everly found herself blindly stumbling down into the dark.

▪ ▪ ■ ▪ ▪

EVERLY DID NOT know how long it took, but she was certain hours must have passed as she inched her way down the hidden staircase. It was a slow process, making her way down the stairs without being able to see an inch in front of her face.

After a while, she put her foot out and was jarred to feel level ground. Breathing somewhat uneasily, Everly put her arms out, feeling the walls around her for a hint as to where she was. Her hands connected with the surface of what felt like another door, and she searched around until she found a doorknob, obscured by the dark. Everly didn't hesitate long before twisting it and, finding this door to also be unlocked, she pushed her way out toward whatever lay beyond.

Dim light pooled into the stairwell from the crack made by the partially opened door. Stepping out, Everly had to squint to see anything beyond her own two feet, so little was the change from the pitch-black stairwell to the space she had just entered. Once she could see a little more clearly, Everly spun around, looking to see where she was.

It was a black hall. The same hall, Everly realized with a shock, that Richard's laboratory was located on.

Or, at least, the same floor.

Maybe, she thought, trying to latch onto something, anything.

Maybe she could find him down there.

Maybe he would help everything make sense.

Maybe he could help her get out.

Or maybe he was the reason for the blood-covered room, a part of her mind tried to intervene. She brushed that thought off, knowing she was running low on options.

Looking around the inky black halls, Everly's mind skipped to Richard's lab, and she shivered, the sterility of that lab reminding her of the white room she had just come from. She rubbed her arms, only to quickly stop when she remembered the blood that was still stuck to her skin, now mostly dried. Hurriedly, to divert her mind, Everly started to move. Besides the color, there was nothing striking about the setting—nothing that indicated what part of the floor she was in, or what direction she should walk in order to seek Richard.

Without much more of an option, Everly set out arbitrarily in one direction, walking down a dark hallway in the hope that it would somehow lead her where she was meant to go. A few minutes of walking brought Everly to a place where the hall widened, then intersected with a separate hall. She glanced briefly down each identical path and on a whim turned left.

As she kept walking, Everly came across nothing but more hallways and more intersections, but no doors. It was a labyrinth of paths and corners, none of which were proving useful. Everly was becoming frustrated, and a little wary. Two more turns went by, and she had to stop.

She was clearly going nowhere. Whatever there was to discover on that floor, it was hidden where even she couldn't find it, and wherever Richard might have been hiding, she felt no closer to him than when she had started. It was beginning to feel dangerous, being down there all alone, and she didn't know if it was worth it anymore. Deciding that it was best to go back the way she had come, Everly spun around, then stopped.

She had no idea where she was. The floor was a maze with no beginning and no end and no center; Everly had sense enough to recognize when she had become hopelessly lost. Taking a deep breath, Everly decided that the only way through had to be forward, even if she didn't exactly know which way forward was. She started walking again, trying desperately to remember which turns she had made on the way in, and thinking all the while that she was heading farther and farther away from her destination.

Half an hour passed (or something that felt like half an hour). In that time, Everly accomplished nothing other than taking a handful of random turns. She was becoming more and more certain that she was going to die down there, lost among the midnight black halls, when a sound nearby made her freeze, and all the color leached out of her face.

She heard footsteps. Coming toward her.

Everly sprinted in the opposite direction, not giving any thought to whether the person behind her could hear the pounding of her feet. She fled blindly through the maze of halls. Out of breath and energy, Everly eventually slumped against a wall, listening for any sign of pursuit.

Her head snapped up as she heard the footsteps again, only much closer now. At that point, she was too tired to run, and whoever was coming near her was too quickly approaching, so Everly waited, looking up from her crouch on the floor to see who it would be to round the corner.

The person she saw running down the hall toward her caught Everly so off guard that she sat frozen and blinking for several moments before moving. It was the man, the one who had teased Sophia that day in the lobby of the Eschatorologic. The one she had seen again in the security room when she followed Jamie down there.

Luca.

He seemed equally as surprised to find Everly down on that floor as she was to find him. He cocked his head to the side, studying her.

"You," he said, in a voice so low it was nearly a whisper. Catching himself, he blinked heavily and spoke again, louder this time: "How did you get down to this floor?"

Realizing how awkward she must have looked crouched beside the wall, Everly made to stand up, and then she considered his words. Considered why she might not have been in a place that was safe for her. Considered why, if she couldn't be down there, this man still could?

"I can be down here," Everly said defensively, offering Luca no further explanation. "And what about you? Does my grandfather know you're down here, sneaking around?"

Luca grinned, though to Everly it looked to be a smile laced with some kind of pain. "Ah, yes. The granddaughter of the great Richard Dubose. I suppose that gives you an unlimited access pass now, does it?"

Everly didn't say anything, but she saw his eyes taking her in, snagging on the blood encrusting her clothes and skin, which she had been desperately trying to forget about. She could see the alarm when it entered his mind.

"What happened?" Luca asked, any smugness from before gone. "Are you okay?" He moved to step closer to her, but Everly quickly retreated until she was pressed against the wall.

"I'm fine," she said shortly. "It's not mine. I—" But she didn't know how to explain how she had come to find herself covered in another person's blood.

Luca didn't comment again on the blood, but she could tell he was still assessing her, trying to understand what she had found herself in the middle of. "You're running from something. Or someone."

Everly held her tongue, but she could see his mind still whirring.

"You are," he said, more accusatory this time. "You saw something, didn't you?" He nodded toward her ruined outfit, his lips pressed into a thin line. "Look," he said, "I don't care what you saw or what you did, all I'm saying is you should watch your back. The Warden has spies everywhere in this building." His eyes roamed the ceiling, and he spoke out of the side of his mouth without looking back down. "There are eyes all around us. If they catch sight of you, there's no going back."

"What spies? The old people upstairs?" Everly snorted, but she watched Luca uneasily.

Luca only stared at her. "You really don't know anything about this building, do you? Why did you come?"

"Why do you care?" Everly asked sharply. "Who are you to care why I'm here?"

"I—" Luca started. She saw his eyes widen, then he sighed. "Clearly you have some trust issues," he said. "You won't survive in this building without friends though—even if you are Richard Dubose's granddaughter—so how about this: I'll prove to you that you can trust me."

Everly crossed her arms, ignoring the flakes of dried blood she could feel rubbing between them. "How?"

Luca grinned, eyes shining suddenly with something that Everly didn't understand, but that made her stomach flip a little on the inside.

(Perhaps it was the sensation of fate, settling into place.)

"I can get you off this floor," Luca said, crossing his own arms. "Better yet, I can get you out of the building."

Everly scoffed. "What makes you think I can't get out of here on my own?"

He raised an eyebrow. "If you could, I'm pretty sure you would have left when you thought a horde of runners was on your heels."

She scowled. He was right, of course. She had no idea how to get off that floor on her own. Reluctantly, Everly nodded. "Fine. You want to prove yourself? Lead the way."

Luca beamed at her and then spun on his heel and started walking away. With the same gut feeling that she was headed down the exact wrong path (or possibly the exact right one), Everly sighed deeply and started walking behind him.

27

Ten minutes after setting out with Everly behind him, Luca arrived at the door that led to the dark staircase. Everly stared at the door, as though in disbelief, and Luca got the sense that she hadn't believed he would bring her where she had asked.

Once in the stairwell, Luca started walking up, but Everly stopped short at the base of the stairs. *She really doesn't trust me,* Luca thought, and he watched her for a moment before speaking, wondering about this strange woman who had somehow wandered into his life, this building. Even though they were encased in the dark stairwell that hardly anyone else used, Luca still found himself glancing around more than was probably necessary. They shouldn't be wandering around like this. *She* shouldn't have been wandering around like this. He needed to get her upstairs. Fast.

"Scared of heights?" Luca managed from where he stood a few steps above her.

"Hardly," Everly said. "I can take it from here is all."

Luca raised an eyebrow, which he knew she wouldn't be able to see in the already dim light. He walked back down until he was standing on the step right before her, then turned his face down toward hers, holding her eyes with his.

"You won't get out alone." He spoke in such a low tone that he could barely hear his own voice and wasn't sure at all if she caught his words. He said louder, "I know this building inside and out. You couldn't manage a single floor. Now, I don't know who you are or what you've gotten yourself tangled up in, but right about now you need to be facing the facts. This building is strange. Most people could live here their entire lives without understanding half of what goes on here. You need help, and I'm offering it. So stop fronting empty excuses and follow me."

Choosing to take Everly's silence as acceptance, Luca grinned, sensing how much she hated being reliant on him, and he turned back, continuing to climb up the stairs. To his relief, after a moment's hesitation, Everly trailed behind him.

They trudged up in silence for only a few seconds before Luca halted.

"Why'd you stop?" Everly called up to him.

"Because," he said back, "we're here."

"And where is here, exactly?"

Luca knew she couldn't see him, but in the dark he shook his head. She truly didn't know anything about the building, did she? *So why was she here?* "Why, home sweet home, of course," Luca said. "Just try to keep it down, okay? I'm not really supposed to have guests." *A severe understatement.*

He pulled out his key ring, causing a metallic jingle to resonate around the empty stairwell. Fiddling with the keys until he found the right one, Luca inserted it into the door and twisted, hearing the satisfying click of the lock releasing. Then the door cracked open, and light flooded in around them. Luca beckoned Everly to follow him and started walking off down the hall that emerged beyond the staircase.

Everly fell into step with Luca as he walked down the green-painted hallway. He could see her taking it in—though beyond the brightly colored walls and floor there wasn't exactly much to see. But her eyes roamed the space around them, and he knew from her bewildered expression that she had not yet been exposed to this portion of the building.

Yet again, he wondered what she was even doing here at all.

Luca tried to speed up his steps, urging Everly along with him. He didn't want to imagine what might happen to her if a runner caught her down here like this.

At the end of the first green hall, they took a turn, and around it they were presented with a series of identical doors. Luca walked up to one about halfway back, grasping the bronze handle and pushing his way in, with Everly staring in bewilderment after him.

Luca's room was small and gray, like all the other rooms on his floor, but he found himself wishing for the first time that it was something more. Something other than four walls and a single thin bed.

And, of course, the figure waiting inside.

Caleb was lying across Luca's bed when they came in, and he raised his eyebrows at Everly as they entered but didn't speak until the door was closed again.

"Found a stray, I see." Caleb's eyes lingered on Everly's bloody clothes, and Luca frowned. What had happened to her? What had she found that Luca hadn't been able to see? Before Luca could sink too far into these thoughts, Caleb looked over at him with a question in his eyes. "This is her?"

Luca met his friend's gaze. Nodded slowly. Then he took a deep breath and turned to look between Caleb and Everly. "Caleb, this is Dr. Dubose's granddaughter—"

"Everly," she interrupted him.

Caleb's eyes widened. "Luca," he said in a soft voice, "why did you bring her here? And . . ." He trailed off, looking over at Everly again. "What happened to her?" Caleb cast nervous, shifting glances between Luca and Everly. Luca realized he didn't have an answer for his friend. Why *had* he brought her here? He didn't know anything about her. He didn't even know if she had been telling the truth about who she was. Luca knew, when he saw her, that he should have turned around. Walked away. Left her to be someone else's problem.

He had too many problems to deal with as it was.

And yet.

And yet when he had found her down there, on the lowest level, cowering on the floor and covered in blood, he hadn't been able to think of anything else. *Help her,* his inner thoughts had screamed, and had been screaming since, filling up his mind with a constant monologue of insistent cries. And then there was the much fainter, less insistent voice that was drowned out by the screaming, the one that he had decided to suppress for now: the one that said *run away from her.*

But he wasn't thinking about that voice.

He was thinking about how he felt like he could trust her, even though he had nothing to support that assumption. How he felt like he *needed* to help her, even knowing what the consequences for both of them could be if they were caught. He just didn't know how to explain that to Caleb. Or to Everly, for that matter.

"Don't worry," Luca decided to say, in an unconcerned voice, as he went over to sit next to his friend on the narrow bed. "She's harmless. And she claims she's fine," he said, referring to the blood. "Anyway, Everly, this is Caleb. Partner in crime and all that."

"Well, as nice as it is to meet you," Caleb cut in, speaking to Everly, "I still don't understand why Luca brought you to his room. They don't let us have people in here—Luca, if you get caught for this . . ."

"I won't," Luca said quickly. He saw Everly looking between him and Caleb from where she still stood near the door.

"How come you get to be in here then?" she asked Caleb.

Luca answered for him. "The Warden recognizes the value each of us holds in this building, and so we are both allowed a certain amount of responsibility and, with that, freedom. As long as we don't break curfew, or go into restricted areas, we have more or less free range of the place."

"Plus," Caleb added, "he looped the camera feed. Right now, if someone was sitting in the surveillance room, they wouldn't see any of us in here. Just an empty bedroom."

Everly narrowed her eyes at both of them. "Have you met him then? The Warden?"

"Not . . . exactly," Luca said slowly. "The Warden speaks through the runners. The people in blue. Well, speaks might be a stretch—they aren't really a chatty bunch. But they work for the Warden, as do the reds, like your dear old gramps. And the Warden's always watching. Always." Luca had the sense that, even when he was functioning as the eyes of the Eschatorologic, the Warden had eyes, too, that were able to peer into even the deepest and darkest corners of the building.

(A very correct and astute assumption, on Luca's part.)

"Do you know who he is?" Everly pushed, leaning forward. "Or where he is?"

Luca shook his head, expression darkening. "The Warden's the Warden. That's all you need to know around here."

She clearly wasn't satisfied with that answer, and Luca could see her face twisting up with more questions. Instead of asking more about the Warden, though, she broached a new topic. "So, what is it that you two do here? Why are you in the Eschatorologic? In this room?"

Luca sat up, leaning in Everly's direction. "The better question is, what are *you* doing here? You seem to be the only one of any of us who had a choice in the matter."

"More or less," she said. "But you didn't answer my question. Are you—" She cut herself off, eyes widening and shifting down. Luca watched her uncertainly, but then Everly cleared her throat and began again. "Were you both . . . taken?"

"I wouldn't say that exactly," Luca said, exchanging a glance with Caleb. "More like we've always been here. We've never known anything else."

"But do you want to leave?" Everly asked, looking between the two of them with a puzzled expression on her face. Luca got the sense she had never found herself as anyone's prisoner—had never found herself without a choice.

Luca and Caleb exchanged an uneasy look. Neither was sure how much to tell her. How much she already knew.

"It's not that easy," Caleb said.

"You don't want to go outside? Breathe fresh air, I don't know, look at the sky?"

"That's all fine and good," Luca said, "but I'm afraid it's not in the cards for us. We're stuck here." He indicated Caleb and himself, but really he meant all of them. The residents of the Eschatorologic.

Everly looked like she wanted to ask more. He didn't blame her. It was a lot to take in. The air in the room seemed to have stiffened, so Luca reclined back against the wall from where he sat on the thin bed next to Caleb, changing tack.

"So, Caleb," he said, looking at his friend. "Everly here needs our help. She's found herself in a bit of a bind, and it seems she needs help getting out of the building unseen. What do you think?"

Caleb's lips flattened into a straight line. Luca could tell he really didn't like the idea. "I think you've already made up your mind," Caleb said, sighing. "So, there's no way I'm going to be able to convince you otherwise, is there?"

Luca smiled broadly, pretending the smile didn't tremble ever so slightly, and spoke to Everly. "It's settled then. You have won yourself two incredibly skilled, not to mention devastatingly handsome, accomplices. You're welcome."

"Whoa whoa whoa, I didn't ask for any help," Everly said, holding up her hands. "I can get out just fine, as long as I know the way."

Luca shook his head, though he could see it frustrated her. "I'm sorry," he said. "Trust me when I say security amps up at night, and if you're trying to hide from something, the dark is the absolute worst time to be out in the open in this building. It's when all the demons come out to play, with no one around to guard against them."

"So, what are you saying then?"

"I'm saying that you're going to have to stay here for a few hours. When I know the coast is clear, we'll lead you safely to your freedom, and you can forget this ever happened. But first, you're going to have to start trusting us."

Luca saw her purse her lips together, but she nodded. "Fine," she said. "What do I have to do?"

"Right now," Luca said, "nothing. You stay here, and you stay quiet. You're not supposed to be here, and I'm the one who'd get in trouble if you're caught, so while I'm gone don't do anything to draw undue attention to this room."

"Wait," she said sharply. Luca, who had already moved toward the door, paused with his hand on the doorframe. He saw her hesitate before saying, "You're not going anywhere until you tell me what I saw up there."

"Where?" he asked.

"There was a room. Upstairs. On the top floor. It was . . . it was covered in . . ." She looked down at herself helplessly. He looked at her, too. At the blood that coated her clothes and skin.

"Was it white?"

"What?"

"The room, was it white? Walls, floor, ceiling, all white?"

"It—yeah. A lot of it wasn't so white," she laughed bitterly, "but beneath all that, it was white. Why? What does that have to do with anything?"

"Look," Luca said, coming back over to her. He hesitated, but then reached down and took one of her hands, trying not to grimace at the feel of dried blood on her skin. "I know you have questions. I know you're scared. But you're safe in here, and we're going to get you out."

Everly looked down at his hand covering hers. Still looking down, she said, "It's some kind of prison, isn't it? That's what this place is. Locked doors, bloody rooms, guards." Her eyes lifted to meet his. "What else could it be?"

Luca held her gaze. "It's a prison," he conceded. "But we're trapped here by far worse than metal bars and security guards. And," he said when he saw her open her mouth, "you really are better off not knowing." He smiled bitterly. "You wouldn't believe it, anyway."

Everly didn't say anything to that, but she dropped his hand, backing away a step.

Casting a sideways look at Caleb, Luca said, "We've got some things we need to take care of before lights out. We'll be gone for an hour or two, and I highly suggest you stay put. There's no use in wandering around out there; you'll only get lost and then be caught. You got that?"

He could tell she didn't like what he was saying, but she nodded. "Good," Luca said. "We need to get going. I'll be back right before lights out. Don't do anything stupid."

As Luca turned to leave, he thought he saw Everly reaching behind herself, placing a hand near the small of her back. Before he could see why, he left, closing Everly in alone within the small, gray room.

▪ ■ ■ ■ ▪

Luca and Caleb walked in silence for a minute before Caleb stopped, forcing Luca to slow down and look at him.

"Are you sure we can trust her?" Caleb asked in a low voice.

"No," Luca said, raising his shoulders. "I'm not. But I think we can, Caleb. I—I can't explain it. I think we need to."

Caleb watched Luca closely for a second before speaking. "Who is she?"

"She's—" But Luca didn't know how to answer that. Who was she, this woman who had formed so solidly out of his living nightmares, his waking dreams? Why did they keep crossing paths, and why did he feel so at ease around her? The dreams . . . they always ended with so much fear. Dread. So why didn't he feel that way when he was around her now? What did it all mean?

Luca sighed. "I don't know who she is. But I intend to find out."

"And you think helping her get out is the best option? Is that even possible?"

"Maybe. People leave—Dr. Dubose, Jamie. It could be that only residents like us are trapped. Maybe she'll be okay."

"But if she leaves . . ."

"I don't know, Caleb. I really don't know anything."

Caleb was silent. They started walking again down the green passageway, headed for the dome. "I don't know how I feel about Everly," Caleb said eventually. "But you clearly see something in her. So, I trust you, and I'll help you. Whatever you need."

Luca looked over at his friend. "Thank you."

▪ ■ ■ ■ ▪

AFTER ROLL CALL, Luca slipped out of the gray-clad ranks and made his way to the laundry room where he grabbed a spare blanket off the shelves lining the expansive walls within the musty room, as well as a pair of gray scrubs. He stood for a moment, considering, before he also grabbed a small towel and dunked it into one of the vats of warm water that were used throughout the day to scrub down the soiled fabrics. Then, his pillage in hand, Luca quickly walked back toward his room.

Everly was still inside, and the sight of her—safe, for now—released something that had been pent-up in his chest. A fear, he realized. For her. Evading her eyes, he tossed her the gray bundle he had collected for her.

"Thought you could use a change of clothes," he said, indicating her bloodstained outfit. "Here," he said, handing over the wet towel as well.

Everly looked up at Luca, her mouth hanging agape. "Thank you," she said.

He turned away to allow her to change. When he turned back around, Luca could see that the clothes he had brought hung loosely on her tall, slender frame, but anything had to be better than what she'd worn before. He saw her sigh with relief at the change, and then she picked up the towel from where she had placed it on the floor and spent a few minutes vigorously scrubbing at her arms and hands, trying to remove any remnants of the red that had dried all over her skin.

Luca wanted to ask her what happened. He wanted to know whose blood it was, what she had seen. What she had done. But every time he opened his mouth to ask, he found that he wasn't sure if he wanted to know yet, so instead he watched as she washed away any traces of red until the towel was dyed a dirty pink and her skin was clean.

Wordlessly, Everly piled up the soiled clothes and towel in a corner of the room and laid out the blanket Luca had offered her parallel to his bed. Luca lay down on the bed, resting atop the thin blanket, and they both lapsed into silence until the lights shut off.

Luca wouldn't close his eyes. He couldn't—not with her lying so close. He couldn't fall asleep because he knew what would come. But against all his wishes, as the minutes bled into hours and he heard Everly's breathing begin to settle into something calm and even, his own eyes began to droop, and Luca found himself falling toward the flames.

28

Another snapshot within the building:

One hundred floors of residents, fast asleep in their gray beds, clad in their gray scrubs, dreaming gray dreams—those who were still capable of dreams.

One single secretary with mind-numbingly beige clothes—sitting at her desk, awake, in a sense, staring at the empty space ahead of her.

A floor below that, in a gray room on a green hallway, a young man, asleep in his bed against his will, with his arm hanging limply over the edge, his hand reaching without realizing.

Next to him, a young woman, also asleep. She lay there, beneath the patchy blanket she was given, curled up into a tight ball with her arms wrapped around her head.

One floor below that, a man in red scrubs with tufted gray hair and blue eyes rimmed in green, pacing the length of his room: back and forth and back and forth and back and forth and back and forth and back. He had been pacing for over a week and would continue to pace for many days still to come.

A few halls over from him, a person in black had been watching the screens on the wall for hours. It was due to this close vigilance that the person in black was able to spot immediately when the young woman was in the stairs, on the black floor, lost in the building. When she found the young man, when he—predictably—led her back up to his room (with camera feeds that were being looped in the surveillance room, perhaps, but not from the dark office belonging to the person in black).

Time passed differently in the building—if it passed at all—and so it was hard to gauge exactly what day it was in the outside world, exactly what that would correspond to for the people inside. But still, something comes and something goes, be it time or something more ethereal than all that.

Staying in the building had consequences—for some people more than others.

The person in black was certain that the woman curled up on the floor of that man's room had no idea what it meant for her to be there. What it would mean if she stayed much longer.

But the person in black knew.

There was a timer in the person in black's head. Again, time passed differently, but still the timer was there, and the digits were rising closer and closer to that sought-after number.

It would be soon. The person in black couldn't suppress a keen smile.

Very soon, there would be no turning back. It always happened. Maybe slightly different every time, but still. It would happen.

And so, things were falling into place. And so, the person in black had more planning to do.

Tick tick tick tick tick.

29

The next morning, Everly was startled awake by a siren-like noise blasting in her ears. At the same time, all the lights in the room flashed on; she held up a hand against the brightness, struggling into a sitting position. She saw Luca already standing, pulling on a pair of limp gray slippers. He noticed her gaze and nodded in greeting. Everly sat up the rest of the way quickly, tossing off the gifted blankets.

"You're leaving?" she asked.

"We're leaving," Luca said quietly. "Hurry up, we need to get out there while everyone else is headed to roll call. There will be too many people flooding the halls for them to keep track of all the cameras. It's a good thing you're still wearing that," he said, indicating the gray scrubs he had brought her the night before. "It'll attract less attention if they do happen to see us."

Everly nodded and hastily got to her feet. Following Luca's lead, she carefully stepped out into the green hall, and they started off away from his room. It was strange, being surrounded by so much green, after her time spent on gray or black floors. She wondered why it was different here, what the color was meant to signify, if anything.

Everything looked the same to her as they walked from one green hallway to another, and she felt at once the relief in not having to find her way out on her own, certain she would still be wandering around the black floor in the basement if Luca hadn't found her the night before.

Luca led Everly silently through a series of halls, his movements confident and sure. Every so often, he would pull up short before turning a corner, gesturing for her to wait until some resident or runner had gone on their way. Every time that happened, she could see a vein on the side of his neck pulse. Could see as his breathing became more shallow, more rapid. *He's afraid,* she realized. And that, more than getting lost in the building, made her afraid in turn, too. Maybe she hadn't understood before. Maybe there really was more at stake here than getting caught by Jamie and given a stern talking to. She thought of the white room, covered in blood, and shivered. For all she knew, it could have been *her* blood in there next, if Luca hadn't found her.

After ten minutes, they reached a single long corridor with gray carpeted floor that steadily rose uphill. As the incline leveled off, there was a single door set in the wall. Luca reached out a hand and nudged it open.

Stepping through the door, Everly was startled to realize that they were back in the lobby. She spun around to face Luca, a question on her lips, but he winked and closed the door back behind him—a door that she suddenly understood was designed to blend in. Once closed, she could just barely make out its outline in the walled surface of the lobby, only a few feet over from the elevator. She stared at it for another second before remembering why she was in the lobby at all. Everly glanced once around her, making sure that no one besides Sophia was there, and then quickly made for the large glass front doors.

Only when she reached the end of the stone stairs that led away from the Eschatorologic did Everly remember to breathe. She'd made it out—she was free. There was too much from the past twenty-four hours to process, too much to think through, and right then Everly wanted nothing more than her own bed.

She went home and found that her steps were dragging the closer she got, the farther she made it away from the building. By the time she had gotten inside her house, Everly was too exhausted to even lock the door behind her. She stumbled back toward her room, where she collapsed onto her bed. She didn't remember her head hitting the pillow, but she was instantly thrown into a deep, muddied sleep.

▪ ▪ ■ ▪ ▪

Someone was at the door. They were yelling, and it had woken Everly up. Rubbing her eyes wearily, she trudged from her room, glancing around from the hall toward the front door, trying to see who it was.

A man was standing in the doorway, but her dad wasn't letting him in. Everly cowered where she stood, not wanting to be seen, but curious all the same. Her dad was yelling, she realized, and it scared her. Her dad never yelled.

"You have no right to be here," her dad said to the man at the door. "None. Get out of my house, get off my property, and leave. Now."

The man held up his hands placatingly. When it became apparent that Everly's dad would only continue to yell, the man resorted to yelling back.

"As a matter of fact, Jacob, I have every right, and you know that. You know what's at stake here. Now let me in."

Everly's dad scoffed, face curling into a snarl. "You and your messed-up deals. You cost me everything, old man. What more could you possibly want from me? What do you want from us? She is fourteen years old." His voice cracked. "What do you want?"

Her dad's words had been rising in both pitch and volume, his face turning a crimson red, veins pulsing on his neck. The man's complexion turned a similar dark shade as he stepped forward, standing barely a few inches away from her dad.

"You're running out of time," the man said in a voice lethally sharp. "Do you know what just happened? It's chaos. I've never seen anything come so close to tearing the whole thing apart." The man took a ragged breath, then said loudly, clearly, piercing the tension in the air, "The fact of the matter is, the building needs her just as much as she needs it. I know what you're going to say, what you always say, but it's the truth. There's no denying it now."

All of this stopped her dad short. He had to shake himself before continuing in a hushed voice that Everly had to strain her ears to hear.

"You can't be sure." The man didn't answer immediately, so her dad said again, voice raised slightly, "You can't be sure that it's her, Richard. And even if it is . . . you can't be sure that the same thing will happen to her as—"

"I am certain. If you saw the others, you'd know, too. She's the spitting image, Jacob. You're going to have to make some decisions on what you want her life to look like. Maybe not now, not today, but sooner or later you will have to decide. Before it's too late."

Her dad shook his head. "We don't know anything. We don't know it'll be the same."

The man looked at her dad sadly, almost pityingly. "Goodbye, Jacob. You'll come to see—it really is all for the best."

And with that, Richard Dubose walked away, and Everly woke up with a start.

▪ ▪ ■ ▪ ▪

HER HEAD WAS groggy and it was taking all of her effort to be able to string two thoughts together.

The dream, Everly realized thinking back. It had been a dream about her dad. And Richard.

It had felt so real, and as Everly shook her head, trying to clear it, she thought that maybe it had been. Maybe it had been less a dream, and more a memory—something she had long ago wanted to forget. If that was the case, then why remember now?

She tried to think back through everything she heard in the dream, but the details were failing her, and the harder she tried to think, the worse her head ached. Her hands clutched at her forehead and she closed her eyes, breathing deeply. It *hurt*—like someone was repeatedly pounding a pickax into her skull. Everly slowly pulled herself out of bed and nearly collapsed from a sudden wash of dizziness. Stumbling back to her feet again, she looked around and saw her bedroom tilt, everything around her flashing in and out of focus. Everly rubbed roughly at her eyes, and when she opened them again, everything was calmer. Breathing deeply, she stood back up, but was hit with the same instant dizziness as before, accompanied by a wave of nausea.

She stumbled toward her door, intent on getting out and finding her dad. He was mad at her, she remembered. But he would help her. She would be okay.

Everly looked down at herself and was startled to realize that she was still wearing the too-big gray scrubs that Luca had given her. And then she remembered that her dad wouldn't be mad at her.

Her dad was dead.

Everly pressed her hands against her forehead, squeezing her eyes closed. What was happening to her? How had she forgotten, if only for an instant, that her dad was gone?

Everly staggered out of her bedroom, but when she reached the living room, she realized that a man was standing at the open front door. At first, she thought it was Richard, and she was certain she had been thrown back into the dream. But then she blinked heavily and saw that it wasn't Richard at all.

It was Jamie.

The shock of seeing him there, in her home, combined with the spinning in her head made Everly fall back against the wall she was standing near. She looked up with dizzy eyes at Jamie, who stood with his hands in the pockets of his red uniform, watching the scene that unfolded before him impassively.

Everly tried to ask what was happening but found that it was exceptionally hard to speak. She swallowed thickly, focusing on her words, then tried again.

"What are you doing here," she croaked out, blinking back tears she hadn't noticed rising to her eyes.

And then her dad was there. She blinked and he vanished, but then she blinked again and he had returned, sitting by her side. He looked pained, unsure of himself. Her father's expression held a rage that was so rare and intense that it frightened her. He held Everly tightly, and in a strangled whisper said, "Evs, why did you do it?"

Not able to summon the will to speak, Everly just shook her head, confused.

Her dad took a shaky breath. "Why did you go to that place? Why—" He shook his head, looking down. "Why didn't you tell me?"

Everly swallowed thickly, then spoke, words slow and drawn out. "No," she said to her dad. "Why did *you* go? Why didn't you tell *me*?" She felt her head drooping back against her dad's chest, and it was an effort to keep her eyes open.

Ridiculously, her mind chose then to trickle back to something she'd read in one of Richard's journals the night before, while waiting in Luca's room for him to return.

> *Mary has been coming by with her husband these past weeks,* he had written. *I think I shall have to resort to telling her the truth, though she might very well have no reason to believe me. She cannot remain at the Eschatorologic.*

Everly looked up at the specter of her dad. "What happened to Mom?" she asked in a croaking whisper.

But then her dad was gone again, and she was alone on the floor in her house, with Jamie still looking down at her with cold eyes.

"You have to come back with me, Everly," Jamie said in a voice void of emotion.

Confused and disoriented, Everly leaned her head back against the wall and eyed Jamie as he stepped farther into her house. She couldn't speak, couldn't find it in her to ask him what was happening. So instead, she could only watch as he slowly approached her.

"You shouldn't have spent so much time in the Eschatorologic," Jamie said.

Everly wanted to deny it, to say that she had been here all night, at home, but the words would not come, and she could only look beseechingly up at him, praying that he would leave her house, leave her alone. He steadily met her eyes with his own cold, hard ones, and she felt an urgent panic rising in her throat.

"You ran out of time," Jamie went on in that same monotonous voice, unsympathetic to the desperation that was overtaking Everly. "Now your energy's all used up. You have to come back."

She wanted to shake her head, to say no, to fight back. It didn't make any sense, and she didn't understand why Jamie had come here, why he was telling her these things.

Jamie sighed deeply, looking annoyed at Everly for not understanding. "You're dying," he said bluntly, peering into her eyes, and Everly shook her head violently, trying to turn away from him. He grabbed her chin, and while Everly tried to make a noise of protest, Jamie didn't seem to care.

"I know you can feel it," he murmured close to her face. "None of the enhanced could survive much longer than this." He frowned slightly, still holding Everly's chin. "I would try to explain it to you, but suffice it to say that your type uses up all your energy by the time you turn twenty-five. I guess happy birthday is in order." He paused, looking at her carefully.

"You can feel it now, can't you? The pounding in your head, the heaviness that won't go away. The hallucinations. You can stay here, if you want, but I promise you won't outlast the week. You need to come with me, Everly."

She wanted nothing more than to deny all of it—to pull out of Jamie's grip and to say that he was wrong, that she was okay. But she could feel it—whatever it was—pulling her down. She thought she saw her dad again, standing behind Jamie with a concerned expression on his face, then a woman with fair features and long blond hair briefly standing next to him, a hand on his shoulder and a frown on her mouth, but then Everly shook her head and they both vanished. Something was very wrong, and though Everly would have given anything for it to be a lie, a part of her knew that Jamie was telling the truth.

Before she could decide anything—before she could know for sure if she would have gone with him or fought against his words and stayed behind—the heaviness within her reached a peak. She felt herself falling, sinking, and right before she collapsed into darkness, she realized that she had heard his voice before.

Jamie's.

He had been the man in that woman's room on the hundredth floor the other day—so cold, so dark, so empty.

And then she sank far and fast into a deep, dark oblivion.

30

Everly tertium entered the building for the last time tossed over the shoulder of a very tall man dressed in blood-red scrubs.

She was not awake to bear witness to her final entrance.

Well, her final entrance for now.

31

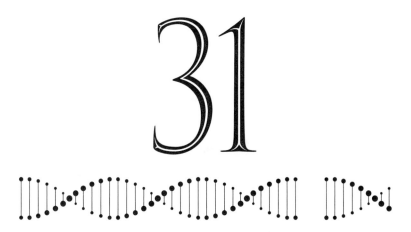

Everything was in flashes.

She was on the ground. There were hands around her, a voice in her ear, a whisper, a sob. Hers? She didn't know.

Then it was all black and nothing and gone.

She was in a car, she thought, but she couldn't open her eyes, she couldn't move her head, she could barely *breathe.*

And then more arms and she felt rocking and *everything hurt.*

Needles, thorns, nails piercing through her blood, her skin, her bones, her soul. Digging deeper, deeper, deeper, deeper. She wanted to scream, wanted to fight, but she couldn't, couldn't, couldn't, she couldn't do anything, and *she couldn't breathe she couldn't bear it she couldn't t*—

But then, with no warning, it all stopped. The relief, so sudden and so blissful, was too much, and Everly succumbed once more to the darkness, giving herself over more willingly this time, free at last from the heaviness, the anguish, the pain. Free.

Everly woke up and had no idea where she was.

Her head hurt, but not like it had before. It was now nothing more than a dull thud at the base of her skull, and she rubbed at her eyes, breathing deeply, trying to remember what had happened.

Jamie. She remembered Jamie. He had come to her house, he had told her . . .

Something about energy.

And she remembered something Richard had said, how people didn't leave the building. She wondered why no one had told her, why no one had *warned* her.

Or maybe they had, and she just hadn't been listening.

But then another thought hit her and she sat up with a jolt.

That voice, the one of the man who had come into the woman's room upstairs—the man who had . . . hurt her. Brutalized her. Jamie's voice, she was sure of that now. Only, he had never spoken to her like that before—so inhuman, so dark and careless. She shuddered at the memory and wrapped the blanket that had fallen to her waist up to her shoulders.

The blanket. The gray blanket. She looked at it, at the bed she now realized she was in, then up and around the room, seeing it for the first time through her tidal wave of thoughts. It was small, empty, gray.

She was back in the Eschatorologic.

A sob escaped her mouth. She hunched over on the bed, and the thin gray blanket slid to the floor. With her hands covering her face, she could feel now, even through the bed, the low thrum that constantly pulsed throughout the building, and so she knew it was true. She was back.

A jolt went through Everly, and she put a hand against the small of her back, pressing into the fabric of her shirt. Relief spread through her as she found the flat bump of the stolen journals, still nestled against her back. Quickly, she pulled them out, shoving them under the thin pillow on the bed.

Besides the bed, there was no other furniture in the room, but Everly did notice a small pile at the foot of her bed, and walking over she saw that it was a set of clothes—the same gray uniform that everyone else in the building wore, the same uniform she was still wearing. Except the borrowed outfit from Luca still felt too large and billowy on her, too much like she might disappear inside the clothes if she tried hard enough. So, as her breathing evened out, Everly studied the new uniform, before deciding to put it on. It fit her perfectly.

Everly looked around her room. Her cell. There was no telling what came next, what was about to happen to her.

But she was all out of choices.

She went up to the door, gripped the handle tightly in her hand, and twisted it.

Part of her was surprised to find it unlocked—she had thought that maybe everyone here would be locked in, trapped, and thought that certainly they would do the same to her.

Though, she supposed, what would be the point? If what Jamie said before was true, she couldn't leave, anyway. The building had become a prison for her, whether there was a lock on her door or not.

The hallway beyond her door was painted a bright, dazzling green, and it was entirely empty. No one else was nearby that she could see, and so she started off walking in one direction, set on finding out, at the very least, where in the building she was.

From the brightness of the color surrounding her, she would guess somewhere on the first basement level—the floor where Luca lived—but she needed to be sure.

Before Everly could make it very far, she saw a tall, lanky figure coming toward her from around a bend. It was Jamie, she recognized, and a part of her recoiled in—what? Shock? Fear? Anger? He was the one who had brought her here, the one who had trapped her in this building of nightmares.

But she had nowhere to run, so she stood her ground, watching as he approached. He was smiling, she noticed, and it made her stomach turn, the way he could pretend like that. The way he could act like everything was normal, like it was all okay. Like maybe he had done her a *favor* by lying to her, by dragging her here.

"Everly," he said as he got closer, lifting a hand in greeting. "Good, you're awake. I was just coming to get you." His smile faltered slightly. "How did you get out?"

Everly didn't know what he meant, so she shook her head slightly, but Jamie shrugged.

"Well, come on. There's much to show you, much to do." He waited expectantly. There was no part of Everly that wanted to go with him, that wanted to be anywhere near him. She wanted to run far and fast in the opposite direction, until the memory of his cold words and the bruises he had left on the woman upstairs had faded.

In that empty hallway, though, she had nowhere else to go. She understood that she did not truly know this man—she had no idea how far he'd go should she refuse him.

And there'd be no one to rescue her. She was all on her own.

She had no other choice. So as Jamie started walking down the hall, talking as he went, Everly was yanked along behind, as though an invisible leash were tied around her throat.

"Unfortunate business, what happened yesterday," Jamie said amicably, "but I hope you understand. You see, the way old Richie describes it, enhanced persons have a limited lifespan out there in the real world. At age twenty-five, the brain stops developing, and at that point with the genetic anomaly, it basically shuts down. There's too much energy, and nowhere for it to go anymore."

"But I'm not twenty-five," Everly protested, still gripping her head. The pain had subsided, but the echo of it still lingered. "Not for another few months."

"That's just the thing," Jamie went on. "Spending time in the Eschatorologic exerts more energy than you think. It speeds up the process, basically. When you're inside, it's no big deal—not now, anyway—but it shortens the amount of time you have in the outside world. So, you spent some time in here, and it shortened your time out there. Spending the whole night in the building must have clinched the deal." He chuckled darkly.

"I don't understand," Everly said. "What are you saying?"

"I'm saying congratulations, you're the newest resident to the Eschatorologic." He said this with a certain amount of pep in his voice that made Everly nauseous.

"You mean . . . I can't ever leave?"

"Nope. Sorry it had to be this way, but I hope you understand. Laws of nature and everything. Nothing we can do about it."

Her head was spinning. None of this made any sense—she was trapped in the building because . . . because she'd gotten too old? Because her body couldn't handle her energy anymore? What did any of that even mean?

"So, all of the people here—this happened to all of them?"

"More or less. You see, it's inversely proportional. The more time you spend in the building, the less time you have outside, but not in a one-to-one kind of sense. For a lot of the residents who are brought in young, they spend a few weeks here and that's that; they become permanent residents of the building, as they wouldn't survive more than a day out there. We're still working out the exact math on it, but it's not pretty to try and play around with. It can get messy quick to have someone out there who's out of time." He gave her a pointed look and she shuddered, remembering what that morning had been like. Or . . . yesterday morning? Everly realized she had no idea how long she'd been unconscious.

"What about you?" Everly asked Jamie. "And Richard—I've seen both of you outside the building."

Jamie nodded, smiling somewhat woefully. "Neither of us are enhanced. It makes no difference if we stay or leave. It's the genetic makeup of your body that keeps you here. Don't try to ask me more than that," he said, holding up both hands and laughing a little. "You'll need Richard to get into the nitty-gritty of it all with you."

"Where is he?" Everly asked. "You said he wasn't available yesterday." Which had been strange, but this was worse: being told she couldn't leave, and not even having the man who'd dragged her there in the first place present to tell her himself.

"Unavailable," was the only answer Jamie provided. "Not to worry, we have you covered in the meantime. Which brings us here."

They had moved from one green-painted hall to another and now stood in front of an equally green door.

Jamie knocked twice, then brought out a large set of keys. After unlocking it, he cracked the door open to reveal a young man with bleary eyes and dark hair that stuck out in every direction. With a combination of shock and what might have been relief, Everly realized that it was Luca.

Blinking, Luca noticed Everly standing behind Jamie, and his face showed his own confusion, replaced almost immediately by what she thought was sorrow, though it was all so quickly wiped away that she couldn't be sure. Luca then looked at Jamie without saying anything.

"Mr. Reyes," Jamie said, gesturing behind himself. "This is Everly, though I believe you two have already been acquainted."

Everly had a moment of panic, thinking that he had found out Luca helped her the day before, that he was now in trouble because of her. But then she remembered the surveillance room, the emergency, the boy on the camera feed.

"She's new to the building," Jamie was saying, "but she will be staying with us now. I need you to show her around, teach her how things work. Have her shadow you for now, until we give her an assignment of her own."

Luca nodded once, glancing back at Everly again with a question in his eyes.

Jamie didn't seem to notice; he clapped his hands. "Good. Skip morning roll, I've told the runners that you're going to be showing Miss Tertium around. I have work to get to, but I trust her in your hands, Reyes. Do this, and the Warden will be pleased."

This didn't appear to comfort Luca much; he remained silent as Jamie walked away, disappearing around a corner at the other end of the green hallway.

Luca and Everly looked at each other, not sure where to begin.

"So," Luca finally said. "Caught, huh?"

Everly nodded slowly. "It would seem that way," she said. She looked at him sharply. "What does it mean? He said—" She halted, words jammed in her throat. "He said I can't leave. Ever." A hysterical laugh tried to escape Everly, but she shook it off, searching for some other explanation in Luca's eyes.

She found none.

"I'm sorry," he said instead. "He's right. You can try, but . . . I wouldn't recommend it." Everly could see the weight of truth in his eyes. Something—some flicker of hope—died at the sight of it.

She didn't trust Jamie, but for whatever reason, she did think she could trust Luca. And he was saying she couldn't ever leave, too.

Luca took her hand, rubbing a thumb over the back of it. "I don't remember life before," he said quietly. "I was too young. So, this is all I've ever known, really. I can't imagine what it must be like to have to leave it all behind."

"It's not even that there's much left for me out there anymore," Everly said distantly. "My parents are dead, I don't have a real job, no friends. But it was the whole world, you know? And now it's just . . ."

"I know," Luca said, still stroking her hand. He cleared his throat. "It's not so bad here. Most of the time."

Everly let out an uncertain chuckle. "Yeah? Not sure how much I believe that."

He offered her a tight smile, lifting one shoulder in a partial shrug. "There are some good people here, and if nothing else they keep you busy. Come on," he said, dropping her hand and walking away. "I'll show you. It should be starting soon, anyway."

"What should?"

He smirked, walking backward. "The day."

Everly was about to ask what that meant, but before she could there was a shrill beeping all around her, and her eyes shot up, trying to find the source. She realized Luca was laughing at her, and she jogged to catch up with him. The beeping stopped, then, and doors started to open all around them, children of all ages pouring out into the hall. Everly looked around with a combination of fascination and horror. All of these children, they lived here? There were so many of them, she thought, and they all lived in the Eschatorologic? Her mind struggled to think up why they could all be there—what prison housed so many kids? Could it be that the Eschatorologic also served as an orphanage or some sort of messed-up group home? Luca said he was young when he came in. Why? What could the building possibly need with them? What could *Richard* possibly need with them? Despite herself, Everly still wanted to assume the best of Richard, but this was hard to justify. Hundreds and hundreds of children, all huddled together, dressed in gray.

The children were moving in the same direction together. Everly started to follow along with the flow, but Luca touched her elbow and shook his head.

"They're all lining up for roll—Jamie seemed to want us to play hooky this morning. Come on." He tilted his head in the opposite direction from the assembling children. "I'll show you around instead."

Luca led Everly down hallways of all different colors, pointing out specific rooms as they came across them—laundry room, storage closets, more and more bedrooms. She nodded along, pretending to listen, but her thoughts were still miles away. On Jamie, who had dragged her back there. On Richard, who had yet to show his face that morning. On the woman she had left upstairs the day before, bruised and mangled, with no way out. And now, it seemed, Everly had no way out, either.

Twenty minutes into his tour of sorts, Luca took Everly down a hall that was filling again with the gray-clad children, who were now streaming toward a set of double doors at the end of the walkway. They joined them, stepping through the doors into the room beyond.

Within was a wide-open area, full of row upon row of long tables. Some kind of dining hall, Everly realized. The room was only half full when Everly and Luca entered, but more and more children were continuing to trickle in behind them.

Seeing them all together like that, in one room, Everly realized that they weren't actually all children. Most of them were—some as young as three or four, and a part of her crumbled to see the smallest of them tripping over their own feet as they filed into the room with everyone else. But there were also others. Some looked close to her age, in their early or midtwenties.

In the corner of the room sat two young men who looked to be about twenty discussing something in intense, subdued tones. Plates of steaming food lay in front of each of them, and Everly felt her stomach growl. She couldn't remember the last time she had eaten.

Luca approached them, and Everly recognized one of the young men as Caleb, Luca's friend from the other night. He smiled when they walked up, glancing questioningly at Everly for a second, then returning to his conversation. The other young man at the table was short and pale with a round face and incredibly shaggy, almost-white blond hair that fell over his eyes, obscuring his features. He paused midsentence as Luca and Everly sat down, looking between the two of them.

"Who's this?" the shaggy man asked Luca through a mouthful of food, gesturing in Everly's direction with his fork.

"She's new," was all Luca said before stealing a piece of bread off the other man's plate. Chewing on his steal, Luca pointed at Everly and then to the man. "Everly, Anker. Anker, Everly."

Anker, apparently satisfied, turned back to his discussion with Caleb, leaning in close and speaking in rushed, whispered words.

"It's others, too. There's been talk. More people getting brought in, every week."

Everly looked between the two of them, her mouth turned down slightly in a bewildered frown. "Getting brought where?"

"For testing," Anker said without turning to look at her. His back stiffened a moment after the words had slipped from his tongue, his eyes widening and lifting first to Everly, then over to Luca.

"Testing?" Everly asked. She thought of Richard, of his long needle and clunky machine.

"Never mind," Anker said, the words leaping from his mouth too quickly. Everly saw him swallow thickly, clearly caught up in something he hadn't meant to broach with her.

Caleb cast worried eyes at Luca, who gazed steadily back. Turning to face Everly, Caleb forced a smile. "You're new, so nothing to worry about yet, I'm sure."

"But what do you—"

"Everly." This from Luca, who spoke the word so quietly, yet so firmly, that Everly's words froze on her lips, shrinking back inside of her as she met and held his steady gaze. When he looked away, he shifted the conversation into talk of tasks for the rest of the day.

It didn't matter. Everly wasn't listening anymore, wasn't even thinking about the strange partial conversation she had stumbled into. Her mind had begun to drift in a way that by now was becoming uncomfortably familiar.

It was this place, she thought. The sprawling dining hall with its tiled floors and uniform tables. It had triggered something, a memory that wasn't hers, a vision of sitting here, in this same cafeteria, eating the same gruel in different company.

Or the same company? In the non-memory, she still thought she saw Luca.

She still thought he was smiling at her, in a way very similar to the way he had smiled at her before.

And . . . someone else?

Blond hair blue eyes fair skin.

It was—

It couldn't be.

It—

It was her mother.

A faint voice whispered the name. *Mary.*

Everly blinked. The vision didn't go away. She saw herself—or rather, she saw through her own eyes—and she saw Luca and she saw her mother and she saw them sitting and eating and laughing and—

Blink blink blink.

The vision continued. The Everly of the vision was staring sidelong at Luca. She was blushing. She was . . . scared? Happy? How could she be both scared and happy?

And the Luca of the vision—he looked scared and happy, too.

The Mary of the vision—her mother—not her mother, it couldn't be her mother—a woman who looked deceptively like her mother—looked happy and . . . concerned? Anxious?

She looked like she was keeping a secret.

A secret she captured with a camera; one shot, caught in a moment of inattention. A photo slid out of the camera and Mary shook it in her hand, then put it away in a pocket. In the vision, Everly barely took notice.

Blink blink blink blink blink blink blink.

The memory that wasn't a memory finally dissipated, leaving Everly still seated in the cafeteria, pale and shaking. Luca had placed a hand lightly on her shoulder, and his brow creased in concern as he assessed her.

"You okay?" he asked her in a soft voice.

Somehow Everly managed a tight nod, though she couldn't meet his eyes. She just kept seeing the Luca of the vision—the joy and terror that had filled his eyes—and she couldn't help but wonder if it was a premonition of some kind.

A glance into their future. And then she couldn't help but wonder what they had been so afraid of. And also so excited for?

And then there was the picture. Everly thought back to the photo album she had found buried in her mother's old things, the single image of herself that she had no memory of taking.

Could it be . . .?

No. None of that made sense. She didn't have any memories of her mother, certainly not memories where they were . . . the same age?

It was all very confusing, and making her head spin, so Everly was grateful when Luca nodded toward the other side of the room and led Everly to a slot in the wall that she hadn't noticed before. He pulled out two plates full of fresh, steaming gruel, and Everly tried not to grimace as he set one in front of her. Catching her expression, Luca passed her a fork.

"Eat. You'll regret it more if you don't than if you do. Trust me."

Begrudgingly, Everly took a few small bites, chewing as she listened to the conversation the others had fallen back into.

"I'll take care of the rounds today," Luca said to Caleb. Caleb seemed grateful, dipping his head before returning to his breakfast slop. Anker looked at Luca, though.

"How come you never offer to do my work, eh?"

Luca slowly rolled his head in Anker's direction, glaring at him until Anker held up his hands, grinning.

"Just asking," Anker muttered into his plate. He rubbed a hand, almost absently, against the side of his temple.

Forcing down a particularly salty mouthful, Everly asked Luca, "So what do these rounds entail, exactly?" Jamie had told her that she was supposed to shadow Luca for the time being, which meant that she would be going with him, it seemed.

"You'll see," was all Luca said.

Caleb rolled his eyes. "It's nothing special. Mainly just chores."

Everly nodded, though she still wasn't sure she fully understood. She wasn't paying attention to what he was saying anymore, anyway. As Caleb spoke, Luca had pushed up the sleeves of his gray scrubs, and Everly's eyes caught on the skin of his forearms that were now bared.

They were covered in thin, red lines, from his wrists up past the fabric of his shirt. Scars. His arms were covered in scars. Everly was staring—she couldn't help it—and catching sight of Everly's stare, Luca's eyes darkened, and he quickly shoved his sleeves back down, going so far as to lower his arms beneath the table.

For another second, Everly's eyes remained fixed on the space where his arms had just been, but then she averted her gaze, fixing it firmly on the plate of mush in front of her instead, trying hard not to think about what the scars might mean.

The four of them lapsed into silence as they all shoveled down the porridge-like substance. Then, plates clean, Luca grabbed both of theirs and walked back to the slot in the wall, sliding them through. Everly tried to peer through the hole in the wall, but she couldn't see anything beyond.

Luca came back over and addressed the table. "We're off. I'll catch you both later." Then to Everly he said, "Let's go."

She waved at Caleb and Anker as she stood. "Nice meeting you," she said to the latter.

He glanced up at her, eyes skirting away from hers rather than latching on. "Sure," he said, with a smile that seemed strangely forced. "You, too."

Once out of the dining hall, Luca plunged them back into the endless maze of halls, with Everly following on his tail. The only good thing to come out of this mess was that Luca was showing Everly the building—finally, if slowly, she was getting some form of answers. "So," she said, "what's first?"

Luca was silent for a beat. Then he said, "First, Sophia."

The desk lady, Everly thought. What were they doing with her?

Everly followed Luca until they reached a door that didn't have a handle. She jumped back as the handle-less door swung open and a young girl, perhaps fourteen or fifteen years old, stepped out with a plate in her hand, bedecked with eggs, bacon, and hash browns. Despite the food Everly had just eaten, her stomach growled loudly.

"You're late," the girl said to Luca.

"You should be more flexible, Katie," he said, offering her a sideways grin as he took the plate out of her hands. The girl huffed, then spun back through the swinging door.

Luca started to walk again, Everly fast on his heels. "Who was she?"

"Katie? Just another resident."

"And the food?"

His eyes jumped down to the plate of food in his hands, as though he had forgotten he was holding it. He frowned. "You'll see."

With that, Luca spun right, pushing open a door that blended in with the wall. Everly followed him and realized that it was the same door they had exited from the day before, when he had helped her sneak out of the building, and that they were now in the lobby.

Luca cantered over to the large desk in the middle of the lobby, plate of food balanced in his hand. "Lovely morning, isn't it, Sophia?" The woman didn't shift in the slightest at their entrance.

"I love what you've done with your hair today—impeccably styled, as always."

She didn't look at Luca, nor did she acknowledge the plate of food in front of her.

Everly glanced at Luca, expecting to see humor lighting his eyes, but instead she was surprised to see a softer expression. Something wistful, contemplative. Maybe even a little sad. Everly frowned, watching him watch Sophia, but before she could say anything he was walking away, back over to the invisible door.

The rest of the afternoon passed in a flurry of mindless activity. Everly helped Luca as he swept halls, wiped dining tables, cleaned a large stack of dirty dishes, and folded a considerable amount of laundered gray clothes. She took in everything around her as they worked. There were so many residents, so many of those residents being children. And everyone seemed to go along with everything they were asked to do.

What was keeping them in line? Did this Warden really hold that much power over them?

After a few hours of chores had passed, Luca led Everly to a new hall. Halfway down, she was surprised to find a door colored differently than the others—a tarnished bronze, stark against the green of the wall it was set into. Luca pulled out his keys, pausing briefly before unlocking the door.

"I want to show you something," he said. "We're not really supposed to be here, but I figured it was something you should know about. So just—try not to draw attention to yourself. Okay?"

Everly nodded quickly, her heart racing.

Beyond the door, Everly's breath caught as she took in the wide, circular space. The room was huge, with a ceiling that extended up in a bowl shape, giving Everly the sensation of being caught in a colorful snow globe. Besides the walls, which were bright and colorful, a large round carpet full of pictures covered the floor, similar to what might be found in a preschool or kindergarten classroom. It resembled a room pulled clear out of an elementary school. Only, there were no children. The room was empty.

"We call this room the dome," Luca said, but before Everly could ask what that meant, he was walking again, across the wide space.

More doors lined the perimeter of the room, each painted its own bright color. Luca approached a light green one, stopping to enter a code into a panel to the side. Everly couldn't help but wonder how Luca was able to have so much access in the building—what made him so special, out of all the other residents?

A beep and a click sounded as the door unlocked for them. Noise erupted around them as they crossed the threshold. Children. Inside, Everly saw so many children, all under the age of ten or so, and they all roamed about the room, laughing and crying and playing.

Everly discerned little to no order in the room. At first, she didn't see any adults, only a raging array of screaming kids. A moment later, though, she was startled by a blaring whistle. The kids immediately fell silent, forming a series of lines throughout the space. The older children helped the younger, and within seconds the chaos had transformed into an orderly assembly. Everly was not sure what she had just witnessed.

With the kids lined up, the adults were easier to spot, and Everly wondered how she had missed them in the first place. She saw five in total, all dressed in dark-blue scrubs that contrasted against the gray the kids wore. All five blue-clad adults were tall and bulky with awkward, stilted movements that made it seem like they weren't meant to wear the frames they possessed. None of them spoke, but one of the adults jutted his head to the side, and the kids began to file through the same door she and Luca had used. She watched as they fanned out into the round room, separating into groups that headed toward the other colored doors within. Each adult headed up a line, unlocking the key code for the doors and leading the kids into their separate rooms. A small group of kids remained behind in the circular room, what looked to be the oldest group of kids that had been assembled. There were about fifteen of them, and one person dressed in blue among them. *Runners,* Everly remembered. Richard had called the people who worked for the building runners.

This one—the runner—was a woman with light-brown skin and thick, curly hair. Everly didn't think she was much older than herself—late twenties, at most. As soon as the other children and runners had filed out of the round room, the woman slumped back against a wall, ignoring the children around her.

Luca, looking more comfortable, walked farther into the room. "This is where the younger kids go during the day," he explained to Everly. "They do lessons, or tests, throughout most of the day. What you just saw was their free time, then they are split up. This lot here," he gestured at the kids who stood talking around them, "they're on their last leg in the educational phase of the building. Soon, they'll be doing work like the rest of us. That, and . . ." Luca trailed off, face paling slightly, and cleared his throat. "They won't be coddled anymore, at any rate."

Everly looked around the room. "So, aren't they supposed to be learning then, if this is the educational phase?"

"Yeah, that's more of a formality," Luca said. "Hardly any of the runners care all that much." He nodded his head at the woman who was slouched against the wall and grinned at her. "That's Julia," he whispered to Everly. "Well, that's what I call her. The runners don't really have names. Or, at least, not ones they like to share."

Everly nodded, taking it all in. As she watched, one of the younger boys broke away from the group and came over to them. He seemed small for his age, with dark wavy hair and bright blue, inquisitive eyes. He beamed at Luca, who bumped his fist.

"Luca! What are you doing here? I thought you had to work."

"I do, little man, I'm just taking a break." He tilted his head in Everly's direction. "Showing my friend here around the place." Luca leaned forward, mock whispering to the boy. "She's new here—doesn't know anything. How embarrassing, right?"

The boy laughed lightly, then looked at Everly with wide, curious eyes. "Hi," he said to her with a smile, sticking out a small hand. "I'm Michael."

She couldn't help but grin back at him. "Everly," she said, taking his hand in her own. When their palms touched, she felt a jolt go through her that made her drop his hand and take a step back. It had felt like lightning piercing her skin, like static electricity in her veins, like . . .

No. No, it hadn't felt like anything, it had felt like the skin of a small hand in her hand, nothing more.

But it had also felt like memories.

Everly shook her head and blink blink blinked but there was no helping the onslaught of images that rained down upon her.

A small boy, swaddled, eyes closed, so small so precious so special, so special, so special.

The boy on a screen and he was small and then bigger bigger bigger bigger.

The boy and she felt love and she felt . . . fear? And she felt disgust.

No. No, she felt . . . she felt uncertainty . . . she felt . . . freedom, she felt like he would carry her away on wings, like he'd break down the doors in her way, like . . .

Everly blinked. *Hard.* She shook her head. She took another step back and stared down at her hand, and when she looked back up, she could see Michael doing the same thing—holding up his hand and looking at it with wide, uncertain eyes.

Had he felt the memories, too?

"Sorry," Everly said, feeling shaken. "I—I'm sorry."

Michael blinked and then looked at her again, face settling back into a smile. "That's okay. Strange things happen here all the time." He turned to Luca. "Can you stay? We have an hour before they send the other runners back in." Michael nodded to the runner Luca had named Julia. "She wouldn't care, I know."

Luca offered him a half smile but shook his head. "Sorry, little man. I have to get back to work. You keep up the good fight, though, you hear?"

Michael beamed at him, nodding vigorously. Everly and Luca started to walk away, and Everly waved back at the boy. "See you, Michael. It was nice meeting you."

He looked at her for a second, eyes brimming with a strange sort of understanding. "Nice meeting you, too," he said to her, then he ran back to join in with the other kids. Everly noticed, though, that he still held the hand she had shaken up against his chest, fist clenched tightly shut.

32

Michael had never entered the building and would never leave.

His first memory was this: a woman with very red hair leaning over him, star-shaped tears streaming down her face and landing in little plinks along the soft skin of his face.

Except that he knew that wasn't real, so actually his first memory was this: Luca. He remembered a sixteen- or seventeen-year-old Luca handing him an orange in the hallway one day, grinning at him and then running off with his friends. Michael had held that orange tightly in his small hands and refused to eat it.

No one had ever given him anything before.

If dreams counted, though, then Michael's first memory was this: a woman (who happened to look quite a bit like the woman with the red hair and starry tears), who held his hand, and swung it back and forth, and smiled at him—and whom he smiled at in return.

That was it, that was the whole dream. As far as Michael could tell, the woman and he would continue to walk down an infinitely long path, always swinging their arms, always smiling, always walking.

That was also the only dream Michael had ever had. It was the repeating episode of a show that came back time and time again, every single night when he fell asleep. Not that he minded. If nothing else, he was always happy in the dream. He never wanted to wake up from it, even though not much of anything happened in it.

So really Michael knew two things: he knew that he liked the dream with the red-haired woman who would swing his arm and smile down at him.

And he knew that Luca's new friend, the woman named Everly, was the woman from that dream.

33

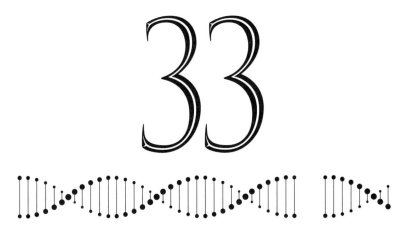

As luca and everly headed away from the brightly colored corridor, Luca couldn't help glancing over at Everly every few seconds. She walked with her eyes cast down at first, but then she turned to Luca.

"Who was he? That boy?"

"Who, Michael?" Luca asked, raising his eyebrows. "He's just one of the younger kids. I've known him most of his life—he was brought here when he was young, like me."

(This is not strictly true, but Luca couldn't know this.)

Everly blinked at that. "You mean, not all of the kids have always been here?"

"No, there are some like you who are brought in when they're older. Though, admittedly, most are much younger than you when they arrive." Luca peered at Everly inquisitively, but she didn't say anything.

"Anyway," Luca went on, "Michael's . . . special. He's different from the others. More, I don't know, bright? Everyone here has this spirit about them, like they've given up. But not him. He's always so upbeat, so ready for anything. He's a good person to have around, especially on the days when you're not feeling so great about things."

This was part of the reason Luca had wanted to bring Everly to the dome.

Michael had a way of making any bad situation look a little better, and Luca could only guess at how Everly had to be feeling right then. He didn't know what had happened—had decided not to ask—but the mere fact that she was back in the building meant that something had gone wrong, and now she was here.

Stuck, like all the rest of them. Luca had to wonder how her grandfather played into all of this. Certainly, the great Dr. Dubose could have some level of control over his granddaughter's place in the Eschatorologic. Wherever he was now, though, he wasn't here, and he wasn't the one who had brought Everly to Luca's room that morning.

Jamie had made it all sound very permanent, and Luca knew better than most how closely Jamie held the ear of the Warden. Everly might not yet be fully aware of the degree to which she was now a resident in the building, but Luca knew it was unlikely she would be finding her way out any time soon. If she was like the rest of them—if she was special in that singular, terrible way—then he knew she'd never be able to.

The other reason Luca had wanted to bring Everly to see the dome was so that she could see them. The children. The youngest residents inside the Eschatorologic, and so she could understand what it meant to live there. What the building did, to even its most innocent of patrons.

"He was the boy on the screen, wasn't he?" Everly asked suddenly.

Luca looked at her sharply. "What do you mean?"

"The other day, when I followed Jamie into that room . . . there was a small boy, huddled alone in a room. He looked . . . very alone."

How had she seen that, Luca wondered. There were so many screens in the surveillance room; how had she noticed the one tiny screen with Michael?

"Yes," he said. "That was Michael. The runners had just gotten to him. He . . ." How to explain? "Michael has these incidents. Times where he tries to . . . escape, I guess." Luca sighed. "It's hard to describe. It's like he falls into a sort of trance, where his body carries him toward the lobby."

"The lobby?" Everly asked.

"Yeah, it's always the same place. No idea why. The kid doesn't know why, either." He was leading her down a new hall, this one the long stretch with its four different colors encircling them. "Anyway, all of that brings us here."

He found the door he was seeking and pushed his way into the surveillance room. Inside, he could see her taking it all in next to him—the dozens of monitors laid out across a wide desk, the machinery both on top of and beneath the desk full of overlapping wires and cords, plugs and lights. He could see her eyes catching on the wall of screens on the other side of the room—the hundreds of windows into the rooms and lives scattered all throughout the building.

A runner sat in a chair at the desk, staring intently at one of the monitors. At the sound of their entrance, he turned and scowled at Luca. Or at least, Luca thought it was a scowl. It was always hard to tell with the plastic masks they wore that covered their jaws. And also their faces. They were just the slightest bit off, to the extent where it was hard to tell if their eyes were narrowed or widened, or if they even cared at all, if they had any response to the world around them.

Not for the first time, Luca wondered why they were used here, in the surveillance room. Their eyes always seemed so unseeing to him, so indifferent. Maybe it made them more objective when watching over the screens, but Luca doubted that.

He doubted very much that the runners were capable of doing anything at all, besides standing tall and firm in front of the residents and bullying little children into submission.

This runner stared at Luca for a beat with those eyes that could have been angry or frustrated or nothing at all, and then he stood, departing from the room without a word.

Once the man in blue was gone, Luca saw Everly shiver, as though brushed by a frigid, unseen wind, and she wrapped her arms around herself. "There's something wrong about those people," she mumbled, eyes cast toward the door the runner had just left through.

Luca sank down into a chair with a noncommittal grunt. He didn't look up, but after a moment he heard Everly come over and sit down next to him.

"So, what's all this?" she asked.

Luca brightened slightly. "This," he said grandly, gesturing at the screens, "is where we're going to be spending the rest of our day." He pointed to one of the monitors and watched as she slowly registered exactly what she was looking at.

The people. Dozens and dozens of people, walking around and sitting and eating and sleeping and working. People of all ages, all over the building. Luca heard Everly's breath catch, and he wondered what she must be thinking, realizing the extent to which they were all watched, every second of every day within that building. He could almost see as it all registered for her—the futility of even thinking about escaping.

And then, without really meaning to, Luca found himself beginning to talk, words building up and then pouring out that he hadn't fully intended to say.

"I've been working with this system for years," he began, his eyes trained on the screens in front of him. He hunched closer to her, speaking in hushed tones, even though he knew no one was listening. Or at least, he hoped no one was. "It was one of my first assigned jobs here. When I was younger, it turned out I had a knack for working with computers. Jamie was quick to take advantage of that, putting me almost full time on surveillance for a while."

"That's . . . incredible," Everly said.

Luca shook his head slightly. "The thing is, it doesn't actually take all that much computer savvy to do this job. It's pretty boring, really. For the most part. You stare at the screens for hours, making sure no one's doing anything they shouldn't, ensuring that everything is in order." He paused, still looking at the screens in front of him. "Jamie—and so the Warden too, by extension—trusted me to do what they asked," he said quietly. "Like a good little brainwashed child. Besides you, and . . ." He trailed off, then went on. "I've never heard of anyone else attempting to deliberately break the rules here—no one likes to go off book. Not when you know what's at stake. So, you could say that, in light of my incredible boredom spent sitting here alone all day every day for more days than I care to recount, I had to find other things to occupy my mind. See, there are cameras in this room, too."

At that, Everly's gaze darted around the ceiling. Luca saw what she was doing and laughed tightly.

"Don't bother," he said. "They're microscopic. Anyway, I'm always monitored, even in here, so there's only so much I could accomplish without seeming too suspicious. Luckily for me, very few people here know anything about computers. Except Jamie, of course, but he's usually too busy to bother looking after me. To all the other runners, and residents for that matter, I could do almost anything and it wouldn't look particularly suspicious. So, I began toying around with the system, experimenting with codes that I learned to navigate myself, and then, slowly, I started to understand the mind of the system, and how to break it."

"Break it?" Everly sat up straight, looking more closely now at the screens around them as though they might hold the secrets to controlling the Eschatorologic.

Luca turned to face Everly fully, leaning even closer to her. "We can't leave; I know that. I'm not trying to break out. I just—" He ran a hand absently through his hair. "I just want to protect them—the people here, those who can't do it for themselves—as much as I can. You know, redirect a camera here, delete a feed there. Hide discrepancies, cover up errors." He looked down, biting his lip. "They don't care much for second chances here, and it's bad enough for all of us as it is."

Luca knew Everly was staring at him, taking in everything he was saying, maybe even wondering why he was telling her all this. He was wondering that himself—why *her*? He barely knew her—other than the fact that she was related to one of the head scientists in the building, one of the people who had done this to him. Just because she had risen like a phantom from his dreams didn't mean he should trust her. If anything, it should make him wary about her, where she came from, why she was there.

And yet.

And yet he couldn't help wanting to trust her. The more he talked to her, the more he wanted to say. The more he wanted to tell her everything that had ever happened to him in that building, and the more he hoped she would want to listen.

And she *was* listening. Everly had been observing Luca with rapt attention since he had begun describing his work within the Eschatorologic. He wanted to capture that expression, her wide eyes and curving mouth. Capture it and bottle it up and keep it for himself.

He shook his head. He didn't know what that was supposed to mean. He just wanted her to listen.

He wanted her to understand.

"Over the years, I've gotten a good enough grasp on the coding here that I can temporarily hack portions of the system. My room, for example. The feed in there hasn't picked up on an actual recording in years. It plays one of two loops—when I'm supposed to be in there, and when the room is supposed to be empty. It's how Caleb can come and go without anyone kicking him out, and why you could hide in there that night without being found."

"This is . . . so unbelievable," Everly said, wide-eyed. "I mean, the fact that you were able to learn all that on your own? I can't even imagine how many hours that must have taken."

Luca huffed out a small laugh. "Trust me, you don't want to. It's paid off, though. I can look out for my friends." Even if it came with the risks. Luca suppressed a shiver at the thought. "Anyway, after you're done following me around, you'll get your own assignment somewhere. It probably won't be here, so there's not much you need to do or learn in here. You can just watch, if you want."

What Luca refrained from mentioning was the darker side to what he did. The parts that he didn't want to tell Everly. Not yet.

Watching the same screens all day every day for as many years as Luca had, he had seen parts of the building that most people never did, and so he had, over the years, been privy to the tail end of what he was sure were many of the secrets the Eschatorologic was trying its hardest to keep hidden.

He had seen, for instance, the people who didn't make sense.

Not all the rooms in the building had cameras in them (or, at least, not all of the rooms in the building had cameras that Luca had access to). The lowest level of the building. Most of the testing rooms.

And, Luca had noticed, many of the rooms upstairs. There were more bedrooms than there were cameras, and he had always wondered, wondered, wondered . . .

The rooms upstairs he *could* see all contained the most peculiar assortment of people.

Or maybe assortment wasn't quite the right word . . .

Luca had his theories. They were words he would never share with anyone—even Everly, this strange girl whom he felt so innately that he could trust. The theories were his most closely kept secrets.

Other than the dreams.

And then there were the secrets that weren't all that hidden. The kind that everyone in the building knew and endured, but that Luca wasn't sure Everly had been told about yet.

Almost unconsciously, he rubbed at his arms. He didn't think anyone had shared with her the truth behind the testing rooms, and he certainly didn't want to have to be the one to do so.

And maybe they wouldn't take her there. Maybe she wasn't here for that reason. Maybe being Richard Dubose's granddaughter would help her, in this one regard.

Maybe she would be spared that one thing, where all the rest of them would never be so lucky.

"Luca," Everly said, startling him away from his thoughts. "Have you ever met a man named Jacob Tertium, or seen him on your screens? He would have been tall, broad-chested, with a receding hairline but dark, curly hair."

"Yes," Luca said slowly, remembering. "I think so."

Everly's eyes were pierced on him, wide and searching. "When," she said, her voice barely above a whisper.

"Not long before you showed up. A week or two, maybe." Luca tried to think back to what he'd seen that day. It had been unusual, which was why he could still call the incident to mind. "I was working in here and I saw him walk into the lobby. Hardly anyone new walks in anymore. He walked inside and sat down on one of those benches—you know, the wooden ones just inside the door? Like he was waiting. A little while later, I saw Dr. Dubose enter the lobby. It looked like he was trying to talk to the man, but the man wasn't having it. I can't hear anything in here," he gestured to the mute screens, "but it was easy to see the man was yelling. Waving his hands around, pacing back and forth."

"Then what happened?" Everly asked.

Luca paused, trying to remember. "Dr. Dubose must have said something to placate him. It looked like the man stopped yelling, and he followed Dr. Dubose into the elevator." Luca shook his head. "I don't know what happened after that. I was curious, so I tried to find them again on the screens, but they must have gone somewhere I can't see."

"Did you see him leave later? The man?"

"No," Luca said. "I worked here a few more hours and didn't notice anything else strange. Then my shift ended. I didn't see anything else."

A single silver tear slid down Everly's face. She made no move to wipe it away, so Luca leaned forward, placed his thumb under her eye, and gently caught the tear.

"Jacob Tertium," he said softly, repeating the name Everly had given. "Someone you know?"

"My dad," she said. "He died. Not long after that."

"I'm sorry," Luca said. He couldn't remember his own parents—couldn't remember anything from his life before the building—but he had people he cared about, too. He knew what it was like to have and to lose.

She shrugged. "It's part of why I came here in the first place. I thought" —she swallowed thickly—"I thought I could figure it out. What happened to him. But this place is a vault with its secrets. There's no prying them loose."

Luca found himself leaning closer to her, until he could make out the freckles that danced across her nose and could count the individual strands of her eyelashes.

"If there's anything to find, I can help you," he told her. "Nothing can stay buried forever."

She tilted her head down, causing a strand of auburn hair to fall into her face. He reached out a hand, brushing it back, and she placed her own hand up, touching the tips of her fingers to his.

"You're a good man, Luca. I'm glad I found you in here."

They were so close now. If either were to lift their head, even the slightest amount, their lips would glance across each other.

And it was this woman—this manifestation of all his best and worst dreams. Part of him didn't think this could possibly be happening. Thought maybe it was all a dream. Maybe she wasn't real at all. Maybe he wasn't, either.

Head swimming in the moment, Luca found himself asking Everly, in a voice barely above a whisper, "Do you ever have dreams?"

"Dreams?" she said, her words wispy and light as a breeze. "Sure, don't most people?"

"Different sorts of dreams," he said, his lips hovering over hers. "Do you ever dream about . . . me?"

Before Everly could answer, Luca heard the door opening behind them, and he jumped away from Everly, face burning as he repositioned himself, facing the screens again. It was Caleb, who smiled at Everly, then walked over to stand behind Luca.

"How's it going in here, then?"

Luca grunted over his shoulder, pretending to be engaged in something. Everly answered for him. "He's a hard worker, this one." Then in a mock whisper, she asked, "Is he always like that?"

Caleb chuckled. "Only when he has someone to impress."

Luca scowled into the screens, but he could feel the back of his neck turning warm. Tearing his eyes away from the screens, Luca leaned back in his chair and stretched out his arms.

"Neck hurts," he said to no one in particular, rolling his shoulders. Then he spun his chair around so that he was facing Caleb, his eyebrows scrunched together in concern. "How do you feel?"

Caleb offered a weary smile that Luca didn't believe for a second. "I'm all right," he responded softly, but Luca could see the deep shadows that lingered beneath his eyes, the hollowness to his cheeks. Luca frowned, and Caleb's smile slipped slightly. "Thank you for taking over earlier."

Luca waved him off. "Anytime. Just don't tell Anker I said that—he'll be on me every other day to do his stupid chores." Luca stood up, offering Caleb his chair. Caleb tried to shake his head, but Luca walked toward the door. "I have to get out for a few, clear my head, look at something besides a million pixels streaming across my frontal cortex. You sit, I'll be right back."

Luca stood in the doorway long enough to watch Caleb sink into the chair, his eyes fluttering in something like relief. Luca's jaw clenched, but he exited into the hallway, shutting the door to the surveillance room before he sagged against the wall.

Caleb was getting worse every day, and Luca didn't know how much longer he could protect him. He didn't know how much more he could do, how much longer his friend could fight.

Luca liked to think there was a solution to everything, but he didn't know if this was something he'd be able to fix.

34

The woman who wasn't her mother was staring right at her.

Well, not at her. At the camera that was propped up in the woman's room, pointed down at her. And even then, Everly supposed that the woman probably wasn't looking at the camera, but rather vacantly staring in some arbitrary direction that just happened to face where the camera was installed.

Nonetheless, her eerie blue eyes had snagged Everly's attention, holding her own gaze tied to the small screen that held the woman who was, and wasn't, and couldn't be, couldn't possibly be—

Her mother.

The woman was sitting alone on her bed in her small gray bedroom upstairs. Bruises were blooming on her face, but other than that she seemed okay. Despite how unnerved she was by the woman and her stare, Everly hoped nothing else had happened to her since yesterday—she hoped Jamie hadn't returned. Hoped he wouldn't for a long time to come.

Everly's mind wandered back to a passage she'd previously found in one of Richard's journals, one that had struck her as just ominous enough to be memorable. It was dated about twenty years ago—right around the same time her mother had died.

I made a mistake. I couldn't see it before, couldn't see how my actions—or in this case, my inaction—would lead to this. It must have been a variable I've noticed in the past, even in passing. The significance of age for them, out there. In the real world. But I never thought to study it, to understand it. And now the worst has happened, and I can't fix it. I failed her. I failed my own daughter.

Everly hadn't understood what Richard meant when she'd first read that entry, which was somehow both days and a lifetime ago, but now she thought she was beginning to. The significance of age for them, he had written. And wasn't that what had happened to her, what people kept telling her had happened? She'd aged too much for the outside world. And if she hadn't returned to the building in time . . .

So, is that what happened to her mother, then? Did Mary Tertium outlive her durability in the outside world, and die because of it?

But how did Richard fail her?

And what could all of that possibly have to do with that woman on the hundredth floor?

A different screen, on the opposite side of the wall from the woman on the hundredth floor, housed that boy. Michael.

When Luca had brought her into the surveillance room, she had recognized it immediately as the place she'd followed Jamie into the other day where she had seen Michael on that screen. Who was that little boy, and why did he try so hard to leave, as Luca had mentioned?

And what had happened when he'd touched her?

"You're probably wondering what's wrong with me, aren't you?"

Caleb's words startled Everly out of her thoughts. She turned to him with wide eyes and lifted her hands, trying to let him know that wasn't at all what she'd been thinking. Consumed in her own worries, she had nearly forgotten about the young man who sat next to her. He just smiled, though.

"It's okay," Caleb said. "I'm not dying. At least, I don't think I am. It's only that I'm not as strong as the others."

Everly sat back, curious now despite herself. "Are you sick?"

Caleb tilted his head, considering. "I'm not sure, exactly. We don't really have doctors down here, you know. At least, not the medical kind. I mainly get tired more frequently than most of the other residents, and I need to rest more. It's not too bad, most of the time."

"I'm sorry," Everly said, but Caleb shrugged and changed the subject.

"So, you're from the outside then?"

"I guess so."

"What's it like?"

"What's what like?"

"All of it. The world."

"The world?" Everly frowned slightly, thinking. "That's a lot to try and describe in one sitting."

Caleb shrugged. "Tell me anything. What's your favorite thing?"

"My favorite thing," Everly repeated faintly, trying to remember anything at all from the world outside the building. She had been in here such a short time—so why couldn't she seem to draw anything to mind?

"Strawberries," she finally managed to say, memories dancing back to the rows of green plants that went back and back and back, sticky red fruit grasped in sticky red hands.

But this made her remember the tainted versions of those memories she had called to mind not long ago—the ones with a version of her father who didn't feel remotely like her father—which made her shake her head, turning away from Caleb so he couldn't see the haunted confusion that she knew must have crept into her eyes.

Caleb was quiet for a moment. "I wish I could remember it," he said softly. "Any of it. Or I wish I could go out, even just for one day."

"So, it's real, then," Everly said, turning back to him. "Jamie said it's something with energy—about using it all up."

Caleb frowned. "The reason we can't leave? I don't know about all that, but yes, I suppose it must be real. They tell us we can't leave. That we wouldn't survive it, and no one is brave enough to test them at their word."

He offered her a dry smile. "I know my odds would probably be even worse than anyone else's."

Before she could say anything else—mention the hallucinations she'd had out there, the pounding in her head that felt like someone driving a wooden stake from one side of her skull to the other—Luca returned to the surveillance room.

Everly met his eyes. For the briefest of moments, everything around the two of them seemed to stop, suspended in a bubble of their own making. The moment passed almost as soon as it had started, and Everly quickly averted her gaze, feeling the tips of her ears turn pink.

She thought back to earlier, when he'd brushed a strand of hair away from her face. When they'd been close, so close. And he'd asked her something about dreams.

There was something about him, something she couldn't put a finger on. Even with everything else that was falling apart around her, her thoughts kept returning, over and over and over, to this man with brown eyes and dark locks who had been by her side the whole morning.

It was like she'd known him her whole life, not like they'd just met a few days before.

It didn't feel . . . normal? Everly had been around other guys before in her life, and she'd never felt like this before, but she couldn't . . . she couldn't put a finger on why . . .

Everly shook her head sharply. Not that it helped.

Caleb stood up as Luca approached them. "I'd better go. I'm not supposed to be in here—you can only cover for me so much, Luca."

Luca nodded at Caleb as he stepped out and sat back in the chair Caleb had vacated. "I miss anything interesting?"

"Not really," Everly said, still thinking about her conversation with Caleb.

Something had been nagging at her, sitting there in the surveillance room looking over the dozens and dozens of screens. When she put a finger on it, she turned around in her seat.

"Luca," she started, but then hesitated. She scanned the screens in front of her until she found the one she was looking for—the one with the woman on the hundredth floor, still sitting on her bed.

"There are adults upstairs," she said. She pointed at a different screen, the one with Lois. "And elderly people. But down here, it's not all kids, is it?" She shook her head. "So, what's the difference? And why so many people? What are they all for?"

Luca was looking at the screens she had indicated, studying them. "To be honest," he said, "I don't really know. It's my impression that everyone starts out down here, and then at a certain point they just take you away. Sometimes you end up there." He indicated one screen, where a woman who looked to be in her early thirties was standing stiffly in the middle of a small gray apartment, her head facing straight ahead.

"See her? That's Vanessa. She used to be down here, with us. When I was younger. They took her away one day, didn't tell us where. Then, a couple of months into working here, I spotted her on that screen. There are others, too," he said. "But some of them . . . some of them never show up on any of the other screens. They're just . . . gone." Luca met Everly's eyes, his gaze more intense than she was used to. "Regardless of what happens to them," he said, voice low, "everyone gets pulled upstairs eventually. You don't see any of the older residents down here, do you? Not even any that are middle-aged. Everyone moves on. I have no idea why."

Everly nodded slowly, but a terrible feeling slithered through her. What happened to the others? Those who weren't given a room upstairs?

What happened when you got older?

There had to be a way out, a way that she could leave this building before she became like the people up there. A way for her to live past twenty-five out in the real world and have a real life. She wasn't ready to accept that this was it, that there was nothing else for her. She wasn't ready to give up even the *idea* of a life beyond this without doing everything in her power to find a way out, to find a way to outlive this genetic anomaly in her veins that apparently wanted her dead at twenty-five.

"Luca," she said, "why are you so sure there isn't a way for us to leave?"

He shrugged. "It's what we've always been told. And it also feels . . . wrong, thinking about trying to leave. You know?"

Strangely, she did know. Right now, sitting in the surveillance room, Everly tried to imagine, *really* imagine, herself walking out those front doors, leaving and never looking back, and it made her almost sick to her stomach. It was like her body had acknowledged, even if her mind hadn't fully yet, that there really was no escape. That this was where she had to be.

She didn't accept that.

"No," she said, shaking her head. "There has to be more than that. There has to be. Where there's a lock, there has to be a key; if we're locked in this building, then there needs to be a way out. There *has* to be," she said, voice rising at the end when she saw Luca shaking his head.

"Everly," Luca said, his voice lowering. "Listen, there's more to it than that. There's something else you should know about the building, about the . . . testing."

Just then, the door snapped open and a runner with blue scrubs and empty eyes strutted in without speaking. Luca hurriedly leaped from his seat, beckoning for Everly to follow as he left the surveillance room. Out in the hall, she wanted him to go on, to finish what he had started to tell her, but he was walking too quickly, and it took a lot of her effort just to keep up with him. They wound up back at the dining hall, where they ate another meal just as salty and awful as the breakfast had been. Still Luca didn't speak to her, didn't mention whatever it was he had been going to say. She wanted to ask but didn't know how to do it without anyone else in the crowded dining hall overhearing. After dinner, Luca led her down a new corridor, where she realized a group of girls and young women were congregating, some of whom were throwing curious looks Luca's way. Luca was looking down, and Everly was amused to see his neck turning red.

"You go through there," he said, his first words to her since the surveillance room. He pointed at the door that the rest of the girls were streaming through. "Get washed up, find a change of clothes—they should be stacked against a back wall." He was already walking away when he called back over his shoulder, "Follow the rest of them back out to roll call. I'll find you then."

Everly's mouth twitched in silent amusement as she watched him go, then she went through the door he had indicated, finding it to be a sort of communal showering space. There was a wall lined with shelves, filled with essentials such as soap and towels. Everly grabbed what she needed, took a quick cold shower, then slipped into a new pair of gray scrubs, throwing the old ones into a large basket near the door that was labeled Laundry.

Luca was right—it was easy enough to follow the other girls as they left the showers and headed down the hall together, winding up, Everly discovered, in the round, colorful room that she had met Michael in earlier. Everyone seemed to be lining up, placing themselves into some sort of order that Everly didn't understand, but that appeared to be roughly by age. She scanned the room, looking for Luca, and when she found him, she made her way over to where he stood, grateful for a familiar face.

"What are we doing?" she asked him.

"We're lining up for roll call," Luca said, in answer to her question. "We do this every morning and every night, so the runners can make sure everyone is accounted for. Here," he said, moving over slightly. "Go behind me. I'm sure it'll be fine for now—you're supposed to be following me, anyway."

Everly did what he said, standing behind and watching as everyone else formed lines throughout the room. A steady buzz of conversation saturated the room, but when one of the doors on the side slammed open, a dead silence took over. Looking over Luca's shoulder, Everly could see ten runners, dressed in their distinctive blue uniforms and black masks, striding into the room. The one in front was a balding man with a stern look in his eyes, who glanced once over the assembled children with the same cold, vacant eyes that all the runners seemed to have. The residents around her stood up straighter at the sight of the runners, and so Everly tried to do the same.

About an hour passed as the runners went down the lines, identifying kids and marking them off one by one on the lists they held in front of them. One of the runners—a woman with thick eyebrows and bushy hair—reached where Luca and Everly stood and Everly froze, suddenly terrified of the person in front of her. What if she wasn't in the right place? What if she did something wrong?

The runner didn't speak. None of them did, as far as Everly could tell. She stood in front of Luca, who told her his name, then nodded back at Everly. "She's new," he said to the runner, who then cast her dead, uncaring eyes in Everly's direction, making her squirm where she stood. Luca nudged Everly with an elbow, mouthing the word *name.*

Everly gulped thickly. "E-Everly," she managed. "Everly Tertium."

The runner barely reacted; her clouded eyes glanced down at the list in her hands, and she must have found Everly's name, for she nodded once before moving on to the person behind her. Everly nearly sagged with relief, but Luca elbowed her again, jerking his head up. She straightened her spine, straining to remain still as the runners concluded their check. The runners all left the dome together in a swarm of blue, and as soon as they were gone the lines of residents began to file back out the door they had come in through.

Everly remained close to Luca, afraid of losing him in the crowd and never being able to find her room again. The people around them eventually began to disperse little by little, heading different ways to find their respective rooms. Everly came up so that she was walking beside Luca.

"You have to do that every night?" she asked.

"Yeah," he said. "Every morning, too. It's not so bad. You get used to it."

He led her down a couple more halls, then stopped in front of a door. "I believe this is you. It should still be unlocked, but don't try to open it after the lights shut off. They lock us all in during the night."

Everly nodded, but her mind drifted to that morning, when she had been able to open her door. Had they just not locked it the night before?

"Thank you," she said to Luca. "For showing me around and helping me." She let out a shaky breath. "It's a lot, you know?"

Luca grinned crookedly. "No problem. All in a day's work." His face turned more serious, and his eyes met hers. "It will get easier. I promise."

This was a lie, and a poorly concealed one at that. It would, in fact, only get much, much worse.

However, since Everly did not know this, she only nodded again, and tried to smile.

I won't be here forever, she vowed silently to herself. *I don't want it to get easier, I want to get* out.

Everly bid Luca goodnight, and she let herself back into the cell that had become her home. Slowly, she made her way over to the narrow gray bed she had woken up in that morning, what now felt like a lifetime ago.

It was still hard to accept that she might never leave the building again. Impossible, really.

Yet so many people kept telling her the same thing, over and over.

Even if it wasn't true, as some small, hopeful part of herself still tried to cling to—even if it was a well-concocted lie and really they were all kidding themselves—there had to be a reason all those people were here.

They're here to change the world, Richard had told her, what seemed like forever ago. But from where she was lying, a floor beneath the ground in an all-gray room, it didn't seem like anyone was changing the world. It seemed like they were all prisoners to a madman's game. Nothing more.

Alone for the first time in what had seemed like a lifetime compressed into a single day, Everly pulled out the stolen journals from where she'd hidden them beneath her pillow that morning.

Angling her body so as to hide them from the view of any cameras that may be above her, Everly dove into Richard's words, trying to find something that contradicted what people had been telling her all day: that she was trapped here.

That she could never leave. That none of them could.

She did not find those words of consolation she so desperately sought. Instead, she discovered an entry dated 1966 that snagged something in her mind.

A fascinating young woman visited me today in the Eschatorologic. That is what I have decided to call it—or rather, what the building has decided to be called. It's strange, this building. I can't quite put a finger on the pulse of what is happening around me, but I know it is something. Something significant? One can only hope.

This woman, she somehow found it, too. Appearing before me, as though from nowhere, with bright eyes and a curious smile. She walked in and said she had a feeling she was supposed to be there. It was the strangest thing.

Her name is Lois. She is a marvelous young woman, with deep blue eyes and dark auburn hair that reminds me remarkably of my dear Miranda. I have the strangest sense that she has come from a great distance away, though I cannot begin to fathom what that might mean. I don't know what it means yet that she is here, but I think it could turn out to be something spectacular—the breakthrough I have been looking for, perhaps.

So, Lois had been there since the beginning. That was a long time to remain in the building. Everly riffled through the remaining pages in that journal, seeking out her name again. On the second to last page she found it, dated a couple of years later.

Lois has consented to being tested, and with the new equipment I have been able to procure, I know that the results are more accurate than ever. I could barely believe my eyes when the results came back positive, though of course it makes sense. Why else would she have felt so drawn to the Eschatorologic? I have suspicions about this location, too—suspicions that I have shared with no one yet. They would help to explain Lois, I think . . .

Miranda has taken quite a liking to Lois. They get along splendidly, the two women. I hope this will be good for Miranda, as I fear my work has kept me away from her more than I'd like. It'll be good for her to have a new friend, especially as she is currently in the family way.

This made Everly pause. Recalling the newspaper snippet she found, what seemed so long ago now, she remembered the wedding announcement for Richard and Miranda Dubose. That implied that Miranda was her grandmother, which meant that she was pregnant with her mom at the point when Richard was writing. Everly quickly scanned the rest of the words in that journal, frustrated when no more was mentioned about her mother or Miranda's pregnancy.

Putting the journals back under her pillow, Everly lay on the narrow gray bed, staring at the ceiling, trying to find a way to put aside the horrors from her day enough to fall asleep.

She didn't cry that night, but later she would wish that she had. Later, she would wish that she had used all the tears she could before the day arrived when she would never be able to cry again.

35

Mary Dubose entered the building for the first time ten years after Richard Dubose had discovered it. Her inaugural entrance was not terribly different from that of Everly—she had been walking and found a strange building arising out of the soil where before she could have sworn there was nothing but densely polluted air. She walked in, found a place, decided not to leave, and then found that she couldn't.

No one, not even Richard, knew who she was. The wonders of the impossible.

Mary Dubose Tertium entered the building for the first time approximately thirty years later (by some accounts). It would have been sooner—should have been sooner, in fact—except that by then Richard had begun to catch on, and he had become significantly smarter when it came to dealings with the building.

Mary Dubose Tertium entered the building for the first time on the arm of her newly minted husband—one Jacob Tertium, a bright-eyed and bushy-haired grad student whom she had become acquainted with in the final stretch of securing her degree in astrophysics.

Jacob Tertium held a particular fatal flaw that he would come to regret much later in life: curiosity. When Mary told him vaguely of her father's work for an unknown lab space on the outskirts of town, Jacob's interest was piqued, and he asked to visit.

Here, Mary hesitated, for the span of perhaps half a heartbeat. But then the allure of new love won out, and she agreed.

Even though she, herself, had never been to the building. She only knew where it was because as a young girl she had often trailed her father to work, halting at the foot of the infinite stone stairs, some form of childish wisdom keeping her away as long as possible.

It had been the first rule her parents had instilled in her, as soon as rules were a concept that could be abided by, that held the possibility of being broken.

You will not go to the building, they had told her, again and again and again until the *will not* in the command had begun to sound more and more like a *cannot*, like if she were to try to enter it there would be some invisible force to prevent her from walking through the front doors.

This was not what happened.

What happened: Jacob and Mary approached the building, hand in hand, and walked up the dozens and dozens and dozens of stone steps. Mary felt a buzzing beneath her feet as she went, though she thought that it very well could have been the nerves making her shake so. Jacob felt a buzz, too, but his was far less physical and far more spiritual: the insubstantial buzz of anticipation that comes with fulfilling a long-kept possibility.

Much to his credit, Richard did not yell when he discovered his daughter and her new husband striding into his place of work. He cast shifting eyes between the two of them, and then put on a smile that Mary could tell was false, but Jacob couldn't. He'd asked if they wanted a tour and showed them the most benign and simple of rooms the building had to offer (which was not much—a few closets and empty bedrooms, mainly). When Jacob threatened (in an entirely polite manner) to linger further, Richard brusquely ushered the two back toward the lobby, more or less pushing them out and closing the doors tightly behind them.

The next day, Jacob wanted to return.

It took a month of this before Richard began to get angry. Not at his daughter or her husband, exactly—because how could they know? More at himself, for the secrets he now realized he had kept too long.

So, back at the Tertiums' home one evening after a month's worth of visits to the Eschatorologic, Richard sat them down and told them the truth.

Or a version of it. He told them of the genetic anomaly that ran through Mary's veins. Told them what she would become, should she continue to return to the building, should she spend too many hours in that cursed place. Told them in the vaguest and most uncertain terms of the powers at play in that building that were more dangerous and unimaginable than the mind could fathom and told them that they could not come back.

What he did not tell them was what his role in those dangerous and unimaginable feats was. Nor did he tell them the things he did not yet know. The doubly cursed life that befell those with the anomaly.

Doubly blessed, doubly cursed.

Jacob nodded at Richard's explanation, saying he understood, and Mary lingered, white-faced and shivering, in a corner of the room, listening to it all without really being able to absorb any of her father's words.

Richard left feeling confident, settled, assured that he had done everything he needed to.

Except that Jacob should never have seen the building at all—would never have, if it hadn't been for his enhanced wife leading the way that first day.

Except the very fact of him having been there at all changed something in him. The fact of his knowing what everything could lead to made him a different person, a different husband, a different father. Some for better, some for worse.

Except one can never play with a safe amount of fire. It will always erupt into an uncontrollable inferno, in time. And always without you seeing it coming.

Jacob Tertium never should have gone in the building.

And Mary Tertium never should have left.

36

Richard perched precariously on the edge of the gray bed, careful not to let his weight shift too much. Beside him, a shallow tray with warm, soapy water balanced on the lip of the mattress. Richard hummed lightly to himself while he worked, dipping a sponge in the water and carefully wringing it out, until the last drops of water fell with nimble plinks into the tray.

"You know," Richard said, only half to himself, "it was never meant to be like this." He gently sponged the skin around a shallow cut, careful not to let it drip. "But it's all for her own good; she'll see that one day."

The woman who was not his daughter said nothing to this. Richard chuckled drily. "Of course, you agree with me, don't you? You'd want the best for her, too."

Jamie had outdone himself this time. The markings on the woman weren't the typical kind made by tools in the white room; this bruising was more personal than that. Richard would have to have a talk with him.

Across the small apartment a door slammed open and—speak of the devil—Jamie came striding into the room.

"Richard, old man," Jamie said jovially. "The Warden passed along a message. Said you wanted me."

"Yes," Richard said, continuing to dab at the forehead of the woman lying in the bed. He thought he saw Jamie's lip curl up in disgust. "It is my understanding that you have brought my granddaughter to be a resident of the Eschatorologic."

"As requested," Jamie said. "Your wish is my command, old man."

"Good. Then I need you to increase the testing—across the board. Time is of the essence now."

"You sure you don't want to do it yourself?" Jamie asked. There was mockery in his tone. Richard didn't like to be made fun of.

He dropped the sponge in the tray, causing the water to splash over the edges and soak into the gray bedsheets. "You will be wise to remember your place, Mr. Griffith."

"My place," Jamie said with a sneer, "is to do your dirty work, old man. Don't forget: your hands get to stay pearly white because of me."

"Go," Richard snapped.

Jamie walked backward to the door, cruel laughter dancing in his eyes, then left without another word.

When he was gone, Richard sank back into the side of the bed, picking up the sponge again. "Oh, how I wish you were here," he said, absently dabbing at the woman's bloodied forehead again. "You would understand. You would see what I have to do."

He knew this wasn't his daughter, his Mary, but still it was nice sometimes to pretend. Looking into this woman's eyes—her now dead, empty eyes—he could almost see a reflection of his Mary there.

It wrenched something inside him but helped him to remember what was at stake.

He wouldn't repeat the mistakes from the past. Everly was in the building, which was good. It gave him more time. And he knew he could do it this time.

He'd find a way to save her.

37

On her second morning as a resident of the Eschatorologic, Everly sat in the dining hall looking closely at Caleb.

The circles under his eyes seemed darker than before, and his head hung limp, like it was too much of an effort to keep up. Everly frowned, watching him, and glanced at Luca, who met her eyes and shook his head slightly. Suddenly, Caleb's face blanched and he sat bolt upright. Everyone else at the table turned to see what he was looking at, and Everly felt a pit growing in her stomach when she saw Jamie striding through the cafeteria, right for their table.

Caleb was shaking, and Everly saw Luca put his hand on his friend's shoulder, watching him carefully. Anker looked nervously between Jamie and Caleb, and it was clear to Everly that they all thought something was about to happen to Caleb. When Jamie reached their table, though, he didn't even spare a glance at Caleb—he looked right at her.

"Miss Tertium," he said in a tone far too chipper for the tense atmosphere that encircled the table. "Would you mind accompanying me for the morning?"

Her eyes slid briefly over to Luca, who was sitting tense, with a pale face and shifting eyes that wouldn't meet hers. Catching her look, Jamie chuckled. "Don't worry," he said. "I'm sure Mr. Reyes will function just fine in your absence. Shall we?"

Slowly, Everly slid to her feet, her heart pounding in her chest. Jamie started to walk away before she could say anything, and with a fleeting, desperate look back at her table, she was forced to follow behind him.

Jamie walked quickly, only pausing once to make sure that Everly was still following. She jogged to keep up with his long-legged pace, panting slightly. "Where are we going?" she dared to ask, her desperation to know where he was taking her outweighing her fear of what he might say.

"Testing room," he said without looking back at her. "It is required for all residents here to undergo frequent testing, to upkeep the functionality of the building."

Everly frowned. Luca and Caleb had both mentioned tests to her, but none of what they had said conveyed anything that would keep the building running. She wanted to ask Jamie more, to find out what he was going to do to her, but before she could find the words, he stopped, pulled out his keys, and unlocked a door.

This. This is where it stops.

Her memories.

She.

Everly.

She can't.

This is where her memories stop and she can't pull them back, couldn't pull them back, wouldn't want to pull them back.

This is where Everly's memories stop.

Not forever, though maybe that would have been its own kind of mercy.

Not all of them, not even all of those from the building.

But from that room.

The Testing Room.

Here's what she knows (knew):

Everly followed Jamie into a room, and it was white, almost blindingly so, and she froze because it was *the* room, the same from upstairs, the same as the one drenched in blood that she had hidden in, and now she was back, only she couldn't be because she was a hundred and one floors lower and this room was white but it wasn't covered in blood.

(Yet.)

A chair stood in the center of the room, a chair with straps by the places where arms and legs and necks and torsos could be inserted, though Everly didn't take any of that in.

Right next to the chair stood a table with a wide assortment of tools varying in length and shape and quality and sharpness. Primarily sharpness. Everly also didn't take this in at the time, which was probably both a blessing and a curse. Maybe she would have been better prepared. Maybe it would only have made it worse, the anticipation of it.

What Everly did take in was a large, clunky machine that was set up behind the chair with the straps and the table with the tools. For whatever reason, her eyes latched onto that machine and remained latched even as Jamie took her arm, even as he guided her (forced her, shoved her) toward that chair, even as he locked her in and pushed her head back and chuckled darkly, though she did not hear because her attention was so focused, so precise, so wholly trained on that machine, and it was calling, calling, calling to her, and she could almost hear it, almost understand it, almost *feel* it there with her, like a physical presence, like a long-lost friend, like a lover in desperate need of attention, of care, of help.

And then:

Steel on flesh on flesh on steel on—

Hot, burning, searing, cleaving, tearing, heaving, fighting, clenching, falling—

Beauty, some would say.

Horror, most would argue.

Death, Everly would have said, if she could have said anything, if she could have strung two thoughts together, if she had been able, after the fact, to retain any of the memories of that room, that chair, that machine.

It's a blessing she can't.

It's a blessing the instant the first edge of the first blade licked the skin of her flesh her mind turned in on itself.

It's a blessing it's a curse it's a blessing it's a curse it's a—

She didn't ask for—

None of them asked for—

The building. The building asked for this.

But it didn't.

But it did.

But it just wanted to exist, and it was people, greedy people, power-hungry people, people who thought they could change the way of things, curious curious curious people.

Everly doesn't remember what happened in that room. She never will.

Others are not always so fortunate.

38

Everly awoke to darkness.

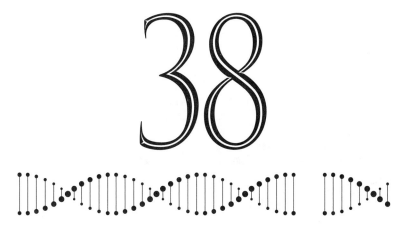

That's not right. Everly awoke to a gray room that was lit by the single fluorescent light above her head, but when she opened her eyes all she could see at first was darkness.

She could not move—only her eyelids, which fluttered open and then clenched tight when she still couldn't see anything and then opened again and fear: Where was the light? Fear: Why couldn't she see? Fear: Where was she?

Blink blink blink blink blink blink blink blink.

And then, as though from far off, a pinprick, small and distant and faint, oh, so faint.

The light grew and grew and expanded and formed, eventually, into the shape and texture of the fluorescent light that hung above her head, and she blink blink blinked at it, and then finally was able to squint around the rest of the room.

Her room. It was her bedroom.

It was—she tried to sit up and—

Flames, up and down and through and within the veins of her arms, legs, skin, bones—

Everly froze. Remained immobile in her thin, gray bed. Tried to remember.

She couldn't remember.

She couldn't remember, but the others could: the invasive memories that flooded her mind then, that told her what must have happened to her, even though she could not recall, even though she had not been there, even though she must have been.

The memories that weren't hers, that had to be hers, that belonged to someone else, but were still there inside her.

The memories told her about the chair that she must have been strapped in.

They told her what must have happened to her while strapped in that chair.

She could not move, could not sit up enough to look down at herself and confirm, but what she could feel told her enough of what must have transpired next.

She could not see her arms, but she could see someone else's—they must have been someone else's—she could see someone else's arms and they were covered in cuts and welts and bruises and burns and they were her arms and they weren't and she could *feel* it.

Whatever they did to her.

He did to her.

Whatever *Jamie* did to her.

She could feel it but also she couldn't because she was numb, blissfully numb, but they weren't.

The others in her memory. In her head.

They weren't numb, and so she wasn't either, because she could feel, was *living*, their pain, was living their experiences, all of their experiences, of sitting in that chair in that white room—

Not a white room.

With straps around her arms and her legs and her torso and her neck.

Not hers.

And the knife, his knife, and other tools that she could not begin to name as they sliced, and skewered, and fought for dominance over what had once been hers but was now *his*—

And had never been hers, this wasn't her story, this was someone else's, many someone elses', because she had no memories of this, of that room, of that chair, so it couldn't have been her, it couldn't have happened.

And yet.

And yet the longer she remained prostrate on that thin gray bed with nothing but the thoughts that weren't hers and the memories that weren't hers and the nightmares that weren't hers, the more sensation returned to her body, the numbness wearing off.

And the more she could feel it.

It was less like burning, and more like the skin of her arms had been frozen and then cracked open and then pried apart and then poorly stitched back together again.

Behind the pain was something else. A different memory—again both hers and not. This one was a voice. A cold, harsh voice echoing around a cold, white room. *We need your pain,* is what the voice was saying in her head, layers upon layers upon layers of that voice, saying the same words in the same mocking sneer. *The building needs your pain. It's something inside you that is released when you suffer. And so, we need to harness that. We need you to feel it.*

Accompanying that voice was the shrill sound of beeps, that a very distant, detached part of her mind paired with the beeps she had heard upstairs, days earlier, after Jamie had . . . *tortured* that woman on the hundredth floor.

It became like a cruel loop: the voice and the pain and the beeps and the voice and the pain and the beeps, memories and non-memories spinning, flying, crashing through her head, her body.

This went on for . . . she did not know how long. Minutes or days or weeks or years, and the reality of it was that in the building it probably wouldn't have mattered, anyway. It all came down to the same, in the end, and eventually it was enough that it overcame her, and she collapsed back against her pillow, though she had never really been able to raise her head in the first place.

Time passed like this. Well, not really, but that is neither here nor there. Everly did not move for longer than she would have cared to recount, for every time she awoke and attempted to shift it would all start over again: the burning that wasn't burning and the pain that was more like death than anything else.

So instead, she tried to remain as still and as silent as she could manage, allowing her mind to wander freely while her body could not.

The layers of pain brought with them other non-memories—these even more confusing than the others because they took place at home. In the house where she'd grown up. She saw different welts and cuts tracing her arms—not given to her in an all-white room with tools of precision, but rather in their living room or kitchen, with whatever her dad had on hand.

It couldn't have been her dad—her sweet, caring father who would never harm her—it couldn't, it couldn't, it couldn't.

So, what was it? Where did the images come from?

Beneath those false memories was yet another: of a room that looked very much like her own, there in the building, except perhaps larger. A woman sitting next to her with fair blond hair and bright blue eyes and worry, worry, worry carved into the lines of her forehead but a smile on her curved, red lips. The blond woman brushed a lock of hair behind Everly's ear and murmured words—of encouragement or warning, she was not sure, but the words were earnest enough, and they almost made Everly listen.

Almost.

And then the woman was gone—was never there? Flashes overlapped, with and without the blond woman. With and without. With and without.

And then she saw a small child, wrapped in a gray blanket, asleep in the arms of a person whom she did not know, being carried far, far away.

And then, Everly woke up, and the memories stopped.

39

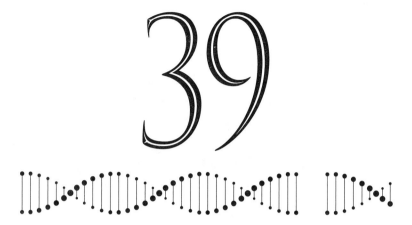

Luca did not see Everly for a week.

At first, he was concerned, because he knew she was being taken to be tested, but he was not anxious. Everyone was tested. It was an inevitability, here in the building. And everyone survived it.

Well, almost everyone.

But then a day passed, and then two, three, seven. Still, she did not return, and though Luca would not speak the words aloud, even to Caleb or Anker who cast him worried expressions at every mealtime now, he was becoming afraid for her.

It didn't usually take this long to recover.

He had been on the verge of asking Jamie about her, which under normal circumstances would never have even been a thought to consider.

On the eighth day, as Luca was sitting in the dining hall for breakfast, struggling to come up with the right words to use to ask Jamie, he glanced up and saw Everly Tertium walking across the room toward him.

Or hobbling, really. Her steps were slow, stilted. An undercurrent of pain laced her every movement, and he could see the strain in her eyes, but he didn't care.

She was all right.

(Here, of course, *all right* is an exceptionally relative term.)

Luca stood up as Everly neared their table, causing both Caleb and Anker to turn and look. None of them spoke as she collapsed into the seat next to Luca's, staring down at her hands, refusing to meet anyone's eyes. A beat passed before Luca rushed over to the counter to request another plate of food, which he brought back and placed in front of Everly. She didn't acknowledge the food or look up at Luca. He felt a tightening in his chest, seeing how small the testing had made her. How helpless.

Normally, they were younger when first brought for testing. Normally they were prepared, in some form or another. They weren't thrown in, unaware, and expected to cope.

Well. They were and they weren't. But it wasn't usually as bad as this.

She had bandages covering her forearms, and he wondered if she still needed them. The testing often marked them, but it was an odd sort of marking that tended to mostly disappear shortly thereafter. Or fade, at least. He didn't know why—no one did, really. The memory of the pain always lasted longer than the pain itself. Memory, and light trails of scars that never fully vanished.

But Everly. From what he could make out of her expression, she still looked like she was in the middle of it. Haunted eyes, pale skin, twisted mouth. She looked like she was trapped, and it broke something in Luca, to see her like that.

At a loss for what else to do, Luca took her hand beneath the table, holding onto it tightly. She didn't react, but he leaned in closer to her, whispering so the others couldn't hear.

"It'll get better," he said, hoping it would be true. "It's always the worst, the first time around, but it will get better. I promise."

She didn't say anything, but he felt her hand squeeze his back, sending a rush of warmth up his arm. They sat like that, together, for the remainder of the morning. When it was time for them to rise to go about their daily assignments, Luca could see that some color was already returning to her cheeks. He still held on to her hand, and she squeezed his again slightly before standing up, causing him to look over at her and see the faintest of grins there on her face—there and then gone, but it *had* been there, he was sure of it, so he was sure it would come back.

She would be okay. She had to be.

40

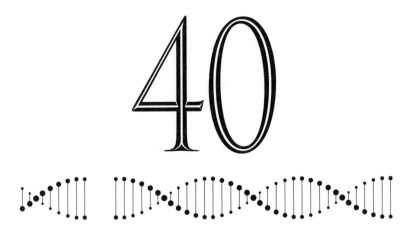

Richard slammed fist after fist into the door, bruising his knuckles until, finally, a harried Jamie yanked the door open.

"What?" Jamie snapped. "I'm busy in here."

Richard pressed both hands flat against the larger man's chest and pushed—oh, how good it felt to be physical, when usually Richard was the one to stand back and observe. He wasn't as strong as Jamie, but he must have caught him off guard as the other man stumbled back a step, eyes briefly widening in surprise, then hardening as he steadied himself.

"You weren't supposed to bring *her* in for testing," Richard yelled. He could feel himself losing his temper. *Good,* he thought. He didn't mind the chance to bite back at Jamie, for once. "Everyone else—you were to test everyone else. But not her."

"That's not what you said," Jamie said flatly. "Increase the testing, across the board. That's what you told me."

"And what did you *do* to her? From what I hear, she was completely incapacitated for days."

Jamie smirked. "It's not my fault she's turned out to be one of the weaker ones."

Richard's face darkened, his eyes slicing into the man in front of him.

"You are never to touch her again. Is that understood? I've gone to too many lengths, come too close, for you to bludgeon it all away with your knives and saws."

"That's not the attitude you had when it came to the father," Jamie said. "You were all too happy to let me have at him with my 'knives and saws.'"

"That is different, and you know it," Richard snapped.

"Look," Jamie said, "between pampering your granddaughter, increasing testing, that kid who keeps running away, and everything else I have to deal with in here, I don't have time to pay attention to the nuances of your requests. You don't want me to do something, fine. But don't expect me to read your mind, old man."

Richard briefly frowned, *that kid who keeps running away* playing through his head. *What kid?* Rather than ask, he poked a finger in Jamie's chest, pressing down hard enough that his finger ached in response. "Never again. Understood?"

Richard stormed away before Jamie could respond. He walked blindly, aimlessly around that bottom floor. He was so close—*so close.* When the news had trickled down to him of what had happened to Everly, he hadn't been able to see straight. It made the reality of their situation—her situation—all too real for him.

She could not die. It would be like failing his daughter all over again.

Now that she was safely housed in the building, they had time. Not an indefinite amount, but enough. He hoped.

But it would all be ruined if Jamie killed her before he could save her.

This would never have happened if the Warden had stepped in. It pained Richard to acknowledge, but he knew Jamie wouldn't disrespect the Warden like that.

That problem may be solved soon enough as well, he knew. Pieces were falling into place already. He knew it was only a matter of time before they all settled right to where they were meant to go.

But what kid kept running away? He didn't know what that was about. But something—intuition or scientific reasoning or the building itself nudging him along, who's to say—told him it wasn't nothing. Something told him to look into it.

And all the same if he bumped *other* things along in the meantime. He needed to shift her out of her new routine, needed to separate her from the attachments she'd begun to form. He knew that'd push her toward the destiny the building had aligned for her—and push her right to where he needed her to be. It was all meant to happen, anyhow.

He'd just be helping destiny along.

41

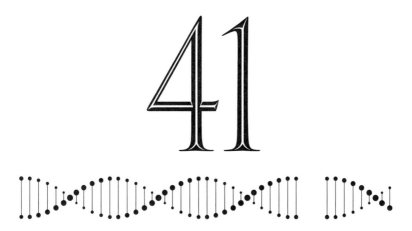

It took all morning, and most of the afternoon, before anyone noticed the absence of Caleb Arya.

People went about their chores, their assignments, their lives as though nothing was different. For most of them, nothing was.

That morning, before meeting Luca for breakfast, Everly had woken up before the alarm, pulling out the journals from beneath her pillow and shielding them with her body, in case anyone was watching.

Not that it mattered, really. They'd already done their worst. What more could they take from her?

Well, they could take the journals, she supposed. And despite the fact that she had stolen them from Richard, she was beginning very much to think of the journals as her own—to think of them, in fact, as her only remaining possessions. The only things in that building that she could pretend belonged solely to her.

She'd turned to the journals more desperately that morning than in mornings past. She longed for an explanation, a reason, *anything* to tell her what had happened to her. Why it had happened. To tell her what she couldn't remember, and what all of this—the pain, the violence, the terror—was for.

She hadn't found anything like that in the journals. Richard never told her what she wanted to know, even in written form. Instead, she'd found an interesting passage, dated 1981.

The data are progressing nicely, though I must admit not as quickly as I would have hoped. The Warden, as she has now asked us to call her, has implemented certain strategies that, while I do at times question, have admittedly led to an increase in results.

The runners she has helped make, for instance, have been able to aid in monitoring the children downstairs, until they are old enough for testing. However, it has become apparent that the tests do not work nearly as well on individuals over a certain age, nor on those who are not in peak physical condition. We may have to do something about that in the future.

Of course, the idea of the runners might help with the latter issue, though I am still not sure how I feel about that process—if it is wise, or good. Or if it matters?

And then there is everything it takes to . . . acquire new subjects, these days. Together, the Warden and I have been able to find a way to temporarily synthesize the genetic properties from an enhanced individual's blood, which I can then use for very short durations of time to venture out into those Other places. It's so I can find them—the enhanced. This, I know, is necessary. But it is hard to remember that in the midst of all the messiness that must take place.

My time at the building, while productive, has been lonelier recently than in years past. Miranda often stays home now, looking after Mary. She refuses to bring her here. We have more than enough children around Mary's age within the Eschatorologic with whom she could play, all very bright and well-behaved. I think it would be good for her to connect with them, but Miranda disagrees. Strongly.

She won't let me test Mary, either. I wish she would. I highly doubt she would have the anomaly, given the extreme rarity of it, paired with the fact that neither Miranda nor I possess it. However, I think it would be pragmatic to check, anyway. One never knows.

Everly had finished reading the entry and had to set the book down. Mary. Her mother. She tried to picture her as a child. What had she been like? Had she been wild and energetic, or more inquisitive and reserved, as Everly herself had been at a young age? Would she have liked it here, at the Eschatorologic? Would she have made the same mistakes Everly had?

She wished her dad were here to talk about her mom. Or Richard, at the very least. Someone who had known her, as Everly hadn't truly been given the chance to.

And then, unbidden, Everly's mind began to stray to different images.

Room after room after room after room of women.

The same woman.

Women who looked an awful lot like how she remembered her mother looking.

No. Everly shook her head, dispelling the awful thought of that floor upstairs. Of those people.

Everly shuddered and had to slam the journal shut to keep her hands from shaking. She now knew what must have happened in that room upstairs to lead to it being so coated in blood.

She now knew.

And something else she had gleaned from the journal: the Warden was a woman.

One tiny clue to this hidden person who held the keys to controlling all their lives.

The one who stuck them all in those white rooms, one at a time.

Later, sitting next to Luca in the dining hall for breakfast, Everly clenched her eyes shut, trying to block out the images—of that room, that floor, those people—but it only made the memories more vibrant, more real.

After breakfast, Everly followed Luca around the building, almost in a daze, trying to block out everything she still wasn't ready to process. She still grunted slightly with the lingering soreness in her bones as she walked but was surprisingly more recovered than she would have anticipated only nine days after what had happened in that white room.

Whatever it was that had happened.

She still couldn't fully remember, and Luca kept telling her that that was good, that she wouldn't want to, that she should enjoy not knowing as long as she could. It didn't help curb her need to understand.

Maybe, she would think desperately to herself, if she knew what had happened, she could stop it from happening again. She could be better prepared next time. Of course, this was a very naive and foolish hope, but often that is what the desperate most need to get through the day: the barest glimpse of a way out.

Everly and Luca made their way from room to room, carrying out each mindless task in a brisk and methodical fashion, until finally they reached the surveillance room.

This, too, began as it would any other day: Luca watched the screens, and Everly watched Luca. She liked to see the way his eyes roved over the faces and motions of residents on the screens, liked to observe the way his brow would furrow when he thought he might have caught sight of something interesting, or something terrifying. It was only because she was watching him so closely that she noticed about half an hour after they sat down when his jaw suddenly tightened, and his face completely drained of color. Everly frowned and was about to ask what was wrong when Luca pushed away from the desk, mumbling something to her about being right back.

With no other choice, Everly leaned back in her chair and studied the screens in Luca's absence. First, she tried to find him, and when that proved futile she simply allowed her eyes to explore the screens, trying to discover what it was that had set Luca off.

There was nothing. At least, nothing obvious to her. No people where they shouldn't be. No frantic children, or adults for that matter. No fires to be controlled, no runners to be diverted.

An hour passed before Luca returned. He seemed calm enough, at first, but there was a wildness in the way he looked across the surveillance room, before settling his gaze on Everly. She stood up, stomach churning at even the thought of what might have happened.

"What's wrong?" Everly asked as Luca came farther into the room.

He searched her face before responding. "I can't find Caleb. I've looked everywhere, checked with everyone I can think of. He's nowhere. He's not in his room, or the mess hall, or the dome. No one I've talked to has seen him since yesterday afternoon, and I can't see him on the screens." He gestured limply to the side of the room dominated by glimpses into the rest of the building, then he lowered his voice. "I don't know where he'd be, Everly."

"It's okay," she said, trying to keep her own voice steady, trying to reassure him. "We'll find him. You don't know that anything bad has happened. Odds are that he's perfectly fine."

Luca released a shaky breath, but he didn't say anything. Tentatively, Everly reached out a hand and set it on his arm.

"We'll find him, Luca. I'll go back out with you, and we'll ask around."

Luca still didn't say anything, but he nodded once, a muscle ticking in his jaw.

For a moment, Everly continued to watch Luca, waiting for a reaction, an outburst, but there was nothing. His eyes stared dully at the floor by his feet, flitting upward every few seconds as though seeking after ghosts in the room that Everly couldn't see. Gently, she took his hand in hers and began to pull him toward the door.

Once they were out in the hall, Everly paused. "Where should we look first?"

As though broken from a trance, Luca straightened, and took in a single, deep breath. "Probably the public access rooms. I checked most of them earlier, but maybe someone has seen him recently."

Everly followed Luca to the dining hall, which was still full of kids, despite the late hour of the afternoon, as well as a handful of runners standing silently around the perimeter.

Luca scanned the sea of faces, growing frustrated when the one person he wanted to be there was missing. Shoulders hunched, Luca turned back the way they had come, gesturing for Everly to follow.

They quickly ran through a series of rooms that Luca saw as possible places where Caleb might have been, having no luck. After an hour of searching, as they were heading away from the dome, they spotted Anker coming from the opposite hall. When he saw Everly and Luca, Anker's eyes widened noticeably. Luca, spotting him, shouted out his name. As if realizing that he had nowhere to go, Anker came over, a tight look on his face.

"Hey, Anker, you haven't seen Caleb, have you? I've looked almost everywhere I can think of, but I can't find him anywhere."

Anker paled considerably, making a noncommittal grunt, and then turned as though to leave. Luca grabbed him by the shoulder.

"You know something." Luca didn't say this as a question, his voice not brokering any room for evasion. Anker made a noise in his throat, like a sharp squeal, and looked between Luca and Everly with strained eyes.

"Look, I'm sorry, man. I wish I could say, but they'd flay me alive if they found out I'd snitched."

"They?" Luca's eyes turned hard. "Runners. What did they do to him?"

Anker held up his hands, trying to back away. "Like I said, I'm sorry." He tried to make a break for it then, but before he could get more than a few steps, Luca grabbed him by the shoulders, slammed him back into the wall, and shoved an elbow into his throat.

"Tell me what you know," Luca said in a low voice that made Everly shiver, even though she wasn't the one being pinned to the wall. She didn't try to stop him, though. Instead, she watched.

"I *can't,*" Anker yelled back, voice shaking, his eyes suddenly wide and frantic. "They'd kill me. You know it. They'd kill you, too, and you would just drag the rest of us down with you."

Luca didn't lessen his grip. If anything, he tightened his hold, and Everly observed as Anker's face began to purple beneath Luca's hands.

Anker clasped at his throat. "Luca," he wheezed, and finally Luca let him go. Anker collapsed to the floor, hacking, and Luca leaned against the wall, arms crossed, glaring at Anker while he recovered. His glare wavered, though, Everly thought. An uncertainty. She saw his eyes flick between Anker's face and his throat, and she frowned.

Once he caught his breath, Anker raised his head, looking between Luca and Everly. "I swear. If I could, I would tell you. I liked Caleb, you know. He was cool. We grew up together here—we all did. I hate that this happened, and I'm sorry, but I can't risk it. I know you two were tight, but see this from my perspective. You've got to be able to understand why I can't tell you anything."

Luca snarled down at him. "Stop," he growled, "referring to him in the past tense."

Anker held up his hands, tossing his head back and forth. "Sorry," he said again.

Luca's eye were slits as he moved toward Anker with a murderous look on his face. Everly stepped in front of Luca, between him and Anker, and shot Luca a sharp look before turning to Anker.

"Look, I get that you can't tell us where, but can you at least tell us what they did with him, or what they're going to do?"

Anker met her eyes, and then Luca's, drawing out the moment. "You know," he said in a too-quiet voice. "You know what they did."

Stomach twisting, Everly looked back at Luca, who had tensed, with his arms still crossed over his chest. Shaking his head, he pushed off the wall and stalked away.

Everly glanced once more at Anker, who she couldn't help but think looked pathetic lying splayed across the floor. Pinching her lips together, she pivoted and ran after Luca.

She found him striding down the hall, banging on closed doors and roaring.

"Whoa whoa whoa," she yelled. "Luca, what are you doing? Someone is going to hear you. *Stop*."

He spun toward her, face white and wet from tears she hadn't realized he'd shed. His eyes were red as they bored into hers, demanding an answer she didn't have. "So? Who cares? I want them to hear me, then maybe they'd find me useless, too, or too much trouble for my own worth, and they'd bring me to wherever they've taken Caleb. In fact—" He brought his hands to his mouth and hollered in a shattering voice: "Come and get me! You hear that? You want me, well, I'm right here!" He rushed up to the closest door and threw his fists into it with enough force that Everly's hands ached just watching him.

"Luca, stop it! *Please.*" Everly ran up, grabbing at one of his arms, but he pulled away from her, face cold.

"Whose side are you on, anyway?"

She gaped at him. "Whose *side* am I on? Luca, you know I'm on your side. We're in this together, right? Hey, look at me." She grabbed his face, forcing him to look at her, to meet her eyes. "We will find Caleb, and we will find a way out of this nightmare. One way or another, we'll make it, but not if you lose your head. I need you, Luca—*Caleb* needs you—but not like this."

Luca was breathing heavily, his eyes flying in every direction, but he had stopped shouting, stopped running. He took a deep breath, as though to say something, but then they heard pounding on the tile floor not far from them. Luca and Everly exchanged panicked glances. He took her hand.

"Come on," Luca said, and they fled, racing down the hall in the opposite direction. He tried random doors, shaking the knobs, encountering only locked rooms. Eventually, they found a door that opened, and Luca ushered Everly in, closing the door behind them with a click and blanketing them both in darkness.

They were in a closet of some sort, with mostly empty shelves and the musty scent of disinfectant in the air. For a moment they stood in silence, the only sound that of them each catching their breath.

"Do you think we lost them?" Everly whispered.

"I don't know," Luca whispered back. "Probably. Most runners aren't all that bright. They probably wouldn't think to check these rooms." He paused. "Everly, I'm sorry. I shouldn't have lost it like that back there. It's just—" He took a shuttering breath. "Caleb is all I have here." Luca paused again, and Everly waited for him to go on, listening to the sound of his heavy breaths. "All my life, I've been alone. Caleb anchored me growing up, made life feel a little bit easier living here." Everly heard him swallow thickly.

"I've failed him, Everly. We were supposed to look out for each other, I was supposed to *protect* him, and I didn't. I let him get taken, and for all I know he could be—"

"No," Everly cut him off. "Don't go down that path. You can't let yourself fall like that, Luca. Not yet."

Luca's breathing turned even more ragged. As her eyes began to adjust to the darkness around them, Everly saw Luca running his hands incessantly through his hair, visibly shaking.

"Everly, I can't *breathe*. What am I even worth, if I can't save—" He stopped short, panting.

"Luca, stop. Stop talking. You," she grasped for his face in the darkness, holding it firmly between her hands. "You can't do this to yourself. You can't blame yourself for everything, you can't control everything, even though I know you wish you could. So, you can't fall apart now because I need you, and I—" Everly's voice cut off. She took her hands from where they still rested on Luca's face and covered her mouth, turning away. She was supposed to be better than this, stronger than this, and so she could barely stand it when she felt him come up behind her, wrapping his arms around her.

"I'm sorry," Everly whispered. "I am so sorry that this is happening."

"No, Everly," Luca said in a low voice that sent shivers down her spine. "You were right. You said we could do it, and I believe you. You—" He sucked in a shaky breath. "Ever since you arrived at the building, I've started to see things differently. *You've* made me see things differently. Made me feel like I don't have everything here figured out, like maybe there's still hope for us, for all of us. So, thank you," he said in her ear. "You saved me. So, I know we can save him, too."

Everly slowly twisted around in his arms so that she was facing him. She could feel his breath against her cheek, his face only an inch away from hers, and she could feel even that short distance between them growing taut, like a ribbon begging to be pulled closer. For a beat, she didn't move, afraid to break the spell that had somehow descended upon the two of them, enclosing them in a world far and away from reality.

But she was curious. So curious.

Bridging the space between them before she had a chance to change her mind, Everly's mouth pressed into Luca's. She heard his breath hitch, and she smiled, with her mouth still against his, reveling in his reaction, in the way he reached up a hand to her face and pulled her closer, the way his mouth now sought hers farther, deeper, longer.

And then she let everything fall away—their situation, what they had both been through, what was still left before them. For the time, it was just them. Him, as he ran a hand up her back, the other tangling in her hair. Her, as she leaned into his warmth, cupping his face in her hands, pulling him toward her like it was the last chance they had, and realizing that it very well might be.

Eventually they broke apart, both breathing heavily—Everly's hands lying on Luca's shoulders, his encircling her waist. She heard him laugh softly beneath his breath.

"Where did you come from?" Luca whispered as he leaned his forehead against hers. Everly searched for his eyes in the dark, barely able to make out more than his silhouette.

"Luca," she whispered. He reached up a hand, brushing a lock of hair behind her ear. "Luca," Everly repeated, a little louder. "We should probably go back." She didn't move her hands, though, and he made no move to break away either. She breathed in his clean scent and sighed, wishing more than anything that they could stay there, in that safe little bubble, separate from everything they would face once they left.

Slowly, Everly took a step back, her hands falling until they reached his, and she squeezed them once. "Come on," she said. "We need to go."

Luca gripped her hands in return, and Everly moved to open the closet door, one of her palms still clasped in his. Before she reached the handle, Luca twisted her back around, pressing his lips against hers briefly once more.

"Okay," he whispered against her ear. Then, turning the doorknob himself, "Let's go."

42

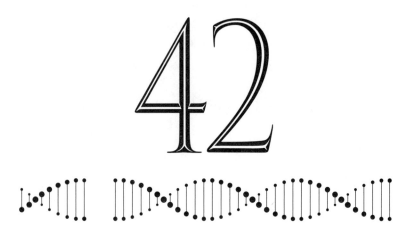

Luca and Everly left the closet quietly, glancing around corners and over their shoulders perhaps more than was strictly necessary as they made their way to his room. Luca's body hummed with energy. Everly was . . . he didn't know. She was so unexpected, in every way. The more he thought he was coming to know her, the more she defied everything he understood.

It was a feeling that left him elated and filled with anticipation.

And also . . . strangely unsettled. He couldn't have said why, not when the brilliance of that fleeting moment in the closet was still washing over him.

But there was almost a nagging feeling, a voice that was trying to tell him something—to *warn* him, he almost would have thought, if he didn't know that to be absurd. What could there possibly be to warn of?

The buzz within Luca dulled as they reached his room, and the reality of their situation returned to him. The reality of Caleb's situation.

People disappeared from the building. This was a fact, like needing oxygen to breathe or gravity to remain tethered to the earth. And like both of those facts, this was one known if rarely acknowledged.

People disappeared from the building, and Luca had never thought to ask why, to wonder where they went, where they were taken.

No. No, that wasn't true. He thought it, but never knew where to look. The cameras didn't show what the building didn't want them to see.

What the Warden didn't want them to see.

So, for years, Luca had watched the feeds of the hundreds of people roaming through the Eschatorologic, and every so often he would become aware of a person who was once there, who once had a pattern and a routine and a purpose in the building, who suddenly just wasn't.

There were hundreds, maybe thousands, of cameras that Luca could watch through, observe through. And none of them showed the missing residents.

People disappeared from the building, but never anyone Luca had known. Not really.

Never Caleb.

It should never have been him—that was supposed to be the point to all of this. Surveillance duty, and the trust he had spent years instilling for himself there in the building. The hours and hours of endless, meaningless tasks they put him through. It was all supposed to be for this. To keep his friends safe.

And he had failed.

Luca had thought the worst thing that could happen to him in the building, the worst punishment for his rebellious actions, would be to vanish himself. Turns out, Caleb going missing was so, so much worse.

It was almost jarring to open the door to his room and find it exactly as he had left it that morning—after Caleb had been taken, but before he possibly could have known. The normalcy of everything around him was almost too much, and Luca had to fight against the nausea that was threatening to undo him.

How had he allowed himself to forget, even for a second, that Caleb was out there, somewhere, all alone? In that closet, with Everly, how had he let himself distance so far from what was happening? Luca felt a spike of fear—immediate and sharp—but he shoved it away, forcing his expression blank again.

Luca heard the door closing, followed by Everly clearing her throat. "Okay," she said. "Okay, so a plan. How do we find him? How do we get him back?"

Luca closed his eyes again and tried to take in even breaths. Then he tried to think. Caleb didn't need him falling apart—that wouldn't help anyone. Everly had been right, before, when she said he couldn't be like . . . like this. So he paused, and he slowed his thoughts. He considered the options they had.

"He has to be on one of the two lowest floors," Luca said, opening his eyes and turning back to face Everly with a new determination. "I know the layout of the whole building, at least where the cameras are. There aren't many places above ground where they could be keeping him—it's all residential rooms."

"And the white room," Everly said quietly, absently running her hands over her arms. "Up on the top floor."

Luca's stomach clenched, and without intending to, he realized he was staring at her arms. At the fresh bandages that ran from her wrists up past the fabric of her gray scrubs—he knew they would extend all the way to her shoulders. And he felt it—the phantom scars that he knew traced his own skin, in the same shapes and patterns as hers.

He hadn't wanted to ask her. She hadn't wanted to say. It was all the same, anyway. Part of what it meant to be a resident. So, he didn't offer her words of comfort, though he wanted to. And he didn't shudder at the thought of the white rooms, the testing rooms, though maybe he should have. Instead, he thought of what could be worse than that—what could be so bad in a building of blades and knives that even here it didn't want to be seen, didn't want to be caught?

Everly eventually broke the silence that had fallen over them. "So, if we assume that Caleb has to be on one of the two basement floors, how much space is there that you don't know of?"

"On this floor, not much. There are a few doors that I've never been through, that are always locked and that don't have cameras inside, but for the most part I know this floor. The lowest level, on the other hand, is full of unwatched, inaccessible spaces. He could be anywhere down there."

"All right," Everly said. "So then he's probably on the floor beneath us. Luca, what do you know about what's kept there?"

"Very little," he replied. "There are files and documents in rooms down there. They've sent me down on occasion, to retrieve them from the archives. But other than that, I have no idea. No one goes down there, really. It's kept locked tight, under strict lock and key, and there's no footage of any of the rooms. If I hadn't ventured down a time or two myself, I might not even believe that it exists at all."

"Richard keeps his office down there," Everly said quietly. "I don't know what else is on that floor, but there are at least more labs and offices, if nothing else." She raised her eyes to meet Luca's, and he could almost read his thoughts mirrored in her eyes. "We should start there. It feels like the kind of place you would steal someone away to in the middle of the night."

Luca felt queasy at the prospect, but he nodded. "Okay. Okay, you're right, he's probably down there. It's just . . ." He trailed off, eyes roaming around the room as he tried to think. "I don't know how we're going to get down there. I have keys to this floor, and the upper levels, but not that floor. All the entrances leading in and out of the stairwell are kept locked, and you need a key to use the elevator at all this far down, not to mention you need to be programmed in for it to work, which I'm not; I'd rather not learn right now what would happen if I tried to use it."

"What do you mean?" Everly asked, a strange expression on her face. "The door leading into the black floor was unlocked when I went down there, so was the door upstairs that I accessed the staircase from." She shook her head, considering. "Do you think someone just forgot to lock them back?"

"No," Luca said slowly, watching Everly curiously now. "Not possible. They lock automatically when they're closed."

Everly looked dumbstruck, and Luca's thoughts mirrored her confusion.

"Seeing as how we don't have any other options," Everly finally said, "I say we go for it, anyway. Maybe we'll get lucky again, and the doors will be unlocked."

"Right," Luca said, but he wasn't convinced. He sagged, running his hands through his hair. "Whether we can get onto that floor or not, does it even matter? What if we do find him, Everly? What would we do next? We can't get out, we can't leave. We'd all be sitting ducks, the three of us, trapped in a building where our every move is monitored. Do you know what they'd do to people like that here? What they'll do if we try this, try and go against the building so blatantly?" The truth was, Luca didn't know himself. What could be worse than disappearing, than going missing in the middle of the night like you'd never existed?

Luca felt his breathing becoming erratic again, the panic from earlier in the hallway returning. It really was a hopeless cause, he knew. They could try to find Caleb, but they'd all wind up dead by the end, anyway.

Everly had moved right in front of him, pulling his hands away from where they'd dug into his head and holding them. "We'll figure that out when the time comes. You all seem so convinced there's no way out, no way around what Richard and Jamie have told you, that you're stuck in here. But I truly believe we can do it. So, when the time comes, we'll find that way. But first," she said, tugging gently on Luca's hands to direct him toward the door, "we go get Caleb back."

A way out, Luca found himself thinking. He could barely even imagine it.

But she was right. One step at a time. First, they were going to find Caleb.

They were going to save him.

43

When Jamie Griffith entered the building for the first time, the building was not happy.

He came strutting toward the entrance with a straight spine and a broad grin, and the building knew immediately that something was wrong. No one smiled when they walked up those steps, when they pushed through those doors. Not even Richard Dubose, who had been searching for the building, or for something like it, for over half a decade by the time he stumbled upon the crumbling stone steps that led him up to the front doors.

No one smiled when they entered the building, but Jamie Griffith did, and this never sat right with the building.

The building was a well-tuned machine that—

No.

The building was a carefully instilled system that—

No. Again.

The building was, well. The building was.

Always had always would within and without and all that jazz.

The building was, and there were certain facets to what that meant. Jamie Griffith's goals did not align well with that of the building, though on the surface it might appear as though they did.

What Jamie Griffith sought: Pain. Power. Dominance.

What the building sought: Order. As simple as that. And order could be achieved by much simpler, much less bloody means than Jamie Griffith chose to go about securing his ends.

However.

However, the building understood its residents. Some more than others. One more than all the rest. And it cared, even if no one knew this, or would have believed it. The building cared, and so it knew the strain that was being put on one Dr. Richard Dubose in being the only unenhanced individual present on the premises. Especially at the beginning.

For a time, after people had begun to first arrive at the building, it had seemed as though they might simply continue to show up, all on their own.

This did not prove to be the case.

Or rather, it did, but more and more often the people were finding themselves on the front steps of the building with so little time left. So little energy remaining to offer.

They needed something newer. Fresher. Younger.

This was Richard Dubose's least favorite component of working for the building, followed very closely by his distaste that came with what he'd realized was the easiest way to harness the energy from the subjects.

The building knew this. Knew it was bad for morale. Knew Richard Dubose would only be game to continue in that fashion for so long before it burned him out.

And the building cared.

Thus entered Jamie Griffith, the third unenhanced person to ever enter the Eschatorologic. One of only four who ever would.

Jamie Griffith sought pain and power and dominance, and he didn't care in what form that came. He would do anything. Which made him, in his own right, perfect. Even if the building still did not like him.

Nonetheless, he came with his own uses, in and outside of the building. One such use happened to be a knack for finding troublemakers and restoring them to their place.

Pain, power, dominance.

The building did not *want* Everly Tertium or Luca Reyes to feel pained, overpowered, dominated.

But order had been disturbed within the building, which never happened.

That is to say, order had been disturbed only once before, and that had been . . . an ordeal.

The building was not looking for another ordeal.

And so it was that Jamie Griffith was led toward a gray-clad figure—one with shaggy hair and desperate eyes—who alerted Jamie as to the actions of two *other* gray-clad figures, who were at that very moment running down a wayward hallway, heading for a locked door into a dark staircase that would lead them down to a nonexistent floor.

The building liked the two gray-clad figures a great deal more than it liked Jamie Griffith. But everyone had a role to play.

44

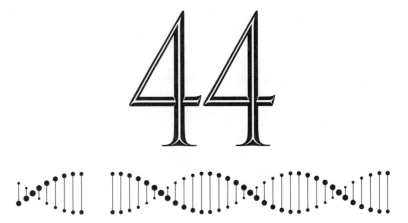

TOGETHER, EVERLY AND LUCA MADE their way through the green-painted halls toward the entrance of the stairwell. Once they reached the door, Luca pulled out his small key ring and fit one of the keys into the lock, opening the door. They descended carefully in the dark, until Everly sensed Luca halt in front of her.

"The door is here," he said back to her, and she heard him reaching for the knob, jiggling it slightly. "Sorry, no luck—it's locked."

Disappointment welled within Everly. Of course, it was locked. Why wouldn't the deepest level in the Eschatorologic be kept behind a locked door? She didn't want to accept it—wasn't ready to believe that their one lead, their one hope, might have ended so quickly in a dead end. Because if not this, then she couldn't think of any other possibilities, any other ways to find Caleb.

She didn't know Caleb that well, but she knew he meant the world to Luca. And for some reason, she was starting to think of Caleb as a sign of hope—almost as if, if they could find him, if they could fix this, maybe they could fix everything else, too. Maybe they really could find a way out, for everyone. If they could get past one problem, then surely they could get past all the rest.

But first they needed to find Caleb.

Everly felt her way forward, hand brushing against Luca in the dark. "I want to try," she said. He made a noise of protest, and she knew it was futile. A locked door wouldn't suddenly unlock for no reason. But she wasn't ready to go back yet. Wasn't ready to give up.

She ran her hand over the surface of the door, seeking the doorknob. When she found it, her hand glancing over its cool metal, she held her breath and wrapped her fingers around it.

Please, she thought. *Please work.*

Clenching her fist around the doorknob, Everly twisted it. And heard a click, and felt the lock give under her grip.

Disbelief spiked through Everly as she slowly pushed the door open, allowing a sliver of light from the space beyond to hit Luca's face, illuminating his stark bewilderment.

"What—but, how?"

Everly didn't answer, didn't know what to say. It had opened, and right then that was all that mattered.

"Come on," she said. "Let's go."

Beyond the door, the hallway was just as inky black as Everly remembered. Orange fluorescent lights lined the middle of the ceiling, casting a pale glow around the hallway that was barely enough to see by. Everly shivered as she stepped farther into the hall, reluctant to plunge herself into the eerie space beyond. Something felt wrong about the floor. More so than when she had been down here before. Something was off, something about the air, and she couldn't put a finger on it.

Luca came up beside Everly and placed a hand on her shoulder. He offered her a questioning glance, and she attempted a weak smile in return.

The passage started off running back in a straight line, with no doors on either side to try, only slick, black walls. They walked in silence, the seconds stretching out with each of their footsteps against the polished black floor. Everly flinched at the thud of every step, certain someone would hear them coming.

Eventually, they reached a place where the hall split off in either direction. Everly turned to face Luca.

"Which way?"

He looked both ways, considering. "Left," he said, and shrugged. "Fifty-fifty shot, right?"

Everly began to nod, began to turn left to walk down the new black hallway, but then her feet stopped. Without really understanding why, her body pivoted so that she was facing right instead, and a dull headache began to form at the base of her skull, a repetitious thudding that spread through her whole body, pulsing with the wrongness of everything around her.

She took a step down the right hallway. And then another. Luca's eyes followed her as she took a third step, and then, unbidden, an image flashed through her mind, there and then gone.

A room. Like the testing rooms, only red. Bright red. Bloody red. A metal chair in the center with straps where a person's arms and legs could be restrained. A monitor.

A table of lethally sharpened tools. An IV full of lethally dangerous liquid.

Gripping her head, Everly stumbled backward, into Luca, who quickly wrapped his arms around her to steady her. He looked down at Everly questioningly, but again, she had no answers for him. So instead, she shook her head, gazed down the black corridor in front of her with clouded eyes, and spoke in a too-soft voice.

"I think we need to go right."

Luca didn't say anything as he steadied Everly on her feet and then fell into step behind her, heading to the right.

The passage went on for some time, and still they didn't encounter any doors—just another long path of silky black walls. For a while, they walked in silence, studying the walls around them and the never-ending hall ahead. After a few minutes had passed like this, with nothing other than the sound of their treading feet exchanged between Everly and Luca, he stepped closer to her and lightly touched her elbow.

"Hey, can we talk about what happened?" Luca asked her, speaking in a hushed tone.

"What do you mean?" she asked, voice equally lowered. Everly glanced over her shoulder as they walked, but, of course, no one was there.

"I mean how you opened a locked door, Everly. Because it was locked when I tried it, and then you—you just opened it. Like it was nothing. How do you explain that?"

Everly walked for a few more paces before responding. "Jamie told me something once, when he brought me down to this floor the first time. He said that some of the doors in this building are coded to scan a person's fingerprints and only open for certain people. That it's a special security measure in place for the more sensitive areas here. I haven't thought about it much since he told me that, but do you think maybe that's how I was able to open those doors? The one for this floor, and the one above?"

Luca thought about that for a few seconds. "Maybe," he said. "But why you? Why would *your* fingerprints be coded into those doors? You haven't even been here that long, and from what I can tell, you're not on a much better standing with the Warden than the rest of us." His eyes glanced down at Everly's arms, where bandages still wrapped her skin beneath the gray fabric of her shirt.

"Richard could have done it," Everly said thoughtfully. "I don't know where he would have gotten my fingerprints, or when he would have had the time, but that could be it. I don't know who else would have done something like that."

Luca seemed ready to argue that idea, but his eyes caught on something behind her. When she turned to see what had drawn his attention, her breath hitched.

Up ahead, there were doors. Lining the walls to either side twenty feet ahead of Everly and Luca ran a string of black doors that matched the rest of the floor. The doors blended in so well with the wall that they might not have even seen them if it hadn't been for the polished silver doorknobs on each. Luca frowned at the first one, casting Everly a sideways look.

"Shall we, then?" he asked, reaching forward to turn the knob.

It didn't budge under his grip. Locked. He frowned, then looked over at Everly. "You want to give it a try?"

She thought he sounded skeptical, but Everly pushed aside her own misgivings and walked up to the door and placed her hand over the handle. She wasn't sure if she was surprised when she heard the distinctive click—the sound of the door unlocking.

Everly looked up at Luca, who was watching her warily. She swallowed thickly, then turned the handle and swung the door open. Everly peeked inside, Luca at her shoulder.

It was empty. The room was small, square, as black as the hall outside, and completely empty.

They moved on, opening the doors of room after room, each empty except a few unadorned shelves, a lab or two that looked like someone had forgotten to stock them with any equipment whatsoever. They found nothing of note, at any rate. Nothing to lead them to Caleb.

With every room they searched, their pace increased. They would check a door, find it empty, and rush to the next, the next, the next. Stalking their every move was the ever-present awareness that they could be seen at any second. Could have *already* been seen, and just didn't know it yet.

They had been searching rooms for nearly an hour (relatively speaking, of course) with no success, and Everly was about to tell Luca that they should turn back and try going in the other direction, when he approached one more door, beckoning, with an uncertain expression, for her to touch it. Unlock it.

Inside was a room she recognized.

"Luca," Everly said with a gasp, grabbing his arm. "This is Richard's office!"

"Really?" Luca's face pinched as he looked around—at the desk pushed to the side, the stainless steel table in the center of the room, the shelves full of equipment lining the back wall. The room was shadowed, with the lingering, dusty sensation that hinted at a lack of use.

"Well," Luca said, "your gramps isn't here. Should we look around, see if we can find anything?"

"Yeah," Everly said, even though she felt wrong about it. She didn't like digging through Richard's life, even here, in this damp basement office that he clearly hadn't returned to in some time. She cleared her throat and nodded toward the back wall, which was filled with a tight row of towering filing cabinets. "Let's start with those. See what's inside."

They went over to the first cabinet, where Everly had to stand on her toes to reach the top drawer. It slid open with ease, and she pulled out a handful of files. Each file had a tab with a name on it, as well as a number. Everly opened the top folder from the pile in her arms, glancing down at its contents.

Maurice Thompson 002, the tab read. Inside was a picture of a man in his midtwenties with sandy blond hair and light green eyes hidden behind thick, seventies-style glasses. Luca came up and read over Everly's shoulder.

"Initiation: October 14, 1967 (first). Mother: Lisa Monroe Thompson (negative). Father: William Thompson (negative). Status: Alive. STM: Positive. Current known iterations: Seven. Room: 207 (note, other living iterations B137, 206, 208, 209). Notes: Rarely stimulated, vague progress, little effect. Kept under surveillance. (Reference iterations 1, 2, 4–9)." Below that was a list of data that Everly was unable to follow, but the name in the file tickled at the back of her mind, just out of reach. Then she gasped.

"Maurice! Luca, I know who this is," she said.

"Really? How?"

"He lives here, in the building. Richard brought me up to see him a while ago, when I first started visiting here. He's one of the elderly people kept upstairs—he's nearly comatose now, barely able to respond to his name." She looked again at the file, at his picture that seemed so young and normal. "I can't believe this is him. I can't believe he's been here that *long*." Rereading the information, Everly's eyes caught on what was listed as his initiation date: 1969. Did that mean he had been in the Eschatorologic for over fifty years? That would also mean, she realized, that he couldn't have been brought in at a young age, like Michael or Luca. He had to have come in much later, as an adult.

Luca was looking over her shoulder at Maurice's file, something clouding over his eyes as he stared at the man's picture.

"Luca? What is it?"

He shook his head, then blinked and looked up at her. "Nothing," he said quickly. "It's nothing. He just . . . reminds me of something. Someone."

Before Everly could ask what he meant, Luca reached up and pulled a new file out of the open drawer. He moved away, eyes pinned to the folder in his hands, and so Everly turned back to the stack she still held herself, opening a new file.

Inside, her eyes were first drawn to the picture—that of an elderly woman whose eyes looked dead, defeated. Her white hair was sparse and damp in the image, and she looked like she was barely able to keep her head lifted. The sight made Everly unbearably sad to look at. There was also something about the woman.

She didn't think that this woman was one of the people she had visited upstairs with Richard during her earlier days in the Eschatorologic, yet something about her appearance pulled at a string in Everly's mind. She was missing something here. She just had no idea what.

Everly looked farther down on the first page in the file and read the rest of the woman's information.

Katherine Morris 089. Initiation: April 11, 1999 (first). Mother: Elena Pemrose Morris (negative). Father: Jacques Leroy Morris (negative). Status: Alive. STM: Positive. Current known iterations: Three. Room: 702 (note, other living iterations B112, 701). Notes: All show strong progress, especially beta. Monitored closely, tested twice a month for further progress. Strong candidate. (Reference iterations 1, 3).

Frowning, Everly put Katherine's file back into the drawer, then scanned the tabs of the other folders in her hands, reading the names and looking for more familiar ones. When she didn't see any, she knelt, set the folders in her arms on the floor, and opened the bottom drawer of the filing cabinet.

Her eyes traced over the labels inside, freezing as she caught on a name she knew, and she yanked the file out, opening it to a picture of a young, bright-eyed boy, staring blankly out of the image.

Michael. There was no last name, just that. Just Michael. The picture they had of him was a younger one—he had to only be about five or six in it. Tearing her eyes away from the image, she looked down to scan the rest of the page.

Her blood froze. She read the first line, then had to go back and read it again. Read it a third time, and still it didn't make sense.

Next to Michael's name it read—*Mother: Everly Tertium. Father: Luca Reyes.*

Her mind went numb, unable to process or understand what she was reading. Why would his file say that? She was not Michael's mother—she wasn't anyone's mother. And besides, Michael was ten, she thought, looking at his birthdate in the file. She would have been fourteen years old when he was born. None of what she was reading made any sense.

Also, there was the part about Luca being his father. Which would imply that they—

But no, they hadn't. Obviously. It was all ridiculous Someone's idea of a terrible joke. Whose? Richard's? Jamie's? This elusive Warden's? What she wanted to know was *why*? Why would anyone put that in the file if it wasn't true?

Everly's eyes returned to the file almost against her will, drawn to her name written in it. Luca's name. Then, she noticed the rest of the information that was included below, and she forced herself to keep reading.

Status: Alive. STM: Positive. Current known iterations: One. Room: B113. Notes: Highly stimulated, rapid progress, great effort. High priority. Kept under surveillance.

What did it all mean? Iteration? Stimulated? STM was the genetic anomaly Richard had told her about, way back when he had first tested her. Is that what this was all about? Everly quickly memorized the text, deciding she would have to think about it more later. As bizarre as it all was, their priority was still Caleb, and they weren't getting any closer to him by looking at these files.

Everly snapped Michael's folder shut, slipping it back into the drawer before Luca could see it. She didn't know why, exactly; she knew he'd be just as shocked to read their names in that folder as she'd been. But there was some voice whispering in the back of her mind. *This secret is mine,* it told her. *Don't let him see it.*

She didn't understand what the voice meant, but she didn't really want to show Luca, anyway. It was all too confusing, and she had enough on her mind as it was.

Something about the file struck her, though. She thought back to the few other files she'd flipped through, and on a hunch, started to leaf through more from the open drawer.

"What are you doing?" Luca asked, noticing as she opened file after file.

"It says in here who each residents' parents were, and if they were enhanced or not. I'm looking for any where both parents had the genetic anomaly." Because if Michael's file *was* true—not that it possibly could be—it was the only one she'd seen so far where that was the case: where both parents were enhanced.

Luca joined her, opening more files of his own. She kept an eye on where he was pulling from, ensuring it was nowhere near where she'd stashed Michael's file.

"All of these people either had only one parent who was enhanced or, in most cases, neither were."

"That's not too surprising," Luca said, eyes locked on the file in his hands. "There aren't too many of us to begin with."

"I know, but . . . what do you think it would mean? If both parents were enhanced for someone?" *What would it mean for Michael? What if it was true?*

No. No, it wasn't true.

Luca shrugged. "I don't know if it would mean anything. And you're right, none of these look like it's ever been the case. So, I guess we have no way of knowing."

Everly mumbled something, half-heartedly agreeing with him as she kept digging through more files, finding nothing.

Luca meandered to the other side of the room, calling out, "Hey," when he opened a side drawer in Richard's desk. "I think these are journals in here."

Happy for a distraction from Michael's file, Everly quickly turned away from the filing cabinet and went to join Luca.

She had become so accustomed to the few journals she'd stolen—the random, thin volumes that she kept stored under her pillow—that she'd nearly forgotten Richard kept a whole drawer full of others down here. Kneeling beside the desk now, Everly's hand roved lightly over the leather surfaces of the journals almost in wonder, contemplating all the answers that may have been here all along, just a floor beneath where she'd been sleeping.

"Richard's journals," she told Luca faintly. "I found these once before. He's documented his years here, going all the way back to when he first started the building decades ago. Maybe even before then."

"Do you think he could have written something in here that could help us find Caleb?" Luca asked.

"I don't know," Everly said honestly. "Maybe. There's so much to look through, though."

"Well," Luca said, gazing longingly down at the journals. "It wouldn't hurt to look. We haven't found anything else useful yet."

Everly knew how he felt. It was like they'd been spinning in circles with blindfolds over their eyes—going nowhere, with no idea which direction they were facing.

"All right," Everly said, reaching a hand into the overflowing drawer.

The two settled together on the floor, each pulling out different volumes to flip through, eyes scanning pages faster and faster, looking for anything that could prove useful.

"Here, he writes about the floors, and the general structure of the building," Luca said after a minute from where he sat cross-legged on the floor across from Everly. "It looks like originally they designated more floors for kids and adults, with no space set aside for the apartments the elderly live in."

"Interesting," Everly said. What had changed somewhere along the way, to have to restructure the building? There was so much she could tell Richard wasn't saying in his entries; she wanted him to spell it all out for her, bit by bit.

"Look," Luca said, pointing at a passage in one of the books. "He mentions the genetic anomaly again here. Didn't you find something about that earlier?"

"Yeah," Everly said. She flipped back a few pages. "Here. *The genetic anomaly is seemingly unpredictable. There is no rhyme or reason for how it generates, which people it might choose. It is not strictly hereditary, though it has at times appeared to be transferred from parent to child. There are no visible indicators of the anomaly, other than the energy spikes. This much we have been able to ascertain, but very little else. As of now, we have only managed to isolate twenty unique individuals with the anomaly. So few, yet so much potential lies with these twenty young individuals.*

"The genetic anomaly is the reason we're all here," Everly said, her eyes meeting Luca's. "At least, that is what Richard led me to believe, when he tested me, and what Jamie implied, when he . . ." Everly trailed off, restraining herself from rubbing at her arms.

"It powers the building," Luca supplied.

Everly swallowed thickly, nodding. Then she hesitated before asking, "Do you think it's true? That the testing is the only way to keep the building alive? To keep *us* alive in it?"

Luca looked at her more closely. "I don't know. It's what I've always been told. I guess no one's wanted to try and see what would happen to the building if the testing suddenly stopped."

Or no one wanted to speak against the runners, ask them to try another way, Everly thought but didn't say aloud. It just didn't sit right with her; why would pain be the only way to give energy? Who was to say there couldn't be another way, one they just hadn't figured out yet, because the people who did the figuring out—i.e., Richard, Jamie, the Warden—didn't have to undergo the testing themselves in order to keep the building up and running? Luca frowned at this, but he didn't comment further. Sighing, Everly looked down into the open drawer, full to the brim with old journals.

They were running out of time—Everly could feel it ticking away, the seconds until they were found here where they didn't belong, the minutes they had left to find Caleb. But one of those journals could hold the answers. There were so many years' worth of notes and memories. It could take a person weeks to go through all of them. Everly turned toward the open drawer.

Just one more, she told herself, reaching for another. When she noticed the year in the new journal she'd pulled out, Everly sat up a little straighter, and then began to riffle through the pages until she found the date she was looking for.

I'm so out of sorts this afternoon, I'm not sure what to do. I don't know what any of this means. I am excited, but also strangely terrified for the prospects, the implications of this morning's events. My hand is shaking as I attempt to document the incredibly unique proceedings.

The child was born today. He is perfectly healthy, a picturesque specimen for a baby boy. The Warden, surprisingly, didn't seem as excited as I would have expected her to be. She didn't linger for long before retreating downstairs. Who knows if I will even be allowed to see her again before her time is up.

The oddity of all of this lies in the overt fact that the child was conceived at all, and now appears to be thriving. This has never happened before, the patterns in the building have never been so blatantly defied. We have tested him, of course, and he has the genetic anomaly. While I cannot say that this is surprising, exactly, it is something new. Something that shouldn't have been possible.

I now feel more desperate than ever to speak with her—I know she is the next, after all. There is no denying it any longer; the resemblance is there. If only Jacob would allow me to bring her here. Though, I understand why he can't. I just wish the circumstances were different. I must try to convince him—for her own sake, her own good.

That had been written on the day marked in Michael's file as his Initiation Date. Everly still didn't understand it. She didn't understand what her parents had to do with Michael's birth, or what Richard was so excited about. She didn't understand why she thought she could see a room, white and cold and sterile, but with a bed set up in the middle, a single chair placed to the side.

A baby, small and dark haired and screaming.

Luca.

Luca?

Luca with wide, fearful eyes. *Everly* with wide, fearful eyes.

What happened on that day?

It didn't matter, Everly tried to tell herself. At that moment, it didn't matter.

She kept looking.

There were only two more journals dated after that one. Everly quickly flipped through one of them, a few lines catching her attention. One entry from a few years ago said, *I saw Lois today, as I suppose I can go back to calling her. If I hadn't known it was her, I would not have been able to recognize her—she has deteriorated so much in the past couple of years.* Then, a year after that: *I can't go up there anymore. I thought I could and it would be all right, but I can't. It's too painful. The proof of my failure, my one great failure—my heart can no longer handle all of this. I used to say I was not certain which was worse—the existence she would have had up there, or no existence at all. What is the worst is knowing I could have saved her, yet instead I did nothing.*

After that there was a considerable gap in Richard's writing. The final journal in the filing cabinet was only half full, and it started about five months ago, which was shortly before Richard had found her. On one page, he had written in frantic, nearly illegible scrawl: *I know what I have to do, yet still I find myself hesitating. Can I really go through with this? Will it all truly be worth it? Will this right my wrongs from so many years ago, erase the distress I have caused to this building?*

He wrote more after that, but Everly couldn't make out most of it. A few days later, he had come back and written: *It has to be now. I have no other choice—it's for her own good; I know she will one day come to understand. Her own good, as well as for the good of the building itself. I have to bring Everly to the Eschatorologic.*

Richard's words made Everly's blood run cold as she tried to process what he had written. He had known what he was doing when he brought her here—he had known what might happen to her. But he had done it, anyway. It didn't make any sense, and Everly couldn't believe that he would have done something like that to her. She didn't *want* to believe it.

Furtively, Everly flipped through the remaining pages of the journal, stopping on the final entry. It was dated the day Richard had tested her, the last time she had seen him before he had gone missing.

> *It all falls into place, and I know what my role is next. She has tested positive, which was of course expected, but now it means that the real work can begin.*
>
> *Everly, if you're reading this—*

Everly stopped. She looked up from the journal, then back down at it, making sure that what she had read was correct. Was Richard *speaking* to her? Had he somehow known that she would be here, that she would read through his journals? Did he *want* her to?

With trembling hands, Everly raised the pages back up to her face and kept reading.

> *Everly, if you're reading this, know that you are very close to the end. I know it is difficult, and it feels like there's no way through, but I promise you there is. You need to know two things: First, I believe there*

is a way out for you. I truly do. I'm trying to find it, Everly. You just need to have patience with me.

And second, the room you are seeking is down the hall, two corridors over to the left. You will know what to do when you find it.

That's where the journal ended—the last of Richard's writing. Everly closed it and didn't know what to do from there. What did he mean about a way out?

More pressingly, Richard couldn't know that she and Luca were trying to find Caleb, could he? They hadn't known themselves before that morning, and Richard had disappeared weeks ago.

And yet.

They were running out of options, as well as time.

"Luca," Everly said, setting the final journal to the side. "I think I might know where to find Caleb."

45

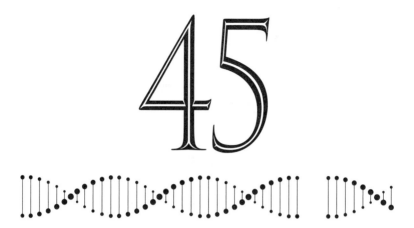

Another snapshot:

One floor above Everly and Luca, a small ten-year-old boy with dark hair and blue eyes was brought into an all-white room by a man dressed in red, who might otherwise have worn a bowler hat and a tweed coat. A needle was inserted into the crux of his arm. A vial was filled with his oh-so-precious blood.

A floor just below that: a very tall man dressed in red lurked in the shadows, preparing for what would come next.

And only a few rooms down from Everly and Luca: the screen with the boy whose blood had been drawn, who now leaned back in his chair with fluttering eyes; the screen with the lurking man in red; and, of course, the most interesting of all, the screen that held the young woman with auburn hair and the young man with dark eyes. The Warden tried to catch those eyes, even though she knew it was impossible, through this imperfect screen.

There was nothing for her to do now but watch. They had found the journals, as she knew they would. Weren't they always meant to? After their friend was taken, was there any other option?

Now they had to find him.

Then . . . well, she was prepared for what would come then.

She was prepared for everything.

The building had prepared her well. It knew, after all, even the small details that she might have neglected. Together, they would succeed. They would restore the order the building so desperately craved. Needed. And then all would be right again within the Eschatorologic.

The Warden leaned back in her chair at her desk, savoring the feel of the worn leather as she sank into it. She would miss this chair, she thought. She knew she wouldn't, not really, but it had been good to her.

She saw as the man and the woman rushed from the lab that they had left scattered with half-open journals. And she took in an uneasy breath, pretending to smile.

It was time.

46

DOWN THE HALL, TWO CORRIDORS over to the left, was a single black door.

Everly glanced at Luca who glanced at her, and she wondered what he must be thinking. She hadn't shown him Richard's final entry, hadn't known how to explain it to him without it seeming like her and Richard were somehow in on this together. That she might have had something to do with Caleb being taken. He hadn't asked her how she knew where to go; he'd only followed her lead.

And she didn't even *know* if this was the right door. It could be any door, could lead into any room.

Because how could Richard have possibly known where they would need to go?

Everly wondered what Luca thought they were going to find, when they finally did open that door.

She wondered if he would be shocked if Caleb actually was in there.

She wondered if he knew about Michael's file.

That last was a question she had been avoiding asking herself again since she had first seen their names, lined up right next to each other inside of that file.

He couldn't know. Could he?

He would have told her, if he knew.

Like she'd told him, right?

She kept wondering if she should bring it up but couldn't find the words. How do you ask someone if they knew the two of you had apparently had a child together ten years ago without either of you being aware?

Or maybe he was aware. Maybe he was in on it. Maybe they all were.

Maybe that didn't matter right now, Everly berated herself. Maybe they should just open the door.

First, Luca tried the handle. He didn't look at Everly as he did it but gripped the silver doorknob beneath his fist and tried to turn it.

It didn't budge. Of course it didn't. So, he stepped away from the door, still without really looking at Everly, and she wondered why he was so unnerved by her ability to open doors here.

She wondered if she should be more unnerved.

Everly stepped forward and felt the lock click open beneath her hand.

Inside, the room was empty.

Of course it was. Why wouldn't it have been, Everly tried to chastise her racing heart. Of course Richard would lead them here, to a room with nothing but walls.

Walls. She could see the walls. In her mind's eye, though, she also saw something else.

A different wall.

Blink and the image vanished, but then blink again and it was back, and even though she knew it wasn't real, it felt real enough to draw her forward, to cause her to raise a hand and reach up, to where the wall should have opened.

"Everly?" she heard Luca say distantly, from somewhere far, far behind her. Far, far away.

"There's something behind here," she said in a voice that even in her own ears didn't sound right. She shook that thought away. Her hand hovered a fraction of an inch away from the surface of the back wall of the empty room.

Luca came up beside her, and though she didn't turn to look at him, she could feel his eyes on her. "Are you sure?" he asked. "How do you know?"

Everly shook her head slightly, staring straight ahead. "I don't know."

Her palm landed flat on the smooth surface of the back wall.

Nothing.

And then, a second later, the telltale sound of a lock clicking into place, and a door sprung open where before there had been nothing but a blank wall, its outline now carved undeniably into the surface in front of her and Luca. Blink and Everly was back, standing next to Luca again, with only the single image of the door she had just opened in front of her. She swallowed thickly and walked forward, ignoring Luca's eyes that she knew were still on her.

Everly edged into the space beyond, aware of Luca following. Inside, it was bright red—bloody red, almost—in a way that attacked Everly's eyes, which had become so acclimated to the poorly lit space of the dark halls outside. She was squinting, waiting for her eyes to adjust, to stop swimming in red, when she heard Luca's breath hitch beside her, and then he was running. Everly blinked into the light, and slowly she began to make sense of the scene around her, to see what made Luca bolt.

It was Caleb. He was lying flat on his back, strapped to a metal table. Unconscious.

But alive.

Luca was by his side, trying to find a way to undo the restraints that pinned his arms and legs down to the table. Everly could only watch, limbs frozen.

Caleb heaved in a sharp breath.

Luca flinched away, then drew closer, brow lifting in concern as he looked down at his friend. The heaving turned into coughing and then, miraculously, Caleb opened his eyes.

"Took you long enough."

The voice was raspy and thick with disuse. It took Everly a second to register the voice, to realize that it was coming from the table, from the lanky young man who was still lying on top of it. "I thought heroes were supposed to be more punctual than that."

Caleb was grinning now, craning his neck to look first at Luca, and then over at Everly. Luca had visibly sagged with relief next to Caleb, redoubling his efforts to free Caleb from his restraints.

Everly took another step closer to Caleb's side. "Caleb," she breathed out, taking him in.

"Nice to see you again, Everly." Upon closer inspection, Everly saw that Caleb looked exhausted—face sallow with dark shadows painted under each eye. He tried to hide it, smiling brightly at Everly when she reached his side. "How have you been?"

"I've been all right," Everly said, smiling down at him, glad, if nothing else, to have found him still alive. "Seen better days. Though I imagine you'd say my day has been a walk in the park compared to yours."

"Wouldn't know," he said. "I've never been to a park."

Everly rolled her eyes, but her grin remained. On the other side of Caleb, she saw as Luca finally managed to undo the last of his restraints—the straps springing free on either side of him.

Gingerly, Caleb lifted himself into a sitting position, offering Luca a grateful smile. Luca was looking at Caleb, his face serious but with a glimmer of hope in his eyes.

"Are you okay?" Luca asked in a low voice. "Really okay? They haven't hurt you, have they?"

Caleb's smile grew, but also tightened somewhat, Everly thought. "Aww, look Everly, he's worried about me."

Finally, Luca grinned back. "Come on," he said. "We're getting you out of here."

Caleb seemed to lose some of his humor, strain carving deeper lines around the edges of his face.

"There's something you should know," Caleb said in a soft voice. Luca froze, his hands halfway down to Caleb, to help him stand up. "I'm really sorry, but I think you were too late. They—the runners—they injected me with something. A toxin of some sort, I think. They told me it wouldn't hurt. And—and that it would be fast."

Everly and Luca could only stare at him, not willing to process what he had just said. "But," Luca said after a moment, "you're fine. You look perfectly fine. So, it must not have worked. Or maybe you heard wrong, and they haven't given you the toxin yet." But Caleb was shaking his head sadly.

"I can feel it, Luca," Caleb whispered. "There's not much more time left."

Neither Luca nor Everly spoke. Everly watched Luca watching his friend. They hadn't made it in time after all. Luca was blinking fast, avoiding meeting Everly's eye.

"No, there has to be a way to stop it," Luca said roughly. "An antidote or a way to slow down the toxin or something." He gripped Caleb's shoulder, eyes fierce. "We just found you. I am not going to let you die."

Caleb lifted his hand to put over Luca's, but he began hacking inconsolably, and had to turn aside to cover it up. Luca's face fell, his dark eyes, once so hard and defiant, now on the verge of softening.

"There's nothing," Caleb said, voice scratchy. Everly decided to back over to a corner of the room, turning away from them. She was having difficulty breathing, thinking, but she knew she didn't have the right to be a part of what was happening between the two of them.

And besides. There were the visions again.

Not Caleb—or not only Caleb—but dozens, *hundreds* of others, just like him. Tied to a table. Needle through the skin. They all fell, hard and fast.

She thought she could recognize some of their faces, but then she couldn't, and she really wasn't even sure anymore.

She couldn't even really see Caleb now. Or rather, she did, but she also saw all the rest: each image superimposed over the last, lined up like a collage of sick and dying and dead.

But she could hear. She could hear as Caleb and Luca spoke in soft, urgent tones, every once in a while interrupted by another string of coughing. Luca mumbled something Everly couldn't make out, but Caleb's voice rose sharply in response.

"No, Luca. Don't. You can't blame yourself for this. It's no one's fault but the runners who brought me down here." Luca started to say something else, but Caleb cut him off. "You were the best part of being stuck here. Living in this building would have been unbearable if I hadn't had you for a friend. I need you to know that."

"I should have been there. It was my job to—"

"It was your job to be my friend. And you were. It wasn't your responsibility to protect me. I'm my own person. I was supposed to look out for myself—I couldn't rely on you for the rest of my life, anyway."

"I failed you," Luca said in a shattered voice.

"Luca, please. I don't want you leaving here with the weight of this on your shoulders. I've always been weaker than all the others, and you knew that. We knew it was probably only a matter of time before they took me away. I wasn't worth their time or effort anymore, and that's that. Please can you not blame yourself for this? Can you do that for me, this last time?"

For a while after that, neither of them spoke, and Everly was caught up once more in all the others—their last words, their final breaths. Some pleaded, some sobbed. Some looked on with stoic eyes and calm resolve. Some already looked vacant, already looked dead by the time they were brought in.

But none of them had a chance.

And so, she knew Caleb didn't, either.

Eventually, the silence was broken as Caleb began coughing violently, not letting up. Everly was able to focus, just barely, just enough to see him bending over, to see Luca patting his back softly, with a pain-stricken expression.

Caleb didn't stop. He bent over, one hand against his chest, the other gripping the edge of the table, knuckles white. Blood began to trickle out of his mouth, and then he was gasping, gasping for a breath that wouldn't come. Caleb's eyes had begun to close, and even through her fog, even through the visions that were continuing to spin, spin, spin around her head, Everly could see that Luca was panicking.

"Caleb? Did you hear me? We'll work this all out." Luca's eyes were red, his jaw hard. "Together. I need you here, Caleb. You can't," his voice broke. "You can't leave me here. How am I ever going to survive this alone?"

Caleb's eyes flickered slightly, his head turning to face Luca. "You'll survive because you have to," he whispered. "You have to, Luca."

Luca grabbed one of Caleb's hands, and Everly wished, she *wished,* that she could walk over and take the other, but she wasn't even really sure that she was there anymore. She wasn't even really sure what was real, and she was afraid to move, afraid that if she broke free of the spiraling images that she wouldn't end up anywhere, that she would just collapse into a great nothingness, and never be able to find her way back. So instead, she stood, and she watched, as well as she could.

The seconds continued on. Caleb's chest was rising and falling in rapid succession, his breaths coming out shallowly. He took in a quick breath then, his lips parting open.

"You'll find a way." His voice faded as he talked, drifting off into the room around them. "If anyone can, it will be you." And with those final words, the remainder of the breath left Caleb's body, and he fell still.

And along with him, Everly saw as all the others fell, too.

And still she watched on passively, waiting for whatever it was that was supposed to happen next.

And still she stood there.

And still she felt nothing.

She felt nothing.

She felt nothing.

She felt nothing.

47

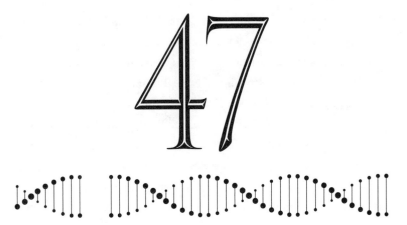

Luca felt nothing.

Not true—Luca felt *everything*, and it was too much, he couldn't do it, he couldn't—

And so instead, his mind had gone numb. He couldn't—wouldn't—think, or feel, and in the moment he was glad for that. Glad for the layer of nothingness that had descended over him as they left that room. The room with . . .

He couldn't think, and so he couldn't figure out what they were supposed to do next. He hadn't really been aware of them leaving that room, but Everly was leading him along, her fingers clasped tightly through his, and he was thankful for it. Without her hand in his, carrying him down one dark hall and into the next, Luca wasn't sure he would be able to move at all. Wasn't sure he would want to.

The warmth of her palm pressed up against his skin, skin that had gone so cold, as though his life had seeped away right along with . . .

It was Everly's warmth that gave Luca a glimmer of light at the end of the empty, caved-in tunnel he had found himself suffocating in. So, he trailed after that, and after her, as they continued to make their way through the inky blackness of the floor they were still lost on.

Luca didn't know how she had done it on her own, but somehow Everly had managed to bring them to the elevator. Creeping in through the mist of numbness grew an awareness that they were so, so exposed in these halls, beneath the cameras that Luca knew ran up and down them. Someone must have noticed they were missing by now. It was only a matter of time before they were found, before they were taken, just like Caleb had been, just like every person in this building was, sooner or later, caught and brought down there, to that dark floor, to that red room, and there wasn't anything any of them could do about it.

This was the threat Luca was realizing had always hung over all of them, like a guillotine blade ready to come slicing down. This is what must happen to all of the people who vanished from the building, never to be seen again.

Just like would probably now happen to Everly and him.

Luca found his breath coming faster and faster and he had to stop, yanking his hand out of Everly's and putting it against his chest until slowly, painfully, his breathing evened out again. Everly stood watching him with empty eyes. As he counted his breaths, Luca settled his features and stood up straight, walking over to stand next to her. Gaze focused straight ahead on the metallic doors of the elevator, he spoke without turning to face her. "We should go. They'll be headed this way soon," and he pushed the elevator button.

A shrill siren pierced through the echoing halls, followed by flashing red lights from atop the elevator doors. The abruptness of the alarm jolted Luca free of his numb reverie, and he saw as Everly, too, was shaken to attention, with her hands covering her ears and her eyes searching wildly around them.

It was the elevators. Luca had been so out of it, so lost in his own head, that he hadn't even realized what they were doing.

Everly had brought them to the elevators. And the elevators had denied them access.

As suddenly as it had started, the alarm cut off, leaving behind only a hazy ringing in Luca's ears. The red lights continued to flash around them, casting an eerie glow across the surfaces of the black walls and shadowing Luca's and Everly's faces in the tinted light. Luca stood with his back to the closed elevator doors, searching the empty halls to either side of them. Waiting.

It was then that he realized the halls weren't empty. Down the dark hallway to the right of the elevator, Luca could just make out the silhouetted form of a person standing in the shadows, turned away from them. It was a silhouette he recognized.

One he knew all too well.

The shadowed man tilted his head, as though observing them. Then he took a step forward, two, three, until he had moved away from the shadows and into the cascading red light.

Jamie.

In the crimson glow of the corridor, Luca could just make out the shape of a smirk, twisted across Jamie's lips. Luca flinched, and his blood stilled. Jamie just crossed his arms and watched them, waiting.

Luca didn't move. Something new bubbled inside him now. Something molten. All those years, time after time of being brought in for testing by this man. Of letting him do whatever he wanted to Luca. Of staying quiet, of not fighting back. It all rushed through him at once.

Then the image of Caleb, lying cold and still on the table in that awful red room, flashed before Luca's eyes. He could so easily imagine Jamie being the one to have dragged Caleb in there, to have stuck the needle in his arm that injected that terribly fatal serum. To have been the one to watch with the same cool smirk Luca saw now as the energy drained away from Caleb, his life fading with every passing second.

And even if it hadn't been Jamie who killed Caleb, he might as well have. He was a part of this system as much as anyone.

"You shouldn't be on this floor," Jamie said flatly, as though he hadn't a care in the world.

"You killed him," Luca heard himself saying, as though from a great distance away. Then a moment later, in a low growl, "You killed my friend."

"Mr. Arya was no longer serving the building as he should have been, I'm afraid," was Jamie's response. "It was out of my hands." As though to demonstrate that fact, Jamie lifted his hands in the air.

"*You killed him*," Luca roared, leaping forward. His motion was stopped short with a jerk on his arm, and glancing over Luca saw Everly, desperately clinging to him in an effort to keep him back. She shook her head once, eyes wide. Luca turned back to Jamie, fire burning in his gaze. "He's gone," he said, voice breaking over the word.

"As I said, Mr. Arya had outlived his purpose. And beyond that," Jamie said, taking a smooth step closer to Luca and Everly, "you needed to learn, Mr. Reyes, that your actions in here do have repercussions. Or had you forgotten?" A cruel smile cut across his lips. "Had you begun to think yourself immortal, beyond the scope of being caught, being turned in?"

Luca froze, going stiff in Everly's grasp. "What do you mean?" His voice turned hoarse over the question. "Someone turned me in?"

It's all my fault, was the immediate thought to follow. *It's my fault Caleb's dead. They killed him because of me.*

"Oh, don't go too hard on Anker. He doesn't hold anything against you, I'm sure. He just realized where he fit into the structure of this building and where his loyalties should lie. Something you could stand to learn from."

Anker? Luca found himself thinking in disbelief. *It was Anker?* Though a darker part of him thought it made sense. They'd been bringing Anker in more and more for testing lately. Luca had seen the bags that had been growing under his eyes, the paleness that had begun to linger in his complexion.

People can only endure so much before they break, and apparently Jamie had found a way to break Anker. Luca thought of finding Anker just after Caleb had been taken, the way the other man had tried so hard to get away from Luca, the wild look in his eyes at being confronted.

It was Anker's fault, it was Luca's fault. But above all, it was Jamie's.

The fire returned to Luca, and he burst away from Everly, charging for Jamie with a sound bursting from his throat that didn't sound human.

He shot forward blindly, aiming only for Jamie's tall form, with no other intention in mind other than to hurt him, the way he'd hurt so many others.

Before Luca could even reach Jamie, however, Jamie whistled out a high, sharp note, and a group of runners swarmed into the dark hallways around them, one immediately beelining for Luca and bear-hugging him. The others circled around behind Everly, preventing them from going anywhere. Luca strained against the runner's hold, but it was futile. The man was inhumanly strong; there was no budging.

Jamie observed all of this with a calm, unbothered expression.

"I am sorry that it has had to come to this. Warden's orders, I hope you understand."

"Who is the Warden?" Everly asked, and Luca could hear a certain desperation bleeding into her voice as she understood the same thing he did. They were caught. "What does she want with us?"

"You'll have to ask her yourself," Jamie said, then he nodded at the runners who had gone behind them, and another pinned Everly in place. As Luca continued to struggle against the one who had taken hold of him, trying without success to get out, to escape, he felt a sharp pain in his neck, and then everything went dark.

48

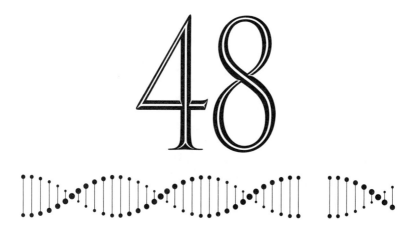

Everly's eyelids were heavy. So heavy. As though they had been pinned down by lead staples, and then glued shut for good measure. With great effort she managed to pry them open, only to shut them again abruptly at the blinding brightness of her surroundings. She took a deep breath, and then cracked her eyes open again, squinting at the room that she had woken up in.

It was the white room. Or, she supposed, one of the white rooms. The walls here were not yet covered in blood, which wasn't necessarily the most comforting of observations. Everly tried to sit up more, to get a better grasp of her situation, but she felt the pressure of restraints pinning her in place. Looking down, she saw metal clamps around her arms, legs, and torso. She couldn't move.

Panic began to settle in. How had she gotten here? What was happening to her? Slowly, so slowly, Everly's memories from earlier filtered back in.

The elevator, Jamie, the runners. The pain in her neck. Reflexively, she tried to reach and touch the sore spot just above her clavicle, before remembering that she couldn't move. They must have injected her with something, knocked her out.

Alarm shot through Everly, fast and hot. Luca. Where was Luca?

She listened, trying to tell if there were any sounds to indicate that someone else—that Luca—could be in the room with her. Nothing. She heard nothing over her own ragged breathing as she tried to keep her rising hysteria under control. Had he been taken, too? Was he—

No. She wouldn't let herself finish that thought. He was fine. He was being kept somewhere else, that was all. The fear was trying desperately to swallow her whole, but she allowed herself an instant to hope, to imagine that he could be safe.

Safer than she was, at any rate.

Why hadn't they already killed her? That was what Everly wanted to know: if she was in here to die, then why hadn't they gotten on with it already? Her fear was reaching a peak when Everly heard the distinctive creak of a door opening behind her, beyond her limited range of view. She tried to crane her neck to see who it was, to no avail. The door closed again with a loud click, followed by the sound of a lock falling into place.

Everly started to sweat, thinking through all the awful possibilities for why she could be here, what they might do to her next. Worse and worse thoughts shot through her mind as she waited in terrible anticipation for her visitor to reveal themselves, to get this over with.

A minute passed, then two, three, and still the person refused to come into Everly's line of sight. For so long the room was still and silent enough that she began to wonder if she had imagined the door opening, the person walking in. Finally, nearing her wit's end, Everly heard the muted click of heels on the tiled floor.

The person didn't come all the way around in front of Everly, but she could feel them lingering just beyond her head. "Well, Everly," said the voice of a woman, a voice that was both familiar and completely foreign to her. "It seems we have found ourselves in quite the predicament here."

"Who are you?" Everly asked, and she hated herself for the tremor she heard in her own voice.

The woman ignored her question but kept talking. "You have caused a considerable stirring throughout my building these past few days. I assume this means you have uncovered what you believe to be the truth of my affairs here and don't agree with my methods. Am I correct in these assumptions?"

"You're the Warden," Everly breathed.

"You are incredibly resourceful," said the woman, who must have been the Warden, with something like laughter hiding in her voice. "And so persistent. I feel I should applaud you for how far you managed to get before being caught. Though, of course, very little of what you thought of as being chance or intuition were as such. There were far more hands at play in all of this than you could possibly know. Still, an admirable feat." The Warden paused, as though in contemplation. "You know, you remind me so much of your parents."

"You mean the parents that you stole from me?" Everly hadn't known that those words would ring so true, but as soon as she said them, she felt the weight of certainty behind them. "You took away my whole life, the lives of all these people here."

"You should not speak of that which you do not fully understand, Everly," the Warden said in a flat voice. "I would think this a lesson most children learn early on."

"Fine," Everly spat. "Why don't you fill me in, then? Tell me all your excuses for capturing and tormenting and *killing* countless people—*children*—for decades."

"It is not so simple as all that," the Warden snapped. "Pain makes you stronger. Clearly, you did not learn this lesson the same way I did. Maybe that makes you lucky—but the inability to handle pain, that just makes one weak." Everly heard the Warden take a deep breath, then Everly felt a hand being placed on her temple, a finger drawing up the side of her skull, sending a shiver racketing across her skin. "And why don't you, Everly my dear, tell me how you felt, watching the life drain out of your friend. What was his name? Caleb?"

"I don't know what you mean," Everly said, but her heart was pounding now. Louder and louder and louder and—

"Oh," the Warden said, with something close to a chuckle. "I think you do. I have felt the very same, you know. The horror of watching something precious fade away, mingled with a very distinct fascination. An unwillingness to look away. A desire to know what will happen next."

"You're wrong," Everly said. The words sounded false in her mouth the moment she said them, but she tried not to let that shake her. Tried not to let it show on her face, the impact the Warden's implications were having on her.

The finger on Everly's temple pressed in, hard enough that Everly winced at the pressure.

"Oh, Everly. Dearest, the sooner you understand how little you actually know, the sooner we can get on with the rest of it. To understand the situation of your mother, and your father for that matter, and even your grandfather, you will have to first understand the Eschatorologic itself." The Warden stopped, her finger freezing somewhere along Everly's hairline. "I wonder, though, if you are fully prepared for what that will entail."

Everly didn't want to give the Warden the satisfaction of asking for the answers she so desperately craved, of begging for them. So instead, she remained silent, lips pinched together.

After a long, heavy moment, the Warden chuckled darkly and took her hand away from Everly's head. Without prompting, she began to speak. "The Eschatorologic was a dream that was first established long before your time. Before mine too, in fact. It began with the stories of people like your grandfather, who first conceptualized the building's creation, and the potential use for it. In the years since arriving at this building, I have spent a good deal of time compiling everything that I could on the origins of this project, everything that I need to know in order to fulfill my purpose here.

"Do you know what this building is fueled by, Everly?" the Warden asked. "People. People like you, like me. We are what keep the Eschatorologic alive and well. And do you know why that is?"

This time, the Warden did pause, long enough that Everly answered, in a creaking voice, "The testing."

"Yes," the Warden said, something like appreciation in her voice. "The testing. It's the reason all of us are here, really. You, me, your boyfriend out there. And tell me, what did your grandfather share with you about the testing, about how it works?"

"There's—there's something in our DNA," Everly said, struggling to remember what Richard had told her, what seemed like so long ago now. "A genetic anomaly. He called it STM."

"Precisely. Years and years ago, your grandfather became aware of this rare phenomenon which occurs in extraordinary individuals: the genetic code implanted in very few people globally, labeled by your grandfather as STM. Your grandfather spent many years traveling the world, testing individuals for the anomaly, and then observing those who tested positive, desperately seeking some sign of what it was that the genetic anomaly may have been responsible for.

"It wasn't until he discovered this building that he had his first breakthrough. He was here, studying the strange pulses in electromagnetic energy, when a young woman walked in through the front doors and gave him all the answers he was looking for. Unintentionally.

"The Eschatorologic requires an immense amount of energy to continue to exist. As I am sure you are aware, it is no ordinary building."

"What is it?" Everly whispered, though she was not entirely sure that was the right question at all. When is it, why is it, how is it. She didn't know.

"It is somewhat of a catalyst," the Warden said. "A zone between zones, a place outside of space and time. What Richard discovered when he stumbled across the building, and that first young woman, was the existence of what he has coined as interdimensional ley lines, as well as what exists beyond them. In other words, places in each world where the boundary of space and time is the weakest, or easiest to transcend. The Eschatorologic lies on one such line, which is how it can exist at all."

"Interdimensional," Everly mumbled. "You don't mean—"

"This is where the genetic anomaly comes into play," the Warden interrupted her. "For you see, it takes a great deal of effort for the building to continue to exist like this. To continue to straddle the planes of existence, of reality. The very otherworldly energy that we, somehow, can produce, is the fuel that the building requires to continue. There are a very select few of us, the enhanced. We are scattered through space, through time, and, yes, as you have surmised, through dimensions."

She said this as though Everly should have been shocked at this revelation, should have held some innate disbelief at the Warden's words. But the opposite was happening for Everly. Similarly to how, while watching Caleb die, Everly was given visions, images, of so many other instances in time, so many other people, now Everly thought she could hear the Warden's words, said over and over and over again, always in the same voice, always the same sentences, tracing the same patterns, and now they were all lining up, clearer than anything Everly had ever seen before.

And so, as the Warden continued to say, "It is important for you to understand that multiple dimensions do exist." Everly finished in her head by thinking, before the Warden could say, "They are not, however, well lined up universes lying parallel to one another, as so many of the stories and fictions which tend to circulate would suggest."

The Warden kept going, and so did Everly, drawn into the Warden's words, her own words, the way the two overlapped:

"Rather," the Warden and Everly both went on, "they are more like tangled up string, intersecting and connecting with one another in random and various ways. As such, while in another dimension a separate version of you—or rather, an individual sharing your DNA and many basic features—may exist, it is incredibly unlikely that the two of you would be on the same time stream or share the same life experiences—in fact, it is nearly impossible.

"Equally unlikely is the probability of a person transcending dimensions and time streams, winding up in a space that is not their own. The genetic anomaly, however, helps with this. In the most basic of terms, it allows you to be open to spaces like the Eschatorologic, spaces that aren't necessarily in your dimension or mine, but rather in all, and equally in none."

"What do you mean?" Everly asked. "It's just—blood and tissue. DNA."

"Oh no," the Warden replied. "It is so much more than that. The anomaly—it calls out to places like the building. Draws you to them. Opens up the building to you because you need each other. We don't live long out there, you know. The enhanced. Without this building, we all die young and tragically, and without us, the building would crumble into nonexistence. But that will never happen. Not while you and I are here.

"We all have a role to play," the Warden said and Everly thought. "We all have a part in the pattern that has always been within this building, and will always, always continue to happen. Mine is to be the Warden—the one that people perceive to be in control, because they need that illusion, they need someone to look to, someone to fear. Do you know what your role is, Everly?"

She didn't know. She was starting to suspect, though, a voice whispering—or screaming—or scream-whispering—in the back of her head.

"There is so much that goes into ensuring that this building continues to run properly. When the first Warden stepped in, she was a broken woman desperate for escape. Here, she found the first place in her life where she wasn't being squashed beneath someone else's heel. The first place where she was important, where she was powerful. That first Warden seized that power and ensured that it would always be hers."

As if from a great distance away, Everly heard as her voice asked, "The first?" From even farther away, she could distantly recall reading in Richard's journals of the first time he had mentioned a Warden. It had been so long ago. So, so long ago. "Who was the first?"

"That's just the thing," the Warden said, and Everly continued to think along with her, answering her own question. "You remember what I said earlier, about people being able to coexist with other versions of themselves, from different points in their timeline, originating from separate dimensions? As it turns out, I was not the first of myself to enter this building. Nor the second, third, fourth. But far, far back, the very first version of myself to enter the Eschatorologic, she took up the mantle of Warden with stride, and so it has been for all the rest. There always comes a time when she can no longer live up to the duties of Warden, when she must step down. And that is when the next comes in, the mantle is passed on, the pattern continues."

Patterns patterns patterns.

"What happened to her?" Everly whispered, though of course, she already knew the answer. She thought, perhaps, she already knew all the answers.

"Oh, don't worry, she's still alive. Just not as mentally present as she once was. She still lives in the building—they all do. I believe you may have even made her acquaintance. Though it was not her—our—given name, she has gone by the name of Lois since arriving at the Eschatorologic."

This last sentence, Everly found herself saying aloud, along with the Warden, in mumbled words that hardly felt as if they belonged to her. She still could not see the Warden's face, but she thought perhaps the woman was smiling. Thought perhaps she had paused in a moment of appreciation for what Everly had done, though Everly didn't understand it herself.

"So, you see," the Warden said, "it has already begun."

"What has begun?" Everly asked the one question, she thought, that she still did not know the answer to. Or was trying not to know the answer to.

"You are beginning to understand. You are beginning to change." A deep breath, and then the Warden said, "I am dying, Everly. Or fading, I suppose. At any rate, I will not be able to remain the Warden for much longer. The role must continue, however—there is still work to be done—and so, as Lois once did, I will soon need a replacement."

Everly's breath briefly caught, and she said in a flat voice, "You cannot possibly mean me," though part of her by now knew that she must.

"Of course, I mean you, Everly. There is no one else." Then Everly heard again the click of heels, and she realized that the Warden was walking around the table, coming into her line of vision.

She stood in front of Everly and then paused, looking into her eyes. Everly didn't understand what she was seeing at first (even though, on some level, she must have always known). The woman was dressed in all black, from head to toe, but that was not what caught Everly's attention. Standing out starkly against the black clothes were the woman's bright blue eyes, rimmed with a circle of green, and her dark red hair. The realization was there, in Everly's mind, but it was so impossible, so unthinkable, that she tried with everything in her to suppress it, to shove away the truth that was standing directly in front of her.

The Warden . . . was *her*. She was older—midthirties, late thirties maybe—but once the realization had sunk in, it was undeniable. That was Everly, standing before her.

Everly sputtered, but no words would come. How could they? It was so unimaginable, beyond anything she possibly could have thought up.

But you know that it has to be, that small voice in the back of her head said, cutting through all the rest. *You know that it's all true.*

The Warden smiled, as though reading her thoughts—and perhaps she could. She continued to look Everly in the eye—her own eyes, staring back at her.

"You understand, Everly? It has to be you, there is no other choice. You have to be the next Warden."

49

Richard Dubose was growing anxious.

He knew what had to be happening right now. He had seen enough versions of the Warden's plan by now to have been prepared for the beats it would enact throughout the building—the so-called pattern that she was so attached to. He knew who she would be with by now, knew what she would be saying. He knew where the other players were bound to be, and he knew the role he was meant to carry out himself before it was all over.

He had his own plan, this time around.

And finally, *finally,* the answers to go along with that plan.

The *solution.*

He'd first had the idea when Jamie had mentioned a kid who kept running away. It wasn't too hard after that to learn the truth of the boy who kept going where he wasn't supposed to. A child with wandering feet perhaps wouldn't have been enough to raise an alarm in Richard's head, until he'd been told who the child was. And then it seemed almost too perfect to be true.

He'd brought him in immediately, of course. Oh, he didn't need to go through the whole rigamarole of normal testing—a vial of blood was all they really needed.

And it was worth it.

Richard knew how to save Everly now.

He just needed her to see, needed her to understand the importance of what he was doing. All those other times, he didn't think those Wardens ever really saw it. What the building was capable of. What the *anomaly* was capable of. But this time—this time it would be different. This version of Everly was different—she *had* to be. So, she was going to listen to him. Agree with him.

And then together, they could make a difference.

Find a way for her to live. The way her mother hadn't.

It was all down to timing, and Richard's had to be perfect.

It wouldn't be long now. In the meantime, all he had to do was wait.

50

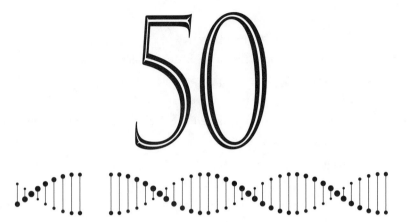

Michael sat up.

It was the middle of the night (relatively speaking, but the lights were all off), and he was not one to wake up like that.

But he'd had a dream.

Michael stood up from his bed and rubbed at his sleep-crusted eyes, feeling his way in the dark across the small room to his door. It wasn't until after he had already opened the door and stumbled out into the hallway beyond that Michael thought to question why the door had opened at all, when it was usually locked at this hour.

Not usually. *Always.* His door was always locked during the night, yet, this night it wasn't. Michael shrugged and kept walking.

His dream had told him where to go, so he didn't question his feet as they trailed down one path and then another. He didn't question them as they led him to a door he had never entered before, and he didn't question the stairs he found on the other side.

The door that, again, unlocked for him when it should not have. The all-black floor that he had never seen before. The unknown directions that were leading him on, on, on. The door that he finally stopped in front of which, again, opened beneath his touch.

Michael rubbed at the bend in his arm where a bandage was wrapped tightly around the skin as he stepped into the room that his feet, and his dream, had led him toward and met the eyes of Dr. Richard Dubose.

"Hello, Michael," Richard said with a smile, placing the bowler hat over his gray hair. "Are we ready to do some work tonight?"

51

Luca came to consciousness slowly, swimming through a pit of molasses to return to the waking world, and when he finally did, his eyes creaked open before immediately snapping shut again.

The room was white. White walls, white floor, white ceiling.

He tried to backtrack in his mind, tried to understand what was happening, but it was like fighting against the tide trying to form a coherent thought.

Where am I?

A testing room. Some testing room.

What happened?

He remembered a heavy darkness spreading through him. He'd been injected with something, knocked out. And someone—runners, probably—must have dragged him here.

What do I do?

Nothing. Luca's limbs felt heavy and his head throbbed. As best he could tell, they hadn't restrained him to the chair he'd woken up in, but they might as well have. He was paralyzed in place, afraid that if he were to move a muscle, it would be enough to signal that he was awake, and that would be the beginning of the end for him.

I need to get up. I need to move.

But he couldn't.

The longer he waited in that chair, eyes clenched shut, the more he could feel the sweat dripping across his brow despite the coolness of the room. Time passed like this—minutes and seconds and hours, they all felt the same to a man who'd grown up outside of time—and eventually he felt his body beginning to shake. It started small at first, a slight trembling in his hands, but as more and more time went on without change, his whole body started to quake. It would be any second, he knew. Any second they could come in. And so, any second could be his last.

Luca didn't want to die. Not yet. Not like this.

The shaking had spread to his lungs somehow, and Luca's chest rose and fell in rapid succession. It felt like he was choking on the air around him. Like it might be that air that did him in, before the runners had a chance to do it themselves.

Sparks were flashing across his closed eyelids, and a pounding was thundering in his head when Luca heard the door creaking open behind him, and he froze, the choked air in his lungs going still along with the rest of him.

Footsteps. More than one pair. A heavy, slower tread. A light and quick one. They both entered, and the door closed back, and still Luca didn't open his eyes, even as he heard the two sets of feet walking around him to where he was certain, if he were to look, he would see the two people standing right in front of where he was propped up.

It took the hand on his shoulder. It was a small hand—warm, reassuring, though he couldn't have really said why—and it didn't shake or rattle or thump when it touched Luca. It just rested there, light against the tense skin of his shoulder. He knew it wasn't Jamie or the Warden or any of the rest, and so finally Luca opened his eyes, dizzy when he found them connecting with the round, blue ones that he knew so well.

Michael was smiling down at Luca, bobbing slightly up and down on the balls of his feet in a way that almost seemed like he was floating in the air, like a kite on the clouds. His smile grew when he saw that Luca was awake, and he shifted, casting a wide-eyed glance over his shoulder at the second person who had come in.

Luca looked over, too, and stiffened, all relief he'd initially felt upon seeing Michael fleeing when he saw who Michael had brought to him. Or who had brought Michael, as the more likely alternative.

Dr. Richard Dubose at least had the decency to look abashed at Luca's state, but still his shoulders were thrown back with that form of authority that comes from presiding over a place for so many years without question. Luca looked between the two—the young boy and the old man—and didn't have a word to say. He could only raise his eyebrows and wait.

"Luca," Michael said in a high, breathy voice as he turned back so that his face was once more close to Luca's. "Do you see? I found Dr. Dubose. And he found you! I saw you weren't at roll call—well, everyone saw, really—and we were *so* worried. Or, I was worried. Some of the others didn't seem so bothered by it, but I *knew* something was wrong, and I tried to tell the runners that, but they wouldn't *listen*. But then there was this dream, and my door was unlocked, and I found Dr. Dubose, and now we're here!"

Luca had to reach up and put both of his hands on the small boy's shoulders to cease his rapid recounting, feeling that his breathing had become labored just from the effort of trying to keep up. "You found Dr. Dubose?" was what he finally managed to croak, his voice sounding rather like it had gone out of use for a millennium or so.

Michael nodded, beaming. "I did!"

With a groan, Luca sat up all the way. He placed a hand to the side of his throbbing temple, looking around Michael to Dr. Dubose.

Luca did not want to speak with Dr. Dubose. He didn't know what the man's stake in all of this was, but he knew that he didn't trust him. However, of the three people in this room, he was the most likely to know what had happened to Everly, and to be able to do something about that. Except . . .

"Wait, kid, did you say you found Dr. Dubose in a dream?"

For a second, Michael stopped bouncing. His eyes grew wide and round, and he nodded once, solemnly, almost reverently. Right after that he was back to grinning, though, and he sprang around to Luca's side, so he could speak close to his ear. In a loud, whisper-like voice, Michael said, "I saw where he was. In the dream, I knew where to go, and so when I woke up, I still knew."

Luca leaned away and tilted his head, just enough so he could meet Michael's eyes, which were now so close to his.

There was something about the kid's eyes . . .

"Michael," Luca said in a low voice, glancing sidelong at Dr. Dubose across the room. "Did you see anything else in your dream? Did you see Everly?"

A beat, and then Michael shook his head.

Luca's shoulders sagged—he hadn't realized he'd been holding them so tense before. He sighed, glanced down again at Michael. Looked back across the room. "You know where she is, don't you?"

Dr. Dubose opened his mouth, but before he could say anything, Luca interjected, "Don't deny it. I don't know where you've been all this time, but it's your fault she's in here. So, you need to help me find her now, and you need to help me get her out."

Luca thought he saw Dr. Dubose swallow thickly. He hoped it wasn't his imagination. "She can't leave," the man said. Luca was opening his mouth to object when Dr. Dubose added, "Not yet."

"What do you mean?" Luca asked. "Why not yet?"

When Dr. Dubose didn't answer him, Luca's gaze hardened. "She's your granddaughter. She didn't ask to be here—none of us did. And I know if anyone can get her out, or any of us out, it's you." He jabbed a finger in Richard's direction.

Dr. Dubose let out a sound that was almost like a chuckle—like a half-suppressed laugh. "You don't know anything, boy, so don't pretend like you do. You have no idea what's at play here, what you've unknowingly become a part of."

A roaring was growing in the back of Luca's skull. It had started off dull and soft—when he woke up, he thought, maybe. But now it was growing. Louder and louder and louder, and now it was in his ears, pushing its way inside of him, filling him up from the inside out. The roar had been nameless, voiceless before, but now he thought it spoke with the words of Dr. Dubose, telling him he knew nothing, he could do nothing.

Through the roar, a thin voice cut like a needle through water. Luca couldn't quite catch it, couldn't quite see what it was, where it was coming from, but he reached for it, sitting there in the testing room they had brought him to. He reached and he reached and he reached and—

"No," Luca whispered. Then said, louder, "You're wrong. Everly believed there had to be more than this, that there could be a way out, and I believe *her*. So, you're going to help me find it."

Dr. Dubose's expression changed. At first it looked as though it was hardening—closing itself off, sealing away whatever secrets were stored up inside that head of his. But then, it all cracked apart, opening up to Luca, revealing—what? A truth. Luca couldn't begin to wonder at what that could mean, but something was there. Something Dr. Dubose had been hiding away before, that he was letting Luca in on now. For a second, only a second, he thought he saw Dr. Dubose's eyes cut to Michael.

"Come on," Dr. Dubose said, already moving back toward the door. "We have somewhere else to be."

52

Everly was no longer in the white room, pinned to a table.

She was in a gray room now, a bedroom, and she was staring down at the prone sleeping form of an old woman.

Lois.

If the Warden was to be believed, Lois was also her, whatever that meant.

No, Everly said to herself. No, it was no use trying to deny it. Trying to call the Warden deranged, or saying that she was wrong. Everly had felt the truth behind the Warden's words the moment she said them, and now she was trapped here, with Lois lying in front of her and the Warden standing silently behind her, and she didn't know what to think anymore. She didn't know what to believe.

"Do you see?" the Warden had asked her. No, Everly didn't see.

But she was afraid that she was beginning to.

"Look," the Warden said, and she walked over to Lois, who did not stir beneath her touch as the Warden gently pushed back her hair, revealing the vulnerable skin at the back of her neck. The base of her skull.

And there, Everly could see the mark: the long, thin scar that so many of the older residents here in the Eschatorologic bore.

"Out there," the Warden was saying, "beyond these walls, Lois here wouldn't even be alive anymore. None of them would be. We are all fated to die at a very young age, due to this . . . *gift* in our blood, our bones. For most it's around twenty-five." The Warden lifted her gaze to Everly's, her hand still resting in Lois's hair. "Richard would tell you that when the brain stops developing, it no longer knows what to do about the anomaly filling up our DNA. And so instead of fighting to find the truth, it shuts down. Too much for it to bear." Leaning forward, the Warden added in a whisper, "But between you and me, I think it's more than that. I think it has more to do with balance—with the building knowing when it needs a replacement for one of us. Knowing when the energy's growing thin."

Twenty-five. The reason she was trapped here. It was the barrier to their leaving, the factor she had yet to find a way around. Though her mind was spinning, spinning, trying to catch up with itself, trying to spot what she had *missed.*

"And in here?" Everly asked, her voice fainter than a whisper.

"In here, the building takes care of that problem for us. It assures the brain that it's okay, that we're okay. So, we live. We get more time."

Everly took a step closer to the foot of Lois's bed. "What happens to them?" she asked. "Why are they all so . . ." She did not know how to finish the thought, but the Warden nodded.

"Being in the building allows our bodies to continue to function. However, the building extracts a toll. Energy. And a person can be stripped of only so much energy before they become—" She gestured down at Lois's sleeping form.

"And the," Everly motioned to the back of her own head, where she knew a scar would be, if she were Lois.

"Ah. You see, they still have the energy. The STM in their systems is still working, it just can't be extracted as easily after they start to shut down like that. So, we have to go about the extraction through . . . other means."

Everly swallowed thickly, but she didn't say anything. She had begun to figure as much. In fact, looking down at Lois, she nearly thought that she could picture the day it happened. The day Lois was first given that scar, the one that since then Everly knew, without knowing, had been reopened again and again and again, fulfilling its purpose until Lois had nothing left to fulfill any longer. Everly thought that she could see a much younger Lois—who was still a much older version of herself—sitting in a chair that was reclined back at a sharp angle. Tied in place. Eyes closed. Breathing deeply. She thought she could see a person dressed in red walk up to Lois's side, blade in hand. And she thought she saw what happened next, too, but she wished that she didn't. Everly tried shutting her eyes but it didn't help. The vision only clarified behind the darkness of her eyelids. With a shudder, she jerked her eyes open again and tried to pin her attention on this Lois, in this moment, and the black-clad woman who stood next to her.

A piece of her leaned toward this, almost wanted this fate, the Warden's fate, Lois's—wanted to become everything the Warden intended her to be. To become cruel, sadistic. To rule the building with an iron fist and never look back. That piece in her head was clawing for purchase against the rest of her that was pushing back with everything she was, with everything she had left. Everly fought instead to remember the room coated in blood, remember listening as the woman upstairs was beaten. Remember the haunted looks on the faces of all the children downstairs. Remember the sensation of her own mutilated flesh.

In Lois's room now, she gripped her head with shaking fingers, ignoring the Warden, who she knew stared at her as she heaved in deep breaths, trying to remember and cling to all those things, the reasons she couldn't, *wouldn't* become like the Warden who stood next to her. Could never turn into that, be a part of this.

She tried to remember all those reasons and remember who she was, why she wasn't a person who could agree with this.

But she could feel the other side of her head, the side that was filling up faster and faster with thoughts that weren't quite hers, as it grew stronger.

It was a battle raging in her own head.

And Everly was afraid she might be losing.

53

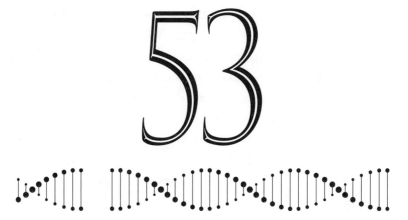

There wasn't much of a crowd, but the people who had arrived were all happy, with bright smiles on their faces and party hats tied loosely on their heads. And they were all singing, voices rising together in an awful, discordant harmony as Mary Tertium sat at the head of the kitchen table, a cake in front of her adorned with twenty-five leaning, burning, dripping candles. She blew them all out, one by one, and when the final candle was extinguished, a cheer rose up among the people who had gathered there to celebrate with her. From the back of the room, a young girl with strawberry-blond pigtails clapped along as well.

"Thank you all for coming today," Mary Tertium said to everyone gathered. "You can't know how much it means to have all of you in my life. So, thank you. Thank you all."

The people cheered again, and then someone found a knife and they sliced into the cake, which Mary was delighted to discover was marbled vanilla and red velvet, her most favorite of flavors. Slices of cake on limp paper plates were passed around the room, and Mary herself piled a large piece, slathered in a hefty dollop of icing, onto a plate that she brought over to the pigtailed girl. Kneeling in front of her, Mary lifted the plate and grinned as the girl's face broke into the widest of smiles before grabbing the cake away and digging in with a fist full of small fingers. *This,* Mary thought. This was worth more than all the other presents she knew were stacked up in the other room. This right here.

She left the girl with her cake and circled around the room, saying hello to the friends she hadn't seen in however long, and thanking others for stopping by, and hugging the ones she wasn't sure if she'd see again because, really, it was a bit of a miracle they had appeared at this event at all—she hadn't seen them in *months* and had begun to worry. An hour or so passed and the people all dispersed, leaving Mary alone once again with her husband and her small, pigtailed daughter. The only two people she wanted with her, anyhow.

"That went well," her husband said jovially, though Mary could see the party had taken its toll on him. His smile had become a little lopsided, and his eyes were starting to squint the way she knew they did when he was getting close to needing to lie down. She smiled softly at him and walked over to place a light kiss on his cheek.

"It was perfect," she said. "Thank you."

"Well, you only turn twenty-five once. Might as well make an ordeal of it."

She grinned, but it quickly turned into a grimace as a sharp pain laced through her head. She raised her hand to her temple, grunting slightly.

"What?" her husband said in a concerned voice. "What is it? Do you need your medicine?" For the headaches had been coming on more frequently of late, and so this didn't seem so out of place just yet. Just another headache. An ill-timed headache, perhaps. But just another.

"No, I'm okay," Mary said, hand still up to her head. She tried again to smile at her husband. "Too much socializing, most likely. I haven't had to host that many people in ages."

"Yeah," her husband said uncertainly. "Yeah, I'm sure that's it. Well, you should go rest. You've had a long day. I'll clean all this up."

"I feel like I should refuse, but really, I think you might be right." She laid a hand on his arm. "Thank you. Wake me for dinner, will you?"

He said sure thing and went about collecting the torn apart bits of streamers and the discarded plates with half-eaten slices of cake and the party hats that had been taken off and stomped on, or perhaps sat on, and he threw them all unceremoniously into a large garbage bag. His pigtailed daughter trailed in his wake, picking up items of her own, some of which were trash and some of which, like the small elephant figurine they kept on the kitchen counter, were most definitely not.

An hour later, the house was in order again, and he looked around proudly, knowing how pleased Mary would be when she woke up. Then he decided to go about making dinner, figuring she'd be half starved by the time she got up. All they'd eaten since breakfast was cake, and he hadn't even seen her eat more than a single small slice.

Another hour and dinner was ready: crab cakes and cornbread and mashed potatoes with cheese and bits of bacon sprinkled on top. All of Mary's favorites.

He went upstairs. He knocked on the bedroom door. He waited ten seconds, and then he knocked again.

No answer.

"Mary," he called out softly, then, a little louder, "Mary? Are you awake in there?"

He pushed the door open. The outline of his wife's body could be seen beneath the white sheets on the bed. Her head was turned away from him, and for a single, peaceful moment he stood in the doorway of their bedroom, watching her sleep.

The moment was over before it had begun, really.

The last peaceful moment for Jacob Tertium.

54

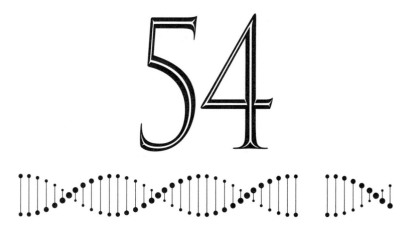

In another world, another life, Jacob Tertium did not have to watch his wife die.

Though, of course, the alternative was much worse, in its own way.

In every other version of this story, Jacob Tertium woke up one morning and, instead of finding his wife's body still and cold beside him, he found no one at all.

No note, no last word, no explanation.

This was the Jacob Tertium who was first angry and then fearful and then nothing at all. This was the Jacob Tertium who forgot he had a daughter, as if she had vanished right along with his wife—until, of course, those terrible moments when he suddenly did remember her. And then he became a man who didn't resemble in the least the Jacob Tertium whom Mary Dubose had fallen in love with.

That version of Jacob lost the ability to speak with words when he lost his wife—and chose instead to speak with fists.

This was the Jacob Tertium who didn't notice when his daughter *did* disappear one night, off to the same distant land of mysteries and secrets as his wife, though of course he would never know this. All he would know was that he was alone.

It was in the house of this Jacob Tertium that Everly always felt trapped. Suffocated. Worse than all that, she felt powerless. She was always searching for an escape, for a reason to leave.

This Everly never remembered her mother, who had found the building and stayed when she was too young to hold any real memories of the time before. All this Everly knew was that her home was cold, and silent (except when it was far, far too loud), and it was not a place for staying.

Then one day, as she was walking nowhere and anywhere, her feet carried her to a building where she met a man with a beeping machine and a wild dream. Again and again her feet brought her back there, until the day they decided to stay.

And then they could never leave again.

Everly never regretted finding the building when the alternative was a father with harsh words and harsher fists. She sought it early, and found it early, and found a home, of sorts, where she had never truly had one. Found a reason for living, where her father had refused to offer her one. And found a place where finally she had a voice.

Finally, she had control.

And she would do anything to keep it that way.

55

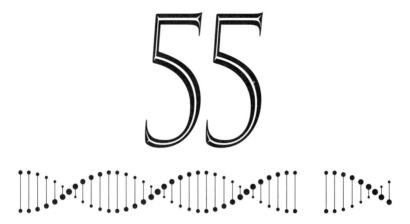

"Where are we going?"

Luca was walking quickly to keep up with Dr. Dubose's increasingly brisk pace as he headed away from the room Luca had woken up in—which, surprisingly, had been a testing room right down the hall from where he usually slept. They were still on the first basement level, but something told Luca that Everly was far, far away from there. So where were they going?

"Down," was Dr. Dubose's only response.

Luca glanced over his shoulder at Michael, who was also plodding along after them, though he looked less put out about it than Luca felt. Michael shrugged when he caught Luca's expression. He thought the kid might have even been grinning, and he wondered what Michael could possibly find to grin about at a time like this.

There was something about that kid . . .

It was picking at the insides of Luca's brain, and he couldn't snag what it was.

They reached the elevator, where Dr. Dubose took out a ring that was full to the brim with different size keys, where he selected a small silver one that he inserted into the panel, right next to the button labeled B2.

Luca had never used the elevator; he'd never had a key before. And, as yesterday had been the proof, it never would have allowed him inside, anyway.

And B2. Even Luca, who knew more about the building than most of the runners and certainly all the residents, still had little idea as to what was on the lowest level of the Eschatorologic, save the rooms he and Everly had searched together looking for Caleb and the few rooms of files he had been sent to in the past.

Is this where they'd find Everly?

Dr. Dubose continued to walk, making turns at breakneck speed as he maneuvered his way across the floor. It was clear he knew where he was going, and Luca had to wonder at that. It was no small secret that Dr. Dubose knew more about what happened in this building than anyone else, except perhaps the Warden. But how much did he know about what was happening right now, after he'd been gone for so long? How much did he know about Everly?

Eventually they reached a door that Dr. Dubose paused in front of. He rummaged through his ring of keys again until he found a gold one with a long stem and a round head.

Inside was nothing but a blank wall.

No, Luca realized a moment later. No, that was wrong. Stepping farther into the room, he saw that what he had initially assumed to be a wall was a divider, set up in front of the door in such a way that it blocked the rest of the room from sight. With a huff, Dr. Dubose pushed one side of the divider away, making an opening that he walked through, to the other side of the room. Luca and Michael exchanged a bewildered look before following him.

On the other side of the divider was an all-black room with a single desk at the back and a wall of screens. It looked oddly similar to the surveillance room, Luca thought. And in fact, walking closer to the screens, he recognized many of them from the same feeds that he was so used to watching, hour after hour, day after day. Only, the more he looked, the more he saw others, too. Other cameras into other rooms that he had never seen before—the hidden spaces that had been kept a secret, even from him. Luca frowned as he looked over all of it. What was this place?

Dr. Dubose seated himself in the chair behind the desk, lips turning up in satisfaction. "It shouldn't be long now," he said. "There's not much to do but wait, so you might as well get comfortable."

Luca looked again around the small room—empty, save for the desk and the screens—and wondered how anyone was supposed to be comfortable in that space.

"What are we doing in here?" Luca asked. Anxiety was creeping back in, right alongside the curiosity he felt as he tried to examine the new windows at his disposal. The new angles into this building he thought he had known so well. "Where's Everly?"

"Oh, she'll be along shortly."

Luca wanted to punch a wall. The old man clearly was set on not giving him answers, even here, even after everything he'd endured to get here.

Michael didn't seem nearly as put out as Luca felt. He walked over to the desk, blue eyes scanning over the contents, as though he'd be able to make any more sense of it than Luca could. It was all junk, or gibberish, or cleverly hidden secrets. Nothing Luca knew how to use. Michael's hand reached out, then, and Luca thought he saw the kid pick up something—a letter opener? For a moment, Michael held it in his hand, wide eyes staring down at it. Then he closed his fingers around the tool and backed a few steps away from the desk.

"I don't know," Michael mumbled, the excited light in his eyes already dimming. "This—this doesn't feel right."

Dr. Dubose chuckled. "Of course, it doesn't. You aren't used to the building's patterns yet, Michael, so of course you would see this as wrong. But it's all right. All will sort itself out soon."

None of Dr. Dubose's words made sense anymore. Luca tried to catch the man's eye, but it was almost like he was *avoiding* him, which did not sit well with Luca. Realizing that he was unlikely to get any answers from Dr. Dubose, Luca instead faced the wall of screens, searching for any signs of

Everly. It was hard, as there were even more screens down here than in the surveillance room, and many of them he wasn't used to. Not like upstairs, where he knew the shape of every angle in every camera, where he could spot when something was wrong almost before it had even happened. But down here, with these new screens, his eyes stumbled blindly from one to the next, looking for any hint or trace or breath of her. Any indication that she was still alive, that she was okay.

"Who uses this room, anyway?" Luca asked as he searched the screens.

"The Warden." This came from Michael, whom Luca had nearly forgotten about, as he was standing so quietly away from them. "This is the Warden's room." Michael's eyes pinned onto Dr. Dubose, who Luca was strangely pleased to see had paled somewhat. "Isn't it?"

A pause. And then, Dr. Dubose let out an uncertain chuckle. "A very perceptive young man, aren't you? Now how did you come to that conclusion?"

Another pause, longer than the first, in which Michael's eyes turned distant and foggy. "I think I dreamed it," he said in a faint voice.

Dr. Dubose was openly staring at Michael. "Fascinating," he said. "Michael, I do believe you and I are going to have some fun when all of this is over."

"She's coming back here, isn't she?"

Dr. Dubose considered Michael for a long moment before responding. "In a manner of speaking, yes. Yes, she is."

Luca didn't know what to make of everything that was happening in front of him. Before he had time to process anything, really, his attention caught on one of the screens, like a magnet drawn to a sheet of metal. His heart slowed, stopped. Jump-started itself and started to spin.

"Everly," he whispered, taking a step closer to the screen. "It's Everly."

And it was, though from the angle of this camera, Luca could not make out where she was—except that it appeared she was standing in a gray bedroom—nor whom she was in the company of.

All he could see was her. All he could ever see was her.

56

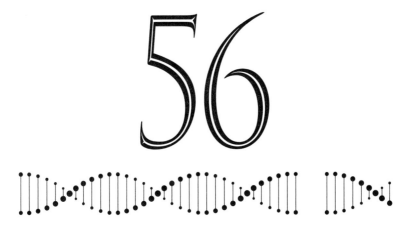

"No," everly whispered, snapping back to herself, away from the torrential thoughts filling her head as the Warden tried to pull her away from Lois's room, tried to drag her somewhere new. It was like the other woman *expected* her to go along with it, to just fall into place.

Probably because that's what she did, however many years ago this happened for her, Everly realized. But it wasn't going to happen to her. She wouldn't *let* it. This was Everly, taking a stand in the battle against herself.

The Warden stood up tall, staring her down, and Everly understood that it was supposed to be intimidating, but by then, she'd seen far worse. Her mind flitted for half a second back to the white room before she shook her head to banish the image.

Everly crossed her arms, not caring if it came across as petulant. "I'm not going anywhere else with you. Whatever you need to say, you can say it here. But it won't change anything."

The Warden's eyes narrowed to slits as she glared at Everly. "Insolent girl, you don't even know why you're resisting."

"I'm resisting because you're *unhinged,*" she said, voice rising. But this felt right. This felt like fighting back against the rogue thoughts in her head, and she embraced that chance. "I don't know what you want from me"—*oh, but how she did*—"but you can't have it. You won't make me more a part of this," she gestured vaguely around in the air, "than you already have. I'm done. I'm out."

"You're out," the Warden sneered. "Fool, where would you go? Would you leave? Run away from the building, you're running away from any chance of living. You'd die within hours of being out there. Is that what you want? Are you so desperate to escape your fate that you'd sacrifice your own life?"

"It's not my fate." Everly shook her head, backing a step away from the Warden. "And it *never* will be."

Lois's room was small, though, and it was quickly apparent that there was nowhere she could possibly run. Before Everly could decide what to do, the Warden clapped her hands. Within moments, a horde of runners appeared at the door—bulky frames, blank faces. A spike of panic shot through Everly, and she backed up until she pressed against the far wall.

"Someone grab her," the Warden said in a flat voice. "Bring her with us. We have more to see."

"No," Everly said, pressing more firmly against the wall, and then louder, "*No!* Back away!"

The runners, of course, did not listen to her, and soon enough two had grabbed her arms, a third wrapping thick arms around her torso, lifting her up off the ground as though she weighed nothing at all.

"*Let me go,*" she screamed, trying to kick out at the runner who held her, twisting in their grasp in an attempt to find some way to bite them, to make them release her.

It was useless. The runner was completely unfazed by her writhing, plowing on steadily down the hallway after the Warden, until they reached the elevator. By then, Everly had gone limp, fear slithering through her restrained form.

They descended to the lowest floor of the Eschatorologic. It reminded Everly now of the day she had stumbled down here on her own, rather than being carried unwillingly in the arms of a runner. That had been the day she found the white room, covered in blood. The day she found Luca. The day she spent the night in the Eschatorologic and set everything in motion.

It was also the day she had seen that woman on the hundredth floor. The one whom Jamie brutalized. The one who didn't speak, or move, or react—likely, Everly now was beginning to see, because she had surpassed that threshold where her body could no longer keep up with her mind.

The woman who looked like her mother.

"What happened to my mother?" she found herself asking, the words spoken in a carrying whisper as Everly was hauled in the bulky arms of a runner down the black hall.

The Warden was already ten strides ahead, and so Everly didn't really expect her to hear the question, much less answer it. Yet, after a pause that was long and thick and crammed with all the things that Everly knew she would never be able to fully see, fully understand, even having the Warden's thoughts filling up her head, came a response.

"She was my friend, you know."

"I know," Everly said. She didn't know how, but somehow the statement felt right. Except clearly, something had gone very, very wrong. Everly twisted again in the runner's grasp, only to have their arms squeeze her in return. "What did you do to her?"

Another pause, longer and thicker than the first, if possible. "I didn't do anything."

"You had to have," Everly pushed, voice rising again. She felt the runner's arms tighten their hold around her, so she lowered her voice again. "She wasn't supposed to die."

"You're right," the Warden said, and Everly's eyes shot toward the Warden at her admission. "She wasn't. That was the beginning, I think. When she left, and never returned. That was the beginning of it all."

"What do you mean?"

"I mean that she was supposed to keep coming. She was supposed to fall into the pattern of the building, and she was supposed to stay here forever, which would have allowed her to live. After she was married, after she had you, she was supposed to be drawn back, again and again. I know, I've seen it."

"So why didn't she?"

Ahead of her, Everly saw the slightest shake of the Warden's head. "I don't know."

They continued in silence after that for a few minutes before Everly asked, in a voice even more quiet than before, "And my dad?"

"He was a disruption," came the Warden's response. Her voice had lost all softness from before, hardening into the cruel sneer Everly thought she was beginning to associate with the woman. Arrogant and controlled. Then, "We're here."

The Warden placed her palm flat against the surface of a door that looked just like all the others surrounding it. Instead of simply clicking unlocked, like all the other doors Everly had encountered in the building, this one let out a shrill beep, and then the door slid into the wall, leaving only a gaping hole in its wake.

She could do that, too. Everly knew that if she had approached that door before the Warden, she would have been able to open it just as easily.

Not that she would. Not that she *ever* would.

She also knew, in the same way she was growing to know everything, what she was very likely to find inside the room with the sliding door when she entered it. Nonetheless, even knowing, in that distant, undefinable way, even amid the suspicions that were creeping in around her, it was still a shock to see it with her own eyes.

Inside were two people. The first was Jamie, who looked up from the computer in front of him with a scowl, only to see who was entering and immediately straighten. His eyes shifted from the Warden to Everly with more understanding than even Everly felt just yet. She wondered how many times he had been through this. How many versions of her he had already encountered. The runner roughly dropped Everly to her feet, but no sooner was she standing on solid ground than she felt a hand roughly grab onto her arm, restraining her from going anywhere.

"Ma'am," Jamie said, his attention focused wholly on the Warden now. His Warden. "It's nearly done. Do you want to see?"

"Yes," the Warden said with a nod. "I want to show her."

The runner shoved Everly forward, causing her to stumble over her own feet. It was strange, the duality of feeling so prepared to wind up exactly here, yet so caught off guard by the reality of it. She didn't want to see what she knew she was about to, but she also knew that she had little choice.

He was propped up against a long sheet of metal with his feet resting on a step, so that it almost looked like he was standing up. His eyes were still closed, his skin still ashen, his lips still blue. Wires were attached to his head and chest and arms, all leading into the computer that Jamie had positioned in front of him. An IV led into one of the blue veins in his left arm from a bag of purplish liquid that Everly didn't want to consider the contents of.

Nearly against her will, she found herself coming up right next to him, watching his very still face for any signs of movement. The body was different, a distant part of her mind was telling her. Bigger, stronger, bulkier. It didn't look weak anymore. He had been transformed. Reborn. Everly knew all of this, without having to be told, because the words were all hers. The Warden's. Everly's. So, she knew the reasons, she knew the process, she knew what was happening inside the stiff body propped up in front of her.

Nonetheless.

Nonetheless, her breath caught when his eyes flickered, shifted beneath their lids, and finally opened.

Everly looked into the dark eyes of what had formerly been Caleb Arya with something like a bittersweet resolution. He looked back at her without seeing her. Without seeing anything, really, she knew.

It was him, and it wasn't.

She was her, and she wasn't.

They all were. They all weren't.

The Warden was watching her. Everly could hear the words she would have said, in a time past, or yet to come. *He wasn't strong enough for the testing,* she would have said. *So, we made him something new. Something better. Something stronger, so that he can continue to serve the building, even now. As all the runners before him have.*

This time, she didn't have to say any of that. Everly already knew. The words were already there. In their place, her hyperventilating filled the open air, breaths coming faster and faster, more and more erratic.

"No," was all she could find it in herself to say anymore. That battle was raging in her head again, voices whispering in slithery voices, *yes yes yes*. She tried to put her head in her hands, but the runner wouldn't let her. "No," she moaned. "No, no, no."

The Warden only watched her. And eventually, she smiled.

57

A LOVE STORY THAT WASN'T meant to be:

Once upon a time, a girl met a boy. A boy met a girl. They fell in love, as only people with no other choice can. They filled the darkness around them with the light they felt when they were together. They were happy.

Girl and boy continued to be in love, longer than they were meant to be, and made choices that in another life, another time, they might not have. They didn't regret these choices, not at the time.

The boy thought the girl was everything he would ever need in life. He thought she was brilliant, and radiant, and fierce beyond all reason. He was a logical person, but he lost all reason around her. He didn't mind this. He would gladly sacrifice reason for her.

The girl thought the boy would show her parts of life that she never would have thought she needed. He showed her what it meant to have someone to look after, to be excited for.

To fear for.

Girl and boy thought they could make it, thought they could defy the odds, the fates, the forces that they already knew were working against them. They knew what was supposed to happen in their story, and they decided together that would never come to pass.

Unfortunately, they both underestimated the strength of said forces that would perpetually be against them.

Girl didn't know that she would find the knife in her hand until it was much too late.

Boy didn't know that he would find the knife in his neck until it was much, much too late.

They had both seen it, but they hadn't believed it.

Girl had loved boy. She had, she truly had.

And boy had loved girl, which made it all the worse when he fell.

All the worse when she rose in the aftermath.

Theirs was a love story that was and wasn't meant to be. It always ends the same. It always will.

58

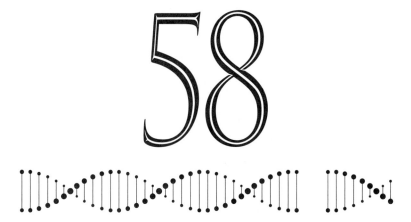

Jacob Tertium knew how his daughter's story was supposed to end.

Years ago, after Richard Dubose had sat him and his wife down and told them the truth of the building, Jacob had thought he could change things. He'd thought he could make a better life for his family, outside of the prison that he knew the Eschatorologic would be for them.

So, they all stayed away.

And yet. And yet his wife still did not survive. Still, he was left alone, looking after a daughter who could never know what had happened to her mother. Jacob did not relish this burden, or the secrets it necessitated, but now he had only her, and he would never risk losing that.

He did not tell his daughter about the building. He did not tell his daughter what had happened to her mother. He did not tell his daughter what was special about her blood, her bones, her very self. He didn't tell her anything.

And for a while, it seemed to work. He knew how it was supposed to go, had gleaned enough from his brief time being part of that world to understand that she should have left already.

She should have found the building on her own by now. So, he thought maybe this time they had done it. Maybe, if she never even stepped foot inside, she would be safe in the ways that her mother hadn't been. Maybe it would all turn out all right.

But then the headaches started—about a year before her twenty-fifth birthday. They were just like her mother's had been, right before . . .

Not long after that, Jacob received a letter, slipped under his door with no signature at the bottom. It didn't matter; Jacob knew who had sent it.

The time is drawing near. You know it is. You need to make a decision, soon. Come and visit me—you remember the way, I'm sure. I think you know what has to happen.

It was all happening again, the exact same as twenty years earlier. And he couldn't—he couldn't lose her too.

Even after all these years, Jacob remembered the way. He remembered how to spot the building his eyes never should have seen.

He thought he was protecting her.

He thought he could find a way, a way where it could end differently than before.

He thought he could make a difference, a change, *anything* that would keep her from that place, from the path he never wanted her to have to face.

Little did Jacob know, that wasn't the reason Dr. Richard Dubose had called him to the Eschatorologic. Jacob, Richard understood, would be too strong a tether to the outside world for Everly. She might still come to the building, but he'd never be able to convince her to willingly stay there if her dad was still out in the real world for her to return to. So, Richard decided to take matters into his own hands—or rather, into the hands of a tall man dressed in red, with sharp knives in a white room.

And just like that, Everly's final tether to the outside world was severed.

Jacob Tertium never stood a chance.

But with his sacrifice, Richard would have claimed, Everly Tertium just might.

59

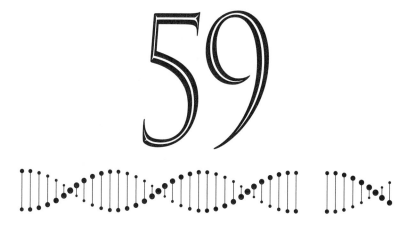

"LEAVE US," THE WARDEN SAID to both Jamie and the runner who had been restraining Everly. As soon as the runner moved away from Everly, she collapsed to her knees, breathing deeply to halt the nausea that roiled through her. Her mind was cracking, splinters of images and thoughts dissipating through her head. Caleb in that red room, dying but not dying. Caleb propped up and unseeing—Caleb but not Caleb. Her parents dying, though she hadn't actually seen either of them die. Luca dying, even though she hadn't seen that, either.

(Yet.)

A baby being taken from her arms and sent away.

Person after person after person with bloody strips on their arms and lacerations on their scalps and screams vibrating from their throats.

Everly, in that white room, that terribly, terribly white room, with the blood and the pain and the screams.

Sometime while Everly had been hunched over, the Warden had approached her, and now stood looming over her.

"It's time, you know."

"*No,*" Everly said, the word starting to lose all meaning. Nonetheless, she lifted her head; through burning tears, she met the eyes of the Warden.

A version of herself whom she refused to become. And in one final stance against the voices filling her head, Everly climbed slowly to her feet. "I might not be able to stop what you do here, and I might not be able to take back anything you've already done. But I will *never* play that part." Everly now stood toe-to-toe with the Warden—both women the exact same height, but for a moment, only a moment, Everly felt taller. She felt stronger, and so she took that strength and placed both hands against the Warden's shoulders, shoving her so that the other woman stumbled back a step. The Warden's face remained stony, not flinching, but Everly's resolve remained.

"And then there's Michael," Everly said loudly, jabbing a finger in the Warden's direction. "Your son, right? Not that you've ever treated him that way. Oh yes, I know all your dirty little secrets. The things you did that you weren't supposed to, all the ways you went against what all the other Wardens before you had done."

She knew this because she could see it now. Without intending to, the story of this Warden's life, as well as all those who had come before her, played like overlapping movies in her head, showing her everything. So, she knew everything about them, including the child the Warden had given birth to, who never should have existed.

She also thought she could see how it had happened. How Michael had come to be. She could now see the threads where this Warden's life had diverged from all the others. Earlier, she'd mentioned how Everly's mother had been a friend to her. Mary Dubose had always been a friend for Everly Tertium.

Until suddenly she wasn't.

Mary Dubose was supposed to come into the building, and she was supposed to stay, and she was supposed to befriend Everly Tertium, and somehow that factor was usually enough to keep all the Everlys and all the Lucas from going too far. Maybe Mary was a voice of wisdom, showing Everly that there was no real future to be had in a building like this. Or maybe with Mary, her friendship was enough, and Everly never needed to go searching for more.

But when Richard had told Mary—Everly's mother, Richard's daughter, the catalyst for all of this—to stay home, she had. And then she had died, when she was very much supposed to live.

Without that friendship, the Warden, who hadn't always been the Warden, had gotten pregnant.

And Michael had come to be.

Now, trembling where she stood, Everly fixed the Warden with the fiercest glare she could manage, hot tears burning at the back of her eyes for this boy who'd never been allowed to experience a normal childhood. For the lives that had been stripped from all of them. "That kid deserved so much better than you for a parent. He deserved so much better than to grow up in a building like this, all alone. We all deserve better than to be here, but he was never even given the facade of a choice."

Through all of this, the Warden hadn't spoken a word. Nor had her expression altered, except now the same sneer as before crossed over her lips.

"The boy was a mistake. Nothing more, nothing less. But he will find his place in the building. Just like you."

Red bled into Everly's vision, blocking out everything else. She heard screaming in her ears—her own screams, probably—and before she knew what she was doing, she had charged up to the Warden again, shoving her once more, but harder, putting all of her force behind the movement, until the other woman's legs buckled, and she fell to her knees, eyes widening ever so slightly in what might have been shock.

"I'm done," Everly said quietly, now looming over the other woman, whose head was tilted down, so her auburn hair fell across her eyes. "I might not know how to leave yet, or how to help the people you've trapped here, but I'm done being a part of this initiation ritual, or whatever it is you think we're doing. You're on your own."

With that, Everly spun on her heel, walking confidently out the door, trying to tell herself she felt victorious. Pretending she hadn't seen as the Warden shifted her head so that the hair slid away from her face. Pretending she hadn't seen the smile that had crossed the Warden's lips in those final seconds while she was still sprawled out across the floor. Pretending the smile hadn't looked triumphant, hadn't looked pleased.

Everly shoved lingering doubts about the Warden away. She'd hinted that she didn't have much more time until she became like all the other people upstairs—until she wouldn't be able to be the Warden anymore. So Everly just had to find a way to wait out the time until then. She had to find a way to survive, and then it would all be okay. They'd find a way out, and they'd make it. She just had to wait.

Without really meaning to, Everly's feet had decided to direct her toward the office. Even though she had never been there before, she knew exactly where to go, and though a nagging doubt at the back of her mind questioned whether she should follow her feet in this one instance, she didn't know where else to go anymore.

She placed her hand flat against the black paint of the door and waited for the click she knew would come. *Let this time be different,* she thought, with her hand still on the door. *I'll do anything for it to be different. Give anything for it to change.*

As she thought the words, Everly felt a strange warmth spreading through her hand, into the wood of the door. Surprised, she jerked her hand away and looked at it, expecting it to be red or singed. Nothing. It was just a hand. Hesitantly, she reached out and tapped a finger against the door. It was cool, solid. Just a door.

Everly frowned but quickly shook her head. There were by far stranger things to have happened in that building. Pushing the door open, Everly encountered the blank surface of the divider that sectioned apart the room. A breath, and then she walked around the divider, to the rest of the room.

And then she saw him.

"Luca," she said. She blinked and she knew him, then she blinked again and she still knew him, but it was different.

She knew how this story was supposed to end now. And she didn't like it.

Blink blink blink and she was back in the moment and Luca had rushed over to her, wrapping his arms around her in a tight embrace that she had barely even registered. He pulled away and looked her over with worried eyes.

"What did they do to you? How did you find us?"

Everly shook her head. "I don't know. I don't know what happened." Her eyes strayed to the desk, behind which Richard was sitting. He was watching her closely, but not with the same concern as Luca. In his eyes was something else. Something more dangerous, perhaps. Or more interesting.

"But you're okay?" Luca asked, pulling Everly's attention back to him. "You're really okay?"

She tried to smile. "Yes," she said, though she wasn't so sure anymore. The Warden hadn't hurt her, not exactly, but she'd done something that Everly thought might have been worse. She'd *changed* her, and Everly still wasn't sure how much. "And you?" Her eyes flicked from Luca over to Michael, who was looking at Everly with a more guarded expression than she had ever seen on the boy before.

"Yeah, yeah, we're good," Luca said, running a hand absently through his hair. He laughed awkwardly, maybe a little unsteadily. "We're all good." He looked relieved, but also unhinged, in a way. Everly knew how he felt. "So, what do we do now?"

Everly's gaze rested on Michael, standing silently across the room.

And she knew.

Almost without knowing what she was saying, Everly whispered the words out into the open: "We leave."

Despite how quietly she had said it, all eyes in the room were on her.

She knew the answer now. Finally, that missing piece clicked into place in her head, and she could see it.

Michael was not brought into the building. Not like Everly. Luca. Everyone else there. He did not arrive, drawn to the front entrance or carried unwillingly in the arms of someone dressed in red.

He was born there.

Ten years ago, Michael was born inside the building, which itself was not exactly a place or a time, so by all reasonable accounts, Michael did not exist anywhere.

Except that wasn't true. He clearly did exist, which led Everly to believe that he in fact existed *everywhere.*

More than that, he was the child of two people with the genetic anomaly. She now knew—oh, how well she knew—that the file she had found with Michael's name on it, with hers and Luca's names listed beneath it, hadn't been a lie.

Michael was born to the Everly who came before her, the Luca who had come before him. He was, as far as she knew, the only person who'd been born to not one, but *two* enhanced persons.

She thought back to what Luca had told her, too. About how Michael always seemed like he was trying to escape, was always running for the doors, without even knowing why.

She thought she could see why now. Michael knew—or his blood knew, or his DNA, or something else inside of him—that he would be okay, if he were to leave the Eschatorologic. He wasn't impacted by the same draw that kept the rest of them tied to the building because his body didn't know to anticipate anything else. Any other way of living, any world other than this half-world that he had always known.

And then she thought of the first time she had met Michael. She thought of touching his hand, the memories that had flown through her. But more than that: she'd felt *freedom* in his touch, as though his very being had been trembling with the need to burst out of the building, to fly far, far away.

Even more than all that was an answer, drizzled in her ear. She almost would have said it was the building trying to tell her something, trying to speak now. It wasn't a voice, exactly. More like a feeling—a feeling telling her she was right.

The secret was Michael's blood. The secret was *him.*

Michael really was their way out of here.

The way to escape this building, the Warden. Her fate.

All this time, the others had all been watching her, watching as she silently processed everything she did and did not know. She saw Richard, who stared at her curiously, a furrow growing between his brows. Luca, whose eyes had taken on a wildness in the course of the day. So much so that he almost didn't even seem like himself anymore. Michael, who looked more wary now than before. He had something clenched in his fist, held tight against his chest.

"What?" Luca asked, breaking into the brittle silence that had settled upon the room. "What is it? Do you know what we need to do?"

Her eyes stayed locked on Michael as she opened her mouth. As she prepared to tell them all what she knew. Their way out.

In the space of the millisecond between when Everly opened her mouth and when the words could come out, two things happened, too swiftly to have been noted by anyone who wasn't observing very closely.

One: in a gray bedroom on the second floor of the Eschatorologic, in a recently prepared bed with gray sheets and gray pillows and a gray quilt, lay a woman with auburn hair and blue eyes ringed in green. As she stared up at the ceiling, she took in her final breath as the Warden, and in the next breath she had become little more than a shell.

Two: all those memories, all those thoughts, all that ability and life and purpose—all that energy, that unnatural, pesky, eternally goading energy—had to go somewhere. So, it did. It fled as far down into the Eschatorologic as it could, to a dark office with screens along one wall, where it found a younger woman with identical auburn hair and identical blue-green eyes, and they filled her up.

Everly took in a breath as Everly Tertium. And the next she took in as someone else. With that breath, the battle ended.

Her eyes cut around the room now. From Michael, whose eyes now radiated a fear they hadn't held moments before. To Luca, who was oblivious but had desperation leaking into his expression the longer Everly took to respond. To Richard, whose grin had blossomed into something wider. Something greedy.

“You did well,” she said in a voice that she both did and did not recognize as her own. Her eyes refocused on Luca, who looked more uncertain than before. “We all did, didn’t we? And look where it’s brought us. Right where we’ve always been. Right where we will always be.”

“Everly, what are you talking about?” Luca asked.

“You know,” she said, “you made an excellent hero for this story. It’s too bad, really, that we don’t need a hero anymore.”

Before anyone could react, she had reached behind her, to the desk, reaching for a perfectly sharpened letter opener, which had never been used on letters. This was how it had always gone before, after all, and so that was what she was searching for. It was always a perfectly sharpened letter opener against the perfectly exposed skin of his neck, and it always ended quickly that way. There was always too much blood for it to be anything else.

Except this time, the letter opener was gone. The Warden before her had left it on the desk, and it should have been there, ready and waiting for her to use, except it wasn’t.

Except it was gone, and it shouldn’t have been.

The moment was nearly over; the others would respond soon enough if she didn’t do something. So instead, she reached for the only other object in sight on the desk: a lamp. Picking up the lamp, which was heavier than it looked, she took two steps and was upon Luca.

The extra second it took her to pick up the lamp, rather than the slim letter opener, allowed something to click inside her head. Something—a voice, an urge, a desire, *something*—made her hands slow as she brought the lamp down along the side of Luca’s temple. Even this lesser thump vibrated up her arms, and time seemed to suspend (even more than usual) as she stood, lamp in hand, staring at Luca.

For the span of a single breath, Luca continued to look at her, and a different part of her head—such a confusing jumble now, that head—worried that it hadn’t been enough. She raised the lamp again, preparing to crash it down over him once more—fiercer, if need be. But no. His eyes fluttered, his knees bending beneath him. She watched as Luca’s body collapsed to the ground at her feet, a bleeding gash now apparent on his forehead.

He did not move again.

Without prompting, the door to the office banged open, and a single runner entered, taking hold of Luca's ankles and dragging him unceremoniously away from the room. This had been expected, clearly. Prepared for. The door clamored shut behind the runner, and silence fell across the office.

60

The warden stared at the just-closed door. Then, from the other side of the room came something that sounded an awful lot like a squeak. She looked in its direction and saw Michael, who had turned pale and wide-eyed as he watched the events playing out in front of him. She began to step toward him, something else trickling aimlessly through her thoughts as she looked down at the small boy, but before she could do anything, he had bolted, running out of the office and down the hall.

"Leave him. We have more important things to discuss," came a voice from behind the desk. The voice of Dr. Richard Dubose. Funny, she had almost forgotten he was there. Now, she sized him up, eyes slowly traveling over his tweed coat, his wrinkle-lined face. Assessing. She had the thoughts of all her predecessors in her head now; they'd never liked the doctor all that much. Mostly, they saw him as a pest, someone who couldn't conform to the balance of the building. She'd taken one life today, why not two?

Lamp still in hand, the Warden took a step, circling around the desk.

"Such as?" she asked, distracting him. But also, she wanted to know. There would only ever be one Dr. Richard Dubose in the building. If she was going to be rid of him, she would at least keep with her the last dregs of his secrets. "What is it you think is so important we need to get into it now?"

Richard's eyes were wide, his breathing erratic. "Your life," he said hoarsely. "I can save it, Everly."

"Don't call me that," she snapped. It wasn't who she was anymore, not really.

She saw Richard swallow. "You don't have to be confined to this," he said. "A life in the building, a life of passing your legacy on, one to the next. You—you're nothing but another in a long line of short-lived monarchs."

"Yes," she answered dryly. "A short-lived monarch in this castle that you trapped me in. You're the reason I'm here, you know. You knew what would happen when you pulled me in here, when you invited me to this building." She scoffed. "You knew I'd never be able to leave."

"Don't you see?" Richard wheezed. "I *saved* you. Out there? You'd already be dead. But in here, we have time now. Time to set things right. And I finally know how to do it—how to give you a full life, rather than having it cut off at twenty-five."

"And then what?" she asked, edging still closer to him, circling around the desk. "So, you found a way, will you save all of them? All of your precious residents, your test subjects locked in this building: will you show them the way out, too? Let them have a life away from the building?"

"Well," Richard stuttered, face turning red. "I don't—that's not the point here. The point is *you,* Ever—" He cut himself off before he could finish saying the name. Starting over, he said, "It's only about you. About saving you, the way I couldn't save your mother. I sent her out there to die, kept her away. That was my fault, but I can give you another chance. The chance she didn't have. That's what all this has been for—bringing you here, increasing the testing. It's why I told your father to come to the building, why I gave him over to Jamie. It's all been for you."

The mention of her father—or someone's father—didn't faze her. Some buried part of her was probably screaming, but the rest of her was numb.

Didn't even care. For most versions of herself, the father of Everly Tertium had not been a man she'd ever want to mourn.

So instead of lashing out at the scientist before her, she studied him: this man who had seemed so large to her when she'd first met him. So vast and mysterious. Now he was just a small old man, cowering behind a desk that was rightfully hers. "Why do you want this so much?" she asked. "Why try so hard to save me? You don't even know me, you realize."

"Because," he said, voice breaking. "It's what she would have wanted."

"Who, your daughter?" The Warden barked out a hard laugh. "The woman you tossed aside to work on this little science experiment of yours? The woman you let die? No, you're not doing this for her. You're doing this because your ego can't stand the fact that you're not always in control. It can't stand the fact that you failed in the past, and so you're trying to compensate for that now. But you know what? I'm not here to appease your savior complex. I'm not your guinea pig anymore."

"That's not what I meant," Richard said, pleadingly. "I can help you, *save* you. I have the answer now; you just need to listen."

"Oh, but I already have the answer," the Warden said. She'd reached the other side of the desk, her fingers tightening around the lamp. "An interesting boy, that one." She watched with cruel pleasure as Richard's eyes widened, taking in her words. "Don't you see? I don't need you anymore. And this 'cure' you so desperately wanted for me? I don't need that, either. Why would I ever want to leave?"

Yes, all the voices in her head now chimed together. *We don't need him. We have everything we'll ever need. All the power we'll ever need.*

"This isn't you, Everly," Richard cried out desperately as she took another step closer to him, lamp still in hand.

And she knew it was meaningless coming from this man's mouth—what did he know about who she was?—but something else echoed in her mind, struggling to reach through, to break the surface. When it did, it was like a beacon cutting through a black night.

Evs, you can only ever be yourself, the voice said. *So, it's up to you to make sure you become the best version of yourself. And that's all you'll ever need to be.*

"No," she mumbled, almost to herself, backing up a step. She gripped her head with one hand, the voices inside fighting more and more for dominance, to take control. "No," she said louder, now doubling over. "*Get away.*"

She didn't know if she was speaking to Richard or to the voices; all she knew was that she had heard her dad's voice—her dad, whom she'd loved, who had died because of this sick man in front of her—and it was almost like he was there with her, fighting for her to be free.

"*No,*" she felt herself scream—a sound so sheer and distant from herself, she barely believed it was coming from her own mouth. But she could feel as her vocal cords shredded against each other with the sound, could hear the ringing in her ears as the scream vibrated through her skull, so she knew it must have belonged to her. "*No no no no no.*"

"SUBMIT," the voices in her head screamed back. "YOU WILL SUBMIT TO US. YOU WILL BE ONE WITH US."

"You can't have me—" she whimpered, but the voices only came back louder than before, intermingling with one another, one layer on top of another.

"YOU WILL DO AS WE SAY AND SUBMIT."

You can only ever be yourself. The second voice—her father's voice—slid in beneath the others, smoother than a stream of pure water being poured into her head. It was softer than the other voices, but stronger somehow, and it was those words that she clung to, that she grasped onto with all that remained of herself and used to pull free of all the other voices weighing her down.

"I am myself," she said, fingers of one hand digging into the side of her head, the other clasped tightly around the lamp. "I won't hurt them. I won't be a part of this anymore. I. Am. Not. *You.*"

And with that, a noise ripped from her throat, somewhere between a growl and a wail. Her eyes flew open, and while all she saw at first was black—black walls, black floor, black ceiling—she could *feel* as the voices retreated, slithering away until nearly all that was left was her.

Everly.

They weren't completely gone; she could feel the shadows of the voices still there, still somewhere inside her. But they were behind a wall in her head now, locked away out of sight. They weren't in control anymore.

And she'd do whatever it took to keep it that way.

"What did you do?"

Everly pivoted, facing the tweed-clad man who still cowered in front of her.

"What did you *do*?" he repeated.

"I am my own person," Everly said. As though to prove her point, she set the lamp down on the desk. There was no need for any more blood to be shed today.

"But you can't be," Richard cried out. "That's not how it works, that's not how it's ever worked."

"Well, today, it is." He should have been relieved to be alive, she thought. But instead he was only concerned for what she'd broken. For the hierarchy in the building she'd defied.

"Fine," Richard said shakily. "Fine, you're not the Warden, but that doesn't matter." She didn't know if that was quite true. She thought, on some level, that she was still the Warden. Everly and the Warden. One and the same. But that didn't seem to be what mattered to Richard right then. "It doesn't matter, I can still get you out. I can still be redeemed for my mistakes. You can still be saved."

"No," she said softly. Richard flinched with the word like he'd been struck. "I won't let you save me. Not if you won't save all the others, too."

"That's not how it—"

"It is how it works, if you let it be." She stared at him hard. "And besides, I won't let you use Michael like that. I won't let him be just another pawn in your elaborate game, in your desperation to absolve yourself of whatever you think you did to my mother. She died, and we're alive. You don't have to make new mistakes to make up for past ones. I know what it's like now to be used for what I am." She rubbed at her arms, which had healed completely sometime in the midst of the mess they'd been living through the past few days. "And if that's truly the only way for any of us to leave—with his blood—I won't ask him to do that. I won't ask him to give more than he's willing to—he's a ten-year-old boy."

And he's my son, she was surprised to find herself thinking. It wasn't true, in a strictly biological sense, but buried deep in her mind were still the lingering hints of the previous Warden's thoughts, her identity. That Warden may not have acted like much of a parent to Michael—may not have even known what parental love would look like, growing up with a complete absence of that very thing—but Everly knew what it was like to be a child who was loved, and she knew she could love Michael. And whatever that distant, aching part of her was that now saw herself as bonded to Michael, it screamed that she couldn't do this. She couldn't use him like this.

Everly knew that Richard was the only person in that building who would even know what to do with Michael's blood, the only person who could get her out. He was offering that to her now—freedom, the opportunity to go back to the real world, to her life.

But it would never be worth it if she left, knowing that hundreds of people remained.

And besides: what was out there for her anymore anyway? She'd never found a purpose in the real world—on that count, Everly and the past Wardens could relate. She didn't have anything to go back to. No family to return to.

But in here . . .

She thought again of Michael. And of Luca, though she grimaced to remember hitting him in the head with the lamp. She hoped—*hoped*—she'd managed to stay the Warden's arm enough that he'd be okay.

She thought of all the other people in that building, all the people who'd endured years of torture and captivity and trauma.

It was a never-ending cycle.

But all patterns have to end somewhere.

She looked down again at Richard, who was hunched nearly in half in front of her, almost as if he were bowing to her, waiting for her verdict.

She clapped her hands.

A handful of runners appeared at the office door, all hefty frames and blank stares.

"Take him away," Everly said, gesturing to the cowering old man. She would deal with him later. For now, it was enough for him to be locked away—to be put somewhere where he couldn't hurt anyone else.

Once they were gone and she was alone, Everly looked around the black office. *Her* office now. She spun in a slow circle, eyes glazing over as they stared at the room surrounding her.

Where to go from here? Where was there *to* go? She had decided not to leave, to remain in the building, and Everly didn't regret that choice, but now she had all the many, many questions of what that was going to look like.

She wouldn't be like any of the past Wardens; that much she knew. Oh sure, the voices were still there in her head, pushing back against the walls she'd put in place against them. But they were contained, for now at least. Should they someday manage to break free, well, she would deal with that when the time came.

For right now, however, it was much more pressing to figure out what kind of Warden she was going to be. The testing would have to go, of course. For the briefest of seconds her mind flicked back to that white room, that chair with all its straps. Yes. The testing would have to go.

But then what? She didn't understand everything about this building, certainly—she doubted anyone, even Richard, could ever truly know everything there was to know about the building—but she'd gathered enough from her time here, from the words of Jamie and Richard and, of course, from the thoughts of all the former Wardens, to understand that it did need their energy to exist. That hadn't been a lie, at least. And for the past several decades, the testing had fulfilled that role. In the absence of testing, the building would be deprived of the energy it so hungered for. And then what? It vanished? And what about them? Would they then vanish along with it? What would a vanished existence look like, Everly pondered. Would they even be aware of it if they were to disappear, right that very moment, along with the building they stood in?

Everly shook her head briskly, stepping closer to one of the walls in the office. There had to be another way. It couldn't just be about . . . pain. That seemed too crudely simple, too barbaric for a building such as this.

The thought surprised her, and she realized that somewhere amid being trapped and tortured and bombarded with many people's memories, she'd begun to form a strange affection for the building it all occurred in. She wasn't sure how much of that was also residual sentiments from former Wardens, but she thought probably this was mostly coming from herself. It wasn't the building's fault she was trapped here, she knew. In a twisted way, it wasn't even Richard's or Jamie's fault, or her predecessor's. By some tragic fluke of existence, she'd been born with the fatal genetic anomaly, and she knew in her heart this was another truth that had been buried in all the lies and misdirects: she would already be dead out there, if she had never found the building.

Which raised the question of which was worse: a life trapped forever in this building, or no life at all?

Everly studied one of the smooth, black walls in the office, laying a hand gently over the surface. Maybe it didn't have to be so bad here, she contemplated. Maybe, together, they could all find a way to change it. To make it less of a prison and more of a home. If they were all going to be stuck here together forever, the least they could do was find a way to make it a more bearable life. Even maybe, someday, a happy one.

But still there was the question of energy. Of finding a way to keep the building alive along with themselves.

Huffing out a frustrated breath, Everly tilted her head so that it was pressed against the wall. Through the wall, she could feel the minute vibrations that rolled through the building.

The Eschatorologic's energy.

I wish I could just give it to you, she thought. *I wish you could take what you needed, and it could be as easy as that.*

Almost as soon as the thought had left her mind, Everly felt a warmth in her skin where her forehead was pressed against the wall, where her hand was still held up on the wall next to it. Surprised, she jerked back, holding up her hand and staring at it.

Could it really be that easy? Could she really just . . . choose to gift the building the energy it needed, without the necessity for painful testing and flashy boxes?

Her mind strayed back to earlier, when she'd touched the door to the office. She'd felt that same warmth where her palm touched the building then, too. It hadn't hurt, hadn't even drained her—but she did remember feeling slightly more tired right after, though she'd been too caught up with other things at the time to make note of it. But it hadn't been the deep fatigue of having your life drained away from you; it had been more the satisfied sort of tired, like when you've finished a long day of work or accomplished something you're proud of. It was like that now, too. She hadn't realized it before, but now she thought she was beginning to see.

Tentatively, Everly reached out her arm again, putting her hand back in the same place on the black wall. She waited, holding her breath.

Nothing happened. No warmth, no tingling sensation. Just the cold surface of the wall against her skin.

Biting her lip, Everly closed her eyes, keeping her hand where it was. How did one give of one's energy? She thought back to the sensation of the former Warden's energy flooding down into her. Thought of what it had been like to have her energy unwillingly stripped from her in a testing room. Thought of the warmth she'd felt just moments before, when the smallest amount of her energy had spread from her hand into the building.

The energy was a piece of her, so surely it shouldn't be that hard to offer.

You can have some, she thought to the building. *I offer it freely to you. So you can live. So we all can.*

Slowly, the same warmth from before began to spread through Everly, starting with her spine and spreading out to the tips of her fingers, which rested against that office wall, bleeding from her flesh into the fabric of the building itself.

She let out an almost involuntary sigh, and it might have been her imagination, but she thought she felt the building sigh beneath her touch, too.

When it was done—when her skin had again gone cold—Everly removed her hand, gazing in awe at the wall, this small piece of a building that they were all connected to. Would always be connected to.

Her fingers flexed at the memory of the energy that had just flowed through them. They had a lot more to figure out, Everly knew. So much.

But this was a start.

A very good start.

61

On the lowest level of the Eschatorologic, in a dark, sweltering room sheathed in metal and hidden away from the rest of the building—for protection, supposedly; to keep all the rest from burning away to ashes just yet—was an incinerator. Large enough to fit a single body.

Inside was the broken body of a man. His arms were twisted over his chest, forming an off-center X. His head was bent to the side with a bloody gash near the temple that no one had thought to clean away.

He was going to be burned.

From across the room, a very tall man dressed in red pushed a button, then stood to the side as a low thrum sounded from within the incinerator—the old contraption gradually groaning to life. The first sparks of heat began to flicker—sparks that were meant to grow until they were hot enough to, well. Hot enough to incinerate a body.

For a moment, they continued to flicker beneath the platform that the body rested on.

But then. Before the sparks could ignite more properly into flames, the man inside the incinerator twitched. Shifted. Took in the barest of breaths.

He opened his eyes, and the building stared back.

This, the building mused. *This is new.*

And interesting.

The man heaved a hacking cough, rolling over sideways, until he collapsed to the floor, just beside the incinerator. Gripping his head, the man elicited a bone-shaking groan.

"Welcome back to the world of the living," a voice spoke over him. Hearing the voice and remembering the distinctly unpleasant heft of a lamp being crushed into his skull not long ago by a woman wielding that same voice, the man flinched. He was crouched down now just beside the incinerator—which, he distantly noted, was quieting down, as though someone had turned it off.

The woman turned to face the man dressed in red, who stood stoically across the room. "Leave us," she said calmly, tilting her head toward the door. And without a word, he obeyed.

Without lifting his eyes, the man on the floor sensed as the woman came over and knelt in front of him, so that out of the blurry peripheral of his vision he could see her auburn hair hanging loosely around her face.

"Luca." The woman spoke the word softly, almost like a prayer. She released a heavy breath that trailed warmly over his skin. He still refused to look at her but felt as her fingers reached out to trace gently over the welt on his head, brushing against the dried blood she had caused. "It shouldn't have happened that way."

The man still couldn't find the words to speak to her—this woman whom he was still so unsure about. His mind flitted back to that black office, to that lamp in her hand, to moments before, when he'd awoken inside the boxy, narrow interior of the incinerator.

But the woman continued, saying in the same soft tone, "I'm sorry," and her voice was so different from before, not at all like that of the woman who had bashed him in the head.

Not quite like the woman he'd been coming to know over the past few weeks, either. The woman he'd been coming to love.

No, it was somewhere in between. And he didn't know what that meant. But it was enough to finally make him lift his eyes.

As soon as he looked at her, their eyes met and held and exchanged a message of . . . a better future. Or the possibility of one. The possibility for a future together, a future all the prior Lucas and Everlys had missed. The woman extended a hand. "Come on," she said, the smallest of smiles beginning to tilt up her lips. "We have work to do."

Yes, the building decided as Luca Reyes took the hand of Everly Tertium. *This is going to be fun.*

ACKNOWLEDGMENTS

FIRST COMES THANKS TO GOD, for, well, for everything, but specifically right now all of my thanks for imbuing me with a creative spirit and filling me up with these stories I can share.

So many thanks go to my parents, Jeff and Twila Miles, who have always encouraged me to follow my dreams and do what I love. I want to thank my dad for always believing in me and being excited for my small achievements. And my mom, who was the first person to ever read a draft of this book all the way through—thanks for not giving up on me after reading that terrible draft, Mom, and for sticking with me and this wild book through to the finish line.

I'm gonna throw out a thanks to my four darling siblings as well—Carl, Jeffery, Felicia, and Madison—none of whom are readers, and who have each, on individual occasions, told me they probably wouldn't read my book, but they'll watch it if it ever gets made into a movie. Love you guys, and I love that you support me, despite not sharing my bookish passions.

Thanks also need to go to my cousin Amanda, who is my science fiction soul sister through and through. Thanks for always being up for nerding out with me, and thanks for your constant enthusiasm.

I also want to thank some of my nearest and dearest friends: Jessica Schultz, Carsyn Bernhardt, JJ Ward. You might not realize this, but I really couldn't have done this without you. Thank you for listening to my endless rambles about my ideas for this story in its way early versions, and for always getting excited for me and my writing, and for being so over-the-moon thrilled when I got this book deal. Thank you for being some of this book's first supporters.

A million thank yous need to go out to the entire CamCat staff, who have changed my life in more ways than one.

Thank you Helga Schier, one of my editors, for your insightful feedback at the beginning that helped me see my blind spots for my own story and helped mold it into something I can be proud of. And thank you Kayla Webb, my other editor, for taking the time to help bring my characters and their stories better to life. Thank you Elana Gibson as well, for your behind-the-scenes editorial work and help with this book, and for all you do on the acquisitions side of things: thank you for being part of the team who decided to take a chance on *The Building That Wasn't* and bring it on. I also really want to thank Laura Wooffitt, both for the time and care I know she puts into marketing and promoting every single one of CamCat's books, but especially thank you for the time and care she's given me. I've learned so much from you, and I'm so thrilled to know my book is being introduced to many readers by the work of your hands. Thank you also to Bill Lehto for your patience in walking through contract logistics with me, and for all you do in ensuring our books will be printed and out there for people to buy. Thank you to Maryann Appel for her absolutely stunning cover design; it's the perfect cover, Maryann, in every way. Thank you to Meredith Lyons for your hard work in helping my book to become its final product, to Gabe Schier and Jessica Homami for the effort you put into social media and the podcast, to MC Smitherman, Camryn Flowers, and Nicole DeLise for the ways in which you support this team and keep everyone afloat—and sane. And last, but most definitely not least, thank you to Sue Arroyo, CEO of CamCat Books, for believing first in me and then in my book and for pursuing this dream that now allows so many others' dreams to come true.

And also thank you thank you thank you to everyone I couldn't list, because writing out all of the friends and family who have been supportive over the years could take up an entire book, and I doubt anyone other than myself would actually want to read that. But I still appreciate each and every one of you, from the bottom of my heart.

And finally, thank you, dear reader, whoever you may be. I'm the kind of reader who always loves turning to the acknowledgments at the end, and it always fills me with joy to see the readers of the world being thanked. So, here's my thanks to all of you: Thank you for finding this book, and for picking it up, and for reading it all the way to the end of the acknowledgments. Thank you for taking a chance on this story. Just . . . thank you.

ABOUT THE AUTHOR

Abigail Miles decided to dedicate her life to stories from a young age, leading first to majoring in creative writing in college and now to spending far too much of her time attached to her computer, composing stories and books. Abigail currently lives in Boston, where all her time (or very nearly all her time) is spent in some combination of writing books, reading books, baking, eating said baked goods, making tea to go along with said baked goods, drinking said tea while eating said baked goods and writing and/or reading said books. Sometimes she does actual work, too.

In 2021, she was part of a Tin House Workshop and has had short fiction published through various platforms, including *Cold Mountain Review, Strange Fictions, Bending Genres, The Quiet Ones, Marathon Lit Review,* and *Bookends Review. The Building That Wasn't* is her first novel.

If you enjoyed
Abigail Miles's *The Building That Wasn't*,
please consider leaving a review
to help our authors.

And check out another suspenseful
sci-fi story from CamCat,
Audrey Lee's *The Mechanics of Memory*.

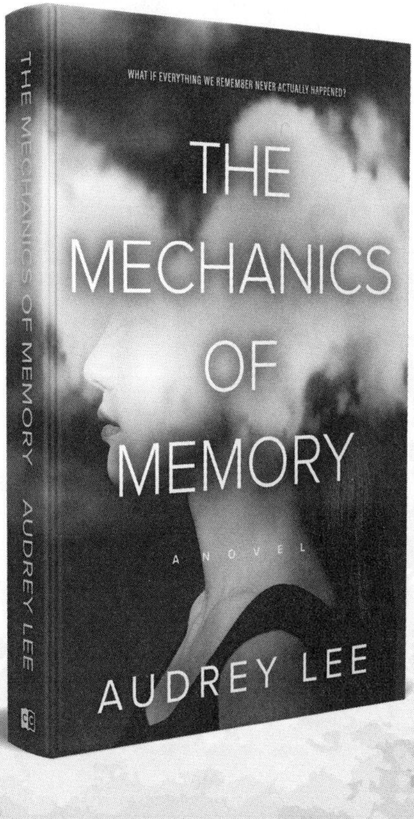

NEVER FORGET

"COME WITH ME," LUKE SAID. "Before it all disappears." He leaned across the kitchen counter and pushed at the lid of her laptop.

Hope swiveled in the turquoise kitchen stool, feet hooked in the rungs. Luke moved through the sliding glass door and onto the tiny patch of uneven concrete in the backyard, black Nikon hanging from a worn leather strap off his right shoulder. Hope watched as he pointed the camera at the sunset, then turned to aim the lens into the house, fingers focusing.

"Don't." Hope covered her face with a laugh. "Yuck."

"Then get over here." He waved at her. "It's magnificent."

Hope slid off the stool and grabbed two lowballs and a bottle of single malt from the counter.

The desert sunset was spectacular. Shimmering sheets of fuchsia and amethyst were splashed across the scarlet sky, palm trees and rough mountain peaks silhouetted against it. And above their outline, a moon so luminous it may well have been dipped in gold, hung lower than seemed possible.

Without meaning to, Hope reached out to touch the moon.

"Didn't I tell you?" he said.

She smiled. "You did."

Luke snapped more photos, from every conceivable angle and with every possible lens attachment. He paced the length of the yard, barefoot, camera case knocking against his hip.

"So antsy," Hope said, depositing glasses on the end table and climbing onto the lounger.

"Stay just like that," he said. He pointed the Nikon at her, shutter clicking, like gunfire.

"You could simply enjoy the sunset, you know," Hope said. "We could enjoy it together."

Luke set the camera on the table and reached for the bottle. The Macallan sounded a hollow pop of anticipation as it opened.

He handed her a glass and settled in, Hope swinging her legs over his. Her toenails were painted dark blue this week, fresh from a pedicure with Charlotte this morning.

Luke didn't care for her nail polish choices, especially when she went blue. Corpse toes, he called them.

"Tomorrow you'll be a big TV star. Are you nervous?"

Luke took a sip of his scotch. "Maybe."

"Is it because Natasha Chen is the host?" Hope asked. "What with your thing for Asian ladies?"

"So now I have a thing?" Luke laughed, hand trailing through her long hair. "You were supposed to be meek and submissive. I was grossly misled."

"At least I'm good at math," she said. "I'll try to work on the meek part."

"Good luck," Luke said. "And it's not because of Natasha Chen; it's because I don't want to make a fool of myself in front of thousands of viewers."

"Impossible," Hope said. "You're brilliant and amazing. And a published author. It's very sexy."

"Nerdy science books don't count as sexy," he said. "And you forgot devilishly handsome."

"I'll never forget." She closed her eyes, focused on the feel of his fingers. "Don't ask her to say something in Chinese, though. Total turnoff."

"Damn, I was going to open with that," Luke said, tracing her earlobe with his thumb. "After the ribbon cutting at the new facility today, Jack hinted this could mean a big promotion."

Hope opened her eyes. "Are you sure that's what you want?"

Luke shrugged. "It's the next logical step."

"I know." Hope sipped slowly. "Just, be careful what you wish for."

Luke pulled her close, and Hope breathed him in, fingernails tapping on the glass.

It made a tinkling sound, like bells.

"Let's run away instead," she said, picking a leaf from his hair. "Scrap it all and start a new land. Become rulers of our own destiny."

"Is this before or after we become dealers in Vegas?" Luke's mouth twitched. "Or start an ostrich farm? Or open a kabob restaurant called Shish for Brains?"

"It has to be mutually exclusive?" Hope laughed.

"Where should we start this new land?" Luke took her hand and pressed his lips against her palm. "Also, we're going to need something catchier than New Land."

Hope closed her eyes. "The Bahamas, of course."

"Of course. And how will we pay the bills?"

"We won't need money," Hope insisted, "because we'll be in charge of the New Land. To be renamed later. But if you must, we can open a waffle stand."

"I do make a damn fine waffle," Luke said.

"We'll call it the Waffle Brothel." Hope twined her legs together like a pretzel. She trailed a finger up his arm, just to the elbow, then back again.

"Horrendous," he murmured. "You're making it hard for me to concentrate."

"We could live in a lighthouse." Hope stilled her finger on his wrist. "And have kangaroos."

"You're like a kindergartener on an acid trip sometimes," Luke said. "Kangaroos aren't even native to the Bahamas."

"Kangaroos are evolutionarily perfect," Hope said. "They have built-in pockets. It's genius."

Luke smiled. "Then we'll import them. And build a kangaroo sanctuary on the beach. So we can see them from the lighthouse."

He lay back and Hope matched her gaze with his, to the endless universe spread above. The red had all but disappeared, the moon even brighter now against the darkening sky. A scattering of stars emerged, blinking at them like jewels.

"Given your exhaustive attention to detail, it sounds like a solid Plan B." He placed a hand on her thigh, a lazy, casual gesture Hope felt far beneath the layers of her skin. "I'm in."

"Promise?" Her voice held the barest of a tremor, almost imperceptible. Imperceptible to anyone but Luke.

He held his face level with hers. Sometimes they shared these glances, moments of razor-edged intimacy. Moments when they were the only souls of consequence, raw and infinite, a singularity. Moments when Hope wanted nothing more than to be swallowed whole, by Luke, and by whatever lay within.

Hope broke the connection, bottom lip in her teeth. Then a grin appeared, and she held her pinky in front of his face. "Promise?" she asked again.

Luke burst out laughing. "A pinky promise? You really are five." But he hooked his pinky into hers, and with his other hand, pulled her on top of him. "I'm sold," he said into her hair. "Waffles in the Bahamas it is."

Hope closed her eyes as she kissed him.

Maybe they could.

▪ ■ ■ ■ ▪

ON THE NIGHTSTAND, Hope's phone vibrated, rattling the jewelry she'd dropped there a few hours before. She typed a hurried response and activated her phone's flashlight, leaving the bed and padding quietly to the bedroom door. As her hand touched the doorknob, Luke's voice cut across the silence.

"Sucker." He was propped up on one elbow, face sleepy and amused. "You know she only calls because of the French fries."

Hope smiled, moving back to his side of the bed. "I don't mind," she said, placing her palm on his bare chest. "She'll have her license soon. And then college. There isn't much time left."

Luke's face softened. "You want me to go too?" He yawned, mouth open wide like a bear.

"No way." Hope touched his cheek. "You'll ruin girl time."

At the door, Hope paused to tap a small white picture frame mounted above the light switch, twice.

For luck.

"She has you wrapped around her finger, you know," Luke called.

"I know." Hope blew him a kiss. "So does her dad."

▪ ▪ ■ ▪ ▪

"SHE DOESN'T GET me *at all*," Charlotte said, popping a piece of gum in her mouth. "If I tell her anything, she uses it against me. I have *no* privacy." She let out a long, theatrical sigh, punctuated with maximum adolescent exasperation.

"It's a scary world out there." Hope glanced in the rearview mirror and changed lanes. "All parents want to protect their kids."

"You don't know my mom. And I don't need protection." Charlie cranked the air conditioning and tapped her blue fingernails on the dash. "Were your parents like that? Nosy?"

"We didn't exactly have open lines of communication." Hope turned down the air. "Remember, I'm first generation. If it wasn't about getting into Harvard or becoming a lawyer, it wasn't discussed."

"So you were a big disappointment," Charlotte said.

"You have no idea." Hope laughed.

"Can you help me with my essay on *Hamlet*?" Charlotte asked. "It's due Tuesday."

"Of course," Hope said, pulling into the parking lot of the Burger Shack. It was the only place open all night, thus the de facto home to anyone within a twenty-mile radius who was hungry or high, or both. Charlie called it the Stoner Shack, but even so, she couldn't deny their chili cheese fries were transcendental. Years ago, it had been a kitschy fifties diner, but today the only remnants of the former Shake, Rattle, and Roll were the defunct jukeboxes welded to the tables.

They stepped from the car, Hope locking it with a beep and a flash of headlights. Charlie led the way across the pavement, walking in a wide circle to avoid a kid throwing up in the bushes.

"I don't know why she isn't like you," Charlotte said, holding the Stoner Shack door open for Hope. "Relaxed."

"I'm far from relaxed," Hope said. "I have the luxury of not being your parent. I just get to be your friend."

"Aww," Charlie held her right hand out, fingers and thumb curled into half a heart. Hope matched it with her left.

▪ ■ ■ ■ ▪

THEIR PLASTIC CUPS were nearly empty, though the silver tumbler on the sticky laminate table was still brimming with Oreo shake. The plate between Hope and Charlotte contained only a few soggy fries, a generous pile of chili and cheese, and a puddle of ketchup.

"Straight out of the fryer," Charlotte said, returning to the booth. She set a fresh basket of fries between them, spots of grease soaking through the paper lining.

"Perfect timing," Hope said. She ran a fry in a zigzag through the chili and ketchup.

"Oh no, now you're doing it too?" Charlotte said.

Hope tilted her head. "Doing what?"

"Making patterns with your food." Charlie made a face. "Is that a two?"

Hope studied the paper plate. "I never realized I did that."

"You guys already share one brain. And the looks . . ." Charlotte mimed gagging. "You act like you're my age. Cringe."

A gaggle of boys entered, calling loudly to one another and jockeying for position at the counter. One was the kid formerly puking by the entrance, but he looked recovered. Another peeled off from the clump, pausing by Hope and Charlotte on his walk to commandeer a booth.

"What's up, Charlie?" he said shyly.

Charlotte's cheeks reddened, and she tucked a lock of hair behind her ear. "Hey."

"I thought you'd be at Brody's tonight." He shoved his hands into his pockets. The kids around here usually had two distinct auras—money or no money—but Hope couldn't tell with this kid. He didn't have an air of entitlement, but he didn't seem like a townie either.

Charlie crumpled her napkin into a ball. "I had to study. We can't all be gifted like you."

"I can help you tomorrow." The boy glanced over his shoulder at the crowd filling their sodas. "I mean, if you want. If you're not busy."

Charlie flipped her hair. "I'm not busy."

Hope pulled on her straw noisily.

"I'll hit you up tomorrow." The boy backed away with a wave.

"What happened to Adam?" Hope asked.

Charlie tapped her nails on the table. "He turned out to be a dick."

Hope made a noncommittal noise.

"Don't be all, 'hmmm, that's interesting,'" Charlotte said. "I know you guys hated him."

Hope tried to keep a straight face. Luke wasn't even able to say his name most days, referring to Adam only as "that arrogant little prick."

"But you were both right." Charlie put her chin in her hands. "Did you ever date an asshole?"

Hope made a face. "Almost married one."

Charlie perked up, looking intrigued, but Hope tilted her head toward the boy. "So, is he a prospect?"

"He's smart. He's different from the boys at my school." She grinned. "But don't tell my dad. He'll get totally triggered."

"Look, Charlie, you're the most important person in the world to him," Hope said. "Which means no one will ever be good enough for you. But it also makes you lucky to be so loved."

"I know." Charlotte rolled her eyes. "I'm so tired of the Adams of the world."

"Me too." Hope nodded. "But there are good guys out there, too. They just aren't as easy to spot. Trust me, the good ones are worth it."

"And that's my dad? One of the good ones?" Charlie wrinkled her nose, still too cool for feelings, though her eyes looked wistful.

Hope smiled. "I'm certain of it."

ONE YEAR LATER

1 | Don't Look Back

HOPE

The Wilder Sanctuary

Rancho Mirage, California

"AND HOW ARE THE NIGHTMARES?"

"Fine." Hope shifted, pushing stringy hair from her face with her palms. "I haven't had any this week."

"None at all?"

Hope shook her head slowly, face impassive.

Dr. Stark looked impressed with his own abilities, as if he'd performed a special magic trick to protect Hope from herself. Perhaps in a way he had. "That's important progress."

Dr. Stark jotted notes on his tablet with a pointy gray stylus. "Are you sleeping any better?"

"A little. An hour or two at a time." It was a lie. She hadn't slept at all.

The sun rose high out the picture window, San Jacinto Mountains ascending against the endless blue. Desert sky. It was hard to think about the dark right now, with so much light around her. "Does that mean I'm getting better?"

"As we've discussed, it's important you get concentrated stretches of sleep." Dr. Stark flipped his tablet to expose the keyboard, typing with a renewed purpose. "It will help you make progress in the Labyrinth."

The word Labyrinth filled Hope with a viscous dread.

She knew she'd visited it dozens of times since arriving at Wilder, though never remembered what happened there. "I told you I'm never going back."

"You did," Dr. Stark said. "But as *I* said, it's important to try and push through. It helps with confronting what you're avoiding."

"I'm not avoiding anything," Hope said. Another lie.

"I'm increasing your temazepam to thirty milligrams," Dr. Stark said. "And tomorrow evening, I'd like you to spend some time with Victor. Say, forty-five minutes?"

Hope glanced at the ceiling. She wanted a cigarette in the worst way.

"Great," he said. "Check in with the pharmacy after our session."

Stark was doing the casual Friday thing today, though Hope remained uncertain if today was, in fact, Friday. He resembled a prep school student, with his shiny polo shirt and immaculately pressed chinos. The polo looked brand new, still creased in the sleeves and too white, almost blinding. Hope couldn't picture Dr. Stark performing the tasks of mere mortals: changing the toilet paper, taking out the garbage, shopping for polo shirts. Maybe his wife did all that. Maybe she bought five polo shirts in different colors from Neiman Marcus, hanging them in an orderly row, next to his dry-cleaned Italian suits in clear plastic bags.

"Is there anything else you want to tell me?" Dr. Stark asked, still typing, fingers thin and bare.

"Are you married?"

"Divorced," he said. "More thoughts about last year, perhaps?"

"Nothing else," Hope said, with a shake of her head.

An artificial chime reverberated through the room's speakers, and a slight shadow of disappointment crossed the doctor's face. "We'll pick up again next week."

Hope wiped her hands on her pants and rose, heading for the shiny glass door.

"Hope," Dr. Stark said.

She paused, hand on the doorknob.

"Be well."

"Be well, Dr. Stark."

· ▪ ■ ▪ ·

HOPE LURKED IN the corridor outside the pharmacy door. Everyone here called it the Roofie Room. Dr. Stark discouraged the nickname, though she'd heard him use it when he didn't think anyone was listening.

She leaned against a wall under a framed print. *I Choose to Make the Rest of My Life the Best of My Life,* the typeface commanded. Wilder was overrun with these platitude posters—inspirational phrases printed on backdrops of pink orchids, mountain scenes at sunrise, soft-focus tree branches with dappled green leaves.

The one on Hope's bedroom wall depicted a wooden plank bridge disappearing into the horizon. *Don't Look Back. You're Not Going That Way.* Graphically speaking, it was a minor improvement over the poster she remembered from seventh grade English class, the one of a ginger kitten with huge eyes, suspended in a tree by its claws. *Hang in There!* in bubblegum pink balloon letters.

The hallway loomed empty and silent, like the whole of Wilder. Staff believed in maintaining a serene, nurturing environment at all times, right down to the soothing smells pumped through the ducts. Today, the scent was a pungent eucalyptus.

Like any pharmacy, the Roofie Room had a high white counter serving as a barricade to a wall of shelves, each one boasting orderly containers of unlabeled amber bottles and plastic baggies full of pills. Willy Wonka's Pharmaceutical Factory.

Dr. Emerson appeared from behind the shelves, smiling when she noticed Hope skulking under another poster: *Healing Begins with a Single Step.* "How can I help you?"

"Dr. Stark changed one of my prescriptions." Hope approached the doctor and craned her neck to see above the counter.

"He seems to have doubled your dosage." Dr. Emerson moved her mouse, perfectly arched eyebrows knitting together. "To the maximum recommended."

Hope shrugged. "I'm having trouble sleeping."

Dr. Emerson removed a nonexistent piece of lint from her white coat. She smoothed her already perfect blond hair, pulled from her face into a tight, sleek ponytail.

Then the doctor launched into her spiel about the side effects and the short-term nature of the meds, how Hope shouldn't do anything like operating heavy machinery or driving.

How she should tell someone if she developed hyperaggressive tendencies or suicidal thoughts. Dr. Emerson sounded like the placid voice-over in a drug commercial. Erections may last more than twenty-four hours.

Death may occur.

Hope smothered a snicker.

Dr. Emerson didn't appear to appreciate being interrupted during her enumeration of drug interactions and contraindications. She resumed typing with bright pink fingernails and pursed lips. "You'll have it tonight."

Another chime sounded.

"Will you please give this to Spencer?" From her coat pocket, Dr. Emerson produced a box of chalk and handed it to Hope. "Also, tell him to come see me. I have a delivery from his mother." Dr. Emerson tapped a manila envelope near her mouse.

"Do you want me to take that too?" Hope extended her hand.

"Absolutely not." Dr. Emerson pulled the envelope away, as if Hope's hand were a poisonous viper. Obviously chalk was the outer limit of what Hope could be trusted to courier. "Enjoy your dinner. Be well."

As Hope turned to go, Dr. Emerson said her name again.

Her tone was expectant, like a teacher whose class hadn't responded with the proper good morning: fake cheer tinged with annoyance, an undertone of challenge.

Hope paused. "Be well, Dr. Emerson."

▪ ■ ■ ■ ▪

THE FOOD WAS, as always, a gourmet affair. All meals at Wilder were perfectly prepared and stunningly plated, served on bone china at a table with a view. This place had a Michelin star under its belt, at least according to their website. Everything passing their lips was clean: nothing processed, no GMOs, all fresh and organic and assembled cheerfully and expertly by in-house chefs. Farm to Nuthouse.

When Hope first arrived, she would have gladly slit someone's throat for a corn dog and a Newcastle. After a month, the urge had mostly subsided. She now ate her whole grains and her sustainable wild salmon in balsamic reduction with little fuss.

Unfortunately, there still wasn't enough Diazepam in the world to make a bed of braised kale pass for a corn dog.

Quinn placed a plate of shrimp on the table, chimichurri sauce sloshing over the side and forming green puddles on the wood. He lowered himself into the seat next to Hope and ran his napkin along the rim. "What I wouldn't give for a good Malbec to wash this down," he said. "A 2004."

Hope raised an eyebrow. "Good luck."

Quinn speared his shrimp, cutting off the tails with deft fingers like a chef at Benihana. He carefully placed each tail, pointy side out, fanned along the edge of his plate. "Did you see the new recruit?"

A few tables away sat a man, much younger than they were, late twenties or early thirties maybe. He was tall and thin, with sandy blond hair and an honest face. He stared out the window with a vacant expression behind his tortoise shell glasses, fork suspended in hand over his untouched salad.

"His name's Carter," Quinn said. There were no last names at Wilder unless you were a doctor. Then there were no first names. "Silicon Valley start-up guy. Rumor has it he invented that word game when he was a kid. Magic Words. High-functioning depression, anger and aggression issues, panic attacks." Quinn held thumb and forefinger close together. "And a touch of PTSD, of course."

"How do you know shit like that?" Hope asked, squeezing a lemon into her infused water and taking a drink. Cucumber. The worst.

"I know all kinds of shit." Quinn smirked. "I think he's pretty. Let's go find out if he's single. Be, you know, a supportive network of healing." He cupped his hand over his mouth. "We should bring him into the fold before someone else does."

In a different life, in her life before Wilder, Hope never would have befriended Quinn. He would have run in an entirely different social strata, too beautiful and polished and wealthy for the likes of her. But here at Wilder, the serfs dined alongside the barons, and Quinn had sought her out and forced a friendship after mere hours, when she still wore the same expression Carter wore today.

"Jesus, we're not in a gang. He doesn't need to be jumped in." Hope pushed zucchini around on her plate, a little yellow boat sailing through the quinoa sea. "Go over there and introduce yourself if you want to get in his pants."

"Has anyone ever told you that you're a giant buzzkill?" Quinn leaned back in his chair, tilting it at an alarming angle. He wore the standard Wilder Weirdo uniform: elastic cotton pants, a gray short-sleeved T-shirt, white sneakers without laces. Yet only Quinn could manage to make it look stylish. "In your old life, did you ever enjoy pushing the envelope a little? Taking a risk?"

"Sorry," Hope said. "I've been a giant buzzkill in pretty much all my lives."

▪ ▪ ■ ▪ ▪

AFTER DINNER, HOPE knocked on Spencer's door. Thanks to Quinn, everyone called him Spooky Spencer, and these days mostly just Spooky. He was the youngest of the residents, thin and slight, a curtain of jet black hair usually hiding his pale face. He didn't speak when he first arrived two months ago, then only a few words, croaked out when spoken to. Spooky spent all his free time with his *D&D* magazines, hand-drawn maps, graph paper, and pencils spread out in front of him, murmuring about campaigns and hit points and initiatives.

Shortly after arriving, Spooky started drawing on the wall in his bedroom, with a stub of a purple crayon he'd nicked from the Creative Connections Room (surprisingly, a clever pejorative had yet to be assigned). Spooky drew a crescent moon in the top right corner of his wall, like that bald kid in the children's books. No one could figure out how he climbed so high to reach, knowing he'd also have some kind of hell to pay for defacing the property. He'd probably be sentenced to three days of mandatory restorative yoga, or a week writing lines in the Zen Garden. Every day is a gift.

Surprisingly, Dr. Stark was delighted when he discovered the purple moon. He thought giving Spooky an outlet for his expression might help him connect with people. So Stark submitted a work order and had one wall of Spooky's room painted with chalkboard paint. He even gave Spooky all the chalk he wanted. Now an elaborate white forest spread across half the ebony surface: bare, eight-foot aspen with sinister cuts in their bark, vines and thorns and brambles winding from floor to ceiling. A path began in the bottom left corner, splintering into several directions as creepy, nondescript animal eyes stared from hidden spots in the trees. Spooky called it The Shade.

Hope knocked again. She examined the box of chalk from Dr. Emerson, its bright green and yellow markings anachronistic against the muted tones of Wilder. The box reminded Hope of her father, who often returned from business trips with a box of crayons for her. It was always the big box of sixty-four, the one with the useless sharpener built in. Impractical purchases were rare in her family, and new crayons were a commodity. Hope would drop to the floor and dump the box onto the ground, smelling the wax and grouping the crayons by color, blunted tips lined up perfectly like a rainbow fence. They always seemed so full of promise.

After the third knock, Hope entered. Spooky was at his desk, watching the door.

"I didn't see you at dinner," Hope said, holding up the chalk. "But Dr. Emerson sent this for you. And she said to tell you there's a message from your mom."

His voice was too soft to hear. Maybe it was thank you. Or maybe it was fuck you. One could never tell with Spooky.

Hope set the chalk on his nightstand and looked at The Shade. Spooky's chair creaked as he rose to stand nearer.

"Where does that go?" she asked, kneeling. She placed a bitten-down fingernail on the fork in the path, smudging it a little.

"Mirror Gate," he said, inclining his head right. "And this goes to Hollow of the Moon." He licked his pinky finger and wiped away the smudge.

"What happens there?" She squinted down the path.

Spooky retrieved a small stub of chalk from his desk to touch up the part she'd smudged. "It's where the souls are collected and cleansed." He added more detail to a birch tree along the road to Mirror Gate.

She wasn't sure she had a soul anymore, but if she did, Hope wasn't certain she wanted it cleansed. So much for connecting with people.

▪ ▪ ■ ▪ ▪

BACK IN HER room, Hope reached far under her mattress for her notebook and pens. Her room was searched daily, including the spot under her bed and the corners of her closet. No expectation of privacy existed for anyone at Wilder, yet she still felt a compulsion to stash her few things away. It was also why she chose to write in code.

It wasn't an elaborate, beautiful mind kind of code. For Luke's last birthday, Hope bought secret decoder rings from a bookshop selling quirky trinkets. Two silver rings with the alphabet running around the bottom half, the top half spinning to reveal a number in a tiny window. Luke had laughed when he opened it, getting it instantly, slipping it on his finger and turning it around and around. For a time, they sent coded messages to each other, quickly discovering it took twice as long to write a note and ten times longer to decode it. Luke had even created a spreadsheet to make it faster. Eventually that exercise, along with so many rituals and routines and secret languages preceding it, was abandoned. Yet in that brief stint, Hope had memorized the twenty-six pairs, and still repeated them in her head when she couldn't sleep. Today the coded numbers came quickly and fluidly, like a native tongue. Sometimes she caught herself thinking in the code too, rather than words: 1-26-18-4-23-17-6-4-14.

It wouldn't take a cryptographer to crack; it was the simplest of substitution ciphers. A third grader could do it. But she also figured no one cared enough to invest the time.

Tonight, Hope opened to the page she started a few days ago, recounting her day in simple, unpoetic prose. When writing in numbers, it was much easier to do it this way. No commentary, no feelings or emotions, just a list of the day. Dr. S. + 30 mg T. Yellow zucchini. The Labyrinth. She never revisited her writing, knowing if she did, it would be unsettling to have forgotten.

She checked the time and flipped to the end of the notebook, to a different section. It was here she tried to recount her life before Wilder, where she tried to parse out her last year, where she wrote about Luke.

Hope wrote what she could, a paltry few lines. She had little certainty these days, and even less stock in her memories. There simply wasn't much to call forth from her lost year, and since Hope restricted her writing to facts, this section had seen little progress over time.

The chime rang, presenting her with a few minutes before her meds arrived, preceding a night which would soon become thick and foggy. This was her most lucid time of the day, and in thirty minutes it would all fade into the ether. She glanced at the door out of habit even though she knew at least ninety seconds remained, then closed the notebook and stowed it safely under the mattress.

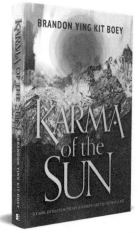